TAKES ONE
TO KNOW ONE

AN ALISON KAINE MYSTERY BY

KATE ALLEN

OTHER ALISON KAINE MYSTERIES BY KATE ALLEN

TELL ME WHAT YOU LIKE

GIVE MY SECRETS BACK

A MARTA GOICOCHEA MYSTERY BY KATE ALLEN

I KNEW YOU WOULD CALL

TAKES ONE TO KNOW ONE

AN ALISON KAINE
MYSTERY BY
KATE ALLEN

NEW VICTORIA PUBLISHERS

Published by New Victoria Publishers Inc., a feminist, literary, and
cultural organization, PO Box 27, Norwich, VT 05055-0027.

Cover Photo by Judy M. Sanchez

Printed and Bound in Canada
1 2 3 4 5 6   2000 1999 1998 1997 1996 1996

Library of Congress Cataloging-in-Publication Data

Allen, Kate 1957-
    Takes on to know one : an Alison Kaine mystery / by Kate Allen.
        p.   cm.
    ISBN 0-934678-74-X (paperback)
    I. Policewomen--Colorado--Denver--Fiction.   2. Lesbian--
Colorado--Denver--Fiction.# Denver (Colo.) --Fiction. I. Title.
    PS3551 . L3956T35   1996
    813' . 54--dc20   96-8841
                                                          CIP

Being a writer is a strange and solitary occupation—if you are lucky, like I am, you have a supportive family of choice. If you are *really* lucky you have a writing circle. This book is for Georgia Megenity and Linda Lane of the Free Range Chickens.

CHAPTER ONE

"They were right," said Michelle Martin firmly, as she tapped her pack of American Spirits against the steering wheel of her truck. Michelle, Alison Kaine's best friend of over twenty years, was an unyielding and total car top. When traveling she not only insisted on packing and driving, but also wanted to hold their shared cigarettes, lighter and food. She had grumbled mightily when Alison had insisted on doing a couple of errands on the way out of Denver, and she was just barely allowing her to read the new *Lesbian Connection* aloud. If Michelle could have figured a way to read and keep an eye on I-25 at the same time, she certainly would have.

"They were wrong," replied Alison, who was itching to handle the cigarettes herself. They were both smoking with the air of doing something pleasurably forbidden and somewhat foolish at the same time. They had kicked the habit together years before, but what was a road trip without cigarettes? Michelle and Alison had taken many road trips over the years; they had gone to Michigan and Yosemite and Canada—and most of those miles had been traveled under the influence of drugs. But now that they were older and more respectable—Michelle was a mother who was going to want her child to Just Say No in a few years, and Alison was a police officer whose captain had lately gotten a bit trigger-happy on the topic of urine testing—they had pretty much slipped out of that loop.

So, since they couldn't do drugs any more, and they had always been too smart to drink and drive, they might as well treat themselves to a few smokes while they discussed the issue of male to female transsexuals at the Michigan Women's Music Festival, a subject which had monopolized the last three issues of *Lesbian Connection*.

"Fuck *that*!" said Michelle, now holding two cigarettes in the corner of her mouth. She snapped out a book of matches. Michelle wouldn't use a Zippo, because they were not ecologically sound, and she wouldn't use the lighter in Alison's car because every time she did she pulled the cigarette away unlit, with a quarter inch of tobacco stuck to the heating unit. This was because she crammed the end of the cigarette too firmly to the surface, but try telling

Michelle how to do anything. "They did exactly the right thing to throw him off the land. The festival is for womyn *born* womyn." Somehow, when Michelle spoke, you knew that she was spelling women with a y. "It doesn't matter if he had his dick cut off—he still had the privilege."

A year before, Michelle might have followed up a statement like this with a line suggesting that random castration might not be a bad way of controlling male violence—cheap, easy, and no mechanical devices to monitor—but she had toned down ever since her lover, Janka Weaversong, had given birth to a baby boy three months before. It was difficult to maintain hard-line politics if you were utterly silly over an infant who was some day going to be part of the group you were maligning. She must have realized this herself because she added sternly, "I'm not going to be one of those women who insists on taking her son into Womyn Only Space." Motherhood was not going to make Michelle Martin sell out.

Alison ignored the side bar. They'd already hashed that one out *miles* ago. They agreed on the idea of separate but equal child care at festivals—otherwise, how were little girls ever going to get the chance to run naked and be leaders? The issue of Male-to-Female transsexual lesbians was a whole other can of worms, one that they should be able to milk right up to the last yard of their journey.

Through Janka's friend Seven Yellow Moons, Michelle and her cement mixer—and by extension Alison—had been invited to spend four days helping to adobe a house on a new piece of women's land in New Mexico. It was an eight hour drive—transsexual lesbians had carried them for a good hundred miles. In addition to day care at festivals they had already discussed Melissa Etheridge (was she selling out?) the new lunch situation at the Mercury Cafe, various friends' disastrous affairs, where they were going to spend New Year's Eve in six months (at the lesbian prom, listening to Monkey Siren!), Michelle's new hair cut (fifty miles—she'd tried something new) and their friend Hazel Thornton's book, *Hung Jury*, which was about the Menendez brothers. O.J. had been declared off limits—it just put them both in a twist.

"They've had at least twenty years of male privilege." Michelle plowed right ahead with the transsexual discussion when Alison took a few seconds too long to answer. You had to be quick if you were going to debate with Michelle—otherwise she'd ease on down the road without you. Alison was usually right on track—she'd had years of practice, but she had been sidetracked by a particularly deep inhale. God, she loved cigarettes! She had better quit fucking with them soon, or she was going to be right back to her old habit of a pack a day. Stealthily, she flicked the pack out from beneath Michelle's thigh and lit another, using the car lighter the right way. Michelle looked at her sideways from narrowed eyes, and pushed the speedometer up another five miles just to show who was really topping this scene.

"Okay," said Alison. "So they don't get to come in because they had the male privilege. What about us? What if someone decides we don't get to come in because we had the white, middle class privilege? Are you going to go for that?"

"Absolutely," said Michelle without hesitation. "Lesbians of Color have every right to have their own gatherings, their own space at festivals. I will respect that totally. And, incidentally, I don't think that wearing dreadlocks makes me Black, which is comparable to what these guys are saying—"I got the plumbing, so now I'm a woman.""

"So it's not the fixtures that make you a woman?" asked Alison slowly.

"Not in this case."

"So it's what's in your head, then? Because that's what transsexuals have been saying all along. That they were women in their heads right from the start, and they were just getting the exterior redecorated to match the interior."

"Male privilege!" said Michelle. "At least twenty years of—"

"Heterosexual privilege," countered Alison. "You didn't come out until you were twenty-one. Twenty years of heterosexual, not to mention white, middle class privilege. So does that mean you don't get to be a dyke now?"

"But I would have given that up if—" Michelle stopped herself, realizing this line of reasoning could be twisted right back around to support the transsexuals. She scowled, her cigarette hanging off her lip as if she were playing some hardened criminal type in a B movie. *Dykes Behind Bars.* Alison looked out the window and hummed happily along with the radio, which was tuned to a country station. She didn't give a rat's ass about transsexuals being thrown out of Michigan—she just liked to best Michelle. It was a game they played often, and she was seldom allowed to win.

She looked down the road and saw that they were approaching a little cluster of houses, the first they'd seen in miles. She wouldn't have really called it a town, but an adobe house set itself apart from the others with a hand-painted sign informing the world that gas, beer, and food could be purchased there. And you could use the two coin-washers in the back while you shopped.

"Map," said Michelle tersely. Alison pulled out the hand-drawn paper that Seven Yellow Moons, who lived on women's land near Santa Fe, had faxed them. It had been kind of a last minute invite. Michelle did not insist on reading the map herself because having a reader meant one more chance to top the scene and get in a tizzy about misinformation. Michelle liked to work all possible angles.

"Turn right after the store," said Alison. Then, "No, no, turn *into* the store!"

Michelle made a turn so sharp that had the road been paved rubber would have been laid. She had to settle for scattering a few chickens which had been sedately minding their own business. "Now where?" she asked, frantic as the chickens, staring at the little *madre y padre* store as if it were going to open up like a secret tunnel. Michelle had been watching too many movies on the Disney channel.

"Now turn the car off," said Alison. "I want to get some cookies."

Alison Kaine was thirty five years old and she had been an out lesbian for sixteen of those years. She had started out as a kind of androgynous, flannel shirt and Birkenstocks kind of dyke, but over the past two years she had really gotten into the butch thing. Her dark hair, starting to show salt and pepper, had become progressively shorter and the mainstay of her wardrobe had become her jeans and leather jacket. They suited her. She had always been a pleasant looking woman, but since she had gone butch she had become positively handsome. She was unaware of this, which made it all the more attractive.

Alison had also been a Denver cop for five years. It was not a career she had planned, but it was a career for which she had been born. Her father, who was also a cop, had been delighted when she had finally given in to his urging, and was still as proud of her as he had been the day she had graduated. There was reason to be proud—she was good at her job and had, in fact, played a crucial role in solving two murder cases that had hit the lesbian community in the previous twenty-six months. Alison dreaded having to tell her father that she might be quitting the force. There were a number of reasons, but the main and current one had to do with her health. Several months before, she had been diagnosed as having fibromyalgia syndrome, a chronic disorder that, during bad spells, made her feel as if she had the achiness and exhaustion of the flu. It had started out hitting her one week in six, but over the past year had crept up to the point where every other week was not unusual. She had not yet spoken to any of her friends about it.

There were only two people in the store, and they were speaking to one another in Spanish. Alison had to bite her tongue to keep from breaking right into the conversation uninvited. Ever since she and Stacy had started taking conversational Spanish once a week through Colorado Free University, her left and right brain had been locked in battle. Her left brain seemed to think that, not only was she fluent, but perfect strangers would enjoy hearing her uninvited comments. Her right brain knew damn good and well that the only conversations she and Stacy had been able to have were about their cats, both of whom were *bueno y gordo*, with an occasional comment thrown in about Stacy's friend Liz's kittens, which were *pequenos y muy malos*. Alison managed, by keeping her mouth shut tightly the whole time, to give the woman ten bucks for Oreos and a twenty-four pack of Diet Pepsi, without making a fool of herself. The conversation—Alison believed that the man was looking for either his horse, his shirt, or possibly his horse's head—continued as the woman totaled Alison's purchase. Alison quivered whenever she recognized a word, like a dog who can pick out 'Walk' and 'Outside'.

"Why did we have to make a cookie stop?" asked Michelle sternly, after she had peeked into the bag to make sure Alison had gotten Oreos, and not Fig Newtons, which she thought were the work of the devil. "We only have forty more miles."

"That's why," said Alison, still wishing sadly that she had gotten a chance to tell the people in the store that *su gato* K.P. was *gris con pies blancos* and Ninetails, *el gato de Stacy* was *negro*. Maybe it wasn't too late—her twenty-four pack of Diet Pepsi had started to look insufficient. "I wanted to stock up," she told Michelle. "Look at the flier— in and out once."

They both looked at the typed list Seven had faxed over to Liz's office—nobody else had access to a machine—when she invited them to the work party. *In and out once*—better for the land—was the first rule, but it was not the only rule.

"*No men's publications*," read Michelle, looking at Alison's TIME magazine. "You better toss that."

"*No men's voices*," read Alison, switching the radio off the country station, and popping in an Indigo Girls tape. "And I'm not going to throw away the library book I brought."

"Put it under the seat," said Michelle judicially. "Put the TIME under there, too. Then we can recycle it when we get home. Besides, I haven't read the movie reviews."

"*No smoking anywhere on the land*," read Alison. They cast identical glances at the American Spirits, and then at each other. Fuck that. They'd have no trouble at all taking care of those babies on the way in.

"*No alcohol or drugs,*" read Michelle. "*They're tools of the patriarchy. No pets as slaves. No meat.*"

"That's why I got the Oreos," explained Alison. "I figured we were going to be eating a lot of soybeans." Both Alison and Michelle, and Janka as well, had recently become vegetarians, but Alison had gotten into the habit of supplementing with sugar. Supposedly the extra calories would not affect her because of the trade-off with meat, but in reality her jeans were getting tight.

"*No drugs,*" read Michelle again. "*No s/m.*" She looked at Alison over the top of her new reading glasses which were still a touchy subject. It hurt Michelle's butch vanity that her eyes, which had always been a firm twenty-twenty, were doing the getting older thing.

"No Stacy," said Alison, spreading her hands, and then, for good measure, "*El gato de Stacy tiene dos anos, y es negro y gordo.*"

"*Si, y Tammy Faye es blanca y naranja,*" replied Michelle, who had been around the cat conversation enough to be able to describe her own cat. "Not at all?" she added hopefully.

"Not as far as I know," said Alison, popping an Oreo. She had invited her girlfriend, Stacy, to drive down and join them, but it so happened that they had gotten into quite a fight the day before. She was not, however, going to give Michelle the satisfaction of this knowledge. Though in reality Michelle and Stacy got along quite well, politically Michelle identified Stacy, who made her living as a dominatrix, as the enemy. Michelle had the idea that if Stacy just crawled back under her rock Alison could be brought back to the fold of righteous women. She was wrong—Alison was firmly entrenched in kink—but it did no good to tell Michelle this. She just couldn't hear it.

To be truthful, if things had been a bit different, Alison was not sure she would have come down for a work weekend sponsored by women so obviously hostile to leather dykes. Seven Yellow Moons, whom they had called for details during her shift at Wild Oats (all the Santa Fe dykes had, were, or were planning on working at Wild Oats) had said, "Oh, come on. I eat meat and keep animals as slaves, and I'm going. It's not me or you they object to, just doing it on their land."

"Methuselah is not a slave, she is the representative of the goddess in your shrine," Alison had replied, referring to Seven's cat. She had not voiced what she was really thinking, which was that women who were avid vegetarians might very well think it was the deed and not the persona of the carnivore that was evil, but Alison's experience with lesbians who were avidly anti-s/m had led her to believe they had totally discarded this fine but important distinction. No s/m on the land might not just mean check your whips at the gate, it might mean leave your ideas there as well, or even stay the fuck away.

But, there had been extenuating circumstances that had pushed the trip. First, there was the baby at home with Janka. Alison had fallen as deeply and completely in love with Sam as had Janka and Michelle. She was delighted to hold and rock and feed him, and had even entered into several conversations about the consistency of his poop, something that, as a childless woman, she had once pledged never to do.

But poor Sam had entered into a colicky stage, and the prospect of a full night's sleep or two was a carrot indeed. Michelle, in fact, had hardly been able to disguise her delight and Janka had been visibly crabby when they left.

There was also the Stacy thing.

"Damn!" said Michelle, hitting a pot hole that knocked the ash off her cigarette and into her lap. "That once in and once out must be to protect your car, not the land!"

Alison, shaken out of her musing, looked out the window and nodded her agreement. The road upon which they were traveling appeared to be carved out of sheer stone, and it had not yet seen sufficient travel for a heavy scar to be cut into the land. Alison could only follow it with her eye another mile or so across the desert. She had been flicking her ashes out the window—now she rolled it up tightly so the red dust rising around the car would not envelope them. The car jounced again, and Alison made a note not to pop any of the soda too soon after arrival. She was glad they had decided to take Michelle's truck instead of her car—not only did it have a covered bed for the gear, it was a lot higher off the ground. She wouldn't want to lose an oil pan out here.

She opened the Oreos and stuffed two into her mouth between heavy drags, just in case there was a No Sugar rule posted on the gate. Yes, the Stacy situation was a main reason she had let Michelle persuade her to use her time off to make the trip. Get away from the baby, get away from Stacy who had said to her last week, "You have intimacy issues." Not asking anymore, as she had been doing for the past two years—"You have intimacy issues, don't you?"— coached as a question to give Alison the chance to open up, to confide, to talk about what she'd tried in therapy, and what had worked and what hadn't. Just you got 'em, I don't like 'em, do something about them or I'm going to be putting on my it's-all-over coat, as Tanya would say. Go on down to New Mexico and hang out with the back-to-the-land girls, maybe it'll give you some time to think about this and (unsaid) God knows you're never here for me anyway except physically.

Which was damn unfair, thought Alison, indignant as if the words had been said instead of implied. She *was* there for Stacy. She was there whenever Stacy, an avid and locally renowned quilt maker, had a show. Unlike all the other friends who showed up and said "Oooh!" and drank the free wine, she was there for all the steps before, for looking at the fabric pieces when they first went up on the wall, and suggesting changes and improvements and commiserating over work that just wasn't coming together. She was there when Stacy wanted a dinner cooked, instead of her perpetual takeout, there when Stacy wanted a little weekend in the mountains, and she had been there twenty-eight months before when a killer had stalked Stacy and put her in the hospital for a week.[1] She *was* there. It was just that she didn't want to move in, didn't want to talk about moving in, didn't want to talk about a commitment ceremony or five years from now when they had bought a nice little piece of land together up in Guffy. This was what Stacy, and Lavender Chrystalpower née Lydia, Alison's previous lover, both labeled intimacy issues.

And they weren't, thought Alison. Or, actually, maybe they were, but what was wrong with that? What was wrong with resisting the merge? What was wrong with still wanting to close the bathroom door when she took a big dump? Wasn't she allowed some lines? Wasn't she allowed to want her own apartment, checking account, tampons and stocked refrigerator? Wasn't she? Wasn't that the sign of a strong, self-sufficient woman who girls should be lining up to date?

Maybe. Unfortunately, this line of defense had lost a great deal of credibility when, five months earlier, she had put up the major part of the down payment to buy into a house with Janka and Michelle. "What about your own apartment?" Stacy had asked in a rage. "What about that refrigerator and taking a big dump *now*?" It had done no good to point out the obvious—that the top floor, with its own entrance, was as good as its own apartment, except when Sam was crying at ten and twelve and two and five a.m. Alison hadn't even brought up the other things—that Janka and Michelle couldn't have swung the deal without her, that their little apartment could not possibly have absorbed a baby. Talk about throwing fat on the fire! Because that was what was at the heart of it, really. It wasn't that Stacy really wanted to cohabit, it was that she wanted a show of loyalty. She wanted a show of romance and daring and "I'll love you till I die," and every time that choice had lit up the board, Alison had instead chosen sensible, and old friends.

Alison shrugged. To hell with Stacy. She tried not to notice that Michelle actually seemed to be driving with one tire over the edge of the arroyo that bordered the road. She lit two more cigarettes as they went over more hills and dips in the rolling, dry land. Michelle was concentrating so hard that she actually grunted thanks when Alison passed her one. It was going to be a weekend of thinking things over—the job and Stacy and when and if she was going to spill the news about her illness to any of her friends. Before the fight she had invited Stacy to go with them, and she had left her a photocopy of the map, but she doubted that she would show up.

"This is it," said Michelle suddenly, at the very same moment that Alison spotted the sign 'Mariposa Ranch.' She was kind of surprised there wasn't a labrys or women's symbol painted below the words, but maybe that was for the sake of security. There had been a note on the little, hand-drawn map specifically warning anyone who got lost not to ask the neighbors or the people in the store for directions. Alison didn't blame the desert dykes. If you were living in a place where the neighbors were few and far between, the best situation was to be on tight terms with those neighbors, and if homophobia and cultural differences drew a line through that choice, then the next best thing to do was try not to draw attention to the fact that there was a bunch of dykes out by themselves in the sagebrush. The gate itself spoke of security. The road opened on either side of it, wide enough for two vehicles to pass, but at the point where the posts had been set down into the stone, it had narrowed to one small lane, bordered on one side by an arroyo, on the other by a steep hill of stone and sagebrush. Once the gate was locked, traffic by this route would be cut off completely. No buildings were visible from where they sat, but beside the road on the other side of the gate was a pile of huge rocks, so large that Alison wondered if they had been moved with a backhoe.

"This is it," said Michelle again. She stopped the car in the middle of the one lane road, and they both sat in silence while they smoked two of the three remaining cigarettes down to the filters. Michelle smoked fast, the same way that she did anything.

Michelle was small and compact, in the same way that a terrier is compact, and just as unaware of size and limitations. Sometimes, because of her size and her cute little baby butch look (still holding at thirty-five, except for the damned reading glasses) women tend-

9

ed to underestimate Michelle. It was a mistake. She was one of the most capable women Alison knew. Her major means of support came from the beautiful stained glass pieces she made and sold at the Book Garden and the Artisan Center, but she supplemented this sometimes iffy income by trading. She could roof a house or landscape a yard or repair a bicycle or lay a patio. Though Alison had put up the major part of the down payment for the house, it had been Michelle who had torn up the old carpets and sanded the hardwood floors and painted over the ugly shades of green and yellow favored by the previous owners, mending and fixing as she moved from room to room. Alison had no misgivings at all about the balance of money—the undertaking would have been impossible without Michelle. Janka would not be pleased to see her hyperactive little darling participating in the smoking ritual. Janka, except for rare moments of gazing contentedly upon Sam's sleeping face, had not been pleased for months. Her pregnancy had gone right from nausea into toxemia, followed by a difficult delivery, sore, swollen nipples and sleep deprivation. Alison felt a little twinge of guilt over leaving her.

"Don't sweat it," said Michelle, who could read her mind so well after two decades that Alison could not even lie to her about birthday surprises. "Janka is going to be fine. I don't know about you, but she was sick to death of me. And your dad is going to treat her like a princess."

So engrossed were they in their firing squad smokes that neither had noticed two other vehicles approach. Both started at the polite tap on the horn.

"Hey, it's Seven!" said Alison enthusiastically, looking in her mirror at the driver of the first car. "And Lydia," she added with much less feeling. Seven Yellow Moons, who was a healer and weaver, visited Denver about four times a year, and often crashed on Alison's futon. About ten years older than Alison, she was a talented and funny woman with a kinky twist in her background. In contrast, Lydia, who was behind the wheel of the second car, was a pill—a black belt at passive aggressive behavior—who felt a three month tryst with Alison years before gave her eternal mooching privileges. Both women stepped out of their cars.

Because both Lydia and Seven Yellow Moons lived on women's land near Santa Fe, they often drove together. Alison had, in fact, never seen Lydia drive a car before—she was one of those women who always expected someone else to pick her up.

"Oh, shit," said Michelle. "Lydia's got a dog now." They exchanged glances. Alison wasn't a big dog fan to begin with, and if Lydia had a dog you could bet on it being untrained. As she opened the car door, Alison braced herself for being jumped on.

"Alison!" Seven Yellow Moons, a tall woman with long hair in braids, whose favorite outfit was sweat pants and a t-shirt, (the one she was wearing was from Womminfest 1992) took Alison's hand into her own as if to shake it, but instead ran her fingers over each swollen joint, testing each with a squeeze. Alison flinched.

"Hmm," said Seven Yellow Moons. "Janka didn't come?" She tested Alison's wrist and elbow in an impersonal way, as if she were examining a live chicken at the market. Seven, who besides being the produce manager at Wild Oats, was a healer and the only one of Alison's friends with whom she had shared her secret—that her swollen hands and back problems and exhaustion were not from playing too much soccer as Stacy thought, but from a disorder the doctor called chronic. Seven was sworn to secrecy.

"She decided it would be too much hassle to travel with the baby," explained Michelle, staring hard into Seven's eyes in an effort to detect anything other than friendly interest. Michelle had convinced herself several years before that Seven had designs upon Janka, who was also a weaver, and no amount of evidence to the contrary had been able to convince her otherwise. Michelle hadn't really wanted Janka for herself lately, but that did not mean that anyone else was allowed to want her.

"I wanted to see the baby!" Seven, who had been Janka's midwife (over the protests of Michelle, who would have preferred she be in the Mayo Clinic from the sixth month onward) had a godmotherly interest in little Sam. "I brought him a present," she sulked.

"You have cigarettes," said Lydia to Michelle, who still had a butt adhered to her lower lip. Lydia now went by Lavender Crystalpower, a name neither Michelle nor Alison had been able to bring themselves to say. Lydia, since moving down to Canyon Land had changed not only her name, but also her dishwater blonde hair. It had gone through a period of being an inch long all over and rainbow colored, but now was in shoulder length dreadlocks, some of which were wrapped tightly with bright crochet yarn in intricate patterns. The wrapping was what made you realize that the dreadlocks were on purpose—otherwise, Alison might have just thought that Lydia hadn't showered for a couple of weeks.

"And you have a dog," said Michelle. "I'm not on their land yet. I can put the butt in the *ashtray*—what are you going to do with that dog?"

"They're going to have to talk to her," replied Lydia obscurely. She turned to Alison, whose hands and fingers Seven was still rubbing and squeezing. "Fat and sugar," she said. "Fat and sugar, am I right?" For a moment Alison wished she was wearing her gun so she could just drill Lydia right through the middle of her forehead. No, cops were treated badly in prison, and Lydia wasn't worth having to share a bedroom with six other adults. Alison couldn't even stand it if Stacy snored.

Michelle snorted and went to sit in the cab to smoke their last cigarette, thus achieving the double motive of blocking Lydia while at the same time not having to talk to her.

"Does it hurt there?" asked Seven Yellow Moons, poking Alison first in the hips, then the lower back. "What about there and there? Is it any worse than it was when Sammy was born?"

"Yes. Yes. No." Alison, anticipating the next question added a second no. No, she had not told her friends yet. Talking in front of Lydia did not matter—Lydia rarely paid attention to anything that did not directly concern her. Sometimes not even then.

"Why not?"

"Because I…" Alison trailed off, unable to even start her list of fears. Because, what if none of her friends or family wanted to hear the word 'chronic'? What if they thought she was a hypochondriac and suggested therapy?

"Fat and sugar," said Lydia again, just as if someone had invited her into the conversation. "What do you expect if all you eat is fat and sugar?"

"Yeah, they're killers," agreed Seven. "You got any more of those Oreos?"

Luckily, Alison had bought the large, economy size. She and Seven stood up by the cab breathing in Michelle's secondhand smoke while Lydia faced the horizon and went into a tai chi routine. Lydia only practiced tai chi in public. The dog, who looked like some kind of scruffy and uncared for retriever mix, snuffled in the dust at their feet for crumbs.

"You poor old thing," said Seven. "Chocolate isn't good for you. Have you got anything else?"

Michelle sullenly handed a leftover sandwich through the window. She was looking at Seven through narrowed eyes, obviously trying to work herself up into some jealous little spat. Michelle did not like routine—if there was no excitement in her life, she was totally willing to create some out of nothing. Michelle needed a holodeck.

"Let's roll," she said abruptly to Alison, after smoking the last cigarette right down to the filter. Seven took a handful of Oreos—eating junk didn't count if someone else bought it—and went back to her van, an ancient Chevy in which she lived while on the road between women's festivals.

"Don't forget your dog," Michelle yelled to Lydia, who was climbing into the third car.

Lydia wrinkled her forehead as if she could not understand what Michelle was saying. "If she wants to come with me, then she needs to make that choice. I'm not going to tell her what to do."

For a moment Alison thought that Michelle (who had loved her own dog so much that Janka and Alison finally had to get him put down themselves, behind Michelle's back, passing it off as a heart attack) was going to leap out of the car and smack Lydia a good one, but luckily the dog finished the sandwich and jumped into Lydia's car just in time.

"Rrrr!" growled Michelle, too mad to even use words. She snapped the truck into drive and roared through the gate and up the track.

The road took an almost immediate dip, which obviously surprised Michelle, because she took it too fast and made everything in the back, and Alison, jump. They were prepared for the second dip, which brought them to the base of a small hill. Even though they had come less than a fourth of a mile because of the way the road went up and down Alison could not see the gate when she looked back over her shoulder. The whole area was hilly, but all the hills were small. Straight ahead of them, standing at the bottom of one of the little hills, stood three women who waved them to a stop.

"Welcome! Welcome sisters!" The woman who greeted them was probably in her late forties. She had a thick head of dark, graying hair, and a great, beaked nose. She was wearing jeans that, though they were well worn, had not come from the bargain bin, and a black tank top with a shitload of turquoise and silver jewelry—bracelets, earrings and a couple of small rings. Alison, even while wondering how much they'd set her back, had to admit to herself she wore them well. Her hands and arms were spotted from a life lived in the sun, and her face showed the same weathering in its network of fine lines. "I'm Hawk," said the woman gravely. She did not offer her hand. Too patriarchal, Alison supposed. "This is my life partner/companion Gaya, and our sister Persimmon." She indicated the two women who stood on either side of her.

Gaya, the woman to her left, did not know how to shop. Like Hawk, her clothes looked as if they had been ordered from Land's End or Bean—however both her shorts, which came down to her knees, and her crew neck shirt bagged a little too much, as if she had ordered them two sizes too big. Maybe she had, thought Alison, pressing the hand that she offered. She was a tall, thin, almost gawky looking woman, and Alison imagined that tall, thin, gawky women didn't get much validation in the land of Madonna and Sharon Stone. A baggy shirt was probably a great defense. She had tried to accessorize with a blue bandanna tied over her hair and some cloisonné earrings, but neither worked very well with the outfit.

Persimmon, who was also fairly tall, was one of those androgynous-leaning-to-femme women that Michelle liked so much. She and Gaya were totally different styles of dykes—she *did* know how to shop, and it wasn't at Land's End—but it was obvious even at first glance that Hawk wasn't just talking semantics when she had mentioned sisters. One look at Gaya's and Persimmon's deep blue eyes told Alison they had the same mama. Their facial similarity was heightened by the fact that they were both wearing scarves over their hair, tied low across their foreheads as if they were Hollywood gypsies. Persimmon's purple batik with fringe worked a lot better than Gaya's. She had a birthmark by her mouth, not a strawberry, but the kind that looks like a coffee stain. How cool to have a lesbian sister, thought Alison, touching Persimmon's hand. All she had was a brother who nagged her about tax loopholes.

Seven Yellow Moons and Lydia came up behind them. From her short phone conversation with Seven, Alison knew that Gaya and Hawk were the women who had actually put up the money for the land, and further, that Gaya had paid the lioness' share.

Seven seemed to know everyone already and there was a little round of hugs.

"I'm Alison," said Alison quickly before Michelle could speak. "And this is Painted Pony on a Serene Horizon." She made a flourishing gesture towards Michelle, who was so horrified that she could do nothing but stand with her mouth open.

Hawk wrinkled her brow. "We don't honor names that indicate cultural appropriation," she said.

"In the City," amended Alison quickly. "Painted Pony on a Serene Horizon in the City."

"Oooh." All three women nodded solemnly, as if this made sense and then engulfed first Michelle and then Alison in the hugging ritual.

Hawk held Michelle an instant too long, sniffing her neck.

"Did you get the rules that we sent out?" she asked, in a voice that was probably meant to sound friendly but came off sounding like a stern aunt.

Alison and Michelle looked at one another. What rule had they broken already? Alison got it first.

"Neither one of us is wearing perfume," she said.

Everyone stepped a little closer and sniffed Michelle as if she were a strange cat.

"Well, it doesn't have to be *perfume*," said Lydia, practically laying her nose right on Michelle's neck. "If you're going to be sensitive to women with environmental allergies then you can't use scented soap or lotion or shampoo, either. I don't use shampoo at all any more—that's just a Madison Avenue hype and it's a lot healthier to keep the oils. Americans bathe way too much." She looked supremely pleased with herself. Michelle looked a little embarrassed but mainly like she wanted to smack Lydia. This was kind of her standard expression when around Lydia.

"We should have made that more clear," said Persimmon. "There's soap and shampoo and skin lotion down by the showers. We're asking everyone to use the same kind while they're here." She gazed long into Michelle's eyes while saying this, as if the words were a cover for something only the two of them understood. Hawk handed them both a copy of the printed rules Seven had already sent them. "We want to make all lesbians welcome in our space, so we have a list of requests which will help make everyone comfortable. You can park and camp up the hill." She nodded towards the road. The main track climbed a small hill and seemed to end in front of a frame house, but there was a less traveled track that led off to the right. It also ended on a ridge, on the crest of which was parked a row of cars and trucks. "We're having an opening ritual and a tour as soon as you're settled—you're the last ones in." Her tone held just the slightest undertone of reproach, as if they'd been keeping everyone waiting. "Bring your car keys with you."

"Oh," said Gaya, speaking for the first time. Her voice was not as deep or melodic as Hawk's. "You have a dog." Lydia's nasty dog, who was obviously also a victim of the no shampoo phase, joined them. Gaya looked at Alison—after all, they had already broken one rule—who jerked a thumb at Lydia.

"We don't believe in keeping animals either domestically or as pets," said Hawk sternly. "We…"

Lydia held up a hand. "You need to talk to her," she said. "I don't own her or tell her what to do. She decided to come by herself, if she's not welcome you need to tell her and ask her to leave." She picked up her ancient backpack and walked back towards the car. Even the formidable Hawk did not seem to know how to answer this.

"What's her name?" she finally croaked faintly, just before Lydia was out of earshot.

"You need to ask her," said Lydia without looking back.

"Lydia calls her Zorra," volunteered Seven. In an aside to Alison she whispered, "It doesn't matter, she doesn't come anyway."

Michelle was looking murderous, so Alison stuck close to Seven as they walked back to their cars.

"Painted Pony on a Serene Horizon?" Michelle sputtered.

"In the City," reminded Alison. "We don't want to get into trouble for cultural appropriation."

"City Pony," suggested Seven, who usually refrained from needling Michelle, but obviously saw this as a chance too good to resist. The truth was that Michelle did look something like one of those wild little moor ponies. "We should unload the cement mixer before we park," she added.

"G-hey!" Seven called to a woman walking down the hill. "Come and meet Alison and City Pony."

G-hey! was as tall as Seven, and about ten or fifteen years younger than Alison. She was dressed in a leather loin cloth and some kind of little leather bikini top that was probably homemade. She looked better in a loin cloth than most women did in full evening wear. Her red hair was shaved except for two strips on either side. She had a tattoo of a phoenix just above her left ear and another of a strand of blue barbed wire around her left bicep.

"Hi!" Braced for another heartfelt hug, Alison was relieved by the casual greeting. G-hey! sprang in to give them a hand with the cement mixer, which came down with a thud in spite of her efforts.

CHAPTER TWO

"Just leave it here," said Seven. "We can move it when we come back down."

"Are you the women with the baby?" G-hey! asked Michelle. "I love babies, I'm thinking about having one."

Alison bit her tongue to keep back all the questions that sprang to mind—like where do you work and how did you plan to get the money and where would you live? Women had been bringing babies into the world long before there were IRAs, Alison, she told herself sternly. G-hey! looked awfully familiar—she wondered if she had met her before.

"He's at his grandfather's," Michelle answered, her confrontation face softening a little at the mention of Sam.

"Oh!" said G-hey! "A male child. I guess you couldn't bring him anyway, could you?"

Michelle's crab face slammed right back down. This was something neither she nor Alison had thought about when discussing the trip. No twelve-year-old boys, yeah, sure, but surely they didn't mean no babies in arms, did they?

"How come Janka's with your dad?" asked Seven who knew when it was time to change the subject.

"He begged," said Alison. Her father had suffered a major upheaval within the past year. With no warning, Alison's mother had left him after thirty years of marriage, leaving nothing behind but a post card which said, 'I'm bored.' With time heavy on his hands, he had spent a great deal of time helping Michelle fix the new house and yard. He had known Michelle since childhood, and looked upon Sammy with as much delight as any of his blood grandchildren, all of whom lived a plane ride away. Staying with him would be a wonderful rest for Janka, for he would cook and clean and get up with Sammy during the night as if it were a privilege.

"I know you, don't I?" said G-hey! to Alison. "Aren't you from Denver?"

Alison nodded. She had long before come to accept the fact that the lesbian underground was really very small. Because of

17

Womminfest, an indoor festival held in Albuquerque over Memorial Day weekend, everybody Alison knew in Denver had at least one friend in New Mexico.

"Oh, I know where I met you!" G-hey! continued, smiling. "I'm neighbors with Marta Goicochea."

Alison felt her own smile freeze and then begin to slide off her face. Oh, my god, she thought, unable to say anything, waiting for G-hey! to continue, to blurt out something like, 'Didn't you have a one night stand with Marta while you were mad at your girlfriend? Boy, she says you fucked her over big time!'

Michelle gave her a nudge in the ribs.

"What?" Alison croaked automatically, though the last thing she wanted to be doing was talking to this woman who, through just a few careless sentences, could break open a secret so well kept even Michelle did not know of its existence.

"Weren't you the cop who came when Marta hit that skinhead with a snow shovel?" G-hey! asked again. "I met you then."[2]

"Yeah, sure, of course," Alison stammered, hoping that her awkwardness would be taken for anything but guilt, even being dumb as a rock.

Seven broke in. "We should get set up. We gotta bring the cars up the hill and then be back down for the ritual."

At the top of the hill were around ten vehicles parked more or less in two rows. Michelle backed into a space flanked by an old truck and a fairly new four-wheel drive vehicle. "I want to be able to make a quick get away," she said to Alison out of the side of her mouth.

Behind the cars and trucks at the crest of the hill, was a small tent village. The tents, again running the gamut from old army surplus to the latest REI, were loosely clustered around two community fire pits. Alison looked at the new sheet of instructions they had received at the gate. As she had feared, this was the only space on the land where camping was permitted. The land dykes wanted, it was explained on the paper, to minimize the impact on the land. Alison could sympathize, but what difference would one tent make in four days? She wasn't going to trench it, and she always carried out her trash. There was no way she was going to be able to sleep with only a nylon wall cutting out the night noises of ten or fifteen other women. She gave a sigh. She would have to sleep in the back of Michelle's truck, a possibility for which she had prepared, but which she had hoped to avoid. What was the point of being out in the country if you couldn't go to sleep watching the stars?

Michelle, of course, had her own agenda for setting up the

campsite, so after she put her medication in the glove box, Alison drifted over beside Seven Yellow Moons, who was standing beside the old truck and talking to G-hey! Looking at the truck, Alison realized that she had seen it in the parking lot of Ms C's, the lesbian two-stepping bar in Denver. It was fairly distinctive, for it showed signs of several different paint jobs and had plastered on the tail gate a black and purple bumper sticker that read, 'First Matriarchy, then Anarchy!'

Further up the ridge they could see the building Alison had already identified as the main house. There were several outbuildings clustered around it—possibly chicken houses and out-sheds in another incarnation. One had been reduced to a heap of gray wood that looked as if it had collapsed in upon itself after too much weather. Down from both the main house and the camp ground were several small houses made of adobe. One, judging from the yard and windows, was lived in. The other, which was close behind the place where the women had greeted them, was just as obviously not. It must be the one they were to help finish. Beyond the unfinished adobe building was what looked like a wooden geodesic dome surrounded by a deck. Next to it was a patch of land that, from the tiny haze of green that covered it, was probably a garden, with something nearby that looked like a solar panel lying on the ground. Surrounding it all was the desert.

Alison had never actually visited a desert until she was an adult, and she had the prejudice of those growing up on Kentucky bluegrass lawns, but even she could see that the land stretching out before them was truly beautiful. Across the whole valley was a fine mist of color from the almost microscopic wild flowers that had bloomed after the last spring rain. Beyond the flatland rose a series of mesas, as stark and multicolored as if their very creation had been intended for nothing beyond viewing pleasure. Above them the sky stretched away for days, a pale blue panorama dotted with clouds. The clouds themselves reminded Alison of a Magic Eye picture—nothing to distinguish one from the other but its proximity. It took her breath away, and for the first time she was glad to be there, rather than just glad not to be in Denver.

"Cool bumper sticker," Alison said to G-hey!, who was rummaging through the gear in the back of her truck.

"You like it?" G-hey! beamed, which made her look even more lovely. Alison preferred women with long hair, but even she could see that G-hey! was knock down gorgeous. "My lover Salad and I make them. You wanna buy one?"

It seemed churlish to refuse, especially since it turned out they were only a dollar and G-hey!'s equipment—all old and/or second hand—made it look as if she were living close to the bone. The transaction completed, G-hey! asked Alison, "So how'd you get an invite?" She squatted down to examine the pebbles and sand at their feet, picked up a small stone and popped it into her mouth. Alison was so fascinated with this little ritual it took a nudge from Seven for her to realize she was being addressed.

"Oh!" she said, and then, "Oh, Seven invited us."

G-hey! rolled the stone around in her mouth as if it were a mouthful of fine wine, and then spat it out in her hand. She held it up to examine again, rubbing her thumb across its face.

"Seven invited you?" she asked in a puzzled voice.

Seven jumped in to explain. "Alison doesn't know. It was hard to snag invites to this party. The rest of us had to go through a questionnaire and interview process."

Alison raised an eyebrow. These women were asking for a weekend of hard labor performed without caffeine or cigarettes and you had to compete for the job?

Seven hastened to explain. "I didn't have a chance to tell you about the retreat. You and Michelle are the only ones who are allowed to leave after the weekend. The rest of us are going to be cloistered for a month."

"Allowed?" Alison seized upon the word with a bit of trepidation. She had never liked being told what to do, even as a child.

"No, not like that." Seven held up a hand. "The rest of us *want* to stay. This is an experiment, and we're all very excited about it."

"You had to agree to give up all outside contact," put in G-hey! who was still pawing through the stones at their feet. "No job, no letters, no phone calls—not everybody was willing to do that."

"I'll bet," said Alison. "What's the point? What are you trying to accomplish?"

"We're trying to create a way of living that isn't patriarchal," said G-hey!, suddenly rising to her feet. Alison saw Lydia's dog, ribs showing through its fur, approaching—she wouldn't want to be sniffed in a loin cloth, either. "We've all been raised in a patriarchy—you know? It's hard to quit thinking in those grooves. Being away from the mass media, men's voices, men's writing—we're hoping that if we spend our time concentrating on common goals…"

"Building the houses…" put in Seven.

"…then we can retrain ourselves to come up with new ways of thinking and working with one another."

"Oh!" said Alison, and then "Why did Michelle and I get to

come?" She did not even mention the photocopied map she had given to Stacy. Obviously that would be frowned upon, and Stacy wasn't going to show anyway.

"You have a cement mixer," said Seven bluntly.

"Oh!" said Alison again. She wondered if she should sulk, and then decided against it. Maybe Michelle's cement mixer rather than their own charm had bought their way in. Either way, they were in and, more importantly, they were going to leave at the end of the weekend. She wasn't sure at all that she would have wanted to stay for the retreat. The idea was interesting, and she was going to want to hear all about it, but the idea of spending a month sequestered was a bit much for her. You might as well be on jury duty.

"They *wanted* to make it six months," said Seven, as if reading her mind. The dog, Zorra, was making the rounds sniffing all hands. She looked at Seven with pleading eyes. "Damn that Lavender," she said, scratching her ears. "I ought to take this dog to the vet's and have her put to sleep."

"She looks hungry," said Alison, joining in for a scratch.

"She *is* hungry," said Seven. "Lavender has the idea that because her ancestors were wolves she can forage for herself. Which makes just about as much sense as dropping me in the middle of the desert and expecting me to survive just because my ancestors could do it."

"Could they really?" asked Alison in surprise, for though Seven had dark hair it had never occurred to her that she might be Native American.

"No," said Seven. "I was just using it as an example. My ancestors spent all their time annoying the English and eating kelp. Her ancestor's weren't wolves, either, not anymore than zebras are horses' ancestors."

The dog was nudging Alison's hands for more pats. One of her eyes looked infected. "What is with this dog? Does she belong to Lavender or not? Are you telling me that she didn't bring any dog food for a whole month?"

"No, probably not," said Seven. "She hasn't bought dog food since she got that dog. Excuse me, since the dog decided to live with her."

"What an asshole," said Alison, hoping that Seven had forgotten that she and Lydia had once been lovers, and that G-hey! need never be told. "How did she get invited?"

"Did you know that Lavender and Alison used to be girlfriends?" Seven said to G-hey!.

"Really!" G-hey! looked at Alison with what she feared was a

21

new and unflattering light.

"Lavender only got in because she looks good on paper," said Seven Yellow Moons, who was obviously on a tear.

"That's not fair," objected G-hey! "She really is into trying to live her life differently. She really does the things she talks about. Like, in her house, you can compost or recycle everything. That's so great! We should all do that."

"I know," said Seven with a note of apology. "I'm just ticked about the dog thing. She and the dog aren't master and slave, right? They're partners. They have this spiritual connection, and Lavender takes care of herself and the dog takes care of *herself* and if by chance they happen to find each other, it's beautiful. But what that really means is the rest of us have to feed that dog, because nobody has the heart to let her starve, and even if we did, Lavender *wouldn't care*.

"She'd say it was the will of the goddess, or something," agreed G-hey!, who seemed to know quite a bit about Seven's neighborhood. Alison wondered if she'd ever lived there. Quite a heavy and brisk trade went on between the Colorado and New Mexico communities. "She'd say that now the dog's soul had a chance to be born on another plane, and that it must have had a lot to work out on this one to be born a dog."

"And do you really think," Seven asked G-hey! "that Lavender has an invite?"

Alison looked at the dog, wondering what she and Michelle had in the truck that could become dog food. The women who owned the land were feeding the workers for the weekend, so they hadn't brought much in the way of provisions, and she didn't think the Oreos were a good idea—the chocolate thing.

"I'll bet that dog is pregnant." Michelle came up behind them, carrying a paper grocery sack that had been torn off two inches from the bottom. She set it on the ground and instantly the dog was on it, eating as if she hadn't seen food in days. Maybe, aside from Michelle's sandwich, she hadn't. "How do you say 'good dog' in Spanish?" Michelle asked Alison.

"I only know how to say cat," said Alison. "She's *una gata buena. Y blanca y negra tambien.*" The dog was actually brown rather than black, but since brown was not a usual cat color Alison did not know how to say it. She couldn't say purple, either.

"Wait a minute," said G-hey! to Seven. "Lavender wasn't invited?"

"Why do you think she's driving herself? I wouldn't take her with me once I found out what she was doing. I wasn't about to leave just because she got eighty-sixed."

"What does she think she's doing here, then?" asked G-hey!, obviously aghast.

"Who knows?" Seven made an expansive motion that washed her hands of the whole thing. "She got herself all in a tizzy when she found out Hawk and Gaya were interviewing—said they didn't have any right to exclude certain women and she wasn't going to play that game! They should have checked invitations at the gate. Right now probably no one knows she's crashing the party—you know, Hawk thinks Gaya invited her, and Gaya thinks Hawk invited her. And when they figure it out she's just counting on nobody wanting to make a scene. What are they going to do—call the local cops and have her thrown off? It'll be easier to put up with her."

"Why didn't you say something?" asked G-hey! disapprovingly.

"Not my problem," said Seven Yellow Moons, doing the hand thing again. "I want to totally stay out of it. Besides, it makes it more realistic. Lesbians are always crashing one another's parties."

Alison who thought that one of the very best things about moving was the fact that Lydia no longer had keys to her place, walked over to see what Michelle was feeding the dog.

"Hey," asked Michelle, "do you suppose the women who are running this place would like to have me throw out Lydia? I don't mind a little scene."

"You, in fact, delight in a scene," said Alison. "And you also seem to be feeding my expensive prescription cat food to this dog. By expensive, I mean that it cost thirty dollars a sack."

"That's what you get for doing errands on the way out of town," said Michelle brightly. "And we'll just make sure you claim that thirty as charity when you have your taxes done."

"Six months?" said Alison to Seven, figuring there was no sense fussing either about the cat food or Lavender's bad behavior, which were both done deals.

Zorra, the dog, began to throw up with the same vigor as she had been eating.

"Mmm, morning sickness," said G-hey!. She had squatted back down, but stood hastily, clutching her handful of rocks.

"That's a thirty dollar puke," Alison said to Michelle.

Michelle waved her off. "Don't worry about it. It'll go down better the second time anyway."

"I don't care how natural this is, I don't want to watch it." Seven turned and led them all down the hill. Zorra stayed, seeing if the food really *did* go down better the second time.

There was a loud clanging noise, and they all looked up

towards the main house. Hawk was banging on a large triangle. Alison had never seen one before outside of a TV western. She made a mental note—one of her and Michelle's endless and private car games consisted of listing things they knew existed but had never actually seen in person. Igloos. Gibbets. Volcanoes. Africa. Around them, women were setting down their gear and drifting up the ridge.

Hawk didn't waste any time with a second welcome.

"We're glad you're here," she said when the group—fifteen to twenty women—had assembled. "This may be one of the most important months of our lives. To start it off, we want everyone to sign a contract agreeing to our goals."

Gaya and Persimmon were passing out paper and pencils. Alison and Michelle, separated by Seven Yellow Moons and G-hey!, looked at one another. Alison tried to jockey close enough for a private chat, but she could feel Hawk's eye upon her, and that made it awkward. Everybody else seemed to be reading and signing without a qualm. She looked down at her paper. Simple, and handwritten. No photocopies here.

I vow and agree that I will dedicate myself to the creation of a new order of matriarchy while I am on this retreat at Mariposa Women's Land. I agree from this moment on to rededicate my heart to the creation of a way of life that renounces racism, abled-bodiedism, ageism, classism, sexism and male dominance. From this moment on I renounce all rules of the patriarchy which are harmful to women and I will do my best to take these vows out into the world once I leave the land.

Again Alison looked at Michelle. What she *wanted* to do was get her to one side and spend about half an hour talking about the pros and cons of signing something this encompassing, but she felt uncomfortable suggesting this with the land dykes standing right there. She had a sneaking suspicion that hesitation might get them kicked off immediately. It was cleverly worded—there was nothing to which she could really object. Of course she didn't want to be racist, or to judge other women by their class background or age. What was the problem? What could possibly happen if she agreed to suspend men's rules for the weekend? It probably wouldn't even come up.

She signed with a flourish and handed the paper back. Michelle signed more slowly, the frown lines around her eyes showing she had gone through the same dilemma and come to the same conclusion.

"Welcome! Welcome!" said all three women again. Alison couldn't help but notice that the welcome of the third woman,

Persimmon, was by far the heartiest, nor did she fail to notice the way that her eye's lingered on Michelle. If Michelle wanted to indulge in a little flirtation while away from the wife and family—and she had shown every sign of jumping at the chance—it wasn't going to be difficult.

"We're going to start with a tour," said Hawk. "That way we can show what we've done, what we're doing and explain our motives behind it all." She pointed back down the hill towards the houses Alison had seen from the campground. They were separated by about a hundred yards. The first was, as Alison had surmised, just a shell built of adobe bricks. This, obviously, was the one they were going to work on. The second was a beautiful little dwelling with two doors set in the front.

"We'll start at the new place," Hawk announced. She strode off down the hill without a backward glance. Alison, who would have had to run to keep up, perversely went into low gear. The path from the main house to both of the small houses was paved with tarmac, which she thought a bit odd. Seemed a bit out of keeping with the back to the land theme.

"Well, what'd you think of that?" she asked Michelle, who was also doing the slow walk thing.

"Makes *me* a little uneasy," Michelle admitted. "I hope that suspending white men's laws doesn't mean there's going to be a human sacrifice, or anything like that. You don't suppose they're going to want to seal someone inside the walls of the new building for good luck, do you?"

"If they do, you're much littler, you'd fit better. I'll be sure to point that out."

"Hmmph!" said Michelle. She angled over towards Persimmon, trying to cut her out of the herd. She'd caught the look, too. Alison looked away with a little flicker of dismay. Oh dear, Michelle wasn't thinking of having too much fun, was she? A flirtation, never to be discussed with Janka, was all well and good—Michelle needed a little pick me up. But anything more would be a disaster—Janka was firmly and immovably monogamous, a stance that, up until this moment, bouncing with childfree endorphins, Michelle had shared. Janka was also proud and stubborn—all she would need in her present mood would be just the tiniest hint that Michelle had sniffed another woman and all of Michelle's stuff would be right out on the lawn. Alison resolved to have a few words with Michelle if she started to get too animated. Part of the best friend job was putting in a few words to the wise concerning women, when needed. (Stacy had snuck in through Alison's back door when Michelle had not been paying attention.)

Hawk who was obviously the mouthpiece, arranged herself in front of the little crowd and began, "We were supposed to have a ritual, but I guess that's not happening right now, so we'll just start with the tour. This is the third…"

There was a stir at the back of the crowd.

"Get off the tarmac," said someone behind Alison. "You can stand on the earth the way that women were meant to stand."

Alison who didn't like being bossed or snapped at either, turned with a tart reply on her tongue. She snapped her mouth shut quickly when she saw the group of women making their way through the group. In the middle, like a queen bee, was a woman riding a three-wheeled, motorized cart. That explained the tarmac, thought Alison. The woman's hair was long and dark, parted in the middle and tied back with a blue band of cloth. She was wearing a white blouse with long, full sleeves, over which lay a heavy silver and turquoise squash blossom necklace. The blouse was tucked into a long, gauzy broomstick skirt with three tiers.

She was surrounded by a three very young women all dressed in a similar fashion, although their hairstyles (*really* short), piercings (nose, tongue, eyebrows, ears and lips) and tattoos (everywhere) were all their own. The way they clustered about her, touching her chair and vying for a chance to help her to her feet reminded Alison of the way the secret service men had acted the time she had gone to see Hillary Clinton speak at the Tattered Cover; everyone jumping to their feet when the First Lady wanted a drink of water.

While everyone stared, the woman climbed from the cart and, with the help of her aides and leaning on a heavy cane, limped up to stand beside Hawk. Alison noticed that, while she was wearing half boot moccasins, her entourage was all wearing Doc Martins.

"You were supposed to wait for me," the woman said to Hawk.

"You weren't here." Hawk looked at her watch. "We agreed on when we were going to start and it was forty-five minutes ago and you weren't here."

"Pah!" Alison had never actually heard anyone say 'Pah!' before. "White man's time. I tell time by the sun and the change of the seasons." She made a broad gesture with one hand, sweeping the sky from horizon to horizon. She was making no effort at all to speak in a private voice. In fact, she acted rather as if she were on stage. "If you're really sincere about changing the way that you think, the male way, then you'll take off that watch right now. How can you listen to what the earth is saying if all you can hear is the ticking of the clock that you wear on your arm?" She held out her

26

hand in an imperious manner as if Hawk was going to take it off and hand it over right that minute. The young women who had followed the cart through the crowd made a collective sound of approval rather like a Greek chorus.

Hawk abruptly turned away from the other woman and back towards the crowd. "We'll do the tour after the ritual," she said shortly. She walked over to join Gaya, using short, choppy steps. Didn't need a Betazoid to tell you she was pissed. Alison raised an eyebrow at Michelle, who had ended up standing beside her. Were we having dyke drama already?

"My name," said the woman, turning to face the group with a pleased air, "is Etonya-kyita."

She was, Alison noticed, also rather tall. What was this, land of the Amazons? She was used to being the tallest woman in her crowd—she wasn't sure she liked being topped by at least three other women. Their age, she would guess from the lines around the other woman's eyes, was probably about the same.

"That name," the woman went on, "was taken from me at the schools of the white man, and I became Sarah Embraces-All-Things, the closest translation that could be understood by the white teachers. I ask that you honor at least the memory of the name taken from me by your people by using my full name. Sarah is not a name of the people. It means nothing."

"Actually," whispered Michelle who could be a font of trivia "it means 'Princess'."

Alison resisted an urge to pinch her. She should have known better than for them to stand together—they were forever been kicked out of serious occasions for behaving badly, starting way back in the fifth grade when Michelle had made Alison laugh so hard in assembly that water came out her nose. They couldn't sit together at the movies, either.

"I was told that being taken from the bad influence of my family and learning white ways would make me successful in the world, would get me out of the 'Red ghetto,' and I was given a social security number so that in case I was another failure I could apply for welfare. But today," she said, throwing her arms out wide, "I am giving that number back! We are all on the verge of a wonderful experiment, we have within us, in this group, the ability to create a whole new way of life, a life that revolves around the Mother and women as her acolytes." The wind fluttered her shirt and her long, dark hair out behind her. Michelle glanced at Alison with an all-too-readable expression—What are we getting into here?

Out of the basket mounted on the front of her cart Sarah

Embraces-All-Things pulled a coffee can and a bundle of sage.

"Come and be smudged," she said, like a revivalist calling backsliders up to the rail. "Come and give us a token of your dedication to this experiment. Come and tell us what you wish for our new world."

What this meant, Alison realized after the first woman stepped up, was put your car keys in the coffee can. Alison glanced nervously at Michelle. She didn't like this idea at all. But Michelle the Control Queen who was uncharacteristically near the beginning of the line, was looking straight forward and tossed her keys in the can without a flinch after she'd had the smudge run up and down her body. For a moment, Alison was afraid that her wish might be 'Get laid', but instead she said demurely, "I want to complete a large job with other women," which, while not quite as encompassing or cosmic as the other wishes—'Change the world', 'Create a community in which there are only lesbians'—was accepted without comment.

It took about ten minutes to cleanse everybody, and then Hawk stepped forward, clearing her throat. Sarah Embraces-All-Things, however, was not yet through with them. She gave a mighty yell, a TV war whoop, and flung the can up onto the roof of the building on which they were to plaster adobe. Alison's jaw dropped.

"Our goal is to have the stairs to this roof done by Tuesday," she announced. "Most of you have committed yourselves to the month. But—and against my warning—we have accepted two women until Tuesday only. May this encourage them to realize our goal."

Alison looked around her swiftly. She didn't want to sulk this early in the game, but did Sarah Embraces-All-Things have to say it that way? It made her and Michelle sound like a couple of freeloaders. And suppose they *couldn't* get the stairs done? She had never worked with adobe, but she *had* helped Michelle with a couple of carpentry jobs around the house, and she knew that it always seemed to take about three times as long to finish a job as you thought it would. From the expression on the faces of Hawk and Gaya, it was obvious they hadn't been in on this little part of the plan. Gaya looked a bit apprehensive and Hawk, as she stepped up again, just plain pissed.

"We want to show you a house that's already finished," she said shortly, her words clipped. "So you have an idea of what it's going to take to finish this one." She turned and began marching towards the finished house. After a moment's hesitation—Is this over?—the women began to follow her in a ragged group.

Alison maneuvered her way over by Michelle. "What did you do that for?" she asked out of the side of her mouth. "How are we going to get home if there's a problem with those stairs?"

"Are you crazy?" answered Michelle in a low, but very pleased voice. "I didn't give them *my* keys—I gave them *your* keys. One of the other women at the campground told me what was coming, so I got them out of your bag while you were talking to Seven."

"My keys!" Alison sputtered. "You mean my house keys, and my car keys and…"

"Listen," said Michelle, holding up her hand like a stop sign, "there is not one single key on your ring that we can't replace easily when we get home. My car keys, however, could be a problem."

This was so reasonably true that Alison snapped her mouth shut.

"Besides," said Michelle, "if we needed those keys, we could get them. I'll bet there are a million ways to get on that roof."

Gaya loped past them to catch up with Hawk. For the first time she looked graceful, rather than gawky, though there was something a little off about her stride.

Before Alison could put her finger on what it was, they had covered the short distance to the finished house, or 'casita' as the land women referred to it. Alison could not help but draw a breath—it was beautiful, a tiny gem that both blended into the desert and was set off by it like a modest jewel in a plain gold setting.

"This is the only dwelling that we've completed so far," Hawk told them. The walk had taken a bit of the anger out of her voice. Then, too, Alison saw that Sarah Embraces-All-Things had not been able to join them directly. They had cut across terrain that must have been too rough for her three-wheeler. She'd had to go up the paved path to the main house, and then back down the paved path that led to the house in front of which they were standing.

"It's meant for two people," Hawk continued, talking fast, as if she wanted to get this part of it done before Sarah Embraces-All-Things rejoined them. "We envision a community of lesbians on this land some day, and we wanted to plan our dwellings so that everyone would have private as well as communal space. None of the casitas will have a kitchen, because we intend to eat together. They do, however, have bathrooms, and are wired for electricity. Oh, and speaking of bathrooms, I should point our shitter and showers out to you." She gestured up the hill, where against the skyline they could see what appeared to be the seat and hole part of an outhouse. Alison could tell, by the way she said the word, that

Hawk was the kind of woman who thought modesty about body functions just a plot of the patriarchy, and who planned to do her part to kill it. "The showers are down by the garden—the garden is watered by their runoff. That's one of the reasons you can only use the soap that we provide. The other is that we are trying to be sensitive to women with environmental illnesses. In the casitas, for example, we have used only timber that has not been chemically treated…"

She continued in the same vein, telling them about the building, but Alison had stopped listening, so taken by the lovely lines of the little house. There were no sharp angles—each wall of the house flowed into the next. From either end of the house two low walls curved around like wings to partition a tiny patio in the back. Small openings had been built into these walls at random points, so that here and there a pot had been set and a plant was growing—a squash, two cucumber vines and several tomato plants. Alison saw that they were connected to a drip system which was in turn connected to a water tank sharing the roof with a solar panel. It looked as if there was probably room for a chair or mattress up there as well. A set of shallow, unrailed adobe stairs followed the line of the house up to the roof. That must be what they were supposed to build by Tuesday.

Hawk was just opening the door on the left when Sarah Embraces-All-Things arrived, obviously in a huff. The three young women who had faithfully followed her were just as obviously in a huff on her behalf.

"Someday," she said with heavy emphasis, "this land is going to be accessible to all women. Until then…" she trailed off, sweeping them all with a hard look to let them know they had behaved badly. She turned off her motor and stood, using the cane. Hawk was still standing with the door open, and Sarah Embraces-All-Things swept past her without acknowledgment. Alison noticed that she was no longer limping. After a moment of hesitation and a tightly controlled gesture from Hawk, the women trailed after her.

The inside of the house was just as lovely as the outside. On either side of a spacious entry way/bathroom area there were two round rooms, obviously meant to be used something like studio apartments. Both rooms had a skylight as well as strategically placed windows. The floor was brick. Only one side—obviously belonging to Sarah Embraces-All-Things from the way that she took aggressive possession—was being lived in.

Sarah Embraces-All-Things had decorated with a heavy mystic hand—there were crystals and tarot cards and dream catchers all laid out or fanned for display, as well as a number of goddess figures and bundles of sage hanging from the eaves. It should have been charming, but Alison was not charmed. What was that all about? she wondered. Was it simply the presence of Sarah Embraces-All-Things herself, whom she had already labeled a bully? Whatever the reason, while Sarah Embraces-All-Things lectured the rest of the group about the lengths to which they had gone to avoid chemical contamination, Alison wandered into the second room.

The second room was very obviously not currently inhabited, which was actually nice, because in its bare bones state Alison could see details that had been hidden beneath Sarah's decor. There was a double bed, neatly made with one blanket, against one wall. Alison realized that it, as well as the bookshelves and desk, had been built into each room. Which made sense of course. It would have been difficult to find furniture to follow the curved wall. She walked over to trail her hand across the back of the desk. It was not just a table, but had two tiers of pigeon holes curved above it. It was beautifully done.

There was a small sound behind her, and she turned to see that Gaya had entered the room behind her, and was looking about with that pleased but shy expression some artists get when viewing their own work.

"This is very beautiful," said Alison sincerely. Twenty years ago, when they had all been discussing communes and women's land, she would have been completely seduced by this room. Even now, when the thought of communal living filled her with only a little less dread than the thought of losing her teeth, she felt its pull. "Did you do all of this by yourselves?" She flung her arm out to encompass the house.

"Yes," said Gaya. "This is our second house. Hawk and I live in a house up the hill. We worked out a few imperfections on it—you know how it is the first time."

"I'm impressed," said Alison. "I couldn't build a birdhouse by myself. Did you do it out of a book?"

"Some," said Gaya. "I was in... I used to be a carpenter. It came in handy."

Now that they had traded compliments and thank yous, there was suddenly a moment of awkwardness between them. All of the things that Alison wanted to ask seemed edged with cynicism. Where do you get your money and what did you ask on the interviews and doesn't this whole idea of a separate life out here in the desert seem strangely artificial?

So instead, she ran her hand over the desk again and then asked, "How did you get the idea for a retreat like this?"

Gaya laughed softly. "It's something I've always wanted to do. My whole life—I've always wanted to be around just women. Men..." she gave a delicate little shudder, "I've always had to be around men. I just don't like them. I don't like the way they do things, I don't like the way they talk about things, I don't like the way they communicate, or the way they compete. I was forced to be around that for years, and now that I have the luxury of choosing, I just don't want to be around them anymore." Her voice was as soft as her laugh, and she looked over her shoulder twice, anxious. Alison realized that she was afraid of upstaging Sarah Embraces-All-Things, a woman who obviously did not like being upstaged.

"We're using this space as a guest room, until we get some more collective members," Gaya added, still keeping her voice low.

"Well, it's lovely," said Alison again. She did not want to continue a conversation that had to be held in whispers—it made her feel manipulated. She walked over to the window and looked out, up the hill at what Seven had told her was the original house.

"I'm impressed," she said again, and then went out to wait for Michelle by the wall.

The rest of the tour was just as impressive. There were no electrical lines, but there was plenty of power—the buildings and the showers all had solar panels and there was a generator run by a windmill as well. The dome *was* a sweat lodge, big enough for at least twenty.

Between the main house, which Hawk told them they could explore for themselves at dinner time, and the sweat lodge ran another arroyo. Several of the women elected to walk on the soft sand in its bed.

"Hey," said one of them, a butch gal whose name Alison had not caught, "look, I found an arrowhead!"

Everyone crowded around to look.

"Arroyos are a good place to find artifacts," said Persimmon, who up until this point had not spoken in front of the group. "The rain washes them down, or it uncovers them. We've found pottery and knives and even a few bones. That's a knife, incidentally."

"What should I do with it?" asked the woman. "Do you sell them? Is that part of the way you support the land?"

There was a rather pained silence—obviously a faux-pas had been committed. Gaya spoke first, and quickly, as if perhaps she wanted to head off a harsher explanation.

"Actually," she said, "you can give it to me. We have some

Native American neighbors, and we give everything we find to them. They pass them on to the appropriate tribal elders."

Someone behind Alison cleared her throat, but before she could speak Hawk jumped in.

"We wouldn't feel right about selling anything," she said. "How would you feel if someone dug up your great-grandmother and sold her wedding ring?"

The woman who had found the knife flushed and handed it to Gaya without asking any more questions. There was an awkward silence, broken finally by Zorra snapping at a horned toad. Everyone laughed in relief, and Hawk turned back towards the sweat lodge. The crowd of women began to speak and laugh again as they followed her down the hill.

The tour over and the rules of the sweat lodge explained—use the fuel sparingly, don't sweat alone, hang the fetish on the door if you're doing a ritual—they started right to work. Michelle, of course, had to get right into the thick of things. Well, it made sense, they were using her cement mixer for the adobe. She was hanging over it and shoveling and looking in the mouth and asking a ton of questions. By the time they started back to Denver she'd be able to build an adobe house all by herself. Michelle picked things up quickly.

Alison, a bit less zealous, found herself on an outer wall facing the desert, Seven-Yellow-Moons beside her. Seven, from the practiced way in which she dug into the tub that Michelle, being important again, lugged over and set between them, had obviously done adobe before. Alison drew on her work gloves—don't forget them! the flier had warned—and copied her.

It was a very mindless, soothing job. She could see right away that even taking the old bell curve into account the very best people were not going to be much better than the very worst. You slapped the adobe on—looking for scorpions, as Seven had warned her—and you spread it with your trowel. That was it. Within ten strokes Alison began to go into a Zen state. Beside her she could hear Seven Yellow Moons chatting up G-hey!, but it was very removed—something like the buzzing of an insect.

Alison had worked this way for perhaps an hour—sitting on a crate and doing the low wall, which was easier on her back and hips—when there was some slight commotion in the women around her that made her look up. Shading her eyes—she was wearing her sunglasses, but they were looking right into the setting sun—she saw two riders approaching on horseback. Well, that was kind of cool, she thought. She'd ridden before herself, but nothing

33

like this. Nothing like riding across the huge vista of the desert from some remote dwelling that could neither be seen nor guessed at. Nothing like moving as if part of the horse. You could tell right away that these two people weren't tourists. Alison sat back on her crate, enjoying the two riders as if they were the big screen. It wasn't for another minute of murmuring that she realized everyone was not as thrilled with this little taste of the west as she was. She looked around, brow furrowed. What was the problem? G-hey! was leisurely putting a long tailed shirt over her outfit—in the back ground Alison could hear Hawk scolding. Oh! That was it! One of the riders was a man. Alison had not bothered to look past their cin-ema-graphic possibilities, so taken in was she by the flying tails and the felt cowboy hats. Now, alerted, she saw that the taller rider was a man, the smaller a young woman.

The air around the house was electrified. Alison herself was a bit curious as to how this one was going to be handled. She looked around for Hawk, who had hustled everyone back into their shirts. What was she going to do? The rule list said, in fact the very *first* rule said No Men On Mariposa. But that meant through the gate, right? Surely it didn't mean neighbors riding over to say hi, did it? That, thought Alison, shoveling up another trowel full of adobe, would be just plain dumb. There weren't many people out here in the desert. Being on good terms with the neighbors might be a mat-ter of life and death in a crisis, although these two people, if they were neighbors, could not live much closer than the town. The view went on for miles, and there weren't any houses in sight.

Also, Alison could see as the riders drew closer that they were probably Latino, and she had a feeling that for a woman like Hawk that might make a huge difference in how they were treated. Straight white men were clearly the enemy, but things might become a little more clouded around a man of Color. Nobody would want their antagonism towards a man mistakenly judged racist rather than separatist. It was a tough life, Alison thought, when you were trying to be a purist. She sat down to watch with interest.

The riders drew right up to the cast and dismounted. The woman—about Alison's age, silver hair in black beneath her hat, dismounted as if she did not have ten pairs of eyes upon her. She spoke to Hawk in Spanish. Hawk replied with a fluency that made Alison burn with jealousy. Obviously they knew one another. Hawk handed her the stone knife that the woman had found in the arroyo, and pointed up at the house to which they walked. Perhaps these were the neighbors through which the Mariposa collective funneled artifacts.

The man dismounted as well, but he did not move towards the women. He lit a cigarette and looked gravely out across the desert, the very set of his back telling Alison that he knew he was not welcome. Alison's heart clenched for him. He was an older man, possibly the girl's grandfather. She loved her own father dearly—he had supported her in every aspect of her life. He did not understand her lesbianism, but she and Michelle were *his* queers, and by god no one would say one bad word about them or their kind while he was around them. She was not yet ready for the kind of separatism that these women proposed, not ready to give up her father and her brother, her partner, Robert, or Michelle's little son Sammy. She stood and moved closer to the man, finding the wall of silence around him insufferable. Out of the corner of her eye she saw a small parade progressing up to the big house—the women who *really* could not deal with even one male neighbor visiting. Gaya, Lavender, Sarah Embraces-All-Things and her court, plus a few others she did not know.

"*¿Tiene usted un cigarette?*" she asked the man politely, because it was something she knew how to say and because—no matter what the anti-smokers said—asking for a cigarette was still the easiest way in the world to start a conversation.

The man looked at her gravely and then smiled, a quite wonderful smile that lit up his face and turned the skin around his eyes into a mass of lines.

"*Si.*" A cigarette was produced and lit. Alison knew that she was not the only tobacco addict who was going cold turkey this weekend—she could practically hear drooling behind her.

"*¿Tiene usted un gato?*" she asked. She could not help herself, but instantly she felt her face flame with foolishness. She waited for the man to laugh, or mount and ride away haughtily.

Instead, he considered the question for a long moment, and then answered in a grave voice, "*Si, dos gatos. ¿Y usted?*"

Alison was so relieved that she babbled, telling him not only KP's name, but his colors and age. He listened to this to this with the same serious consideration, and then volunteered that his cats were brothers, and black.

Who knows to what cultural bonding this exchange might have eventually led, but at that moment the young woman returned and Alison's conversation was pre-empted. She could not follow the quick exchange between the two of them, which was fine, because Miss Manners would not have approved of her listening anyway. The only sentence she caught came when they had wheeled their horses in preparation to leaving.

"Look at the chickens," said the old man to his granddaughter in Spanish pointing with his chin. Alison, as well as the other woman, looked up the hill, but all she saw were the women who had left earlier, standing by the door of the house and looking at something in the dirt to which Sarah Embraces-All-Things was pointing. Alison turned back, thinking that she had misunderstood, but it was too late to ask any questions for they had turned away. They were speaking in Spanish, their heads close together, and they laughed before they started off again across the desert.

"Need a refill?" Michelle appeared, carrying a tub of adobe. She looked critically into the bucket Alison was using and for a moment seemed about to make a comment about her speed or progress. One good look stopped that.

"Neighbors?"

"I guess." Michelle shrugged. Obviously she had been concerned with much more important things.

"Hawk speaks Spanish really well," said Alison just as if she were a good sport and not burning with jealousy.

"Yeah. Persimmon says that she does a lot of stuff well. She says that she and Gaya practically built those first two houses by themselves from the ground up. Drew the plans, connected the solar, everything."

"Wasn't Persimmon living here?" asked Alison, dipping her trowel into the bucket. Ooh, there was a scorpion, just as Seven had warned her there might be. She picked it out carefully with the tip of the trowel, walked off twenty feet and threw it into the sagebrush. She did not know the official policy on the insect kingdom and she didn't want to ask. She was afraid Sarah Embraces-All-Things or one of her minions might make her wash it off and give mouth to mouth.

"Oh, yeah," replied Michelle. She put down the tub and put both hands on her back to give a little stretch. "She says she's only a scut worker—she's only good for carrying bricks and putting on adobe. But she brings in money with her stained glass," she added hastily, as if Alison was getting ready to accuse Persimmon of not pulling her share.

Alison didn't care if Persimmon had a round trip ticket on the gravy train. "That must have been hard work," she said, looking up the hill at the little house where Sarah Embraces-All-Things lived. "They were smart to get some help on this one."

"Persimmon used to live at Canyon Land," offered Michelle. Canyon Land was the womyn's land on which Seven Yellow Moons,

Lavender, half a dozen other women and twenty dogs lived.

"Gaya too?" asked Alison. She needed to scratch her nose, but she knew from experience that taking off her gloves without washing them first would result in adobe everywhere. And it stained. She rubbed her nose on her shoulder.

"No, only Persimmon. Gaya lived out on the east coast, I think. Persimmon hasn't said much about it—I gathered that there were some family problems and they were kind of estranged for a bunch of years. At least, nobody I've talked to met Gaya before they bought here." Michelle always felt that it was her job to keep Alison up on the gossip. And she did a good job, too.

"How come Gaya has money and Persimmon doesn't?" Alison asked, doing a creative little wavy thing with the trowel. If she knew anything at all, Michelle would know the answer to this. Michelle was very interested in other people's money.

Michelle did not fail to produce.

"She had a rich godfather," she replied promptly. "Died and left her a bundle. Persimmon says she's sunk almost all of it here."

"Hope it pays off," said Alison, who was becoming more and more immersed in the pattern on the wall. "Hope they get some new women this weekend."

"This isn't the final coat," pointed out Michelle. "Someone's going to plaster right over the top of that."

Alison gave her a sulky look. Was it continually necessary to rain on her parade?

Michelle was obviously going to ignore the sulk, so Alison decided not to waste her energy.

"How'd they connect with Sarah Embraces-All-Things?" she said, sotto voce.

As if summoned by the thought, Sarah Embraces-All-Things herself appeared from the other side of the building. Alison was glad she had been watching her voice. Sarah Embraces-All-Things was carrying a bundle of burning sage in her left hand. In the right she clutched the heavy cane which Alison was becoming convinced was only for show. She was followed by the same three young women who had accompanied her at the tour. Alison didn't know how they ever got a chance to take a shit—she hadn't seen them step away from Sarah Embraces-All-Things for a moment. But Sarah's room had not shown signs of more than one person living there. Perhaps the Ducklings detached at night. Making a broad stroke with her trowel, Alison tried to remember the names of the three women. Seven had told her, and she knew that they all went together, but she could not think of the category. Flowers? Birds?

Sarah Embraces-All-Things aggressively smudged the area around Alison, coming right up close enough to touch Michelle. She ignored her instead.

"He didn't come this far," said Alison without turning her head. "He stayed over there—look at the boot tracks."

"You didn't have to *welcome* him," said one of the Ducklings in a shrill and confrontational tone. She had a somewhat longer hair-cut than the other two, and really bad acne. Sarah Embraces-All-Things gave her a look obviously meant to remind her that she was just the ring bearer and she snapped her mouth shut with a click, looking chagrined.

Sarah Embraces-All-Things walked up behind Alison and began smudging her from the back, blowing smoke into her hair while one of her assistants chanted and another played a recorder.

This was too much. Alison stood so abruptly that she toppled her crate and came close to doing the same to Sarah Embraces-All-Things.

"I do not need to be smudged," she said in a cold, controlled voice. "I have enough good energy to survive a ten minute conversation with a man about cats. You, on the other hand," she pointed at the Duckling with the acne, "need to shower. You smell bad. Smudging is not a replacement for deodorant." She stalked around the corner, following Michelle who had already beaten a hasty retreat and practically ran into Seven Yellow Moons.

"I don't know how you're going to put up with a month of *that*," she said, jerking her head back towards the recorder music.

"Mmm," replied Seven who was standing on a crate to do the high part. "This is stupid. They must have some scaffolding."

"Maybe they don't want to break it out until Michelle and I leave," said Alison snippily. "Maybe we won't do our best job if we don't have a motive to get those stairs done."

Seven turned around to look at her and then stepped down off the crate. "Fuck that," she said. "I'm not doing anything above shoulder height until some scaffolding shows up. Blow Sarah off," she suggested. "Go have a Diet Pepsi."

This was such a good suggestion that Alison could not think of a single reason to resist. However, she could not keep from muttering as she headed up to the car.

"Six months," she said aloud as she walked up the hill. "I don't know how they thought anyone could have put up with six months of that crap!"

CHAPTER THREE

"Six months?" said Alison in an undertone to Seven Yellow Moons when they finally sat down for dinner. There was a hole in her stomach that the tail end of the Oreos had done nothing to fill. It was almost ten o' clock, and they had worked all afternoon. Alison hadn't thought that simply spreading mud on the walls of a structure would be so taxing, but it had turned out to be unexpectedly hard work. She was exhausted. If it hadn't been for the food issue, she would have gone straight to bed. But she hadn't eaten a real meal all day, and she knew that she would pay dearly the next morning if she didn't pack in something substantial before sleeping.

Dinner had been the first hurdle in releasing the patriarchy. Alison, along with all of the workers—there were eighteen in all, counting the four land dykes—had assumed that their hostesses had things under control, and would ask for kitchen help if it was needed. When seven o' clock had come and gone with no sign even of preparation someone had asked.

"We all need to make some kind of arrangements for feeding," Hawk had told them solemnly. "In the patriarchy, there are certain expectations about food—expectations about who will provide it, who will prepare it and who will serve it. If we are truly going to use this time to break old patterns, then we need to approach each of our daily rituals without expectations, with new and open minds."

Michelle, who had been standing across the half circle from Alison, had turned so red that Alison had feared the top of her head would blow off, but nobody else seemed to think this was too out of line. There were some musing nods, and after Hawk had stopped speaking and melted back into the circle without further suggestion, various women had offered either to cook or voiced ideas about scheduling.

Luckily they had not, as Alison feared, been forced to go out and hunt and gather. The back room of the communal house was as full as a warehouse—enough food for twenty women for a month. But neither was there any hint of a preplanned menu. Hawk had drifted off towards the sweat lodge, followed by a little bevy of women who must have had a hell of a lot of confidence in their sisters. Alison hoped they were planning on cooking breakfast. She and Michelle were leaving in four days—she'd fast before she became a kitchen drudge. She didn't care what she needed to work out from her last life—she'd rather come back as a dog than a dishwasher.

Although the good news had been that there *was* food, the bad news had been that none of it would take less than an hour to prepare—and the time had been nearly doubled for twenty people. It had occurred to Alison, while chopping onion after onion, that if the six women who had ended up in the kitchen *really* wanted to push the envelope, they could just make dinner for themselves. That would have shaken a few expectations.

But she hadn't the heart for it, and it must not have occurred to Michelle, who of course had ended up in the thick of the burritos—how could a good job be done without her supervision? After all, these women were going to have to spend the next month together—they didn't need to start off on a vengeful foot. Besides, even though Alison's first impulse had been to pull Hawk's head off—she didn't handle low blood sugar well—her challenge certainly *had* made her think. It was obvious from the conversation in the kitchen that the whole kitchen crew was pondering the same question—How was the community going to make sure everyone pulled her own weight without reverting back to a familiar system of bosses and workers? Alison had spent a couple of summers at Girl Scout camp, and she knew that no matter how well you worked the old patrol system and kaper chart, there was always somebody dicking around when it was time to clean the biffies. She was going to want a full report from Seven Yellow Moons after the experiment ended.

"*Six months*?" she asked again when they had finally all gathered at the huge table. "That's a hell of a long time to be sequestered, isn't it?"

"Yeah," said Seven, helping herself to a rather strange-looking salad-type dish. The woman who had put it together had obviously *really* liked carrots. "Kind of like being on the O.J. trial, huh?"

Alison was a little surprised by this reference, and she had to remind herself to be careful with the stereotypes. Even though Seven Yellow Moons lived in a small, woman-built house that had no electricity or running water there was no reason to think she hadn't heard of TV. She took the bowl of salad and, following Seven's suit, dumped a couple of helpings right onto her burrito.

"Yeah," Seven continued, taking a long hard look at a plateful of cornbread that had obviously gone wrong somewhere in the process. "It was a great idea. Really. Wonderful things have come from cloistered groups. Probably the only reason that written language survived during the Dark Ages is because it was kept alive in monasteries. I mean, there's been a lot of craziness, too, but if you're free to work on those things that concern your community— you know, not worrying about wage work or the mortgage or what's happening in Congress, then that's a lot of time for process and meditation."

Alison was not sure if she wanted that much time for process and meditation. Her tolerance for process had diminished greatly since her early bookstore days.

"But they decided not to do it." Seven had gone back to the six months issue. "There weren't enough women who were willing to agree, or who could afford to take the time off from work." She took a piece of the oddly shaped cornbread and placed it all by itself on the corner of her plate, as if to prevent possible contamination.

"I imagine," said Alison, hesitating over the bread. She finally took a piece—Zorra would probably enjoy it even if she did not. "I mean, I'd still have house payments, even if I was staying down here."

"Actually," Seven lowered her voice in what was obviously preparation to gossip, "I think they could have gotten enough women. What they *couldn't* have gotten was enough of the right kind of woman. You know," she gave a little nod down the table towards Lavender, who was in the middle of some long story about a dream either she or possibly the dog had dreamt the night before. "I mean, what the women who own this place are looking for eventually is women who are willing to come and live here permanently. You know, they want to build a planned lesbian community. But there's a lot of work to do here. They want women who are open to new ideas, sure, but they also want women who are hard workers." Neither needed to mention Lavender by name. She was a well-known lily of the field. "They've got some pretty big plans." Seven made an all encompassing gesture with her fork. "Did you know that they want to open the ranch to retreats eventually?"

"What do you mean?" asked Alison.

"Well, you know, if your Wicca group or your bookstore staff or your soccer team—something like that—wants to do a retreat they can come and camp and use the sweat lodge and all that and the Mariposa women will provide meals."

Alison thought about this before answering, wondering who

41

was the cook among the Mariposa women. She'd bet it wasn't Sarah Embraces-All-Things or Hawk. On the other hand, it did sound like a great income idea, and it also explained why the sweat lodge, which they had been shown on the tour, was so particularly nice. Alison had expected a lodge similar to the one on Canyon Land, which was covered with old blankets and had a dirt floor, so she had been surprised by the finely sanded wooden floor and the benches which lined the perimeter of the spacious dome.

"That's a good idea," she said finally. "I went to a retreat like that once—there's a Buddhist place up by Boulder that does it. Except I'm not sure if I'd want to camp out if I was on a retreat."

She gave a little shudder, thinking of the night ahead. And she used to love to camp. She gave a little sigh and then forged ahead with the conversation in order to keep from getting mired in self-pity.

"I'm pretty impressed with what they've done already," she admitted. The woman who had chopped tomatoes next to her during the preparation of dinner—she hadn't caught her name—had told her that the house they were in had been the original ranch house. (Alison supposed that was the correct term, although she had no idea of what type of farming or ranching could be done in an area that seemed so barren.) The house had obviously been through fairly extensive remodeling. The kitchen had been designed with collective cooking in mind—there was tons of counter space, as well as a huge freezer, an industrial-size double sink and two refrigerators, one a walk-in. Suspended from the ceiling above the two large ovens was a wooden rack from which hung a variety of pots, pans, colanders and bowls. You could cook for three or ten or twenty. There had also been a more than adequate selection of slicing, mixing and stirring tools, although nothing in the food processing family. The tomato woman, who was chatty, had told Alison that the four women who currently lived on the land believed in the mantra 'Chop wood, carry water'—that is, satisfaction and peace could be acquired through the carrying out of everyday chores.

The dining room was also huge. Like the cookware, the three tables at which they were sitting could be arranged to comfortably accommodate a small, large, or in-between number. The cooks had pushed two together and they were all sitting family style. There was still plenty of room left over to walk around the edges. Alison suspected that a wall or two had been knocked out to open it to the kitchen, and consequently, make it easier to serve. Full bowls and platters could be put onto the counter from the kitchen side and removed from the dining room side, and the process reversed during clean up.

Alison had not had much of a chance to look at the rest of the house, but the quick tour she had taken on her way in gave the impression that it was just as pleasant and roomy as the two main rooms. There was a large library of women's books and publications, and what appeared to be a music/reading/socializing room, which opened off onto a lovely secluded patio paved over with flagstone and lined with pinon pine trees. There were also several smaller rooms that were being used for storage or crafts. All of the rooms were decorated with a wonderful abundance of women's artwork—the walls were hung with paintings and weavings and quilts, and the ceilings with mobiles, chimes and ornaments. The house reminded Alison of Michelle and Janka's apartment in this way, right down to the beautiful stained glass pieces that hung in several window. Tomato Woman who had apparently been on the land a couple of days already, said those were made by Persimmon, who had a workshop up behind the communal house. The only difference was that Michelle and Janka operated on a budget. Whoever had collected the artwork in this house did not.

Thinking of Michelle made Alison realize that her friend had not been heard from once during the meal, a state of affairs so unusual that for a moment she was alarmed. She glanced quickly down the table to her right. Michelle had a satisfied look and a sunburnt nose. She was in deep conversation with Persimmon. Alison caught only a phrase or two of their conversation, but it was enough to tell her the topic—stained glass. Michelle must be in heaven—like Stacy who was a quilt maker, she seldom ran into lesbian peers. Maybe that little twitch of worry about Janka and Sammy had not been necessary.

Turning back to Seven, who was nibbling on the cornbread with a very peculiar look on her face, Alison asked, "So who's got the money here?" She wanted to see if Michelle's gossip concurred with Seven's. It was obvious that *somebody* had money—neither the building nor the retreat was being financed by any of the cottage industries in the back rooms. You'd have to sell a hell of a lot of bleeding pads to pay for this kind of remodeling.

"Gaya," said Seven. "Don't try the cornbread."

"What's wrong with it?" asked Alison, looking down the table, where about half of the women opposite her were mirroring Seven's sour face. She took a little nibble off her own piece despite the warning.

"Ew!" she said, shaking her head like a dog coming out of

43

water. After a brief moment of recovery she said, "You know, I thought there might be a little problem in the recipe reading department—I've never seen baking soda measured in cups before—but I didn't want to make any assumptions."

Seven gave her a look. Alison suspected that if they had been alone it was a pretty fair assumption that she might have gotten smacked with a spoon.

"Very open-minded of you," Seven said dryly, pushing the offending hunk of cornbread completely off her plate and onto the table. "Gaya is the one with the money," she repeated, picking up her mug of water. They were all drinking water. As far as Alison had been able to tell from the pantry, water was all there was to drink. She thought of her twenty-four pack of Diet Pepsi with a smug satisfaction, and hoped the coffee drinkers had thought to bring their own stash. Otherwise tomorrow morning was going to be ugly.

"I heard she inherited a big hunk," continued Seven, going back to her burrito. They were good burritos. "That's really about all that I know. Hawk and Gaya aren't from around here, you know. I think they're from somewhere on the East Coast—nobody but Persimmon knew them before they bought this place last year."

Alison almost said, "Must be nice," but she realized it would come out sounding ugly and envious, when she truly meant that it must be nice. She admired women who put their money and energy back into the lesbian community. She had long since outgrown her own desire to get back to the land. Her own issues about toilet paper and TV and how often the kitchen should be cleaned made living communally seemed rather horrible to her, but she had also long since come to realize that there was no one 'lesbian community', but rather hundreds and thousands of groups needing to be nurtured. She now thought of the lesbian community as she thought of the rain forest—the extinction of even one small part lessened them all. The elephant really does need the salmon.

Alison was so pleased with this analogy that she nudged Seven and repeated it to her. Seven, who had been chatting up one of the Ducklings seated on the other side of her, just grunted.

Alison looked down the table again, trying to put names to all the faces. There was G-hey!, Seven's beautiful young friend with the shaved head and the loincloth. Like the rest of them, she had put on a sweater and jeans once the sun went down—now she had to count on her piercings and hair for her fashion statement. She was talking in an animated manner to Tomato Woman—damn, she had to find out what her real name was, or she'd end up saying that

to her face!—and at the same time absentmindedly trying her cornbread over and over. She would take a tiny bite, look supremely
surprised, discard the cornbread on the side of her plate and then
the next moment, pick it up for another try.

Hawk had also put on a sweater. While G-hey!'s looked as if it
had lived a long and vigorous incarnation—there were holes in
elbows of both sleeves, and the cuffs were coming off—after being
purchased at a thrift store, Hawk's was obviously hand knit. Unless
she had knit it herself—and who knew, she didn't look like a knitting kind of gal, but Alison was trying to get out of the stereotyp-
ing mode—it had cost a bundle. In fact, if Alison hadn't heard the
scoop from Seven, she would have guessed that Hawk was the one
with the money, rather than Gaya. It was not just the cut of her
clothes—her jeans and boots were worn, but they had come from
Land's End when they were new, and Alison got their catalog, she
knew what their stuff cost—or the heavy silver jewelry she wore on
her wrists and ears, but also the air of satisfaction with which she
had handled the equipment and supplies, right down to the shovels and gloves. Well, thought Alison, it was probably just as nice to
be the girlfriend of a rich woman as it was to be a rich woman.
She'd had a taste of that herself—every once in a while Stacy would
decree that there must be a weekend away, with hotels and room
service and massages and don't-worry-about-money-baby. It was
nice.

She knew from listening that the slight blonde woman sitting
between Hawk and Sarah Embraces-All-Things was named Lisa.
She had overheard one of the kitchen staff saying something about
her earlier—"I'm surprised to see Lisa here." That had been all. She
had been shushed down by a friend who had glared around the
kitchen—she didn't want to start off the new order with gossip, did
she? Lisa was only picking at her food, despite the fact that she and
Michelle had handled the most strenuous job on the work site. Her
face was pinched and sun-burnt, and she seemed to radiate an
unhappiness that went beyond mere exhaustion. She had scarcely
exchanged a word with Sarah Embraces-All-Things, which seemed
strange, for Alison had seen Sarah Embraces-All-Things call her
down to sit beside her at the beginning of the meal. Perhaps they
were ex-lovers—that was always a good guess about two lesbians
who seemed ill-at-ease.

Then again, perhaps not, for Sarah Embraces-All-Things did
not seem to be sharing Lisa's discomfort. She was talking expan-
sively to Lavender, who was sitting on her right. From the few
words that Alison was able to catch across the long table, it sound-

ed as if the dream analysis had ceased and Sarah Embraces-All-Things was telling Lavender how to make fry bread. Alison wondered if anyone had yet realized that Lavender was a gate-crasher.

By now, most of the women at the table had tried the cornbread and quietly pushed it to the side of their plates. As Alison watched, however, Sarah Embraces-All-Things took a large bite from her untouched piece. Her mouth puckered and she washed the piece down quickly with a gulp of water.

"Who made this?" she demanded, in a loud voice that silenced all other chatter at the table.

No one answered. Without consultation, everyone else had obviously decided not to embarrass the woman who had made the cornbread by making an issue of it. Alison caught a glimpse of her sitting down at the other end of the table. She was the same woman who had found the knife, and Alison still could not recall her name. She was big butch gal, nearly as tall as Alison, and perhaps forty pounds heavier, though she carried her weight differently—and was the only woman at the table, aside from Sarah Embraces-All-Things who looked puzzled rather than embarrassed. Alison saw that she had not taken a piece of the cornbread and recalled having overheard her in the kitchen telling one of the other women that she tried to avoid foods with wheat flour or leavening in them.

"I did," she said somewhat hesitantly. The silence at the table made it obvious that nobody thought whatever was coming was going to be a compliment.

"You've put far too much baking powder in it," said Sarah Embraces-All-Things brusquely. "It's ruined. It's inedible." She pulled one of the compost buckets—empty peanut butter buckets meant for peels and cores—towards her and crumbled the piece of bread into it.

The silence continued, but even though no one spoke, several flushed, and Alison could see that she was not alone in thinking this exchange inexcusably rude.

Sarah Embraces-All-Things looked around the table as well. "Oh," she said, "I see. White men's 'politeness'. Lying so that no one will 'be hurt'." She turned and addressed the woman who had mixed the cornbread—suddenly it popped into Alison's head that her name was Jerusha—and said, "I'm not telling you to be unkind. How can telling the truth be unkind? I'm telling you because that's how we learn—by hearing the truth. Baking soda and baking powder are leavenings—they are never used any way but sparingly. If you put more that a spoonful or so in anything, you know that you are doing something wrong." Her tone was condescending—

Alison would not have spoken to a child in the same manner—not even a child she disliked. "Now," she added in a self-congratulatory manner, "you've learned a lesson that you will remember for the rest of your life. You'll never make that mistake again! Wasting food is an insult to the Mother—perhaps after dinner is over you will want to take this out to the compost and explain to her that this won't happen again." She picked up the compost bucket and passed it to Lavender, motioning her to place her cornbread into it. Even Lavender, whose strong suit was not social skills, was a bit hesitant to participate in what looked more than anything like a public humiliation. Sarah Embraces-All-Things ignored her hesitancy and took the piece off her plate herself. She handed the bucket to the woman on the other side of Lavender. Alison had not met this woman but had noticed her while they were working because she seemed to have limited use of one hand, which had made things a bit awkward for her once or twice.

The woman took the bucket, but rather than passing it on she stood and announced in a loud voice, "Time for dessert! G-hey!, come help me! Jerusha come help me!," and then, to Alison's surprise, "Alison, come help me!" The three women named jumped up gratefully. Jerusha practically tipped over her chair in her haste to escape the table.

"If you're done, scrape your plates and put them on the counter." Michelle jumped in to fill the void, holding her plate in one hand by way of demonstration. "There's a bucket on the counter—we didn't use any meat, so everything can go in. There's a bucket for left over water, too, we can use it for the house plants."

"I'd advise you drink it," said Hawk, above the tentative voices that were once more beginning to fill the awkward silence. "It's hot out there—most of you probably lost a lot more water this afternoon than you were used to."

On the other side of the kitchen counter, Alison found herself next to the woman who had seized the bucket. "How did you..." she began in a voice that was almost a whisper.

"Oh, I don't know anyone at all here. I just yelled out all the names I could remember hearing this afternoon. " She replied in a voice that, like Alison's was not meant to carry. The kitchen was wonderful for its convenience, but it was not a place into which one could retreat and bitch aloud. "Christ, what an ugly thing to do! I just hope you made dessert, or we may just have to walk out the back door and not come back."

Luckily, they *had* made dessert. There had been no refined sugar in the pantry, but one of Michelle's at-home-standards was a wonderful honey cake, and she'd just tripled the recipe. Anything to wash the bitter taste of the scolding out of their mouths.

During the following commotion and chatter—everyone seemed to be on the same wavelength about smoothing the whole thing over—the woman with the twisted hand introduced herself to Alison as 'Claw.' Alison could not help but give a slight start of surprise, and Claw smiled.

"What that woman," she pointed with her chin in the direction of Sarah Embraces-All-Things, "was doing was bullshit. But, it is true that some Native American people tend to be more blunt about names. You know—if somebody is a cheat, she's called Cheater." She held up the hand. "I was in an accident a couple of years ago. I got kind of tired of everybody noticing and nobody saying anything. I'll probably pick something else after I've shocked all my friends."

Michelle came up behind them and said in a whisper, "I found another one of those knives this afternoon. Do you know where I should put it? I don't want to find out that Big Sister is watching me."

Claw pointed with her chin again, this time towards the back of the house. "There's a box in the guest room," she said. "I've been here before—sometimes they send the bigger stuff with me. You know, the stuff that can't go on horseback."

Michelle disappeared furtively. She reappeared just as Alison and Jerusha, or Rusha, were serving up the last piece of cake. Giving a theatrical shiver upon her return, she took the plate and sat down again by Persimmon, entering immediately into conversation.

It was close to midnight when dinner was finally over, and Alison gave Michelle, who was once again chatting up Persimmon, the high sign across the room. Let's blow this pop-stand and catch some zzzs. Michelle returned the look with one Alison had not seen since the days before Janka. If she had not known better, she would have translated it as 'Get lost and don't wait up, Girlfriend'. It ground her to a halt in the doorway and produced an immediate worried look. Surely she had misunderstood, hadn't she?

But before she could follow this theme, Hawk made an announcement from the doorway of the kitchen.

"We are going to be having a cloistering ritual," she said in her firm strong voice. "Sarah Embraces-All-Things is going to be leading us all in a ceremony by the main gate in fifteen minutes. It will be short—I know you're tired, but we'd like everyone to be there."

"We will need the energy of all to be successful," announced Sarah Embraces-All-Things mystically. With the heavy use of her cane she had walked over to her three-wheeler, which was parked outside the front door. The basket on the handle bars was now filled with dried flowers, a rattle, a round drum, and a woven bag. She started the cart with a little flourish and lead the way down the hill. The Ducklings crowded around her to part the crowd, reminding Alison of Clint Eastwood running beside the President's car at the movie theater.

It was not the announcement of Sarah Embraces-All-Things which made Alison walk down to the gate with Seven and Michelle. Given what she had seen at dinner, she thought it was probably nothing more than a little spiritual blackmail. But she was curious, and perhaps a little apprehensive. She had not been prepared for that act with the car keys. She wondered what else they had in mind, and whether everyone remembered that she and Michelle had only signed on for the weekend. What if they were going to blast the mouth of the road?

Michelle was still talking with Persimmon, though from their conversation—soldering, glass cutters and design—Alison thought that she must have misread Michelle's I-want-this-woman look. Seven Yellow Moons had lagged behind to speak with G-hey! and Tomato Woman and Alison found herself matching step with Lisa, the woman who had sat so silently by the side of Sarah Embraces-All-Things at dinner.

"Hi," Lisa said, after a moment of walking side by side in silence.

"Hi." Alison was not up on proper ritual etiquette, and she wondered if they were supposed to approach the site quietly and meditatively. But everyone else was talking and laughing—spirits seemed to be high in spite of the hour. "Did you enjoy dinner?" Only after she had asked the question did Alison realize how tactless the question had been. She herself had seen that Lisa had not enjoyed dinner, even before the scene with the cornbread.

"The burritos were good," said Lisa finally, in a voice they both knew lacked conviction. Like everyone else, Lisa had shed her shorts for warmer clothes, but her sweatshirt did not seem to be doing the job. She was hunched inside it with her arms crossed, holding herself as if she were chilled. Or, perhaps she was not cold, but just miserable, thought Alison.

Lisa's next words told her she was right on the money. "I heard...Seven Yellow Moons told me...Is it true that you and your friends are the only ones leaving after the weekend?"

"I heard that, too. I mean, yeah, Michelle and I are leaving Tuesday morning, and Seven told me that the rest of you are staying."

"Could I....I mean I don't want to inconvenience you. But I drove with a friend..." Lisa groped for the words.

Alison, who had already begun to suspect what might be coming, wondered why they were so hard to find. She gave Lisa a long, hard look. The moon was full, and at its zenith, and the same silver light that was lending such a festive feel to the walk showed Lisa's face tight and unhappy, with a broken flush of emotion spread across it like a rash.

"Would you give me a ride into town?" she finally said in a rush. Her voice was low as if she were telling a secret.

"Which way are you going?" Alison asked. Perhaps she was still oversensitive because of the incident at dinner, but as soon as the words were out of her mouth they seemed unkind. It didn't matter where Lisa wanted to go—she knew that Michelle would be willing to swing a couple of hours out of the way to rescue any woman who seemed so wretched. She opened her mouth to amend, but Lisa responded so quickly that she could not get the words in first.

"Anywhere," she replied. "Any way you're going. You can drop me off in the nearest town that has a bus stop. I don't care. But...please."

Alison was more ashamed than ever. "Of course," she assured her. "Where do you live? Santa Fe? Albuquerque? I'll check with Michelle, but I bet we can give you a ride home."

It was obvious from Lisa's tight stance that she was trying hard not to show her emotions, but she could not help a sigh of relief. "Thank you," she said tightly, and then, if those two words were not enough, "Thank you," again.

"Didn't you sign on for the full month?" asked Alison curiously. Her father, Captain Kaine of Denver's finest, always told people that he had known Alison would make a great detective by the time she was ten years old, because she had always been the nosiest kid on the block. That hadn't changed.

"Yes," Lisa agreed, in a low voice that held such a myriad of emotions Alison was hard put to pick out any single one. Shame? Sorrow? Anger? Fear? "I did. I wouldn't break the contract if there was any way around it—I got a writing grant from the Mariposa foundation; I wanted to show that I was grateful. But I'm not going to last the whole month—I can see that already. And it's better for me to leave at the beginning than to disrupt the whole community after the first week? Don't you think?"

"Yes," Alison agreed, thinking that it was also damn smart of Lisa to get going while the going was good. Once she and Michelle were gone there was no way Lisa was going to hitch a ride to town—she didn't think the mailman or any delivery trucks were going to show up at Mariposa. "What's the problem?" she asked, not because it was any of her business, but because she had offered a favor and knew when she had the power.

Lisa bit her lip and looked the other direction. "It's just that...it's not really...I guess it's everything, I guess. I thought I was ready for this, and I'm not." She looked at Alison sideways to see how she was buying this.

Not at all.

"You know," Alison said after a moment, "the very best thing about me and Michelle being here is that we hardly know anyone. We don't have any ex-lovers here—we can pretty much just do what we want and go home, and nobody will even notice. Cool, huh?"

For the first time since dinner had begun, Alison saw Lisa smile.

"Yeah," Lisa said. "Cool. I guess you're right. But I really don't want it talked around, okay? Promise?"

"Okay. Promise," said Alison, mentally adding a codicil stipulating that telling Michelle would not really be talking it around. Telling your best friend—and particularly a best friend as honorable as Michelle—was like your lawyer talking over your case with another member of the same firm—they were all protected by the same seal of confidentiality.

"I didn't know that Sarah was living here," said Lisa. "They didn't tell me that when I did the interview." She was the first woman Alison had heard deliberately violate the full name rule. Their voices had never risen much above a whisper throughout the whole conversation, but now Lisa spoke even more softly, glancing around first to see if anyone was trying to overhear. No one was. The moon, if possible, had grown bigger and was floating above them in a manner you never saw in the lights of the city. Not only had the noise level risen, but several of the women, truly moonstruck, had begun capering and skipping down the road. No one was paying any attention to Alison and Lisa.

"I can understand," Alison sympathized. "Did you used to be lovers?"

"No!" The only word to describe Lisa's reaction was horrified. She attempted to recover quickly. "I mean, no. I'm really not comfortable talking here. Okay? I'll be glad to tell you the whole story in the car."

Alison nodded. They were almost at the gate at any rate. The women who had already reached it were bunching themselves together in a rough half circle that would automatically preclude any private conversation.

"And Alison," Lisa caught at the sleeve of her jacket before she turned away. "Don't tell anyone that I'm planning to leave. Okay? I don't want any trouble."

She went off to the right, to stand between Rusha and Persimmon. Alison, circling the opposite direction, watched her, trying to keep a line of worry from forming between her eyes. She had not considered, when she had agreed to Lisa's request, that there might be any kind of trouble. What exactly was Lisa worried about? She didn't think that anyone would try to stop her physically, did she?

No, Alison decided, joining hands on one side with Seven Yellow Moons and the other side with Tomato Woman. Lisa probably just didn't want to be guilt-tripped.

Sarah Embraces-All-Things parked her three-wheeler over by the side of the gate. She removed her long, woolen shawl and using her cane, walked to the middle of the circle. One of the Ducklings, the one with the shaved head and the eyebrow piercing, came behind her, carrying her props.

"We are here in the full moon to make an offering to the Goddess," said Sarah leaning on the staff. "We are going to offer her our freedom. Willingly, we are going to renounce contact with the outside world for one full moon, in the hopes that by giving this gift we will return to the world of men changed, purified by the fire."

Glancing around the circle, Alison saw more than a few faces reflecting trepidation. What the hell did Sarah Embraces-All-Things mean by this? Apparently Alison was not the only one who was not sure if she wanted to be purified by the fire.

Sarah Embraces-All-Things turned her head to the side and suddenly breathed out a huge flame. Everyone except the Duckling was caught off guard—the whole circle exclaimed and jumped backwards, though to their credit no one dropped hands.

Alison, who had done a few fire scenes herself, was quite impressed. She had seen a number of fire eaters and breathers—all at leather dungeons—but Sarah Embraces-All-Things certainly beat them all in the area of showmanship. She glanced over at the Duckling. Why the hell hadn't she jumped like the rest of them? Oh,

52

of course, she was the prop man, the shaman's acolyte. They must have practiced together. And the fire breathing explained why Sarah had removed her shawl—she hadn't wanted to risk the fringe.

The fire breathing was the only real surprise. The rest of the ceremony was kind of what Alison anticipated. Sarah Embraces-All-Things smudged the circle, and made offerings to the four directions. Alison could see across the circle that Michelle was trying hard not to fidget. Although everyone's presence had been requested, Alison noticed that Lavender was not there. Lying low until the gate was closed, Alison suspected.

Sarah Embraces-All-Things now had a rattle, and was chanting in what Alison assumed to be her native tongue. She must not use it often—the flow was a little bumpy. Alison shifted from one foot to the other. She had no desire to interrupt the ceremony, but she was tired, and the grueling work had made her ache in places she had not ached in years. If this did not stop soon she was afraid that she was simply going to burst into tears.

Luckily, Sarah Embraces-All-Things came to an abrupt halt.

"You," she said, pointing her staff at Hawk. "And you, and you and you." All told, she picked eight women out of the circle. Except for Hawk and Gaya, whom Alison assumed had been chosen because it was their party, she picked the women who were very young, preferring those who were also large. In short, the six women in the circle who were probably the strongest. And also, Alison could not help noticing, no one who had obviously disapproved of her at dinner. Jerusha was not chosen, though she fit the other qualifications, nor Michelle nor Lisa nor G-hey! nor Tomato Woman nor Alison herself. Even in the midst of the cornbread scene Sarah Embraces-All-Things had kept her head and noticed what kind of expression each woman had been wearing on her face.

The circle was broken as the eight women were directed to the side of the road.

"What the hell?" murmured Michelle, who had some how ended up beside Alison in the shuffling. Both watched in rather apprehensive silence as Sarah Embraces-All-Things choreographed the women around the pile like a dance team. They circled, they bent, they lifted one rock all together. In the moonlight, Alison could see the strain on their faces—even with so many, those rocks were *heavy*. Twenty little shuffling steps, awkward because some of the women were moving backwards, and the first slab was placed in the middle of the road, two inches in front of the gate. It had been an incredible show of working together, so incredible that Alison wondered if it, too, had been practiced before the ceremony. Smash your fingers beneath one of those hummers and you'd be out for the month.

"I don't like this," whispered Michelle with a frown. "What are they going to do next? What if they decide they need to bury someone under those rocks for a sacrifice?"

Alison was worried as well, though her fears were not quite so morbid. What she was wondering was if Hawk, despite her assurances, *really* remembered that she and Michelle were supposed to leave on Tuesday. Those babies looked *way* too heavy to fuck with unnecessarily.

As if she had read her mind, Hawk caught her eye and gave her a reassuring little wink. Okay, then, she didn't need to worry. It was pointless, at any rate, because she wasn't willing to interrupt the ritual. It might not be her church, but obviously a lot of the women watching were into it, and she had the same feeling about religions as she did about dykes—as long as they were engaged in trying to channel the benevolent parts of themselves and/or a god being, rather than organizing gay-bashing or killing the infidels, they made the universe richer and more interesting.

Sarah Embraces-All-Things had wandered back into the middle of the now ragged circle and was giving some little lecture about the symbolism and how they were going to bless it. By now it was far too late, and Alison had been on her feet far too long to pay attention. She wished she had been as smart as Lavender, who was probably sound asleep. It was a relief when Sarah Embraces-All-Things began to sing 'Isis, Astarte.' The chant, which named six major goddesses from various cultures, was a lesbian standby that was kind of like 'Row, row, row your boat' to lesbians of Alison's age—everybody knew it and could sing along. Chanting helped numb the pain she was feeling in her legs and back, although she always just hummed over the part where you called on Kali. She had read a bit of Indian mythology, and thought it unwise to bring oneself to the attention of Kali.

Mercifully, there was not a whole lot more. The women moving the rocks got into it. G-hey!, who had not been one of the original eight, beckoned to a couple of friends in the audience and butted right in, organizing a line that was more like a bucket brigade. Michelle jumped in to help, though Alison held back. Sarah Embraces-All-Things got a sour little look around her mouth—she was obviously the kind of woman who liked to top the scene *way* too much—but what was she going to say? Wasn't that what the whole retreat was about—working together and doing things in new ways? She tried to gain center stage after the rocks had been stacked into a credible wall, but Alison wasn't the only one who was tired. By ones and two women were beginning to melt away in the darkness. Up by the tents Alison could see that someone had already built a little campfire. She hoped there would not be singing. She could not bear to hear a single chorus of 'Kumbaya'. She estimated that she had about fifteen minutes left on her feet before she became too exhausted to care for herself, so she was overcome with relief when Sarah Embraces-All-Things, obviously deciding to make the best of a bad situation, wound up abruptly.

Alison performed only the very most necessary of bedtime rituals—brushing her teeth could be skipped, taking her medication could not—before crawling into the back of the truck. Michelle had everything laid out as nicely as if were the Hyatt Regency. Alison's mummy bag was tucked underneath three blankets—she was well known for sleeping cold at night. Camping with Michelle was always a wonderful, effortless experience—she liked to pack and set up and break down, and she always knew just what to bring to make everyone comfortable. It was something to remember when Michelle was being a pill.

Alison hastily undressed and then pulled on a pair of long underwear—according to REI you could wear them on expedition to the North Pole—and a pair of thermal socks. She was asleep the moment her head hit the pillow.

CHAPTER FOUR

Perhaps it was because she was too tired, or perhaps it was because she was in a strange place, but Alison slept poorly that night. Her foam pad seemed lumpy and insignificant and she had forgotten how constricting a mummy bag could be, how few choices it gave for sleeping positions. She tossed and turned, and finally fell into an uneasy sleep from which she woke several times—first to unfamiliar noises and then because her hips and arms were aching.

Around dawn she finally drifted into a dreamless slumber, but this was shattered about forty-five minutes later by loud and unmelodious chanting. Alison pulled her pillow over her head, but it made an ineffective barrier. She pushed the back window of the camper shell open a few inches. All around her, through the thin walls of the tents she could hear disgruntled stirring and mumbling. The word 'coffee' was mentioned more than once.

She thought that perhaps she could wait out the chanting and catch at least a few more zzzs, but after five minutes it became evident that the chanter—and she had her suspicions as to who *that* was—had a strong, long-winded set of lungs. Women around her were giving up as well. She could hear sounds of rising—some were even joining the chanting. She had only two choices—get up and try *really hard* to be a good sport, or lie there in the back of the truck and work herself into a real tear.

She opted for the first, although what she really wanted to do was storm out of the truck stark naked and wring the neck of Sarah Embraces-All-Things as if she were a Rhode Island Red.

The whole tent village was stirring by the time she crawled out of the back of the truck, wearing nothing but a t-shirt. She pulled her jeans and clean panties after her and put them on standing up outside her door. It was just easier.

In spite of the fact that she had only gotten five hours sleep—max—even she could see the beauty of the dawn. There was not yet a hint of the heat that would beat down upon them so heavily later in the day. There was even a slight breeze, and a few drops of dew clung here and there to the yucca, glittering jewel-like in the rising sun. Across the broad stretch of desert that swept down and away from the ranch the buttes were still in dark shadow which made them appear as purple as an angry sea.

It *was* Sarah Embraces-All-Things who was doing the chanting—had there been any doubt?—but by now several other women had joined her on the edge of the arroyo that was the back border of the camping area. The whole ranch was ringed by arroyos, the dry washes through which Alison had heard water poured whenever there was a cloud burst. There was this one, and another down by the sweat lodge and garden.

Everybody was just kind of doing their own thing in the ritual department. Sarah Embraces-All-Things, dressed in another long skirt and shawl—today red was the predominant color—was standing facing the rising sun shaking a rattle and chanting in the same tongue she had used the night before. Beside her was Lavender, doing a slow dance of tai chi, a second woman playing a recorder and a third—G-hey! wearing nothing but her Doc Martins—singing "Morning has broken" in a voice surprisingly strong and beautiful. She was the easiest to follow and, male voice or not everybody either knew Cat Stevens or had gone to church, so one by one everyone who was not too crabby joined in. Their voices bounced back from the hill behind them, then were thrown down the arroyo and lost. It was beautiful. Alison saw Sarah Embraces-All-Things give G-hey! a cross look—oops, upstaged again.

Alison groggily performed her toilet by the truck, using the hood as a table. She threw a Rockies cap over her hair, which needed gel and a mirror to be its cutest. She longed for a nice hot shower to take the kinks out of her bones, but she didn't know how warm the solar showers would be at this time of day. Besides, she didn't want to stand in line with the group of younger, hardier women who had headed in that direction—she was afraid that she would squeal if the water was too cold. She remembered, with a touch of nostalgia, the freezing cold showers at the Michigan Women's Music Festival the first year she and Michelle had attended when they were nineteen. They had even crawled briefly into one of the big barrels and immersed themselves. That would kill her now.

She fished her own solar shower out of the truck and put it on the hood of someone's black car. The car was a Taurus, and its paint was peeling. There had been a bad lot of paint slapped onto those '87s.

She wondered if anyone was going to pull together a collective breakfast, and remembered the pans the dinner crew had left soaking in the sink. All she really wanted was one of her Diet Pepsis, but she waited until Sarah Embraces-All-Things finished her chant and mounted her cart before breaking one out of the cab. The list of no-nos had not specifically mentioned soft drinks, but Alison had the feeling that was only because the Mariposa collective had not specifically thought of them. She was not ready for a scene this early in the morning, and no one was taking her Pepsi until they pried it from her cold, dead hand.

She sat on the cab of the truck, dividing her attention between the sun creeping its fingers across the desert and the morning rituals of the other women. No one was making much of a move to head up towards the big house—apparently nobody felt very communal before six. Several women were making fires in the prescribed pits, and before long she could smell tea—all herbal of course.

"You got another one of those?" asked Seven Yellow Moons, slouching beside her on the truck. Alison hesitated, frankly hoarding. "I'll give you a thousand dollars for it."

Alison laughed and went back into the cab. Michelle, who did a lot of caffeine in the morning, had installed cup holders onto both doors. Alison removed their traveling mugs and poured the soda into them, so that they didn't get hit on by anybody else. She could not afford to keep the whole camp in caffeine. Let them drink kefir.

After handing Seven her cup, from which she drank long and gratefully before walking away, Alison walked over to give Michelle's tent a good shake. If she had to be up at dawn, then so did Michelle. When there was no response, she unzipped the top of the door and stuck her head inside, and then pulled it out with a frown. Michelle, obvious from the pristine condition of the sleeping bag, had not slept in her tent. Alison was filled with an immediate and unnamed dread. Although she did not yet want to invoke the power of naming, she knew what the dread was *not* about—being eaten by coyotes or adobed up in one of the walls. It was about something the consequences of which were even more horrible and irreversible.

As if her fear had conjured the person, suddenly Michelle was right there, asking in a rather miffed voice, "Well, did you find what you need?"

Alison stood up slowly, taking an inventory. Michelle's hair was wet—she had already showered, though she was dressed in the same clothes she had been wearing the night before. There was a shower and flush toilet in the main house, and Alison knew from kitchen gossip that Persimmon lived in her studio, which was a converted shed immediately behind it. The clothes and the showers were real clear signs, and the rudeness was the third—Michelle always attacked if she sensed a confrontation coming.

"You fucked that woman, didn't you?" Alison asked, too shocked to be anything but blunt.

"Oh, right, like I fuck every woman I spend time with! Just because I'm interested in her work! You're the one who is always telling me that Janka and Seven Yellow Moons are just friends and Janka needs a chance to talk to her peers…." Michelle tended to get a little shrill when she was indignant. "Just because you…"

"Oh, bite me, Michelle," Alison broke in shortly. It was too damn early in the morning to bottom to Michelle's indignation. "So what, you were just exchanging blessings and letting the goddess in you embrace the goddess in her? You should have fucked her—Janka's not going to like that any better. Come on, Michelle, you have a wife and a baby!"

"Well, just call her and tell her!" Michelle sputtered. "Like she would care! Like she would even care if I *had* made love with Persimmon! You don't always know what's going on! I know I have a wife and a baby! Believe me, I know it! So what does that mean, that my life is over now? That the whole rest of my life is going to be getting up at five in the morning, and listening to Janka complain about her varicose veins?" Whereas her first shot of anger had been a smoke screen, this outburst was obviously genuine—so real, in fact, that Alison was knocked speechless for a moment. Which Michelle didn't even notice, because she was on a roll that was carrying her right over the top of everything in sight.

"I have had sex exactly twice in six months! Twice! Because Janka had morning sickness, or she was tired, or Sammy was in the room, or he *wasn't* in the room and she was afraid he had stopped breathing. Jesus! I didn't think I was signing on for…" she struggled for a word, and then finally was forced to make do with, "This! This! What the hell does it matter if I had slept with anybody else?" Even at the height of a tantrum, Michelle could not bring herself to describe any act of passion with another woman 'fucking'—men fucked, women made love. "Which I didn't! But do you think Janka would have cared? Do you think she would even *notice*? Hell no, not as long as I'm getting the bills paid and remembered to stop at the store for milk on the way home!"

"You sound just like a man," said Alison—it just popped out, and it was much more amazement than judgment, but of course she couldn't have said *anything* that could have pissed off Michelle anymore if she'd tried, and on top of no coffee as well. The moment the words were out of her mouth she instinctively threw her free arm up above her head as if she were afraid the sky was going to fall.

For a moment this appeared to be a distinct possibility. Then with a strangled hurumph Michelle hoisted herself off the cab of the truck and headed up the hill towards the main house. She was so offended that she entirely forgot she was a tough little butch (Michelle and Janka insisted they didn't do roles, but come on) and flounced up the path as if she were Stacy in all her petticoats.

Alison drew a great breath and tried not to freak out. Too early in the morning, too little sleep and too large a dose of Sarah Embraces-All-Things to deal with Michelle getting a crush. All she could do was hope it remained on the spiritual level. She might have followed and tried to do a bit more nipping in the bud, but as she turned to pick up her shoes she saw walking up the road towards her none other than the lovely Stacy. Oh, dear. Alison could not help but give an apprehensive little gasp.

Stacy, luckily, was too far away to have heard the exchange— luckily, for it wouldn't have gone over well, and Alison didn't need to have *both* her girlfriend and her best friend mad at her at the same time. (It was odd, actually, how often those two seemed to coincide.) Stacy gave Alison a beautiful smile, and continued up the road at a leisurely pace. Stacy, who was tall, with dark curly hair and a beautiful hawkish nose that might have overwhelmed a woman with less personality, looked as if she had been dressed entirely from pricey catalogues—possibly Banana Republic colliding with Sundance. She was wearing a pair of tailored khaki pants, a matching French cut t-shirt so new Alison could still smell the store on it, and little lace-up, black half-boots that would have complimented almost *any* outfit, girlfriend. Topping it off was a *really cute* green cap that brought out the sparkle in her eyes (and didn't she know it!) and a truckload of silver bracelets. She was going to give Hawk a run for her money in the jewelry department, that was for sure. In one hand she was carrying a stove top espresso pot.

"Hey!" she said, obviously just as pleased with herself as she could be. "I made it!" She held out her arms for a hug—all was forgiven. Alison hastily tried to put a pleased look on her face. Okay, Stacy hadn't done one thing wrong, Alison had invited her to come, she had left her the map, and it just hadn't occurred to her that Stacy was going to stand out like a sore thumb. Compared to G-hey!'s tattered sweater or Sarah Embraces-All-Things' batiked skirt, Stacy looked as if she had come from a completely other and more upscale planet. There was going to be no pretending she had been here all along.

Released from the hug, Alison noticed for the first time that Stacy's best friend, Liz, was also standing there in the road—Stacy tended to eclipse. Liz who, like Michelle, was another big spirit in a compact package, and who had been personally and abundantly blessed by the goddess of freckles, was not doing the Sundance thing, but unfortunately what she *was* wearing with her tight jeans was a short leather vest over what looked like a black jogging bra. Liz currently had no girlfriend, so lately she had been dressing to troll. There was no denying she looked cute enough to turn the city girls' heads, but what would go over well at Ms. C's was not necessarily going to be greeted with appreciative looks here. With a guilty start, Alison realized that she had neglected to give Stacy a copy of the rule sheet along with the map. Well, hell, it had only been a token invitation, really—she hadn't thought for a moment that after that last fight Stacy was really going to show.

"Well, hey," said Stacy, "I sure am glad to see that you're still the cutest butch in the western states. Because that drive was a bitch—I don't think it would have been worth it for anyone else."

Alison's heart filled with a gush of love that temporarily shut out any other feeling. She hated it when she and Stacy fought, and she adored it when Stacy let her know she was the butch of her dreams.

"I hate it when we fight," said Stacy, taking her hand. Stacy had no qualms whatsoever about stripping down at a play party, and it didn't much bother her to be caught by strangers fucking up against the side of the bar, but in some ways she was very private and proper. Alison knew that she wouldn't give her more than a chaste kiss in front of the women who were watching from beside their campfires.

"We were on that goddamn cow track at five this morning," said Liz in a grouchy, pre-coffee voice. "Her highness here got a bug up her ass at about nine o'clock last night."

Alison did not bother to ask why Liz had given in to Stacy's bug—it was a best friend thing, and it would all come out even in the end. You didn't have long-term best friends unless you were willing to indulge a few of their wild hairs. For the same reason, she didn't ask why Liz had shown up at all, when there had been no mention of her in the initial plans. Another wild hair, no doubt.

"Hey, there's Seven Yellow Moons!" said Stacy perkily, waving. "She'll let us put our coffee pot on her fire." Already she was walking towards it. She seemed awfully pert for someone who had been up all night. Alison wondered if perhaps illegal substances had been involved. When Stacy and Liz traveled together, they often were.

"You'd better take that scowl off your face if you're cruising," Alison said to Liz. Maybe Seven would break the Bad News to Stacy, because she certainly couldn't think of a way to do it that wasn't going to cause a tantrum. Serve her right, too—she'd be pissed herself if she'd driven all night long just to find out that she wasn't invited to the party. "My mama always said you'd catch more flies with honey than vinegar."

"I had your mama and she wasn't all that good," said Liz rudely. "And I'm not interested in catching anybody who wears a loincloth. I'll bet nobody here even owns a pair of high heels."

Alison reached back into the cab of the car and pulled out another Diet Pepsi.

"Drink this, or I'm going to shove it up your ass," she said in a sweet tone, handing it to Liz.

"Better watch out," Liz replied, taking it from her with no sign of thanks. "I might like that so much that I'd imprint on you."

"That's okay," Alison said. "I can use someone to fetch and carry, and you'd look cute in a dog collar."

"Woof!" said Liz, downing half the Pepsi in one gulp.

Stacy, of course, was already in full scale conversation with the gals around Seven's fire, who had magically doubled the moment the smell of coffee hit the air. Stacy in center stage included many gestures and tosses of the head to make her earrings and ponytail dance.

"I might as well tell you," said Alison to Liz, watching Stacy's face to see how she was reacting to receiving the same news, "that I kind of made a mistake about this party."

"Gee, Alison, does that have anything to do with the rocks blocking the gate?" Liz asked in the dumb blonde voice that she and Stacy shared between them when sarcasm was needed. "And I thought that was a Native American welcome sign!" She was looking hungrily at Michelle's cab. The one Pepsi had taken the edge, but it hadn't really touched the need. Alison looked the other way, pretending not to read the sign. Come on—she had to conserve, and if she knew Stacy, there was at least a twenty-four pack in her car, and probably three kinds of gourmet coffee. Lawrence, Stacy's cleaning faggot, also packed for her trips, and he did a good job—she was always ready for a full-scale expedition on short notice.

"Guess what I just found out?" Stacy trilled from behind them. Definitely on some kind of high—nobody was that happy about being dumped. "We have a little problem. We're not invited to this little do at all!"

Liz groaned, and wisely went down to the fire pit to guard the coffee pot. Even on a crab high, she couldn't help flexing her pecs a bit and running her hand over her hair to see if it was still cute.

"I'm sorry," said Alison, taking both of Stacy's hands and gazing into her eyes with a look that was meant to say she was the loveliest woman on the face of the earth. Stacy dealt better with rejection if it could be tempered with blind devotion. "It was my fault. I didn't understand. I thought it was an open party—I couldn't imagine any group of women who wouldn't kill to have you join them for the weekend. Would you and Liz mind doing a Santa Fe weekend and coming back for us? I'd pay for a hotel."

"Actually," Stacy replied, doing a little earring toss for practice, "we have a little problem." She still sounded awfully cheery. "You see…"

So intense was she on the Helen of Troy look that Alison had no idea anyone else was around until she heard a throat being loudly cleared not more than two feet away.

They looked to the side. Standing beside them were Sarah Embraces-All-Things and Gaya. Gaya looked rather apologetic—Sarah Embraces-All-Things furious.

"Excuse me." Gaya spoke first. "I think maybe we weren't clear about what was happening here, but…"

Sarah Embraces-All-Things broke in, in one of those firm, assertiveness training voices which bring those upon whom they are used to a full and immediate boil. "You are not welcome here!" she said in a voice that was much louder than it needed to be. Everyone turned their heads to watch the show. "This is a spiritual retreat! It is a spiritual experiment that could rock the lesbian community! We are trying to do something that has never been done before, and we don't need…" She stared at Stacy with loathing, groping for a word to describe her total inappropriateness. Alison was not sure what exactly it was that had set her off, but it didn't really matter. Some lesbians just hated Stacy on sight, and Sarah Embraces-All-Things hadn't even *seen* Liz.

Sarah Embraces-All-Things turned to Gaya, still shaking with fury. "I *told* you we shouldn't have made an exception for these, these…" again she groped for a word.

Gaya, obviously afraid she would find one, cut in quickly. "It was our mistake," she said, smiling an uncertain smile of appeasement at everybody in sight. "I think we just weren't clear. We probably shouldn't have made any exceptions—you know, no short termers, and that's our fault—"

Alison had not had either a good morning or a good night, and the caffeine meter was still running low. "Excuse me," she broke in, "but are you telling *me* that Michelle and I have caused any problems in the purity of your little retreat? Because I worked like a dog yesterday. Like a dog! And so did Michelle! You couldn't have done a thing unless she had been there to fix that mixer when it died! Plus, we *both* made you dinner while you were doing the spiritual thing in the sweat lodge! So don't be giving me any shit about us contaminating your gene pool! Because we can pack up and leave any time you want us to! Just clear that gate!" Alison didn't throw tantrums a whole lot, but when she did, they were good ones.

Stacy took her arm and gave her a look of some admiration. Stacy appreciated a good tantrum. "Actually, Sweetheart," she said, "that packing and leaving thing might be a bit of a problem…"

"No, no." Gaya tried to soothe. "It's not that. There are some problems. The dog, for example…"

"That's not our dog!" exploded Alison. "Lavender Crystalpower brought that dog onto the land. I don't have a dog. I don't even *like* dogs!"

"Then why have you been feeding it?" demanded Sarah Embraces-All-Things. "Good food wasted on an animal that should be foraging for itself! The People never fed their dogs, they knew that the Mother was offended…"

"Well, then just let me go apologize to the compost heap," cut in Alison who was on a roll. "Or isn't that good unless there's a public humiliation scene to go with it?"

Stacy who could see things getting out of hand, attempted to mollify by pulling out a pack of cigarettes and offering them around. Of course, they had to be American Spirits. Why not? Already in the course of less than five minutes they had offended everyone in sight—why not add PI cigarettes?

"I can't believe…" stuttered Sarah Embraces-All-Things. "Tobacco is a holy herb, it shouldn't even be *sold* for any other purpose, let alone—"

"I'll chant," said Stacy rudely. "'Berkock, ata aduno.'" Alison realized that she was repeating some of the words from Sarah's wake-up chant, which she must have heard while coming up the hill.

For some reason, this made Sarah Embraces-All-Things snap her mouth shut with an audible click. Gaya gave her a cautious look before proceeding. If Alison had been Gaya she would have smacked Sarah on the side of the head with her checkbook, just to remind her who was holding the—mighty hefty—purse strings, but she supposed that was not Politically Correct, and certainly not the way to start building a new matriarchy.

"Okay," said Gaya tentatively, still looking at Sarah. Sarah was glaring at Stacy, who was blowing smoke rings and looking out across the desert with an artistic eye as if she were Georgia O'Keefe. "The dog is a problem. The cigarettes are a problem. The caffeine," she looked pointedly at the can in Alison's hand—damn, she was busted!—"is a problem. The extra people are a problem. Like I say, it's partly our fault—we shouldn't have let in anyone who we didn't interview, we shouldn't have made any exceptions for short termers. But we have to ask your friends to leave."

"Can't do it," said Stacy in a perfectly reasonable, we're-all-friends-here voice. "Sorry. We just didn't know we weren't welcome, and we don't have a car. We're not going anywhere until Tuesday."

"What?" asked Alison. She tried to make her voice come out anything but horrified. She was not successful.

"My car broke down," Stacy explained, still sounding as if this were the most reasonable of explanations, and that it had not occurred to her that anyone might object. It probably hadn't. "So Liz said she'd bring us in her van, but Lawrence has been really depressed and we'd already said that we'd hang with him this weekend and he'd met this Santa Fe guy on the Internet..."

"Stop." Sarah Embraces-All-Things joined in again. "Are you telling us that you brought a man onto sacred ground?"

"No," said Stacy. By now she could not help but know everyone was miffed, but she had obviously decided not to acknowledge it. "What I'm telling you is that we were dropped off at the gate and don't have a car." She looked around. "Why is this sacred ground? I don't see a church."

Alison had been paying attention for the last couple of years—she knew Stacy was playing Sarah Embraces-All-Things.

Sarah Embraces-All-Things, however, swallowed it hook, line and all the rest. "*You cannot be here,*" she said, in a voice so measured and stern that she could have been Moses coming back from doing lunch with God. "You weren't invited, you are obviously not the kind of women that we wanted to be involved..."

"Oh, get over it," said Stacy, growing tired of the whole thing. "What are you going to do—stake us out to an ant pile just because I don't have an ugly lesbian haircut? Here," she dug into her pocket and came up with a roll of bills. She peeled off three hundreds and held them out towards Gaya. "Okay, we weren't invited, you didn't plan on us—well, this should more than pay for using your showers. We brought our own food—you don't need to worry about us. Okay? You can buy another windmill or something."

Alison could not tell which of the group surrounding them was the very most offended, nor by which gesture. The Ducklings made disparaging noises and looked at Sarah Embraces-All-Things as if they were attack dogs just waiting for the word. Alison might have tried to enter the conversation as a mediator, but at this point Liz bounced up from the fire pit and entered full into the fray. Liz who was a successful criminal lawyer pulling down big bucks, was the world's biggest negotiator. Alison had absolutely no doubts that she would iron out a deal within minutes from which she and Stacy would emerge smelling like roses.

"*You* are going to kick us *off*?" she asked Gaya in a tone of great amazement—there must be some misunderstanding here. Like Stacy, she had immediately discerned that the thing which would fluster Sarah Embraces-All-Things the very most would be ignoring her. "We drive forty miles out in the desert to help you, we bring you presents and you're going to kick us out in the heat forty miles from town to starve?"

"You brought your own food," said Sarah Embraces-All-Things angrily. "She just said that. Don't try to manipulate us."

"Takes one to know one," retorted Alison. It was out of her mouth before she knew it was happening—she tried to cover by saying quickly, "What kind of presents did you bring?"

"I brought a hot tub," said Stacy, unable to keep a little tone of satisfaction from her voice. Stacy was a generous woman, and she always gave good presents, but this was outdoing even herself.

Most of the women at the campfires had trailed Liz up to watch the commotion, probably hoping for a chance to slide in their two cents. Lesbians liked to share. There was a stunned silence following this announcement. It seemed to mean something especially to Gaya and the Ducklings who gave one another meaningful looks.

"A hot tub!" Sarah Embraces-All-Things was the first one to get her voice back. "Of all the wasteful…"

"Get with the program, Pharaoh," said Stacy, still not looking directly at her. "Happy slaves are productive slaves."

"A hot tub!" said Gaya, so low she was almost talking to herself, "We have a hot spring here, you know—we've wanted to—"

Sarah Embraces-All-Things made a sharp, cutting off gesture towards Gaya. The audience didn't like that—Alison could tell by the looks. She took in a deep breath, obviously girding herself for a show down, but Liz jumped into the gap.

"And I," she said, "Sent you scholarship money for a poor dyke. Last month? Remember? When you sent out letters?" Everyone looked at each other. Liz herself was careful not to look at anyone but Gaya, although the letter must have been something from one of Seven's faxes. Liz, just by virtue of the fax machine, often got information Alison missed. "If we have to leave, then I am definitely going to want my money back. Which I guess means whoever I paid for has to leave as well. So you should be deciding who is going out with us. Or," she paused, a bit of courtroom theatrics, "we can make a compromise." A long look at Gaya. "We camp outside the gate, and feed ourselves. You get the hot tub and the scholarship money—in return we get to use the tub and any of your bathing and bathroom facilities."

Sarah Embraces-All-Things began to sputter again. "You can't…"

Stacy looked over at Liz to see if she was using the dumb blonde persona. The dumb blonde was like a magic cloak of invisibility—it could only be worn by one at a time.

"Well," she said, putting on a Valley Girl accent that made it come out like 'wull', "I can read a little bit, I mean, not big words, but I do know that the signs on the way in said 'National Forest.' Like, right?"

Both Gaya and Sarah said nothing.

Stacy was still being Barbie. "So, like if we want to camp in the National Forest, we can, right? I mean, like, unless you want to call a park ranger?"

Gaya looked around at the other women, virtually all of whom had a yearning look in their eyes that seemed to be saying, "Hot tub! Hot tub!" Everyone had been tired and sore the night before.

"It seats eight," said Stacy, reading her indecision. "And it's sitting on the trailer with all our camp gear outside the gate."

Seven Yellow Moons, who had joined the crowd, spoke up. "You know," she said to Gaya, "this could just be one of the challenges that we're going to have to face. Just because we've shut ourselves off from the world doesn't mean that the world isn't going to come to our gate." Seven was doing a very credible job of pretending that she had never met Stacy or Liz before, even though she had to be the one who had hit Liz for the scholarship money. "I think that the whole idea is not to pretend that the world has gone away, but to try and find different ways to deal with the curves that it throws us." She looked around at the other woman and gave a benevolent little nod, as if she were a homespun prophet addressing the clan.

"How many people would it take to carry that hot tub?" asked G-hey!. Stacy held up eight fingers. Alison could see everyone immediately start counting their neighbors.

Gaya, at least, knew when it was time to retreat with dignity. "You're right," she said to Seven, and then to Liz, "welcome." She tried to reach for the money Stacy had been holding in her hand, but it had disappeared without a trace. Stacy knew what had been in the terms and what had not.

"We're going to be the Fun Camp," Stacy said to the assembly. "Open twenty-four hours a day."

"First things first," said one of the older women. "I want that hot tub fired up to one-oh-five by the time we get off work tonight."

CHAPTER FIVE

"That woman is not Native American," said Stacy scornfully half an hour later, when the hot tub had been seen safely over the gate and up the hill. It had actually only taken about six to lift it into the bed of the pickup truck that Gaya, guarding her excitement, had backed down the hill. As far as Alison knew, it was the only immediately operable vehicle on the land. There were more than enough women to unload at the other end, so Seven Yellow Moons and Alison had stayed to have breakfast in the Fun Camp. Michelle, who had walked down to the gate about fifteen minutes later, was also sitting in a lawn chair and listening to Stacy. "I heard her chanting when we walked up the hill, and it wasn't in *Indian*."

"What do you mean, in 'Indian'?" said Michelle, helping herself to a cup of coffee without asking. "God, that tastes good! I haven't been able to take a shit since I got here! There isn't any such thing as 'Indian'. What—you can recognize Navajo or Cherokee?"

"She's scamming the whole bunch of you." Stacy slid a perfect omelet out of the cast iron skillet and onto a paper plate. Stacy, who cooked so very little at home that Alison's phone number came behind Wok to You on her automatic dial, underwent a metamorphosis while camping, suddenly becoming a kind of lesbian Girl Scout version of Julia Child. Nobody else was allowed to touch either the food or the fire at any of Stacy's campsites, although she would permit help with the washing up. "I'd *never* be able to take a shit if I had to use one of those things."

The shitter had been pointed out to her on the way back to her campsite on the wrong side of the gate. "I mean, an outhouse is one thing, but...No, and I don't speak Ogalala Sioux or Omaha, either, but I do recognize Yiddish when I hear it. My grandma spoke Yiddish. And you saw how—what is her name? Sunshine?"

"Sarah Embraces-All-Things," said Alison, looking longingly at the Dutch oven from which wafted the smell of buttermilk biscuits.

"Oh, honestly!" said Stacy. With a pair of tongs, she lovingly rearranged the hot coals covering the lid of the Dutch oven. "She read that in a book! I'm surprised that she doesn't call herself Leaphorn, or Chee! Anyway, you saw how she shut up when I said a couple of words back—she knew she was busted."

"She was speaking Yiddish?" Alison was confused. She leaned back in the beach chair, one of half dozen trucked in by the Fun Camp girls, all in assorted cute colors, resting her back. She was getting old—sitting on the ground just wasn't as much fun as it used to be. "Wouldn't that mean she was Jewish? Why pretend to be Native American?"

"Because of the status," Stacy said, still scornful. "Who has the most status among a spiritual, Southwestern crowd of lesbians? Could it be a Native American dyke in a wheelchair? And, incidentally, I don't think she needs the wheel chair any more than she's Native American, and I sure as hell don't think she's Jewish. The words I picked out of that chant were words any kid with a Jewish friend would know—you know, the blessings, that kind of thing. I'll bet she put together a little Yiddish, a little Spanish, a little French, made up a bunch of words and listened to the Navajo radio to see how to accent it."

Alison was stung. "If she had used Spanish, *I* would have recognized it," she said stiffly. She hated looking dumb.

"Yeah, but maybe she wasn't talking about her cat. Actually, you're probably right—she doesn't use Spanish because there's too great a chance of running into Latina dykes. She probably doesn't say she's Navajo or Hopi, either, for the same reason." She stirred the fire and then pulled her stick back with an audible sigh of satisfaction.

"I still think..." began Michelle, feistier than ever now that she had done the coffee. She was going to be bouncing off the walls—they just might get the stairs done today. Hell, another cup of coffee and Michelle could finish the whole job by herself.

"Actually," interrupted Seven Yellow Moons, "you're not the first person to think that. There's kind of a consensus around the community that she's running a scam."

"So why doesn't somebody do something about it?" asked Alison.

"Like what? Sarah's got backing in the right places—the one woman I know who tried to confront her was *crucified* by her supporters. You know, there are a lot of really sincere women out there who can't imagine lying about something like a disability, or who your parents were, and anybody who *can* imagine it must just be a bigot. This woman I know—she was publicly harassed. I saw her being turned away from a concert, and I read an article that gave her name and all but called her a member of the KKK."

"That's disgusting," said Liz. "Why should we be so *rampant* about policing ourselves on any possible prejudice, but allow a woman who's running a scam to go unchallenged? She's doing more harm than anybody else. When it all comes out—and it will—she's going to fuck with the credibility of *every* Native American dyke, and *every* differently abled dyke—anyone who's already been scammed by her is going to think twice about believing anyone else."

"I agree," said Seven, risking all and poking the fire. Stacy stiffened a bit, but since Seven *was* a guest and not a family member, she said nothing. "And I know Native Women who agree as well."

"Well, why don't *they* confront her?"

"Because, Michelle, if they confronted every single lesbian who was claiming to be Native American or selling dream catchers they wouldn't have time to go to work! Half the lesbians I know think they're Native American. It's the happening thing to be, and everybody wants to cash in! Have you been following that thing in Lesbian Connection, where one sixteenth women are trying to crash the Women of Color tent? Admittedly, Sarah is trying to take it a bit farther…"

"Yeah, I guess," said Stacy. "A whole lot farther. And what's the deal with her and this place? I tell you, if I had big bucks, I sure as hell wouldn't give her a backstage pass. And I can't believe that Gaya and Hawk really *like* her. Who could? She's a bully. Took me about two minutes to tell that."

"Maybe she has Munchausen's," suggested Alison. "You know, that syndrome where they pretend to be sick for attention. People go to huge lengths for that. I read about a woman who pretended to be blind for years."

"She doesn't have Munchausen's," said Stacy scornfully. "She has PTS."

"Well, I'd certainly die to know what that is," said Liz, sticking her head out of her tent. While Stacy had been cooking, she had been arranging. Through the door Alison could see that it was furnished with opulence—there was a thick, double-wide air mattress made up with sheets and a comforter, two huge pillows on the bed and a sheepskin rug on the floor. It was no wonder that Stacy and Liz traveled well together. The whole camp was furnished with the nicest and the best, from the grill over the fire to the huge pop-up awning under which they were all sitting in Stacy's cute little festival chairs.

"It's Power Tripping Syndrome," Stacy told her. "Certain lesbians are particularly susceptible to it."

"Yeah," said Seven, *really* pushing the envelope by stirring the fire again. Stacy stiffened, ready to cause a scene if she attempted to displace the Goddess of the Hearth. "Oh, don't worry," Seven told her, throwing a pebble into her lap. "Nobody's going to try to take over your fire. PTS has to have a certain climate in which to flourish. You know—like orchids. They just won't grow in some zones. This one is perfect. Only it's really," she paused for a moment, picturing something in her head, "called PCPTS—Politically Correct Power Tripping Syndrome. There has to be some guilt involved for it to really bear fruit."

"That's the kicker," said Michelle. She looked at the woodpile, and then at Stacy with a calculating glance. There were going to be blows soon if they weren't careful. "Women like her prey on women who truly are sincere. These women, for example. They really *do* want to make some changes in the world. I know," she said, gesturing to Stacy, "you just think it's funny. It's just a joke. But how many women do you know who would be willing to actually put money into something like this? Persimmon says it could be important, it could be as important as anything that came out of the sixties."

Stacy looked up from the rule sheet which Alison had belatedly handed to her. "No pets as slaves?" she read. "What am I supposed to do with Nine Tales—set her free to forage? I guess that would be one way to support the coyote population." She gave Alison a look. "I find it very Freudian that you forgot to give me this," she said. "These women don't sound like fun at all. I don't think I would have driven eight hours if I'd seen this part of the invitation." She looked at the list again. "I think we broke something like ten out of fourteen rules the minute we walked past the gate."

Liz stepped out of tent and looked over Stacy's shoulder. "Eleven, actually. We brought a keg."

"You did *what*?" Alison was aghast.

"It seemed like a good idea at the time," said Stacy. "Hospitable. A party and all that. We brought a case of Dos Equis for us and the keg for the little people." Now that breakfast was under way she had out the Oil Of Olay and was doing her face. Not one single UV ray had touched Stacy's skin for years.

"Why didn't you tell her what this was going to be like?" Alison asked Liz. "You've been on women's land before."

"Oh," said Stacy scornfully, "she and Lawrence got into the truck and talked about sex the whole way down. I thought they were going to ask me to pull over so they could do each other."

Everyone looked a little queasy over this image.

"I wouldn't do Lawrence," Liz protested. "I draw the line somewhere."

"There's a surprise," said Michelle. Stacy had to be treated civilly most of the time because she was Alison's girlfriend, but Michelle and Liz couldn't stand one another and rarely tried to hide it. Generally neither pulled any punches, although they could, in emergency situations, close ranks and work together.

"Hello!" said Liz. "That's my coffee. That's my cup you're drinking out of. That's my chair you've got your ass parked in. If you want to dis me, then you just take it on up the hill. Maybe the nature girls have boiled up a nice pot of chicory and loco weed by now. And you," she said to Alison, "I've been to Michigan. That's what I've been to. I had no idea we were sailing into a nunnery."

"Well, at least you should have known better than to wear *that*," Alison replied. She was still feeling a bit grumpy. Michelle might like to start her day with a quarrel, but she didn't.

"Pardon me," said Liz, "but there are plenty of gals wearing leather at the festivals. I didn't know I was going be strip searched at the door here."

"That strip search scene certainly is a re-occurring fantasy of yours," observed Stacy, who was applying just the tiniest bit of lip-gloss with the help of her compact. She made a kiss to blot. The gesture made Alison wet immediately. She looked up the hill, wondering if *she'd* get thrown off if she threw Stacy down in her tent instead of rendezvousing with the work crew. "And you wouldn't have to actually fuck Lawrence—you could give him a wine enema and make him bark like a dog—that would hold you both for a while."

"And you wonder why these women don't want you here," said Michelle, sneaking a peak at Liz to see if this was considered dissing. She didn't want to be thrown out before the biscuits were done.

"Why?" said Stacy, genuinely confused. Now that the skin was taken care of, she was ready to deal with the Dutch oven again. First things first. "They don't want us because we talk about kinky sex? That's why they don't want us? Their loss—Liz and I work hard and we're compassionate and fun to be with. I was even willing not to fuck while we were guests. My mama told me that was rude, anyway. To hell with them if they think they're better than we are. That was only if we camped inside the gate, Sweetie," she added in an aside to Alison, who had looked stricken when she heard the no fucking rule.

"You don't understand where these women are coming from,"

argued Michelle, still keeping a wary eye on Liz, who was now set-ting up a little table with attached benches that had put somebody back a couple of hundred dollars. Liz, who understood that argu-ing was one of the spices of life, was letting this whole thing pass. Michelle was like the prosecution or the defense—you kind of had to let her have her say as long as she stayed within the boundaries. "Stacy, you've only been out a few years." She said this almost apologetically, for it was known to be a touchy subject.

"Yes, I know," said Stacy crossly. "And you've all been out for twenty and you fought side by side in the revolution together and never fucked a man and wore flannel shirts and cut your hair short so that someday I'd have the right to vote and marry my girlfriend and because of that I'll never be as good a lesbian as any of you no matter how hard I try or how long I live. Right? Did I get it all?" She moved back away from the Dutch oven. Everyone gave Michelle a hard look. Couldn't she have waited until after breakfast?

But Stacy was merely prepping. If she was going to the trouble of cooking, then by golly everything was going to be just right. She opened one of the two large coolers and took out a tub of soft but-ter and two squat jars of homemade jelly, courtesy the grandma who didn't speak Yiddish. When these were arranged in a nice lit-tle Zen arrangement on a tray with good silver and cloth napkins, she went back to the biscuits.

There was quite a long pause while everyone had a small spir-itual experience. Only after she had fought the good fight with three biscuits—one with honey, one with jelly, and a third just plain, did Michelle attempt to pick up the threads of the conversa-tion.

"No," she said, standing and shaking the crumbs off her lap onto the ground, where Zorra pounced upon them eagerly, "It's not about that. It's not about being better than you. I'm just trying to tell you where these women are coming from. When we joined the team, there was a pretty big movement of lesbians who were trying to get back to the land."

"It wasn't just dykes," put in Seven Yellow Moons who was about ten years older than the rest of them, and had spent a good part of the seventies in various mixed communes. "It was a hippie thing as well. It was an outgrowth from the war protesters and fuck the establishment. We didn't need them! We could take our Mother Earth magazines and move out to the country and live in an old school bus and raise our own food and not pay taxes to the war machine. And the lesbian/feminist movement was just part of *that* outgrowth and so of course we wanted to do the country thing, too."

"I'm getting bored," Stacy warned. "I don't like being lectured."

Luckily, Alison knew how to handle the Getting Lectured situation, which was to switch from speaking directly to Stacy into conversation mode.

"Do you still feel the same way?" she asked Seven quickly. "I mean, I guess obviously you do, because you still live on women's land."

"Yeah, I do," said Seven. "About a lot of it. I want my main energy to go into other dykes. I want to live around other dykes, and I really don't like living in a city."

"But you don't seem as exclusive as these women are," said Liz.

"Yeah," said Alison, who was looking longingly at the biscuit still on Liz's plate, "and can anything that's run like a monarchy work—even if it's in a different guise? From what you say the women who are living on your place—I don't know if they're changing the world, but most of them are living the way they talk. But most of what I've seen here has been about doing things in exactly the same old way. The only difference is that there's somebody different in power, and there's a whole new set of rules. What does it matter if I drink five cups of coffee in the morning? How does that make me a lesser person, if I'm willing to do my share? I'd almost rather deal with somebody who says up front, 'Well, I'm going to treat you different because you're queer, or because you're a woman,' because at least they're coming right out and saying it— at least there isn't all this fencing. At least if you know what's happening, you can fight against it."

"You haven't seen some of the women who are living at Canyon Land right now," said Seven moodily, staring into the flames. "I never thought I'd say this—I've always believed in open women's land, I've lived on it for ten years. I helped start Amazon Farm! But I've found myself being really envious of Gaya. And you know why? Because this is her place! She can kick people off if she wants! We've been dealing with a couple of women all winter long—they moved into the main house without asking. Hell, specifically *against* anything any of us said! One of them's a runaway— she can't be any older than sixteen. She's okay for a kid, but the other one is twice her age, really obviously preying on her, and we think she was involved in a ripoff at one of the stores in town—a place where some of us work! We don't want them there, but what are we going to do? First we had to get consensus, which took weeks and when we finally got that all we did was write the older one a letter telling her to leave. Guess how much good that did. She just said no—what are we going to do, call the cops?"

"But is it better here?" said Alison. "I mean, I guess Gaya and Hawk are in charge, but I'm not sure how far they're willing to push it."

"Well, they threw Stacy and Liz off the land," said Michelle to Seven. "Or they would have if it hadn't been for you and the hot tub. And I suppose it's not much fun to be the beggar at the gate." She looked hopefully at Liz, obviously hoping her feelings were hurt by being eighty-sixed.

"Whoa there, City Pony," said Stacy. Liz went off into a little spasm of laughter and Michelle gave Alison a dirty look.

Alison raised her hands in defense."I did not leak that,"

"She didn't have to," said Stacy, still preoccupied with the kitchen thing. "The campfire of the coffee drinkers was fraught with tales of the amazing City Pony of Denver." The Dutch oven was soaking over the fire, and the coolers were in the shade. Okay, life could go on. "Actually, it's just fine being the beggar at the gate. I don't know why you bothered with the negotiations," she said to Liz. "I'm happy right here."

"I want to pick up girls," said Liz, taking the last biscuit. "And to do that, I have to run with the herd. You should encourage me. I'm so horny that you're starting to look good."

Stacy preened happily, though if she had thought there was even a note of seriousness to Liz's claim she would have run like a bunny. Just like Alison and Michelle, she knew that what she had with Liz was better than any affair and should never be tainted by the dirty word 'sex.'

"And Lavender and her dog are still here, and they weren't invited," said Michelle. Zorra raised her head from Michelle's lap and gazed reproachfully at Alison. "Lavender's still there," she amended, patting Zorra on the head. "And the only reason they were able to throw Stacy and Liz off is because Stacy and Liz are fairly civilized and fairly respectful of other people's rights. Lavender's not."

"Don't say that I'm civilized in front of other people," Liz protested. "I'll never get another date." She took a square tin with a picture of an orange cat on the lid from beneath her chair and started cleaning what looked like about two pounds of pot. Liz liked to buy in bulk.

"Lavender has Lesbian Passive-Aggressive Disorder," said Stacy. She paused to recall the initials. "It's worse than PCPTS— sometimes you can confront those gals in the end, but you can't do a thing with PADs. They just do whatever they damn please, and nothing anybody else says even registers."

"I'm depressed," said Seven dolefully, leaning back on her elbow. "There's not going to be a revolution, and I'm getting too old to be carrying my water from the creek."

"Oh, don't let it get you down," Stacy consoled. "Sarah's going to get hers some day—and in a big way, too. Tell us some gossip to cheer everybody up. Do you know why Gaya and Hawk are letting her cleave unto them?" Stacy had been married once to a religious fanatic, and it sometimes crept into her conversation. "Are they just being politically correct?" Both of her coolers were run on solar batteries—she arranged the fold-up panels facing south.

"Well," said Seven, perking up, "the general consensus among the con-Sarah camp is that she has something on them. Why not? She's got something on everybody else."

"She's a blackmailer as well?" asked Alison in surprise. She thought about Lisa asking for asylum the night before—okay, that would fit.

"I think of her more as an outer," said Seven. "Blackmail is such a harsh word. And doesn't it have to involve money? I don't think Sarah does what she does for money."

"Ah!" said Stacy, carefully placing two sticks from the pile side by side across the pit. She slapped Michelle's hand away.

Michelle looked cross. "Everyone *should* be out," she said in a voice so peevish it made Alison, who agreed with her, want to argue the other side. "If everyone was out, look at the voting block we'd have. Look at—"

"Yes, yes, I know, I know," interrupted Liz, who even in a time of truce could not resist a small squelch on Michelle. She put the last lick on a perfect joint. Liz scorned women who had to use two papers. "But don't you think that everyone has *some* personal rights about who and how?"

"It doesn't matter anyway," said Seven. "That's not quite what I meant. I mean, she's the kind of person who knows everybody's nasty little secrets, and knows just where to drop them to cause the most furor. Then she's all confused about why everyone is upset, because all she was doing was Telling The Truth, and isn't that what life is really about? The Truth?" She put on a virtuous, aggressive tone and face for the last two sentences, and Alison flashed back to the previous night's supper.

"Oh," Alison said to Stacy and Liz, "she used that theme last night. You should have seen it." Quickly she filled them in on the details of the corn bread scene.

"Ugh!" Stacy shuddered. "That girl needs to drink lots more caffeine and double up on sugar."

"Her life does seem rather joyless," admitted Seven. "I think she'd benefit from keeping a couple of animals as slaves—I mean, I've never seen her spontaneously happy about anything that I would enjoy."

"She liked the sunrise," said Michelle, leaning over to give Liz a light. Getting high was like meeting in Switzerland—immediate truce.

"Bullshit!" said Alison rudely. "She liked waking us up. She liked being spiritually superior. That's not a convenient place for someone in a wheelchair to do a daily ritual. I'll bet she usually does that up in back of the house. If she does it at all."

"Me, too," said Seven. "And I agree with Stacy. She doesn't need to be in a wheelchair. She says she has MS. Well, my mom had MS, and Sarah doesn't act the right way."

"Doesn't MS fluctuate?" asked Michelle with a frown. "And doesn't it manifest itself in a lot of different ways?"

"Yes," Seven admitted. "And of course, that's why she chose it. But if she had it bad enough to be in a chair, she would be in pain at least some of the time. And she's not. Not genuinely. Oh, she puts it on occasionally like a performance, but if you watch her, she can move pretty much any way that she wants—it doesn't hurt unless she wants something. Did you see her pitch that can up on the roof?"

"Something we missed?" asked Liz. Alison, with a great number of side bars from Seven and Michelle, described the cloistering ritual.

"Well, I *never* would have given up *my* keys," said Liz, looking at Michelle as if she had just one-upped her.

"You gave your keys to *Lawrence*," said Michelle. "At least I know that my car's not going to be *impounded*." Everyone looked politely off into different directions without comment. Lawrence, Stacy's housecleaner, was well known for little adventures that started out, 'I was just sitting there minding my own business when this cute guy walked by,' and ended up in jail, or stranded in some little town where the locals were beginning to menace. "Besides, I can get those keys down and drive off that hill anytime I want to."

"Yeah," said Seven, "except for the fact that you're completely parked in and some of those gals aren't going to like it if you start moving their cars."

Michelle got a picked-on look and Alison who thought everyone was being a bit hard on her, changed the subject.

"Did you say that Lawrence was depressed?" she asked Liz.

"Oh, always. Manic/depressive was invented to describe that boy. We're hoping the Internet stud will cheer him up."

"I don't know why Sarah didn't just say that she has chronic fatigue syndrome," said Stacy, scornful again. "Everybody who doesn't want to work has that." To Michelle, who was once again attempting to put wood on the fire, she said, "I will break your hand if I have to. You can drink my coffee and eat my chocolate, but I am topping this fire scene."

Michelle sulked. Alison grew cold and quiet. The chronic fatigue comment was just what she would have predicted from Stacy. And Seven Yellow Moons thought she should talk to her about the fibromyalgia syndrome? Right.

Stacy got into one of the big coolers and began offering bottle of Dos Equis.

"Isn't it a little early in the morning for beer?" asked Michelle.

"Listen," said Stacy, "the only reason I came down here was because Liz said we could party with our shirts off in the middle of the desert. And they don't want me to help." She popped a top for Liz and herself.

Alison looked at her watch. Plenty of time for a collective breakfast to have been made and eaten.

"Well," she said, standing and looking at Michelle and Seven. "I hear Dinah blowing her horn."

"You have that backwards," said Michelle, also standing. "Dinah blew her horn at supper time, not when it was time to start work."

"Either way, I hear the adobe calling."

"Bye," said Stacy, starting to pull off her shirt. "Don't forget to visit. Remember, we're the Fun Camp."

CHAPTER SIX

"Michelle." Alison caught her friend by the sleeve as she passed, carrying a tub of adobe for the women working on the inside walls.

"Hmm?" Michelle set the tub down and wiped her face with her sleeve, leaving a big streak of adobe across her forehead. Michelle was in her element—working with other dykes, and doing the hardest and very most essential job. What could be better?

"Cover for me. I've got to go lie down. I just can't work anymore." Indeed, the wonder was that she had managed to accomplish anything at all, for she had been overcome with fatigue almost two hours before, and it was only a kind of desperate pride that had pushed her.

"You do look dreadful," observed Michelle who was not known for tact.

"I feel like I'm getting the flu," Alison answered. It was not a lie. The onset of what she had come to think of as 'bad times' felt exactly like the aches of a fever that used to herald a bout of vomiting. The only difference was that this was not something which would happen once or twice a winter, and then recede within a few days time.

"You sure have had the flu a lot this year," commented Michelle, as if she had been reading her mind. "Maybe you should get a flu shot. Sure, if anybody asks I'll tell 'em you didn't feel well." She picked up her bucket and strode off. Women were waiting. She was needed.

Finding a place to nap was difficult. Not her tent, or Stacy's, or the main house—they were all too noisy or too hot. What Alison really wanted was someplace cool and quiet that also was wired for electricity. She thought perhaps if she took two of her sleeping pills—FMS was linked to sleeping disorders and the doctor said that she probably woke up as many as twenty times a night without even being aware of it, thus depriving herself of much needed non REM sleep—and turned on her white noise machine she might be able to repair the damage caused by the restless night.

But it seemed that this particular combination might be too

much to ask for here. She thought for a moment of Persimmon's shop, but it was awfully close to the main house—she was sure she would hear any noise from the patio. And since G-hey! had told her they'd filled the hot tub, and it would be up to temperature by mid afternoon, she was sure there would be people on the patio. She stood by the car, feeling sicker and sicker, almost incapable of making a decision.

Finally, however, just before the moment when she might have collapsed into tears, she remembered the little house in which Sarah Embraces-All-Things lived. Gaya had said that the empty half of the duplex was meant as a guest room, hadn't she? Alison was fairly sure that Sarah was up at the main house. It was just a guess, but it was almost time for lunch, and Sarah Embraces-All-Things was the kind of woman who liked to be in the thick of things. Even if she did come back to her room, how much noise could one woman without a stereo or TV make? Resolutely, Alison put aside the memory of the morning chant. It was the best option she had.

She took two pills with an Oreo—take with food—and forced herself to walk slowly down the hill. One foot in front of the other, and soon you'll be able to sleep, she promised herself. She tapped on Sarah's door, just in case, and was flooded with relief when there was no answer. The guest room was just as she remembered it, welcoming and cool. She pulled a blanket out of the cupboard. The sheet should have been enough, but when she was like this her body started shutting down and the heating system was the first thing to go.

All that remained was a final trip to the bathroom. She had never before had outhouse anxiety, but the public shitter was a bit much, and so it was quite a pleasure to use the flush toilet. Sarah Embraces-All-Things, she noticed, as she looked around the bathroom, did not seem to be planning on a housemate any time in the near future. The counters and shelves were spread with her personal things. Even the towel rack was full, clothes mixed in with the heavy, terry cloth towels. Everything was nice, right down to the glycerin soap. Apparently the fragrance ban didn't reach into Sarah's private life. Unless she had a private income, which Alison somehow doubted, she had somehow managed to climb onto the gravy train with Hawk. Was she lovers with Gaya as well? There had been nothing about monogamy on the rule sheet, and Alison remembered years ago reading several back-to-the-land books in which the lesbians were in open relationships or triads. Of course, they had all been doing that then.

Well, it wasn't any of her business, and she supposed that just because both women dressed expensively didn't mean that they weren't economizing in other places. Still, she felt just a little scammed. When it all came down to it, Hawk and Gaya were getting a month of free labor, plus some substantial housewarming presents, in return for meals. Oh, what the hell, if they'd put it in an *Earth Watch* catalog as an anthropology experiment they probably could have gotten a crew who would have paid to come. It was time to go to bed. Seldom before had the thought of sleep seemed so inviting.

As she turned away from the sink—after lathering her hands lavishly with the glycerin soap—Alison bumped against the wall and jostled the towel rack. Two towels and a jacket fell to the floor. The jacket was quite beautiful—the fabric looked as if it had been hand-woven in an elaborate pattern of black, red and a touch of orange. When Alison picked it up, a prescription pill bottle fell out of the pocket and rolled across the tile floor. Alison cornered it by the tub. The cap had not come off—lucky for her, because it was almost full. She glanced at the label but the name of the medication—Norpramine—meant nothing to her. Neither did the name, Katie Baxter. Probably the name Sarah Embraces-All-Things used when she wasn't doing the Native American scam. She dropped it back into the pocket of the jacket and went into the guest room, closing the door behind her. She turned her noise machine to the 'night train' setting and was out the moment her head hit the pillow.

She slept deeply, and did not wake until after dusk. Sarah was still not in her room, though she must have come and gone, because her jacket was no longer in the bathroom. Alison thought that if she hurried, she'd still have time to catch dinner in the main house. But she felt self-conscious about joining the women who had worked all afternoon. She didn't want to sit down to a meal she had not helped prepare, and she didn't want to explain herself. She decided to visit the Fun Camp, instead. On the way, she stopped at the truck and changed into warmer clothes. She also picked up her towel. The long nap had taken care of the fatigue, but she still felt a trace of the ache. A sauna sounded good. And maybe, if everyone else was feeling social and sticking to the hot tub, she and Stacy could oil up and play a little kissy-face on the wooden benches. They had done that one other time in a private sauna that they had rented, and it had been very exciting. Alison could still remember the feel of Stacy's skin sliding beneath her hand, covered with hot oil and her clit grew hard with the memory. Hot oil was wonderful and sensual, but it was a mess in the house. Carpe sauna was her motto.

The Fun Camp had taken on a settled look that surpassed what Alison had managed to achieve in her own house since the move. Stacy had been decorating. There was a row of multicolored Chinese lanterns strung around the canopy. A rainbow banner was waving from its apex and various bits of jewelry and clothing draped artfully on the poles showed that Stacy had found it necessary to change outfits several times.

Wonderful smells wafted up from the fire pit. Stacy had loosened control of the fire just a bit—she was allowing the crew, which looked identical to the breakfast crowd, toast their own marshmallows.

"Hey!" said Michelle, looking up from the fire. "I though that if I hung around here long enough that you'd show up!" She transferred her marshmallow, which was burnt to a crisp, onto a graham cracker. Patience—except for her artwork—was not one of Michelle's stronger virtues. This was something that she and Janka had not thought to figure into the baby thing.

Stacy who was sitting at the table with Seven raised her head.

"Hi! Michelle said you were sick—are you feeling better?" I saved some dinner—the gals said you didn't make it up to the main house." She stood, and Alison saw that Seven had been reading her tarot. The round Motherpeace cards were spread out on the table.

"Did I miss anything?" Alison asked Michelle, who was already loading another marshmallow. Never a wasted motion.

"Mmm, not too much. There wasn't another big cornbread scene, if that's what you mean."

"That's what I mean."

"No. Sarah Tops-the-Scene gave a little lecture about respect and woman energy that nobody understood."

Alison looked at Seven, who nodded confirmation. "Nope, I couldn't figure it out either. As near as I could tell, someone had used something of hers."

Oops, thought Alison, the soap. Well, she'd be damned if she'd confess.

"Was the hot tub ready?" she asked.

"Was the hot tub ready?" repeated Seven. "Oh, was the hot tub ready!" She leaned back in her chair and kissed the tips of her fingers as if she had just tasted a fine wine.

Stacy handed Alison a plate heaped with beef and vegetables on a bed of rice, looking pleased with her culinary efforts.

"Shiskabob," she said, and looking even more pleased when Alison moaned with delight.

"Where'd you get that tub, anyway?" asked Michelle. She had

lost her marshmallow into the fire and was attempting to block Liz from the best spot while she reloaded. "I know you're rolling in the dough," she paused significantly so that everyone would know that she knew why, too, and disapproved, "but isn't that a little lavish, even for you?"

Stacy smiled. "Well," she said, "it was just the best deal. One of Lawrence's friends was repossessing it from an ex-lover, and he didn't have anyplace to put it—he just wanted to make sure the ex wasn't enjoying it. Bad break up."

"Aren't they all," murmured Liz. With a bold move she swept her stick beneath Michelle's and claimed the prime territory.

"Well, anyway. So he wanted to get rid of it, and when he heard about where we were going and how the locals had left that dead dog on these gals' mailbox, he practically donated it."

"That wasn't these women, Stacy," said Michelle, pretending that she had graciously given the spot to Liz. "That was the women at Camp Sister Spirit. In *Mississippi*." She sounded pained by Stacy's ignorance.

"Oh!" Stacy looked momentarily nonplused. Then she waved it away. "I'm sure these women have had *something* unpleasant happen to them. I'll bet the locals are rude to them in the store. And it was the perfect deal—he got a little money, we got a hot tub and the ex-lover got screwed. Talk about closure!"

Alison, who had been packing down dinner as fast as possible, looked up. "So the ardent separatists are up there sitting in a faggot hot tub? Don't tell them, 'kay?"

"Oh, we wiped it out," said Stacy, taking a bottle of wine out of one of the coolers. Alison saw that the keg had been tapped as well. It was sitting by the table. Its top was rimmed with plastic cups, each with a name written on the side in permanent marker. The Fun Camp had been busy. "Faggot cooties aren't that hardy."

Liz finished her marshmallow and went into her tent. She came back carrying a jar of silver polish. She took off her bracelets one by one and began polishing them, using one of the coolers for a table.

"How's the reading?" Alison asked Seven, who was still sitting at the table, studying the cards laid out among the silverware.

"Weird," she answered, in a voice both puzzled and troubled. She looked up at the moon, which was still almost full. "I'll be interested to see what happens tonight." Stacy had obviously switched from reading to chatting mode, so she swept the cards back into a pile and put them into a small bag made of blue, handwoven cloth.

Liz put her bracelets back on and peeled off her sweatshirt. Beneath it she was wearing an open leather vest and nothing else.

She began attaching a silver chain between her two nipple rings, which made Michelle, who disapproved of such things on principle, screw up her mouth in censure. Liz had an extensive collection of nipple jewelry.

"What are you getting all dressed up for?" asked Stacy, a bit miffed because *she* was not the center of attention. Oh, well, she got to be in charge of the fire.

"Oh, I'm going to do a three-way with that red-headed gal from Denver and her girlfriend," said Liz in a supremely satisfied tone. "They're heading down here after they shower."

"You're going to do a three-way in that tent that is not more than five feet from my head?" asked Stacy. "You know, tents are visual privacy only. I'm going to have to listen to you all night long!"

"Guess you'll just have to eat your heart out," said Liz sweetly, still sounding smug.

"How did you even get to *talk* to them?" asked Alison. She knew Liz was a smooth mover, but she had not seen either G-hey! or the woman she thought was her girlfriend leave the construction site all morning.

"This afternoon," said Liz. "They like coffee." She really was supremely pleased with herself. "I felt just like a blackmarketeer trading candy bars for sexual favors. Hey, maybe we can work that into the scene!"

Michelle stiffened with indignation, which of course was why Liz said it. Their truce was like that of the Klingons and the Federation—ready to blow at any moment.

"You sure are getting to be a chicken hawk," said Stacy, breaking one of the brittle sticks of wood from the fire pile into five pieces. She was obviously trying to burn down to the perfect bed of coals. Alison hoped she had no intentions of walking on it—there were just some places where the line had to be drawn. "First it was Carla…"

"Don't mention that name, please," begged Liz, crossing her fingers in front of her as if to ward off a vampire. Carla was a young woman she had dated for less than a year, having paid for Carla's therapy, and who in the aftermath of being attacked by a serial killer had turned on the leather community in general and Liz in particular and trashed both all over town.[3] It had been unpleasant for everyone. "I haven't heard from her for months—let's not invoke the power of naming."

"Well, I hope they're over-age," put in Michelle, jumping at the chance to get Liz back for the nipple rings. "*That* could really fuck things up here, and imagine how it would look for you in the newspaper if their parents brought suit…"

"Oh, get over it," said Liz crossly. "They're not that young and you know it. At least I'm not fucking around behind my girlfriend's back."

There was a startled silence during which no one looked at anyone else, except for Michelle, who gave Alison a pained and betrayed stare.

"I didn't leak it!" protested Alison, who really *hadn't* leaked it. "You're always blaming me for leaking your secrets, and I never do!"

"Get a clue, Michelle," said Liz, smug again. "She didn't need to leak it. Lesbians can't keep secrets. Jerusha told Claw and Claw told G-hey! and G-hey! told Salad and Salad told me." Whatever else Liz had been doing that afternoon, she certainly had gotten into the loop.

"I knew, too," said Seven Yellow Moons. "Lisa told me."

Michelle got to her feet with a haughty dignity and strode off into the night without a good-by, unless you counted giving the finger to Liz. She and Liz greeted and took leave of one another in this manner so often that it actually could be counted as kind of a cultural thing.

"Thank you," said Alison to Liz. "It's going to be fun to spend eight hours in the car with her. I appreciate it."

"Oh, she shouldn't be such a judgmental little bitch," replied Liz, unrepentant. "Or, if she is going to be such a judgmental little bitch, she should curb it while she's fucking around behind Janka's back."

"Just for the record," put in Alison, "she says she's *not* fucking Persimmon. She says they're doing a spiritual thing."

"She's lying!" said Stacy. "Come on, you can practically smell it on her!"

"And everybody knows what 'spiritual connection' is in dyke speak, anyway," put in Seven. "It's like 'back rub'."

"So, how come Sarah has all the dirt on everybody?" asked Alison, thinking that it was time to change the subject. Maybe if they didn't discuss Michelle's infidelity—consummated or just inevitable—it would just go away. "*I* don't have the dirt on *anybody.*"

"You do, though," corrected Seven. "Take what's happening with Michelle right now. Any one of us could pretty much drop a bomb on her life by calling Janka tonight and telling her what's going on. It would be The Truth."

"She says nothing's going on," Alison protested.

"She's *lying!*" said Liz in exactly the same tone that Stacy had said it.

Seven continued as if there had been no interruption. "But none of us will, for a variety of reasons. Because we're hoping it will blow over, or it's none of our business, or because if anyone tells it should be Michelle. But Sarah would not only tell, she'd do it in front of other women, so that Janka would have to kick Michelle out immediately to save face. It's a gift to be that confrontational, really. To really get a kick out of fucking up people's lives. I'll bet that when Sarah was ten she was one of those nasty little girls who would sneak up behind you and say, 'I saw what you did,' just on the off chance of getting a bite. Who hasn't done something they're not proud of?"

"So what has she got on Gaya and Hawk?" asked Stacy, stretching like a cat over the warmth of the coals.

Seven shrugged. "Nobody knows. She'll spill it when she's done with them. This month will be exciting for her—we'll be like having a box of ants to shake. But I can't imagine her staying out here after that. She needs a larger population to prey on. To tell the truth, I'm tempted to leave when you do. I don't think I would have agreed if I had known that Sarah was going to be here. She's bound to destroy someone, and that's not going to be pretty." Alison thought briefly of Lisa, but remained true to her promise.

"What's with those kids she's leading around by the nose?" she asked instead.

"Oh, the Young Muscle?" asked Seven, who was obviously getting on a Sarah-bashing roll.

"The Healing Circle," suggested Stacy who was washing her hands under one of the solar shower bags.

"The Chain Gang," said Liz. Everyone laughed, and Alison knew they would never be referred to in any other way for the remainder of the retreat.

"They got names?" Stacy asked when the laughter died down.

"They do," said Seven, "but I can't remember what they are."

Stacy lifted an eyebrow at Alison, who shook her head. "I can't remember either. But they go together. You know, Camas and Lupine and Sego Lily, or something like that."

"Huey, Dewey and Louie," suggested Liz.

"Snip, Snap and Snur," said Seven.

"Flicka, Ricka and Dicka," said Stacy.

"How about Snap, Crackle and Pop, if we're going to be silly," suggested Alison.

"Why don't you know their names?" Stacy asked. Now that

dinner and marshmallows were behind her, she pulled a piece of handwork out of her tent and sat down close to the lantern. "Why don't you know everybody's names? Didn't you do some get acquainted activities when you got here? Whenever I go to a conference or a retreat we always play some get-acquainted games, or at least introduce ourselves."

"Dykes don't do that, Honey," said Alison. "We bond over our power tools."

"Dykes," said Stacy, snipping a thread, "should get with the program."

"What kind of retreats do you go to?" asked Seven Yellow Moons curiously.

"Well, I usually go to a couple of quilting retreats every year. And I go to Powersurge." She named the big women's leather conference that was held in Seattle. "Come to think of it," she said thoughtfully, "we didn't play any get-acquainted games there. But then, we didn't have to. Those gals kind of like to just jump in."

Alison could see that this was going to become a Powersurge conversation in a minute if she didn't take the reins.

"So where did these kids come from?" she asked again, hastily.

"Well," said Seven obligingly, "Sarah ran this little scam where she put on these 'authentic Native American' sweats. And white girls paid to go. This is all according to my sources, of course. I wasn't there." She obviously wanted that to be really clear. "So I believe that she picked those young women out of those sweats and cast her net over them."

"Like a big, old spider," contributed Stacy. "She made a trap and then she waited."

"Is she fucking any of them?" Liz asked. She clearly had fucking on the brain.

"If my information is correct," said Seven, "she's had sex with all of them. Sparingly. As reward. I believe she refers to herself as a 'sacred prostitute'." She gave a little Mona Lisa smile, obviously looking forward to the reaction this little tidbit of information was going to produce.

She was not disappointed. Liz and Alison both went off into spasms of laughter.

Stacy snorted indignantly. "Honestly! And that woman treated me like a whore just because I was wearing nail polish!"

Liz recovered and looked for something on which she could wipe her eyes without ruining her outfit. Stacy handed her a paper towel and gave one to Alison as well.

"I am going to steal that," said Liz. "What a way to get laid!"

"You don't have the sincerity to make it work," said Alison. To Seven she said, "Do you really think she has something on Hawk and Gaya? You don't think that the Native American/differently-abled stuff is enough?"

"Could be," admitted Seven. "I'd almost rather think that she was blackmailing them, though, than to think that they've been taken in so totally."

"Maybe they haven't," suggested Alison. "Even if they suspect they're being had, they're in the same boat as the rest of you. Even more so. What are they going to do? Say, 'You're not disabled—get out of that chair!' That'd go over big. Stacy or I might be able to do it just before we left—she probably doesn't have the facilities to hunt us down. But Gaya and Hawk are tied to this area because of the land, and to top it off, they're trying to attract other women. She could screw them good—didn't you say she drove another woman out of the community by trashing her? They've probably just decided the best thing to do is wait it out—you said yourself she's going to get bored soon."

"Why are they in this area, anyway?" asked Stacy. "I mean, what brought them here?"

Seven opened her mouth to speak, but at that moment they heard crunching on the road, and G-hey! and Salad appeared out of the darkness. Salad was none other than Tomato Woman. Both of the young women, dressed in tight, torn jeans and sweaters, looked hale and healthy and utterly delectable. Seven, Alison and Stacy exchanged only one glance and then stood as one.

"We're going to go do a sweat and a shower," Alison told Liz.

"I need to meditate," said Seven. Brief hugs and handshakes were exchanged and all three were on their way in less than a minute.

"Oh," said Stacy when they were out of hearing, "I hate it when I'm attracted to really young women!"

"I didn't leave because of that," said Seven. "I left because I haven't gotten laid in almost a year, and I didn't want to listen. Why do you hate it?"

"Because it just makes me think that I'm becoming a dirty old woman, and that soon I'll be having to worry about controlling my bodily functions in public."

"What I hate," said Alison, "is when I'm attracted and smile at them and they smile back in this really confused way, like they're trying to remember if you're one of their friend's mothers."

"Liz doesn't seem to have that problem," observed Seven.

"Liz is a pig," replied Alison. "And don't think you can blackmail me by repeating that—she knows what I think."

They parted ways by the little tent village. Seven headed up towards the house where, she confessed, she really had her mind on leftovers rather than meditation. Alison and Stacy cut down on the path towards the sweat lodge. They held hands. In her free hand Stacy was swinging a little gym bag that, though Alison knew was at least two years old, looked just as cute and new as the rest of her outfit. Stacy believed heavily in Scotchgard. The moon was up and still almost full, so they could see far across the desert floor, until it became lost in the shadows of the great buttes. Closer they could see the sweat lodge. There was steam rising from its roof, indicating recent use, though there was no sound of conversation, and no one at the showers. Alison hoped they were not interrupting anyone, though she could not see the 'Occupied' signal of feathers and cloth that Hawk had shown them, hanging from the door. She wondered how Stacy would feel about getting all oiled up and fucking on the wooden floor of the lodge before going to bed. She looked at Stacy and was once again struck almost dumb by her loveliness in the moonlight. What had she been thinking—jeopardizing her relationship with this woman by sleeping with Marta Goicochea? Stacy was not one to put up with anything that she thought made her look stupid or second class—she made no bones about wanting to be the belle of the ball. Never again, Alison vowed. She was a bit troubled by the fact that an aftertaste cut through the fervor and purity of the vow—the memory of the way Marta had seemed to enter her mind and fantasy totally, so they had moved together as if they were one.

Closer to the door they saw that the lodge was indeed in use. A shirt and jacket hung on the clothes rack by the door and there was a pair of boots lined up neatly toe to toe on the wooden walk. They looked at one another. Alison shrugged. She was still tormented by the memory of the previous night, when she had tossed and turned in pain. She knew from experience that a sauna and four Advils before bed would make a great deal of difference. They had been talking the whole way down the hill—whoever was inside already knew they were there, and, as Alison had already noticed, the feather fetish was not hanging in front of the door and was in fact nowhere to be seen.

"I really want to do this," said Stacy in a low voice. "I've got to wash—I really stink."

"Never, my sweet," Alison replied on a gallant whisper. "Stink is not a word that ever appears in reference to you. I'd rather go down on you after three days in the desert than kiss any other woman fresh from her bath."

Stacy, already stripped down to her French cut panties, snapped a towel at her. Alison dipped her hand into the bucket of water sitting outside the door—it felt like ice—and flicked a handful at her. They were both still giggling as she pushed back the blanket which covered the door.

The moonlight had been so very bright that at first it was almost impossible to see inside the sweat, though there were two burning candles stuck in the pots of sand. Alison hesitated by the side of the door until she could see that there was only one other woman in the tent, lying on the bench on the far side. This surprised her. Hawk had been adamant about the sauna rules on the tour, and the first one was that everyone use the buddy system. According to the endless information of Tomato Woman—oh, got to remember her name was Salad—Persimmon had done a marathon solo sauna and passed out a couple of weeks ago. If, Salad had told Alison, Gaya hadn't gone looking for her, there could have been big trouble. Hence the buddy rule.

"Hi," Alison said, feeling just a bit foolish. "Hope we're not bothering you."

The woman—in the light and from across the room Alison could not tell who it was—made no sign that she had heard, but lay still with her back to them. Oh, well, thought Alison, I guess she's not in the mood to chat. She had probably thought that no one would join her uninvited this late at night. Boy, she really had the heat cranked up! The sauna was heated by a small potbellied stove that sat in the middle of the dome, surrounded by a sand pit. It was vented through the roof, and reminded Alison of several of the yurts she had seen at Canyon Land. Sitting on the stove was a huge metal basket filled with rocks. A few feet away from the stove, where the sand ended and the wooden floor began, was a wooden bucket of water, in which was both a ladle and a whisk.

Stacy, a big barrette held in her mouth, had already seated herself beside the door on one of the wooden benches which lined the lodge. She had her hands up over her head braiding her hair off her neck. Alison started to join her, but something about the way the other woman was lying made her uneasy. Tentatively she went closer, all too aware that if the other woman was simply ignoring them she was going to look insensitive and pushy. Even from a few feet away she could not identify the woman—she did not know any of them well enough to be able to tell from the curve of her back or the feather tattooed on her right shoulder. A mass of hair hung down across the woman's shoulders, but even that was no help—it was so damp from sweat and steam that really all Alison could tell was that it was dark.

Motivated by that same vague sense of uneasiness she reached out and put a hand upon the woman's shoulder.

"Are you okay?" she asked.

"Is she all right?" asked Stacy at the very same moment. They were both answered by the sudden movement of the woman responding to Alison's tug by rolling onto her back, and then onto the floor with a dull, yet somehow deafening plop.

"Eek!" Stacy gave one short squeak as if she were Blondie Bumstead, and then visibly reined herself in. "Jesus, Alison, has she passed out, I'll get some water…" She turned towards the door, but remembering the icy water in the bucket Alison stopped her with a hand.

"No, we don't want to put her into shock—help me get her out of here."

Carrying the absolutely limp body between the two of them was a problem, even charged as they both were by adrenaline and they wasted a few moments. Finally Stacy dashed outside and grabbed her beach towel. They laid it beside the woman on the wooden floor, and after rolling her onto it managed to drag her to the door. She might have a few splinters, but Alison hoped fervently that would be her only problem. Alison, in fact, was beginning to hear a little voice in the back of her mind which she most definitely did not want to hear, and that voice was saying, "Dead."

Out in the moonlight, so suddenly clear and bright that Alison felt almost blinded, they were able to see that the woman who they had tumbled onto her back was Sarah Embraces-All-Things. Alison checked for a pulse while Stacy wet another towel with water from the shower—it was much cooler than the sweat lodge had been, but not so cold as the spring water. She made a quick compress across the woman's head, and then scooped up a cup of the spring water, diluting it with the warmer water.

"Is she coming around?" she asked anxiously. "Can you get any water down her? Jesus—there's no telling how long she's been in there! She must have passed out from the heat—she must be completely dehydrated! See if you can get her to drink something, Alison. Liz has some Gatorade up in the cooler—do you think I should run up and get it? Do you think she's going to need to be hospitalized? Damn it, if she has to go to the hospital we're going to have to open that gate…"

"I don't know if it will do her any good. I don't even know if she's alive," said Alison shortly, as she started CPR.

CHAPTER SEVEN

"What we need to do," said Alison, "is leave the body right here where it is, and close off the area. Then we need to move the rocks out from in front of the gate, and open the gate and go get the police. The local sheriff. Whoever there is around here." She was speaking very slowly, in simple sentences. Hawk must not understand her—that was the only explanation that made sense to her. Hawk didn't understand, and that was the reason she was still standing there, shaking her head.

"Of course not," said Hawk, in turn speaking as if to a child who was not only slow but a bit naughty. "Why would we want to do that? This is a horrible tragedy." She bent her head to illustrate the depth of her angst, although truthfully it was already etched so deeply upon her face that Alison felt a private apology for doubting the sincerity of her feelings towards Sarah Embraces-All-Things. "But communities *have* tragedies. We have to learn to deal with them just as we have to learn how to share our chores. Death is natural—a part of our connection with the earth." She had repeated the speech many patient times in response to Alison's demands—she was as immobile as the buttes in the distance, now glinting with the first rays of the sun.

Alison rubbed her gritty eyes. Hawk had the advantage of at least a few hours sleep. They had woken her from her bed when, at last, Alison had finally given in and admitted nothing she was doing was going to make any difference. Sarah was dead and probably had been dead before they had even entered the sweat lodge. Not long dead, but in the end it didn't matter whether it had been minutes or hours.

"You can't just..." Alison began, starting again on the explanation she thought by now was so simple even an idiot could understand it. You can't just go off from society and say you're going to live by your own rules and think that saying so is enough to divorce you from the laws of the outside world! My god, they had fought a fucking civil *war* over something not so very different!

"No," said Hawk, finally. This time she turned away from Alison, and went to stand beside the blanket-draped body of Sarah

Embraces-All-Things. Gaya was already standing there. Hawk took her hand gently, so that they stood together, silent, their backs to Alison.

Alison shivered. At some point during the nightmarish attempt at revival Stacy had taken down someone's solar shower and had begun to run the tepid water over Sarah's head, shielding her eyes and nose with her hand, and then over her body, up and down and around to the head again until the water had run out. Alison had no idea at all if this had been the right thing to do. Her total experience with heat exhaustion had been at World Youth Day, and then all they had done was taken the faithful to the first aid tents. If Sarah had still been alive, it might have been. As it was, it hadn't mattered one way or the other, except that it had made Stacy feel as if she, like Alison, had tried. Oh, and it had covered Alison with water as well, so that even now, after she had put her jeans and sweater back on, she felt chilled and achy.

"Come on, Baby." Stacy was at her elbow, looking tired and concerned, pulling on her gently. "Come on, these people are crazy, there's no sense talking to them anymore." She kept her voice low, for almost the whole camp, apart from the women they knew to be trysting, had somehow caught the urgency in the air and appeared from their tents one by one. They were now spread out around them in a kind of half circle. Here and there small groups were talking in quiet voices, but many of the women were standing alone, their faces somber. Alison allowed Stacy to pull her past them, trying to read in each the depth of their commitment to this experiment. Who agreed with Hawk? Who could be swayed to side of the laws of men?

She had to turn her head when they passed the Chain Gang—she could not bear to see such raw despair, verging upon hysteria. Earlier she had pulled one of the girls off Sarah's body, and the two others girls, comforting her, gave her baleful looks through their tears, as if it had been some kind of desecration.

Stacy guided them back to her own camp, where she fired up the gas stove and rebuilt the fire. Alison sat in a lawn chair with her arms wrapped around her chest, too far gone to even pretend to help. She felt dreadful, exhausted, pushed so far beyond her limits she had no control what-so-ever over the loop that was running through her head. Plop. The sound Sarah's body had made when she jarred it loose onto the floor. The way her head had rolled back onto the floor as if it no longer had any connection to her body...

"Put this on." Obediently Alison held out her arms and let Stacy wrap her in her own down parka, pulling the hood up around her face. It was awkward, for she seemed to be wearing some kind of coat that she neither recognized or remembered putting on. Not that it made any real difference. Alison felt that the cold had seeped into her blood, as if her heart had stopped pumping blood in favor of ice water.

"Is it possible that you could keep it down before 5:00 in the morning!" Liz's angry, hissing whisper cut through Alison's fog, but she was able to register only the voice, not what was said. I'm cold, she thought, I'm so cold.

In the same daze she listened to Stacy reply, "There's been an accident." There was much more—there was explaining and questions, but she could not grasp any of it. I'm cold, she thought ...and the way she had sounded when she had hit the wooden floor... and they should call the police she knew they should...and she was tired and so very cold...and the way her body had sounded.... At some point Stacy put a sugary cup of tea in her hand and Alison sipped at it obediently, thinking I'm so cold. Then the tea was gone and she could hear a voice, familiar but somehow unplaceable saying, "Come on, Alison, let's just lie down..." and then nothing.

Alison awoke because it was hot, way too hot, and had been way too hot for awhile. She had been floundering with her covers out of dreams so deep that she had to struggle to consciousness as a diver struggles for the surface. But even throwing all the blankets back was not enough, and she woke covered with sweat, her heart pounding.

She lay for a moment on her back, remembering what had happened early that morning. If it was still the same day. She felt as if she could have slept the night round.

She remembered Stacy curled up against her back, with her arms around her. She remembered wondering how Stacy could stand it, for by then the cold had invaded her entire body, and it had seemed to her that Stacy must feel as if she were clasping a woman made of ice. She remembered—or was it a dream?—Seven Yellow Moons appearing as if out of a fog and saying, "Take this, it will make you feel better." Propping her up with her arm and urging a cup of vile smelling tea upon her. That was probably why her bladder was so full now. Then she remembered nothing, until she had begun the slow and difficult climb back to consciousness.

She took care of the bladder problem, and then walked around to the kitchen. Stacy and Liz were sitting beneath the canopy. Stacy, wearing only a long skirt and a heavy, festie necklace was reading a textbook. Stacy, who had married and done the housewife thing right out of high school, had been taking a couple of classes at D.U. and was currently suffering through Shakespearean literature, which she loathed. Liz was taking a Mensa pre-test, frowning and tapping her pencil.

"How you feeling?" Stacy jumped up at her approach. "Want a Diet Pepsi?" She pulled one from the cooler without waiting for an answer, and popped the top.

"Dreadful," said Alison, and then "better," after a long pull on the soda. "What time is it?"

"It's almost two. You slept a good eight hours. You needed it. I was really worried until Liz went up and got Seven—it was like you had gone into this—oh, I don't even know what to call it. You weren't really awake, but you weren't resting, either. You kept moaning and mumbling." Which meant, thought Alison, that Stacy had been unable to sleep as well, but was too nice to say so. She gave her a grateful look and opened her mouth to finally tell her just what the problem was, but Liz cut her off.

"If 'conscience' is to 'morals', do you think 'referee' is to 'game' or 'team'? Do you think maybe you're cursed? You sure have been in the dead body business a lot lately. You're going to be like Jessica Fletcher pretty soon—nobody is going to want to invite you to dinner for fear their girlfriend will kick off. Although I guess that could be a service, too."

This might have been funny in a kind of black humor kind of way if Alison had not just crawled out of bed in the middle of the day—as it was, she had to restrain herself from slamming her soda can into the back of Liz's head.

Stacy caught the look. "Jesus, Liz, you're just always the Queen of Tact, aren't you! She just got up! Can't you keep it to yourself for a while?"

Liz gave an offended sniff and turned haughtily back to her test. She quickly checked two boxes with hard, unerasable strokes just to show that she didn't need *their* input.

"Have you been up long?" Alison asked Stacy, sitting in the chair beside her. There was a box of crackers beside Stacy's chair. Alison picked it up and began devouring them like she was being paid money.

"Oh, yeah, hours."

"I guess nobody went to get the police," Alison said, looking first up at the stones by the gate, and then back at the tent in the middle of the road. "How come you didn't do that?" She had not meant this to sound as it did—snappish and critical. Stacy responded to the tone immediately.

"Because, even if we could have gotten a car out, I was letting *you* sleep," she said shortly, obviously feeling unappreciated. Unsaid was Because you were sick I was the one who had to take charge even though *I* was up *just* as goddamn late and *now* you're sitting here eating *my* food.

"We didn't know what the hell to do," said Liz, defending Stacy. She gave Alison a frown to let her know that she shouldn't have to defend Stacy. "Those women down there—I went down and talked to them after Stacy told me what had happened, and they were totally immovable. I sure as hell wasn't ready to walk forty miles into town and go get the cops to deal with an accident with them saying right in my face that they didn't want any interference. Why bother? If they want to bury her in the desert or put her in the compost, who am I to butt in? And you were sick, girlfriend, and I don't mean just twisted. If we'd gone to the town for anything—and if we'd been able to get help moving those rocks and getting those goddamn keys off the roof—it would have been because we were taking you to the hospital." She gave Alison another hard look—'We were concerned, so get over it, Bitch.'

Alison did not resent this. It was the best friend's job to alert that friend if the girlfriend was not treating her right. She herself certainly could not discern when she was doing the in-love thing—Michelle had saved her from many a sociopath and freeloader. Yet another reason not to want Michelle and Janka to split the sheets—she didn't want to have to start screening Michelle's dates again.

"Well," she said, washing down another mouthful of crackers. She was not yet able to say thank you—that would require ten minutes and another Diet Pepsi. "So I guess that now that I'm up we'd better figure out a way to get in and notify the coroner, huh?"

Liz and Stacy exchanged a look. Didn't take a Betazoid to tell that they'd discussed this already.

"Alison," said Stacy carefully, "What's the big deal about this? I mean, it's a tragedy, but accidents happen. She fell asleep in the sweat lodge. It happens. That's *why* they have that two people rule. People *die* from heat stroke. Why expose these women to outside contact that they don't want? You've been hassled by the police yourself, Alison. Can you imagine what the local rednecks are going to make of these women living out here in the desert by themselves? Jesus, they couldn't even begin to explain the retreat without practically teaching them a new language! It would be just like highlighting a place that they've worked really hard to have remain low key. Is that what you want to do? We might as well just send a telegram to the *National Enquirer*."

"You've certainly become compassionate all of a sudden," said Alison grumpily, popping a second can of caffeine. She hated sleeping during the day—it made her feel like a laggard. She should have been notifying and organizing and roping off, and instead she had been lying on her back with her mouth open, snoring.

"And you've got control issues," said Liz, shutting the pamphlet with a little whoosh. "What's it going to hurt anybody if they bury that woman out here instead of paying a mortuary a thousand bucks?"

"Well, duh! Of course I have control issues! Why would I be a cop if I didn't have control issues?"

There was no answer to this. Liz handed Stacy the book and the pencil and said, "Do the pattern part for me."

"You know," Stacy told her, taking them from her, "they're not going to let me come to the real test with you."

"Why do you want to join Mensa anyway?" asked Alison.

"I want to pick up hot babes with high I.Q.s," said Liz, who did not care if the world thought she was a pig.

Stacy opened the booklet to the pattern part. She looked at her watch and began to make check marks, humming in a pleased little way. *Macbeth* was cast aside, face down in the sand.

Alison was trying to put her finger on the reason that she thought it was important the law be in on this one. It wasn't a feeling, was it? Oh, dear, Miss Jane Marple solved things with feelings. She couldn't bear it if she turned into a blithery little old lady who solved crimes by noticing that the killer had been wearing her good hat backwards at church. "I guess even if they bury her, she can always be exhumed," she said trying the words aloud to see if they would pacify her.

Stacy held up her hand. "Don't talk to me," she said, "I'm getting Liz into Mensa."

"We have bagels and cream cheese," said Liz. "Do you want some? Watching you eat those crackers is making me sick." She stood up without waiting for an answer and began rooting around in the cooler. Over her shoulder she said, "I think they're going to vote on it at dinner. People keep drifting over here and giving us the latest update."

"What's the general feel?" asked Alison, putting down the crackers, which were making her a little sick, too.

"Oh, everybody is doing the death thing. You know, all of a sudden she was a lot more likable and admirable than she was yesterday. But there's a big undertone of relief from the women who actually knew her. I think Seven was giving us the straight story last night—she was a nasty woman who enjoyed jerking people around. I probably would have ended up dating her eventually—she sounds like just my type."

"You're not allowed to date anyone anymore without bringing her by first," said Stacy, without looking up from the test. "You have no sense."

Liz who had quite a strong little mothering streak, handed Alison a bagel spread not only with cream cheese, but piled high with avocado and cucumber as well. Alison took it pensively without remembering to say thank you. She was lost completely in her thoughts, still wondering why it was that she felt so strongly about interfering in this particular death. Being a cop did not mean that she was always on the side of the law—she smoked an occasional joint and listened to her head phones in the car, both of which were illegal, and she was sure you could get arrested for some of the sex she'd had with Stacy. Who would it hurt if Sarah Embraces-All-Things was buried here on the land without interference? Why couldn't she just let it go, as Liz and Stacy seemed to have done?

There was a shout and a whistle, and Michelle came walking up the road, followed by Zorra, carrying something in her mouth. It looked nasty.

"I came to see if you were still alive," she said to Alison. "We were worried." She did not look worried—she had a definite well-fucked glow. "What are you doing?" she asked Stacy.

"Taking a Mensa pre-test," said Stacy. She shut the booklet and handed it to Michelle.

"Oh, that's so elitist." Michelle opened the booklet. "Give me your pencil—a couple of these are wrong."

"They are *not* wrong," defended Liz, jumping to her feet.

"Oh, right, and pencil goes with refrigerator? It goes with titanium."

"It's not elitist," said Stacy, settling back in her chair with *Macbeth* on her lap again. "We're trying to combat the rumor that lesbians are stupid. Is there anything more dreadful or boring than Shakespeare?"

"I didn't know there was a rumor lesbians were stupid," said Alison absently, still trying to grapple with the Sarah problem. "I thought we were just good at sports, and I try to combat that by being the worst player on any team that I'm forced to join."

"Oh, it's not so much that we're stupid as that we don't have any common sense. That we marry everybody we date."

"That's not a rumor, that's God's own truth," said Liz, standing on tiptoe to look over Michelle's shoulder. "No wonder the straights don't want to give us spousal benefits—it'd be a bureaucratic nightmare. And we don't have any sense about who we date in the first place. Come on," she said, "the *farmer* doesn't fit in there, because he *grows* things."

"Plumber doesn't fit, because she *fixes* things," countered Michelle, busy with the eraser.

"You picked me," said Alison to Stacy. "That showed good sense."

"Darling," said Stacy, still looking disdainfully at her book "that was what we call pure luck. I date women because they are hot. I can't help myself—doesn't matter if she's an ax murderer, if she's hot I date her. You were just a little gift from a god who likes to make us think he's benevolent now and then to fuck with our heads."

"*I* date women who I have things in common with," said Michelle smugly, still holding the test out of Liz's reach.

"Gee, Michelle," said Stacy with a snort, "I'm so glad that you're not a dumbass like the rest of us. I wish I could think of something really stupid that *you'd* done within the last, oh let's say forty-eight hours."

"Yeah," said Liz. "Gimme that test."

Michelle tossed Liz the test. "What are you going to do about that body?" she asked Alison, obviously feeling that it was time for a subject change.

"What do you mean, what am I going to do about it?" asked Alison, as if this something she had not even thought about. "Why is it my job to do something about it?"

"Well," said Michelle, planting herself in the chair that was right next to Liz, so that she didn't have to look at her when she was talking to Alison, "You're the law. Or the closest thing that we've got. Besides, you *are* the biggest busybody in the whole world. I'll bet you've been fussing about it since the minute you woke up."

There's a good guess," said Stacy. "Maybe you really are smarter than the rest of us."

Liz couldn't let this pass without a comment. "Hmm, unsafe sex is to lesbians as fucking another woman behind Janka's back is to…come on, fill in the blank—the answer for both is 'really stupid'."

"Why do I need you to lecture me!" asked Michelle. "I don't need anybody to lecture me, but everybody has *been* lecturing me. And how do you have the nerve to lecture me any way? You let women beat you! You fuck in public! You date eighteen-year-olds! Since when is it your job to be my Jiminy Cricket?"

"And what do all those things have in common that what

you're doing *doesn't* have in common? Well, my gosh, they're consensual!" Liz was on a roll.

"Who's been lecturing you?" asked Alison curiously.

"Seven Yellow Moons! You'd think she was my mother. You know, anybody else here would have been able to have a little fling, and nobody would have said a word about it. But not me, oh, no. Not that I am," she added hastily.

"That's because everybody knows you," said Alison. "Except Liz, and she's just trying to piss you off. You don't have flings. You've never had flings. You have long term relationships. You have marriages. You have children. And I don't want to see that child and his mother move out of their house because being on women's land gave you hot pants."

"Oh," said Michelle, "but it's okay if you and her highness over there set each other—and the house!—on fire?"

"That was a year ago, Michelle. It's passed the statue of limitations. It can't be brought up in court anymore."

Michelle looked at Liz, who said, "That's right. Chrystalpower vs Bornwomyn, 1992."

"I am a little princess, aren't I?" said Stacy in a pleased voice, although everyone knew that had not been intended as a compliment. Stacy was quite good at taking insults and putting her own little twist on them. It was a talent which Alison envied.

"What are you hearing about the body?" she asked Michelle, who she figured had taken just about as much scolding as she was going to take without blowing up. There wasn't anything they could do about it, anyway—Michelle knew that they all disapproved and she was going to have to make up her own mind.

"The last I heard, almost everybody was in favor of building a funeral pyre and sending her out with a ceremony while the moon was still full. I mean, everybody who thinks it's a do-it-yourself job. There are a couple of women who think we should try to find her family, but they're going to be outvoted after dinner."

Alison was so dumb-founded by this little tidbit of information that Stacy was actually the one who spoke first.

"They're going to *burn* her? Jesus, that's going to smell just dreadful. I don't think I'm going—I might never be able to eat barbe-que again." She gave Zorra who had been nosing around the fire pit looking for scraps, a perfunctory pat on the head and then pushed her away.

"They should boil her down and make soap from her," offered Liz. "That would be much more ecologically sound. I think I'll put it in my will." She, too, pushed at Zorra. "Go away," she told her, "you're nasty and stinky."

"She's not nasty and stinky anymore," protested Michelle. "I took her down to the showers and washed her this morning."

Alison who knew that Liz and Stacy were just doing their dry, witty, 'we're stoned' act, could not help but protest. "I know nobody liked her," she said, "but still, she *is* dead. There could be a little respect."

Liz sniffed Zorra who, now that it had been pointed out, *was* looking much improved. She also looked about ready to pop. Those puppies were coming *soon*.

"You are lecturing *me* about how to deal with death?" asked Stacy. "Pardon me, but are your parents still alive? Because mine are dead, and until you've gone through that, I don't think that you have anything to tell me."

"You're right," said Liz to Michelle, "she smells great. What did you use on her?"

"Apple pectin shampoo," replied Michelle. She did not look at Alison, who knew damn good and well that there was only one person in the truck who'd brought apple pectin shampoo and it was not Michelle. "That other shit doesn't work on hard jobs."

"Like Lavender Crystalpower," said Stacy, who never lost a chance to zing any of Alison's exes.

"What does that dog have?" asked Alison, trying for another topic change. She was being shot down from all sides. "She may not be nasty, but whatever she has in her mouth sure is."

"I can't believe you washed her in the showers," said Stacy. "I'm surprised you didn't get confronted about offending the goddess—if she feels that strongly about cornbread, it must really put her in a twist when you waste water washing a dog."

"Oh, I didn't waste it," Michelle assured her. "I showered at the same time. It was a memorial wash, actually. You know—the same way some people donate to a cause instead of sending flowers. It was the Sarah Embraces-All-Things Memorial Dog Wash."

"When you die," said Alison grumpily, "I'm going to have you stuffed and then let the leather community use you for a prop."

"Oh, dibs on the first three months," said Liz. "What *does* she have? Is it a dead bird?"

Stacy, who wasn't nearly as fussy as one might think, pried the object out of Zorra's mouth and held it up. It was pretty gross. "It does have feathers, but I don't think it was alive recently."

Michelle, who actually was a lot *more* fussy than one might think—hence the dog washing—took it from her gingerly with two fingers.

"You know what that is?" she said. "That's the thing that used to hang on the door of the sweat lodge. If you wanted privacy," she explained to Stacy and Liz. "You know, you put it up so no one would barge in if you were meditating."

"Or fucking," said Liz thoughtfully. "I'll bet you could have a nice hot oil scene in there."

Michelle gave Liz a look.

"How did that dog get that?" Alison asked with a frown. "Why wasn't it up on the pole?"

"Must have been on the door," said Michelle, tossing the whole thing in the fire. "Nasty," she said to Zorra. "Find a nice stick."

"Jesus, Michelle!" said Stacy, scrambling up out of her chair and fanning her hand in front of her face. "Wet feathers! What could smell worse!"

"You may have a chance to find that out tonight," said Liz. She was going back through the Mensa book suspiciously, lifting her head now and then to give Michelle a hard look.

"Not tonight," said Michelle. "Or, at least I bet not tonight. Hawk wanted to just burn her in a bonfire on the ground, but the Chain Gang doesn't think that's enough of a show. They want ritual; they want a pyre. It'll take a day to build."

"Are they going to drive her car up underneath it and shoot it and burn it with her?" asked Liz, erasing an answer with furtive movements.

Alison was looking at Stacy's vacated chair. "Whose jacket is that?" she asked, pointing to the garment draped over the back of it.

"I don't know," said Stacy, throwing a handful of kindling on the coals. If they were going to burn the feather fetish, at least they could burn it quick. "I have no idea where it came from. Oh, no, wait, that's not true. I think that's the jacket I grabbed down by the sauna when you started getting the chills." She held it up and examined it. It was the same jacket Alison had seen in Sarah's house—the distinctive weaving on the back was unmistakable. "I guess that makes it Sarah's. Nice, isn't it? I saw some fabric like this out at Cloth World, and it cost fifty dollars a yard. And that was before it was made into anything." Stacy always knew not only what everybody's clothes had cost, but also what they would have saved if they'd made them themselves.

"You ought to keep it," said Michelle. "There's no sense burning it with her." Michelle was honorable, but practical.

"I'll bet that woman smells bad by tomorrow night," commented Liz. "I left a piece of chicken out of the cooler yesterday, and I sure wouldn't eat it now."

"Ah," said Michelle dryly, "so it's not true what they say. You do draw the line somewhere."

Obviously Liz knew she had been insulted, but she couldn't quite figure out how deep it went. Was Michelle accusing her of necrophilia or cannibalism? While she was pondering Stacy got in, "Well, Liz is right, that could be a problem."

"Nope," said Michelle, scratching Zorra's ears. "Do you think her eyes are infected, or do you think that's just from being neglected? I could smack that Lydia! Incidentally, she's one of the We Want a Pyre ringleaders. I think she's hoping that she'll inherit the spiritual leader seat. No, it's not going to be a problem because they have her in the walk-in refrigerator."

"I'll bet that's cutting down on midnight snacking," said Alison. She couldn't help it, it just popped out. Now she was in no position to point out anyone else's insensitivity.

"This whole thing is beginning to horrify me," said Stacy, slipping the jacket on. It looked pretty good. "Do you suppose someone planned this? You know, as a little challenge to bond the group? They were always doing this kind of thing at Girl Scout camp—you know, pretending there had been a fire or something, and we had to build emergency shelters and survive on k-rations."

"There's a name for it when it's planned, Doll Face," said Liz, throwing down the pamphlet in disgust. "Then it's called murder. And let's not even go *there*—you know how Alison is."

"She should get another hobby," agreed Stacy. "My last girlfriend drank and beat up people—maybe she could take that up."

"Did you know that Persimmon grew up in Los Alamos?" asked Michelle.

The three of them looked at her. Even though there had been several conversations going on at one time, this bit of information didn't seem to fit into any of them.

"She told me a Girl Scout story while we were working on the adobe today." Michelle explained the connection. "Kind of like Stacy's. They were working on some kind of special award while they were in junior high…"

"The Sign of the Arrow or the Sign of the Star," put in Stacy, who had been really heavy into the Girl Scout thing.

"I guess. Anyway, what they had to do was spend four days in a bomb shelter."

"A bomb shelter?" said Liz. "Where in the world did they even *find* a bomb shelter?"

"It was probably the sixties," Alison reminded her. "Everybody was worried about the cold war. And Los Alamos was a first strike target. They were doing a lot of nuclear testing there. Is that why Persimmon's and Gaya's family was there?" she asked Michelle.

"Yeah," she said. "Their dad worked in the lab."

"So why do you know so much nuclear history?" Liz asked Alison.

"Oh, I read it in my Mensa newsletter. No, really I have a friend who lived there as a kid. Her dad worked in the labs, too. He just died of cancer. They're going to court."

Stacy was bored of talking about people she didn't know. She did a little pirouette. "What do you think about the jacket?"

"Pretty cute," said Alison. "Isn't your conscience going to bother you at all about robbing from the dead? Maybe you should go up to the kitchen and see if she's wearing any jewelry or has any gold teeth."

"Oh, get over it," said Michelle. "You robbed from the dead yourself last year when Tam died. Everybody knows where those whale bowls and Nancy Griffith tapes came from." It was rare that she defended Stacy from Alison—she looked a bit surprised with herself after she was done.

"Oh, honestly, I'll take it up and throw it in the fire myself if it's going to offend your rigid little cop scruples," said Stacy to Alison. "You sure are in a mood this afternoon."

"I don't feel good," Alison mumbled, too low for anyone to hear. She was aching all over, and still felt tired, despite her long nap.

"You don't have to throw the jacket in, the majority block wants her to go sky-clad," put in Michelle, obviously pleased to have all the dirt.

At the same moment, Liz said, "One of the best songs Malvina Reynolds ever wrote was 'Bury Me in My Overalls'."

"And 'sky-clad' is?" asked Alison. "Do I want to know?"

Michelle was looking at Liz with a completely baffled expression, as if she could not imagine her even *existing* in the same world as Malvina Reynolds. The question had to be repeated.

"What? Oh! No, probably not, but I'll tell you anyway. It means buck naked."

Stacy got a horrified look on her face. "Promise me, all of you, that no one sees me naked after I'm dead."

"What's all this voting about?" asked Alison. "I thought that was way too patriarchal. What about getting consensus? I think I'll make it up to dinner, bring it up and then block consensus."

"You can try," said Michelle, shrugging. "I don't even know if you'll be allowed to eat, though, since you didn't work today. There's currently a very 1984 overtone to the whole camp. I expect there's going to be a coup soon."

"This just gets weirder and weirder," commented Liz. "What about G-hey! and Salad—they didn't have anything strange to say last night."

"I don't think they're involved," admitted Michelle. "Not everybody is. A bunch of women are just kind of blowing everybody else off and doing their own thing. The ones who are struggling are doing it because that's what they like to do. You know?"

"The last of the big-time collective members," said Liz who had been a big-time collective member herself in the seventies.

"Kind of. I mean, not that they're not sincere, the ones who want consensus and really want to process. There's some real old time, grassroots women up there—women who helped create Owl Farm and ARF and Doe Farm." She named three pieces of women's land with which they were all, except maybe Stacy, familiar. "There's historic material up there. If I was going to take sides, I'd be on their side. Persimmon says that the process is just as important as the outcome."

"What's the other side about?" asked Stacy. She put her hands into the pocket of the jacket, and pulled out a brown prescription bottle. "Oh," she said, looking at the label, "Sarah was a little depressed. I guess maybe it's lonely being a blackmailer."

"Oh, the other side is the real rigid no-drugs, no-animals, no-tits-showing, no-impure-thoughts side. They're kind of the lesbian Puritan side. You know—the Puritans fled England to escape religious persecution, but once they got here they persecuted the hell out of everybody else."

"I'm glad I wasn't a Puritan," said Liz, throwing the Mensa test on the coals. "I would have been in the stocks every day. Of course, I might have liked that. See what you made me do?" she said to Michelle. "Now I'm going to have to spend fifteen bucks for a new one." Michelle gave an evil little smile that made her look like Wednesday Adams.

"What do you mean, she was depressed?" Alison asked Stacy.

"Who's leading the Puritan group?" Stacy asked Michelle. To Alison she said, "Well, she was taking Norpramine."

"Pretty much Hawk," Michelle told her.

"Gee, there's a surprise," said Liz. "Mmm, got the money, got the land—what else do I need? I know! A rabble to subdue and rule! She's damn lucky she married a rich girl."

"I don't know," said Michelle. "I mean, she does have a point

106

with a lot of stuff. I'd be a little hesitant to open up the land to any-body. Remember that story Seven was telling about the drama at Canyon Land? I guess Hawk has the right to be really specific about who she wants and doesn't want on her land. Persimmon says they've had a lot of real flakes drift through. She says they're not out here to drop out, they're out here to re-create."

"I thought you were going to be on the side of consensus," accused Stacy.

"Well, I probably would be if I were going to stay," Michelle admitted. "I'm just playing devil's advocate."

"Norpramine is an antidepressant?" Alison asked Stacy.

"Yeah, unless they use it for something else, too."

"How do you know that?"

"I took it myself for about ten months a couple of years ago."

"Did you like it?" Liz looked up with interest. "I took prozac, and it made me completely numb from the waist down."

"You could bottle that side effect and sell it," said Alison. "I've often thought that life would be much simpler if we could just go to the vet's and get neutered along with our cats."

"Don't you think," said Michelle, getting a lecturing tone in her voice, "that antidepressants are just the in fad right now? I mean, a lot of people who should be working on their issues are being lulled into thinking everything can be cured with chemicals? Persimmon says…"

"Oh, fuck *that!*" interrupted Liz. "You obviously are not depressive. I think antidepressants are the best invention of the twentieth century. Before velcro. Before ziplock bags. I think they should put them in soft drinks. I think you should be able to go into 7-11 on a bad day and buy a Pepsi-Pro. A Grand Slam."

"I thought it was a great little drug," said Stacy, trying the jack-et buttoned up. "This itches."

"I would guess that you'd usually be wearing it with a shirt," said Liz. "Although, knowing you, it's not a given. Were there any side effects?"

"A couple, but they weren't too bad. Real dry mouth. I had to pee a lot. The worst thing was that at first I greyed out a lot."

"Toss me that bottle," said Alison. "What do you mean, 'grey out'? Is that a real expression, or did you just make it up?"

"Do you suppose people said that to Lewis Carroll? Well, if it's not, it should be. You know, grey out. Like black out, only not as bad. I'd stand up and get woozy. I went down a couple of times. Both in connection with something else. One time I had the flu, and the other I'd been in a hot tub too long. That one was kind of a drag—I hit my head and went back in the water. Luckily my sister was right there and pulled me out, otherwise I would have been in big trouble."

"Speaking of hot tubs," Stacy said to Michelle, "how's the hot tub?"

"Great!" Michelle answered. "They have it hooked up to this mineral springs behind the house—it's naturally hot water, they're not even running the heater and it's up to a hundred and five."

"If there's a hot springs," asked Alison fussing with the child-proof lid and looking inside the bottle, "why isn't everybody just sitting around in *it* naked? Why do they need a hot tub?"

"It's not that kind," said Michelle, scratching Zorra's ears. "There's not a place for a pool. Persimmon showed me—it's up behind the house. It's a delicate environment. I guess they'd been arguing about it—I mean, a hot springs would be a real plus to draw in retreat people. Sarah wanted to dig a pool that only the land collective could use. She was all bent out of shape when Gaya and Hawk decided to pipe the water into the tub."

"What do you have on your fingers?" asked Stacy, looking first at Michelle's hand and then Zorra's belly. Both were glittering.

"Oh!" said Michelle, wiggling her fingers in front of her face. "Persimmon's been painting constellations on her ceiling. With phosphorus paint. They glow—you know—at night. I was helping her." She looked at her watch, "It's been fun, but I gotta go."

Zorra had rolled onto her back to let Liz scratch her stomach.

"She's due soon," said Liz. "I'll bet she has those pups by the end of the week."

"How do you know?" asked Michelle in a doubting voice.

Liz who had caught the Malvina Reynolds look, replied in an exasperated tone. "I grew up on a farm, Michelle! What do you think—that I just sprang fully grown from the head of Satan?"

Michelle pursed her lips, as if this had indeed crossed her mind.

"Wait a second," said Alison. "I want to go up to the house with you. Didn't I see your bike lock in the truck?"

"Yeah. How come?"

Alison turned to Liz and Stacy without answering. "While we're gone," she said, "I want you to find Seven and see if you can persuade her to help us move those rocks. See if she's got any friends who'll help. I want to drive into town."

"Oh dear," said Liz, "I sense Jane Lawless."

"Oh, man," said Michelle, "You're going to try to lock that body up, aren't you? You're just not happy unless you make everything into a mystery, are you? It's really getting to be an obsession.

Persimmon says you really need to heal in some ways."

Alison held up the bottle, miffed with the whole lot of them.

"I saw this bottle yesterday. It was almost full." She tipped it onto its side so they could see for themselves the four pills that remained inside.

"Oh!" said Stacy, making the connection immediately. "Okay!" Then, being Stacy, she added, "But I gotta shower if we're going into town."

"Stacy..." began Alison.

"Oh, I'll be done by the time you are. You don't think you're going to just walk in there and slap that lock on, do you? Believe me, there'll be processing. Or do you need me for strong arm protection?"

Michelle, glancing at Stacy's bare breasts and jewelry, looked pained. "I think I can take care of that."

Alison was glad that Stacy had chosen to dress très femme—she didn't know if Michelle would have been on her side otherwise. She was starting to sound a little brainwashed.

"Come on then, Cordelia," said Alison.

CHAPTER EIGHT

Stacy, of course, had been right. If there had been a way to do it, Alison would have slapped the lock on the door of the refrigerator without even a note, and left the back way without saying a word to anyone. After the night before, when she had been unable to make anyone listen, Alison had had enough.

But that was a dream. The work day had ended, and the main house was the happening place to be. Jerusha and Claw were sitting on the front porch, listening through the open window to Joan Baez's *Gracias A La Vida* album. Alison nodded at them, pausing a moment to listen to the lyrics of *De Colores*, which she hadn't heard in a good ten years, though at one time she had owned the album herself. "*Canta el gallo*," sang Joan Baez in the song about the farm animals, "*canta el gallo con el keri, keri, keri, keri, keri…*"

Michelle shifted restlessly beside Alison who pushed the front door open, sensing that Michelle could become a loose cannon at any point. It would be much better to act while she was at least minimally behind her. Hopefully they wouldn't run into Persimmon. Whether or not they were sleeping together, it was obvious that for the moment Michelle thought her word was god.

Immediately she regretted her decision to go through the front room, for it was obvious that they had walked into something personal. Kneeling before the couch, her face buried in the cushions, was the young woman who had attached herself, keening, to Sarah Embraces-All-Things' body the night before. She was rocking back and forth on her knees, making a horrible moaning sound. Though they could not see her face, they could see her scalp—covered with ragged clumps from a haircut that had probably been done with a knife rather than scissors. The other two members of the Chain Gang and Lavender Crystalpower were hovering about her, patting her on the back and making comforting noises.

"I want to die!" wailed the girl, her voice muffled by the pillows. "I want to just climb into the fire with her!" She lifted her face, shiny with tears. "I can do that, can't I?" she asked the other women eagerly, as if it were a question of law. "I can do that!" Alison noticed that her arms were covered with dull stripes of dried blood from gashes that were probably self-inflicted.

"Do you need…" she started, automatically going into police girl mode and thinking about doctors and suicide and intervention.

"We don't need anything from you," snapped one of the others hostility. "We don't need anything that you have or that you can give!" Alison saw that her upper arms were covered with the same stripes of blood—okay, then, some kind of ritual. Maybe, like the hair, they thought this was a sign of Native American mourning. She hoped none of them felt obligated to put out an eye or sever a finger.

"Please, Alison," said Lavender, stroking the girl's back, "haven't you caused enough trouble? I mean, just by coming here and bringing your male energy with you?"

Had it not been for Michelle's hand firmly on her back, Alison would have mixed it up right then and there.

"Don't bother," said Michelle in her ear, and then, "they're hurting." Michelle who could be cold and distant and the queen of just-get-over-it to those outside her family sometimes had unpredictable little waves of compassion that took Alison by surprise.

"What am I going to do now?" she heard the girl wail as they hurried down the hall. "She was healing me! I don't even have my medication any more! What…"

They passed the door of the bathroom behind which was coming a series of curses, rattles and bangs.

"Goddamnit!" someone said. The door flew open with a bang. Salad, a scowl on her face, strode out, almost bumping into them. "The goddamn doorknob came off!" she told them. "That goddamn doorknob's been coming off ever since I got here—I wish somebody would fix it!" She brushed past them. In the kitchen she picked up a big knife and began chopping peppers with a vengeance. Alison followed.

There were five or six women, all with sunburned noses, in the kitchen chopping and dicing. Alison only knew G-hey!, Salad, and Lisa by name. Whatever else was going to be worked out during the retreat, at least the dinner crew was working as a unit.

Without saying anything, Alison stepped into the walk-in refrigerator. She had thought that Sarah Embraces-All-Things might be laid out in an open coffin, maybe surrounded by little gifts for the journey, but she was not. She had been rolled in a quilt— Rocky Road to Kansas—and put on a bottom shelf, displacing a case of lettuce and a box of apples, which were now sitting in the way on the floor. At least, Alison assumed the bundle was the woman, though she didn't really want to peel the quilt back unless she had to.

She stepped back outside the door.

"In the quilt?" she asked Michelle in an undertone.

"Yeah. I helped do it."

"You're not supposed to go in and out of the walk-in," said one of the choppers. "It warms it up too much. We're supposed to get everything all at once."

Alison had noticed her at the job site. She was loud and vocal and began a lot of sentences with, "You need to." She didn't know what her real name was, but she had overheard G-hey! saying to Salad sotto voce, "Sandpaper Woman—she grates on everybody." Her voice held an undertone of irritation, which Alison took to mean that her absence on the job had been noted. Damn it! she thought, momentarily side-tracked. That was just the kind of thing she had feared would happen if she displayed her illness.

"Then I guess you have everything that you need for dinner?" she asked, her voice cold in response. "Do you need anything else?"

"I need some more onions," said G-hey! wiping her eyes on her upper arm. "Are they in there, or are they in the back?"

"Why do you care?" Sandpaper Woman asked Alison. "You're not eating with us, are you? I mean, you haven't been helping."

"Fuck you," said Alison, surprising herself with her own vehemence. "Who put you in charge of monitoring me? For your information, I have been as sick as dog ever since I got here."

"Yeah, fuck you," said Michelle, who was bored with standing around.

"Isn't that funny," said Sandpaper Woman, who was obviously not in the mood to let anything go, "how some people are always sick as a dog when there's work? What do you suppose that correlation is all about? And isn't it funny that the very same women who think they can break all the rules are the same ones who aren't around to help?"

That tore it. Alison had been planning on allowing one last trip into the walk in, but now as far as she was concerned every single one of the women in the kitchen could go to hell. Without hesitation or remorse she slipped Michelle's lock through the handles of the doors and snapped it shut.

All hell broke loose.

"Just what do you think you're doing?" Sandpaper demanded in an angry voice, turning from the stack of apples she had been paring. She wiped the sweat off her face with the sleeve of her t-shirt. Several of the other women chimed in.

"I'm closing off a crime scene," said Alison, slipping into her most detached cop mode, the one that allowed her to do things that her regular, compassionate self wouldn't.

"You have no right to interfere with what we've decided to do with that body! You aren't part of this community!" screamed Sandpaper. Her face had turned such an ugly shade of purple that it was distracting. Alison hoped she wouldn't have a stroke. That would complicate things. She wondered if denouncing the rules of men included their hospitals.

At the same moment Lisa said, "What crime scene? She was killed down in the sweat, not in the refrigerator!"

Although Sandpaper had been the louder of the two, it was at Lisa that everybody turned and stared. She opened her mouth, and then shut it, looking as if she were just as startled by what had come out of her mouth as anyone else. Suddenly, she turned a deep crimson and turned back to her cutting board, thwacking loudly through the cucumbers on her board.

"She wasn't killed at all!" said Sandpaper, pushing herself right up into Alison's face. It was unpleasant—obviously she was another one who thought Americans bathed too much. "She died of heat stroke—you were there! It's up to us to decide what to do, and we're going to do what she would have wanted! You have no right to try and tell the rest of us what to do! Do you think that Sarah Embraces-All-Things would have wanted a bunch of men to paw her body and cut her open after she was dead? If you think that, then you didn't know her! I did! We talked about it! She wanted her body to be burned, and she wanted her ashes spread on the land, and that's what we're going to do! You can't stop us!"

"Indeed I can," said Alison, growing all the more remote. Actually, of all the discussion that she had heard, this one—that police intervention would have gone against the dead woman's wishes—was the one which came the closest to moving her. She might even have been willing to honor their wishes, had the circumstances been different. But presumably Sarah Embraces-All-Things, when planning her funeral, had not known that she was going to be murdered. "I'm a police officer, and I not only have the authority to seal off and secure a scene, I also have the authority to demand civilian assistance and to forbid anyone from leaving the scene." They didn't need to know she was not at all sure her authority crossed state lines.

The announcement that she was secretly a man could not have caused a more perfect silence. All of the women, except for G-hey!, who had pretty much continued chopping onions without pause throughout the whole scene, stared without speaking. In spite of her impassive pose, Alison could feel her own face reddening.

"We should have known," said Sandpaper finally, her voice bitter and betrayed. "We should have known when you showed up with that dog. You know, I was against it when Hawk and Gaya wanted to screen applicants. I said no, it's bound to be discriminatory, it should be open for all lesbians. And look what happened. A cop," she said, in the same way that one might say Nazi or wifebeater. "We end up with a cop."

Alison could feel her face growing hotter, and she cursed her mother's fair-skinned, Norse ancestors. But even more, she cursed the women standing in front of her. They were the same women who had allowed a bully like Sarah Embraces-All-Things to dictate the rules for a community, and yet scorned Alison without hesitation when she did what she believed was right. For a moment Alison hated all lesbians and their causes.

Lisa, her head still bent, hurriedly left the room, and Alison followed her. What was the point in staying? There was nothing she could say to Sandpaper, a woman who had devoted her life to battling sexism, racism, homophobia and able-bodied privilege, that would even touch the depth of her prejudice towards Alison.

Outside the door, Alison hurried to catch up with Lisa.

"Lisa!" she called. "Do you still want a ride in to town? Because you could come with us now, instead of waiting." It was not what she wanted to know, merely the first thing she could think of to stop the woman's flight, as well as a ruse to enlist her help with the rocks.

"No," said Lisa without looking at her. "I don't need to, now. I mean—oh everything I say is coming out wrong!"

"You mean what you said about the scene of the crime?" asked Alison in a sympathetic voice that masked the fact she was going in for the kill. She glanced over her shoulder and saw Michelle trailing them. With a small movement she waved her away. "What did you mean by that?"

"Nothing. Nothing! Only that Sarah was so awful…"'

"That it wouldn't be surprising if someone killed her," finished Alison, nodding her head with understanding. "I thought of that, too. I heard that she had dirt on a lot of people, and she wasn't hesitant to use it."

"Yeah," Lisa agreed. Her arms were wrapped so tightly around her body that it looked as if her hands were reaching for one another across her back.

"What did she have on you?" Alison asked quietly.

Lisa looked longingly up the arroyo, obviously wishing she

were back at the house, *anyplace* but here.

"Come on," Alison urged. "Lisa, she didn't just die accidentally! Somebody *killed* her! Don't you think that person should pay for what she did?"

"No!" Just the one word, burst out with such verve that, from the look on her face, surprised Lisa herself as much as it surprised Alison. "I mean…" she tried to backpedal, and then, obviously realizing it would make things worse said again, "No. Alison, I really don't. You want to know the truth? I think that whoever killed her should be given an award! And I'd pitch in for the first hundred dollars! She was a terrible person, Alison—you're not from around here, so you don't know. And I'm not the only one who feels that way, I know it. I'll bet she had stuff on half the women here, just like she had on me."

"Was she blackmailing you?" asked Alison, deciding it best not to respond to the rest. She was going to have to regroup her thoughts—if Lisa was right, if her feelings towards Sarah had been the norm, then no one was going to rally to Alison's little speech about at least catching the killer.

"No," said Lisa with a heavy sigh. "Yes. Or, at least, she wasn't really trying to get money from me or anything like that. That didn't ever come up. Sarah liked power. She liked knowing you were sitting right there next to her pretending to be civil, kissing her ass. And any time she wanted, and for no reason at all, she could just pop out with something that would devastate you."

"Something about your past?" asked Alison, puzzled. "Did you have a record, or…"

"Oh, for Christ's sake!" said Lisa, throwing up her hands. "Why would I want to tell you? Don't you get it? It died with her! I don't have to worry about it any more!"

"Yeah, except that people who are being blackmailed are usually pretty big suspects if the blackmailer is killed."

"Who cares? No one will be able to pin this one on anybody here! They're not even going to be able to prove this was a murder! By the time you get out of here, that body is either going to be too decomposed for an autopsy, or it's going to be burnt."

"Ever hear of accessory to murder?" Alison asked, trying to keep the irritation out of her voice. "That's what we've all got to face if we cover this up." The last thing that she wanted to do was alienate Lisa who might be the quickest route to the murder motive. But she couldn't believe these women, whose disregard of the law seemed to go right past passive resistance into contempt.

However, for all her attempt to sound neutral, Lisa picked up on the thought immediately.

"Look," she said, obviously trying to keep herself in check, just as Alison had, "you're the one here who's being stupid, not me. What do you think—that just because you managed to lock that body in the walk-in, it's going to stay in the walk-in? Come on! You don't even know if it's still there *right now!* Somebody could be there with a hacksaw already! For all you know, somebody has already pulled that body out and is getting ready to bury it, or is getting ready to burn it, or just fucking drag it out into the desert for the coyotes to eat! And it doesn't even have to be the murderer! You have no idea how committed some of these women are to this experiment. You think that just because you and your friend came here to cruise for the weekend that nobody else is taking it seriously."

"I didn't come here to cruise," said Alison, stung.

"Well, you didn't come with any kind of commitment for change, with your bag of Oreos and your Diet Pepsi! But some of us did! The rest of us—we had to be interviewed to get a space in this retreat. This isn't just a weekend thing for us. There are strong feelings here. Maybe we can't change the world, but if we work really hard, maybe we can change our little corner. So don't be surprised if you don't get any cooperation in trying to take Sarah Embraces-All-Things back to the world of men. For most of the women here, taking care of her body is just another hard choice that we're going to have to make here in isolation. It's not any different or worse than deciding what to do if the windmill breaks down."

"I can't believe you," said Alison, sitting back on her heels. She was still ticked about the cruising remark—she sure as hell didn't want Stacy to get hold of *that* ugly rumor—and vowed to scold Michelle for her libido as soon as she got the chance. "All this stuff about women love and women's community, and you're willing to let a killer—someone who killed another *woman*, let's be clear about that—go free while you throw the victim's body on the compost heap. Is that it? Murder is okay as long as it's dyke to dyke. Better tell me now, because there are a couple of women back up at that house who I'*d* like to strangle."

"You can't put meat in a compost heap," said Lisa coldly. "And she was a blackmailer. She was an evil, evil woman. Did it ever occur to you that maybe this is exactly what happens to evil women in a closed community? Some cultures leave people on the ice floes when the tribe moves—maybe this is just another version of that."

"Infants. Old people who they can't care for any longer," Alison protested. "Those are people who are living on the edge—

one extra mouth could be the difference between life and death for them all."

"Infants who are deformed. Or twins. Or girls. Everybody has their own criteria. And if I had to pick—if I could add my own to the list, I would still put Sarah Embraces-All-Things on an ice floe, because she was evil, and she was spreading that evil into the community. What if we had all agreed to strike just one blow in the dark, so nobody knew whose blow killed her? Would you be able to accept it then?"

This was a hard one. Alison had only really ever had to face it on tv and as always, she felt pulled two directions. When did vigilantism step over the line into something that was just as bad as the original bullying?

"No," she said finally. "There has to be a right way and a wrong way to do it—otherwise it's all just chaos. If Sarah was causing a problem, then why didn't Hawk and Gaya just put her off the land? Nobody needed to kill her!"

"She probably had something on them, as well," Lisa said matter-of-factly. "Come on, don't look so surprised! I'll bet she had something on half the women here—why should they be any different?"

"But, what..." Alison began hesitantly. What had these people been doing? How could so many have dark secrets? She was no saint, but she had no secrets for which she would kill.

"Come on!" said Lisa impatiently. "Don't you get it? It didn't have to be anything that was a secret from the whole world. Come on! It just had to be a secret from one person—the right person. And if Sarah knew that one person, that was all she needed to know."

Alison was getting a bit tired of being called stupid.

"No," she said shortly. "I *don't* get it. What are you talking about?"

Lisa was silent for a moment. "Okay," she said finally. "I'm going to tell you a story. About some friends of mine. This isn't a story about me with another name—this is something Sarah did to somebody else I know. It just illustrates the point." She had been standing, illustrating her conversation with jerks and great sweeping gestures. Now she sat down on the rocky ground and wrapped her arms around her knees.

"Okay," she said again. "My friend...I had this friend. Renee, her name was. And she had this girlfriend. And it was really good between them. I know that for a fact. I saw it. And the girlfriend went out of town for a week. To visit her mother. So Renee said that she would come over and take care of the cat and dog. And the girlfriend said okay, thanks, but please don't leave *your dog* there when you're not there, because she bothers the cat. And Renee says, you're paranoid about the cat, and if he's bothering her, she can get up on the bookshelf. But, okay, I won't leave him there."

Lisa paused, looking out over the desert as if in search of a sign.

"So what happened?" coached Alison, seeing already that there was not going to be a happy ending.

"So," Lisa continued, still looking out over the desert. Her voice had grown cold and brittle. "So, the girlfriend went out of town. And one day when Renee was in a hurry, she left her dog. And the cat got on top of the bookshelf, just like she'd said she would. But the *dogs*," she was speaking in a halting voice, and Alison saw that her eyes had filled with tears. "The dogs....when there are two of them, they start acting like a pack. The girlfriend's dog loved the cat, they were friends, but when Renee left the two of them together, they starting acting like a pack and they knocked the bookshelf down, and they killed her cat." She raised a hand to wipe at the tears on her cheek.

Alison was very soft-hearted—animal stories could easily make her cry. But Lisa's pain seemed excessive for something far in the past, something, according to her, in which she had not been involved. Also, she could not see how the evil of Sarah Embraces-All-Things fit into the story.

"And Sarah?" she asked.

Lisa took a huge breath, the kind that is meant more for bringing a wavering lip back into line than anything else.

"Sarah didn't like Renee," she said. "Not that like has anything to do with it. Sarah didn't divide people up the same way that other people do. Like you and I do. You know, people you like and people you don't like. All Sarah cared about was people she had power over—people she could hurt—and people she didn't have power over yet. She didn't like Renee—Renee had told people that Sarah wasn't Native American, that she was a compulsive liar. She didn't like the girlfriend, either—she had agreed with Renee about Sarah." She paused again to catch her breath. Up the hill, Alison could see women gathering around the main house.

Out by the front gate, she could just see a corner of Stacy and Liz's rainbow-striped awning, and carried on the wind, very faintly, she could hear a snatch of the Nancy Griffith tape that they were playing, another rule breaker because there were men in the back up.

"Renee didn't tell her girlfriend what happened," said Lisa, resuming the tale.

Wise move, thought Alison. She was *never* going to tell Stacy, or even Michelle, about Marta, and as far as she was concerned the cat thing was much more serious than the sleeping around thing.

"She told her girlfriend that the cat'd had a seizure, and that she died on the way to the vet's. Wrapped in an old nightgown of the girlfriend's, so that she smelled her and thought she was there holding her. She had her cremated at the vet's before the girlfriend got back in town. It was Renee's vet, not the cat's regular vet.

"But Sarah lived downstairs from the girlfriend. And when she heard the story, she told her what really happened. She knew that the girlfriend could never forgive Renee if she knew the truth, even though she was the love of her life. So she told her. She said it was just because it was the truth, and the truth should always be told, but it wasn't. It was just out of evil. Because she was right—the girlfriend couldn't forgive Renee. Even though she was the love of her life, even though she wanted to. She could not forgive her."

She was crying openly now, and Alison had given up all pretense of thinking this story was about anyone else.

"So you," she started. "The dog…"

Lisa was shaking her head. "No," she said, "I told you this wasn't my secret. It was Renee's secret. But I was the one she told it to. Why did she have to do that? Why couldn't she have let me have a picture of my cat—I'd had her for sixteen years, I'd never been a grownup without her!—why couldn't have she have let me believe that she died painlessly? Why did I have to know that she had been terrified, that she had been torn to bits by a dog who she thought loved her? Why?"

They sat that way for a while longer, Lisa wiping her face with the tail of her shirt, and Alison looking up at the house and the women milling about on the porch. Several women pointed her way—no doubt the lock on the walk-in was a hot topic.

"I won't help you move that body," Lisa said finally, after a silence so long that it made Alison start. "I won't help you move the body, and I won't help you move the stones. Because I don't care who killed Sarah. I hope whoever it was sleeps well at night, and I hope she gets away."

No sooner had Lisa made her escape down the hill towards the showers, than Seven Yellow Moons came walking up the same way, and said by way of greeting, "How are you feeling?"

"Tons better." It was true. She still ached all over, but it was better than the night before, when she had been stupid with fatigue as well. "Stacy says you came by and gave me something?"

"Skullcap tea. And your own meds." She pulled a prescription bottle out of her pocket and tossed it to Alison. "I saw you put them in your glovebox, and I figured that you were just too tired to remember you had them. I've seen that before."

"Thanks," said Alison again. "What do you think about this burning the body idea?"

Seven was neither stupid nor easily distracted. "So, did you tell Stacy what was wrong? She and Liz were both awfully worried."

Alison made a little noise in her throat that was meant to suggest that this topic be dropped, but Seven, who had been obliging for several months, was relentless.

"Really!" she insisted. "Do you think that's fair—for her to be worrying that you have a brain tumor or are going to go into convulsions, when the answer is so much more tolerable?"

"To you, maybe!" Alison burst out, unaware that the words were even lurking until they hung between them in the air. "To you! But I'd almost rather *have* a brain tumor!" She was horrified by her own words, and struggled quickly to try and explain them. "At least with a tumor you…you…"

"You have evidence? Is that it?" Seven finished for her. "You have the x-ray and the doctor's report and evidence you can hold in your hand in case anyone wants to hassle you?"

"Yes." Alison sagged with relief. As twisted as it might be, Seven seemed to understand. It wasn't that she wanted to be in the center of a death-bed scene, it was just that she wanted her illness to be something more concrete, less trendy than just another form of chronic fatigue. Fibromyalgia syndrome—what was it really except a doctor's guess based on a series of responses? Does it hurt there? Does it hurt there? There was no blood test, no test at all to explain the aching pain and fatigue that overcame her more and more often, sometimes without warning. And she wasn't willing yet to say the word 'chronic' aloud to her friends. Would she be greeted with derision—Oh, great, now Alison's jumped on the environmental illness bandwagon? She remembered Stacy's reaction to the community soap. And could the timing possibly be any worse? If she had not spent the day sleeping, the issue of Sarah could already be resolved.

"Well," said Seven, reading her mind. "I don't think you're giving your friends credit. But it's your call." She said this last in a reluctant tone—obviously committed to the intellectual ideal of women dealing with their own illnesses however they saw fit, but still *wanting* to butt in. "See you at dinner?"

"Sure," Alison replied, aware this might not be true, but willing to stretch the truth just a bit in the name of escape.

Alison had expected a flurry of camp-breaking activity back at the gate, but Stacy's tent had not even been taken down. And—oh damn it!—she had been standing right there talking to Seven and in the face of the FMS drama she had not even asked her about the stones. Stacy herself was sitting beneath the awning cleaning her face with Ten-o-six and a cotton ball. She was so into it that Alison knew she had to be high.

"Stacy!" she said, trying to keep herself from scolding, which would not set any show on the road. Stacy reacted badly to scolding, turning immediately into the queen of passive resistance. "Let's go! Let's pull the tent down and go get some help with those rocks. I don't know how far we're going to have to drive to find the law around here."

"Give it up, Alison." Stacy's tone was sweet, but firm. "It's not happening. You can't make it happen, and I can't make it happen. We're not going to find enough people to move those rocks. There's only three of us—you, me and Michelle—and that's not enough."

"What about Liz?" Alison asked, grabbing at straws. She hated nothing more than feeling helpless. Any activity was better than that feeling.

"With her back? I don't think so. I stood there at those showers and talked to every single woman who came by about moving those rocks, and every single one of them said no. And these were women who drank my beer and smoked my dope and broke my bread—I mean, they're not open for bribes, and they're not caught up with rules just because they're rules, either. They've thought about it and they've talked about it and they've decided that they're committed to doing it this way. So who the hell am I to try to tell them different?"

"Did you tell them she'd been *murdered*?" Alison asked. She felt as if her grip on reality was doing a slow slide. With that information, how was it possible that the decision was still to burn Sarah's body? Not in her world.

"Nope. That's your theory, Babe. I thought you ought to be there to support it, because I'm not sure if even *I* believe it."

Alison felt like smacking her. If she did, she thought bitterly, she would probably be cast out into the desert without shoes or water. But if she killed her—oh, she was safe from retribution then! She turned away, trying to get control of her anger. It was too much, feeling so helpless.

At this moment there was quick rattling of stones and Zorra suddenly appeared between them, practically upon Stacy's lap. She was carrying a stick in her mouth. Two days of loving and being cleaned and fed had changed her from a particularly wretched looking stray to a rather handsome bitch with strong collie tendencies. She appeared more pregnant every time Alison saw her, but she was still just a puppy herself—she still wanted to play.

Michelle appeared close behind. "You satisfied now?" she asked Alison. "Too bad you missed the scene she made in the kitchen," she told Stacy.

"Somebody doesn't want that body autopsied," said Alison shortly. "That's what the burning is about. Find out who started that idea, and you'll find out who the killer is."

Stacy raised a skeptical eye. "Isn't that jumping? Couldn't it just mean somebody doesn't want you to interfere with the ritual? Not because of foul play, but just because they don't want you to butt in?"

Alison pondered. It was true that feelings were running high back in the main house. "I don't think so," she said. "I think it's because whoever it is wants to make sure Sarah is good and gone before the cops get here."

"Alison," said Stacy. "Maybe there was no foul play. The pill bottle seems to me like pretty slim evidence." She broke off, shaking her head. "Listen to me," she said. "I'm saying foul play. I've said it twice. I never thought I would ever even *say* foul play, let alone be involved in it. Liz is right, you are going to get a Jessica Fletcher kind of reputation. People are going to start inviting you to visit relatives they don't like."

Alison ignored this side bar. "Well, they can try to keep me from getting into town, but they must know that it's only going to make us more suspicious—it's only going to make us want to get out of here even more."

"Not me," said Stacy, holding up our hands. "I mean, I'm perfectly willing to follow right along in your wake like the faithful girlfriend that I am, but I have no self-motivation whatsoever. Personally, the woman sounds dreadful."

"You haven't heard the whole of it," said Alison. Briefly, she described her conversation with Lisa.

Stacy shuddered. "Dreadful! Just dreadful! What is it about blackmailers that makes them think no one is going to blow up in their faces? I ran into Seven down at the sweat lodge, and she told me a story that was pretty much the same—apparently Sarah found out that the mother of some child she knew had been a prostitute in her youth, and she insisted on telling the kid 'To clear the air for everyone'. A fifteen-year-old!"

"Ouch!" said Alison. "Was it someone here?"

Stacy pursed her oh-so-kissable lips. "I don't know. Seven was awfully vague about names—I guess that could have been the reason."

Alison hit herself in the head with the palm of her hand. "You were in the sweat lodge? Damn, I should have closed that off as well!"

"No point," said Stacy, who now had a nail file going. In Stacy's book, camping out was no excuse for poor grooming. "I'll bet every single woman on the land has been through it since last night. But I did think of something strange."

Alison's attention was elsewhere. "Do you think anyone could saw through that bike lock with a hacksaw?" she asked Michelle.

"Well, you're not supposed to be able to. That's why I paid thirty bucks for it. But I tell you what someone *could* do with a hacksaw—saw through one of the handles on the refrigerator."

"So in other words, that was just a token closing."

"A ritual," Michelle agreed.

"This is scaring me," said Stacy to Alison. "One woman has already been killed. Okay, let's say you've convinced me. Whoever did it thought it was just going to be passed off as an accident. And it would have been—it probably still *could* be. Except for you."

"And us, by association," said Michelle, checking the Dutch oven to see if there was any cake left.

"I don't think I want to play with you any more," said Stacy, a worried wrinkle appearing between her eyes. "I think my mother wants me to go home now."

"Somebody here doesn't want you to go home at all," said Michelle, scarfing down the last bit of devil's food and looking sadly at the crumbs. "We can't move those stones in front of the gate, even all four of us together. The keys aren't such a problem—they must have scaffolding or a ladder somewhere, but until we get a crew on the rocks, we're trapped here with a murderer." Unlike Stacy, Michelle did not seem too worried by this. Michelle liked a little drama in her life—she was probably already having stalk-the-killer fantasies. Plus, thought Alison, if they were talking about the murder, no one could be scolding Michelle about Persimmon.

"Do you think we need to worry about her getting hit on the head?" Stacy asked Michelle, the worried line deepening. Stacy and Michelle had their ups and downs, but the one thing upon which they were consistently and deeply united was their concern for Alison. She sighed, pretending it was a trial, but truthfully feeling herself cherished and lucky.

"I'll stay with her," Michelle responded immediately. You

could see her envisioning a snappy Ramba outfit with a black beret.

"It would be smarter," said Stacy, "if the two of you went up there and took that lock off that freezer. Tell whoever is around that you changed your mind, the goddess spoke to you, whatever you want, and then hightail it back down here until they burn the body. Once that body is gone, you're not a threat to anyone. We have enough food and water down here that we can all wait down here together until those stairs are built or Lawrence shows. Nobody is going to try to keep us from going once the body is burnt. They'll be just as glad to see the last of us as we'll be to see the last of them."

Michelle sulked. You could see that she had been counting on the Ramba thing.

"We can't do that," Alison protested. "Just let someone get away with murder?"

"They wanted to deal with things in the community, I say we let them deal with things in the community," said Stacy. "I'm sorry, Alison, but I don't think it's worth risking our own lives to avenge this Sarah person. It's not as if this is a serial killer! Sarah was a blackmailer—that's why she got it."

"We don't know that," Alison protested.

"But it's a pretty damn good guess. What is it that you're always telling me—look for the obvious? If her husband beat her up and she's found dead, then he's probably the killer."

"Except for O.J.," put in Michelle. "And I hear there were mysterious killer elves involved there."

Stacy ignored her. "If she's a blackmailer and she's found dead, well then, somebody probably got tired of being blackmailed. The only reason the killer would have for striking again would be if she was afraid she was going to be exposed, and gee, who does that mean the next victim will be? Possibly the Queen of the Busybodies?"

"I am *not* a busybody," Alison protested. "I just have a very strong moral code."

"The one does not rule out the other," said Stacy. "In fact, now that I think of it, most people with what they call strong moral codes are busybodies. Look at the CFV people," Stacy named Coloradan's For Family Values, the right-wing group that had pushed through Amendment Two, the anti-gay rights law, in the 1992 election. "Their whole spiel is about their strict moral code, but what it really is, is being busybodies. If Will Perkins just got a time-consuming hobby, he wouldn't have to worry about you and me kissing."

"Oh, Will Perkins gets off on thinking of you kissing," protested Michelle. "All straight men do. They just can't stand the thought of *faggots* kissing—it offends their manliness."

"I hate manly men," said Stacy. "Give me a nellie queen any day."

"Hello!" said Alison. "Have we gotten off track again? Have we forgotten that we have a body in the refrigerator up the hill?"

"Give it up," said Stacy.

Alison looked at Michelle. This was the point in the conversation when she would usually say something like, 'Let's guard it. Do you have your gun?' This was a situation that could have been specifically written for Michelle.

But Michelle looked down the road, and then up in the direction of the house and then, without looking at Alison's face, suggested, "Maybe Stacy's right."

This from Michelle who *never* said, 'Maybe Stacy's right,' and *never* turned down the opportunity to drum up a little excitement or confrontation.

"You *are* sleeping with that woman," said Stacy. "I don't care what you say. You've become a Stepford lesbian. I'll bet you let that woman call you City Pony while you're having sex."

Michelle flushed, but did not attempt to defend herself, another omission so uncharacteristic that she might just as well have pleaded guilty.

"Give it up," said Stacy to Alison. "We can't call, we can't drive in, we can't bike in, we sure as hell can't *walk* in—let's just try to not call attention to ourselves until they build the damn pyre and burn the damn body. They'll help move those rocks then—believe me, some of them want us out of here just as much as we want to get out! Hell, let's send Michelle up there to *help* with the damn thing!"

"It really is the best idea, Alison," said Michelle, still not looking at either of them. "I'm sorry. But I've got to go right now. I told Persimmon that I'd take a sweat with her—she likes to take regular sweats with anybody who's important in her life. She says it's really important to allow regular time to dialogue."

They sat silent for a moment. Stacy got up and went to the back kitchen area. She came back with a cutting board and cucumbers.

"Have you seen my pocket knife?" she asked Alison.

"No." Alison shook her head, lost in thought.

Stacy put the board down and went back over to the table. Sitting on it was one of those big wooden camping boxes, the kind that fold out with a tailgate and have shelves for pans and utensils and salt and pepper inside. She flipped the lock, let the front down and stuck her head inside it.

"Damn that Lawrence," she said, her voice muffled from being stuck in the box. "I'll bet he washed the damn thing and didn't put it back inside." Stacy, who hadn't done her own dishes in years, was just as anal about her camping box as she was about her fire. She pulled her head out of the box, making an exasperated, clucking sound with her tongue, and then stuck it back in again.

"Oh!" she said after a moment. "Look at this!" From out of the lunchbox she pulled a blue and white fake Tupperware box Alison had seen her purchase as part of a set at the fleamarket. It had come with three square, flat pieces that were almost identical. Alison had seen her use them for both sewing and eating.

"Cool, honey," said Alison absently.

"Don't say 'Cool' in that condescending tone," said Stacy, struggling with the lid of the box. It flew off with a an unexpected pop, strewing notebooks and pens and a dictionary—a term paper in a box. And something else. Stacy picked it up and waved it.

"Ta-dah!" she said. It was her cellular phone.

"What? How?" began Alison.

"Lawrence must have packed the wrong box. This one goes in my brief case for school—there was another one that had some kitchen things in it." She strutted around the fire pit, doing a little Yes-I've-got-the-phone dance.

"You are a real woman," said Alison admiringly. She felt a huge load of responsibility roll off her back. They could call the local law, and be out of there before sundown.

"I am," agreed Stacy. "I truly am!" She held the phone up to her ear and pressed the 'Power' button. Her face fell. "Unfortunately," she said soberly, "it needs to be recharged."

Alison could have screamed with frustration.

Stacy looked into the box again. Her face lit up. "Fortunately," she said, her tone triumphant, "the recharger is in here, too." She held the cord aloft and began her little dance again.

Alison looked at the phone and then turned and looked at the main house.

"This isn't going to go over well," she said. "I don't think we should go back up there right now. I have a feeling they're hanging me in effigy and sawing off the handles of the walk-in refrigerator."

"But not tonight," said Stacy, finishing the dance and ending up in Alison's lap. "Tonight they're having a big bonfire and a poetry slam."

"A poetry slam?" asked Alison. She could not see Hawk at a poetry slam. But as Stacy's shirt fell open, she could see those beautiful bare breasts right in her face. She could not resist sliding her

126

tongue along her right nipple.

"Stop it, stop it!" said Stacy, pushing her mouth away. "We're planning here, in case you hadn't noticed. I think that it's being billed as something else—a chance to share erotica that doesn't include penetration, or something like that—but G-hey! and Salad are determined to turn it into a poetry slam."

Alison did not care about G-hey! and Salad. She buried her face between Stacy's breasts, hoping she would be permitted to stay as long as she didn't attempt any tongue action.

"So nobody should be in the main house, right?" Stacy took hold of her ears and shook her head. "So we can go up and recharge the phone and have the hot tub all to ourselves while we're waiting. Pay attention here, Jane Lawless."

"Great plan," Alison agreed, her speech jittering a bit from being shaken back and forth. She would have agreed to anything. "In addition to having the body of a goddess you are a shoo-in for Mensa. They shouldn't even make you take the test." Stacy, looking pleased, stopped shaking and allowed Alison to cuddle up to her again. Stacy was a beautiful woman, and she had been told that many times. The girlfriends who stayed around, however, remembered to also mention that she was smart or creative or talented as well.

"I think you made my nose bleed," said Alison, touching it gingerly.

"Don't be a baby," said Stacy.

"Where's Liz?" Alison asked, trying to look around and getting a tit right in the eye for her trouble.

"She's infiltrating the politically correct camp," said Stacy, leaving her breast in Alison's eye. Alison didn't move. She'd take what she could get. "She did adobe this afternoon and she's going to go to dinner this evening."

"Won't they throw her out?"

"After she worked all afternoon? Their work force is down, honey. The pharaoh is dead and some of the slaves are freaking out. I don't think they're getting things done as quickly as they hoped."

"A murder does tend to slow things down," Alison agreed. She pressed herself closer up against Stacy as slowly and stealthily as if she were a cat.

"Didn't you hear me say, 'Stop it, stop it!'?" asked Stacy.

"Yes," Alison admitted. Lying would do no good—in fact it would just set off a whole long thing about honesty and did she think Stacy was *stupid*?

"Well," said Stacy, leaning down into her, "start it, start it!"

CHAPTER NINE

They waited until after it was dark and they could see the bon-fire up by the tents before heading towards the main house. Liz, who had popped over to the Fun Camp for a few hits on the bong after dinner, walked part of the way with them. She had not been thrown out of dinner, though there had been talk. There had been, in fact, a lot of talk. Even name calling, but according to Liz she had just been nice until everyone had seen the error of their ways. Which probably meant that she had sat there with a big, old Cheshire cat grin on her face chewing grits like she belonged until everyone had run out of steam.

Liz was full of information. As Alison had suspected, Sandpaper and Lavender *were* in subtle competition for the next Dalai Lama and kept making vague references to the afterlife. Hawk was mad at everyone and she had snapped at Lavender when she tried to point out, for the good of the community, of course, that she was letting her power flow into some really male patterns. Jerusha was obviously having an affair with Claw and in a cloud of lust had replastered a whole wall that was already fin-ished. The Chain Gang had quit work on the house altogether and had spent the afternoon alternately freaking out and collecting materials for a pyre, which they intended to build down by the arroyo that ran past the sweat lodge, whether it was voted in or not. They had appropriated the roof beams for the bunk house, and this was causing tension. Nobody wanted to look insensitive, but those things were *expensive*. There had indeed been talk of a hack saw, but as far as Liz knew, no one had yet removed the lock from the door of the walk-in. And G-hey! had tried to introduce anal sex as a din-ner topic and had been soundly scolded by Persimmon, who seemed to count that as s/m and told her to read the land rules again.

"It doesn't sound like you were the center of attention at all," said Stacy.

"I wasn't," agreed Liz regretfully. "Just bad timing, I guess."

She peeled away from them at the camping hill, promising to do her best to keep anyone from returning to the main house early.

"Oh," she called quietly when she had gone a few feet, "don't go to Sarah's old place—I think the Chain Gang moved into it. That one kid is really freaking out—they'd be doing her a favor if they got her out of here."

The main house was completely dark. Alison guessed that you got really good about turning out lights when you were hooked to a solar generator. She had thought to bring a flashlight, and used it to locate an outlet in the front room. She didn't want anyone to look up from the poetry slam and wonder who was raiding the refrigerator. The phone gave a little beep when she plugged it in.

"How long will it take?" she asked Stacy.

"Actually," Stacy said, carrying her big bag, "I think that you can use it in a few minutes, as long as it's plugged in. I charge it up all night, and then I just stick it in my briefcase in the morning." She walked through the open glass doors which led out to the patio and the hot tub. Her mind was not on dialing 911. She had already made that clear.

Alison stood by the phone for a moment, watching her disrobe. Would it really matter if she called the sheriff right this minute, or in half an hour or even an hour? Nope, she decided, not in the grand scheme of things. Sarah was already dead and Alison was willing to bet the county wouldn't get anyone out before morning. And there was Stacy lifting the top off the hot tub and descending like Artemis bathing…

Luckily Alison was wearing a t-shirt, or she would have scattered buttons all over the floor as she followed Stacy into the tub, only a heartbeat behind her heart-throb.

Stacy had already ducked her head and come up sleek and wet. In the moonlight Alison could see the set-up that Michelle had described. A metal pipe was trickling sulfur-smelling water over the side of the tub. The pipe was jerry-rigged to a sawhorse and the ladder of tub, and Alison could see it snaking up the hill, glinting in the moonlight. She couldn't see how they were draining the run off. Maybe it hadn't been a problem yet, or maybe they just unhooked the pipe at the top when the tub was full and let the spring follow its natural course. The lid of the tub was the type that folded in the middle and could be locked down to keep out kids and pets. Stacy had not bothered to lift it off, but had simply folded it back. The dark vinyl cover shone in the moonlight.

Even with the lid like that the tub was roomy. Stacy moved behind Alison and pulled her forcefully against her, back to front. Alison felt herself opening, mind and body, towards her immediately. All afternoon she had teased her and flirted with her. Alison loved that part of the game, but she was ready now for the next level of play. She wanted to be taken roughly and used hard and then held, floating in the water, afterward.

Stacy must have felt the same way, for she did not bother with foreplay. Stacy was not a foreplay kind of gal—she didn't like to spend hours kissing and touching with the tips of her fingers. Her foreplay was flirting, dressing sexy, putting out compliments with sexual innuendoes and knowing looks, and she had been having it all afternoon. She held one arm, stiff, across Alison's chest to hold her to her. The other hand she slid down her long back. She parted Alison's asscheeks and put on finger on her asshole, just pressing. Alison tightened her asshole involuntarily, and then pushed back against Stacy's hand. She loved being fucked in the ass. She loved it when Stacy took her from behind, commanding her to spread her asshole so that Stacy could then enter her with a well-lubed dildo; loved the way that Stacy would fuck her hard and deep, not afraid to push her limits. She liked it because it was nasty and forbidden and it hurt and felt good and made her come like nothing else did.

Stacy's finger slipped up her ass a quarter of an inch and stayed, pulsing softly. It felt dry and tight, which was exciting by itself. Stacy always used lube—this felt like half-remembered sex play, like the touching you did before you knew what was supposed to feel good, or why—hit and miss. Alison pushed back against her again. Despite the friction, she wanted Stacy to fuck her ass this way. She wanted to feel forced—it clicked in immediately to so many of her fantasies.

"You'd love me to fuck your ass in this hot tub, wouldn't you?" Stacy whispered into her ear. "You'd like me to push it in as far as I could go and just fuck you 'till you came, wouldn't you?"

Alison moaned low in her throat, a noise that could be taken any way that Stacy wanted.

"But don't you think that would be a little rude? Fucking your ass in someone else's tub? Who knows what kind of nasty diseases we might expose them to?" She moved the arm that lay across Alison's chest to her right breast.

Alison made a deep sound of frustration. When Stacy was teasing, she liked to know that her victim wanted it enough to beg. The strong, silent type was likely to just end up without.

Stacy pulled on her nipple, first softly and then harder—a series of pulls like a strobe light flashing. She was interposing two realities. When she tugged, the pull was the only thing that existed—then when she rested Alison could only feel Stacy's finger in her ass, barely inside, barely moving.

"I know that you'd do it if it was your choice," whispered Stacy. "You wouldn't care. You wouldn't care if you left lube floating on the water like an oil slick or if somebody tripped on a big dick that you left on the deck. But I was raised a lot nicer than that." Tug, tug, tug on Alison's nipple, bringing back memories of times that she had used clamps, times that she had put Alison in spread-eagle bondage that had included a rope to each breast.

"I don't care," Alison whispered back. "Fuck me. Fuck me in the ass." Not just because she wanted it, but because she knew that this was what Stacy wanted to hear, that part of her excitement came from feeling that she was the one who was in control, the one who set the limits and boundaries. "That's so easy," said Stacy, shifting her hand from Alison's right breast to her left. "I can make you come like that any time that I want, can't I? Just spread your ass and fuck it hard with a big dick. But I can't do it like this." She moved her finger just the tiniest bit, such a small amount that it could have been Alison's desperate imagination.

Alison moaned again. She didn't want to be played with. She wanted to be fucked deep, fucked so hard that her ass was sore the whole next day. She wanted to feel taken and used—the focal point of a desire Stacy could not control. But she knew it would do no good to protest—if Stacy had her mind set on control, then control would be the only thing that would happen. The best thing to do would be to become one with it.

"Put your hand on your clit," Stacy told her, tugging hard on her nipple. It was like sending a direct wire to her brain, like bypassing step one and two and three and going almost directly to the climax. Alison obeyed without hesitation. Stacy loved watching her get herself off, and she had a thousand variations on the scene. Sometimes she would make Alison go for a week or more under direct orders not to touch herself at all. It was hard to fall asleep those weeks, but it was worth it when Stacy finally gave permission—and watched greedily. Sometimes she got Alison up to speed with whispers and promises and then made her fuck her own cunt with a dildo before she'd make her come. Once Stacy had set up a video camera and taped Alison as she made her fuck herself in the ass until she came. Then she had made her do it again, this time watching herself on tape as she did it. Or, Alison pretended that Stacy made her—nothing else made her more excited than pleasing her lover, and she had yet to deny her anything that she had asked.

"Tell me how you want your ass fucked," Stacy ordered into her ear, and Alison knew that it was just one more way of making her fuck herself, to hear her say the words.

"On my hands and knees," Alison gasped, circling her clit with her finger. "With my ass up. I want you to fuck it hard." Stacy moved her finger, that slight in and out motion in her tight asshole and Alison could feel her mind magnify it to fill her fantasy, to become the deep thrust, the hard movement that pushed her head down into the carpet. "I want you to use a big dildo. A hard one. Push it all the way in the first time—don't warm me up at all." She was choking out the words now, not yet approaching orgasm, but approaching that plateau from where she knew orgasm was possible. She began to turn inward, starting to play back the loops of fantasy that, with occasional updating, had made her come during masturbation since childhood.

She was totally unprepared for Stacy's sudden movement, shoving her up and out of the water so that she was bent over the edge of the tub. Stacy knocked her feet apart with her own foot, so that her legs were spread and her ass open.

From behind, Stacy pushed three fingers into Alison's cunt, at the same time pushing her index finger farther into her asshole. Again Alison was aware of the dry, almost painful feel of it, and again it kicked into the most forbidden of her fantasies. She pushed herself back on Stacy's hand, taking her hard thrusts as deeply as they could go, imagining herself a toy, a sex slave used only for the pleasure of her mistress. The first time that Stacy had ever fucked her she had used a dildo in her cunt and her ass at the same time—or had that just been the fantasy she had used to make herself come? Either way, she flashed back upon it, remembering herself face down upon the bed as Stacy has fucked her from behind with a double-headed strap on, filling her cunt and ass with the same long, deep strokes that she longed for now. Stacy was pumping harder, slamming her hand against her cunt with a force that would leave her bruised the next day, but Alison did not care. If a bruising was the price she must pay for being taken hard, then it was a price that she would pay gladly. She pushed her ass back to take the full length of Stacy's fingers. Then, suddenly, with a stifled scream, she came in a spasm.

Stacy peeled the glove—Alison wasn't even aware that she had been wearing one and had no idea when she had put it on—off her hand and tossed it over the side of the tub. She caught Alison as she slid back down into the hot water. For a moment she and Stacy cuddled in a strange, weightless way. Alison was reminded of the time that she had seen the walruses at Sea World swimming around and around in great, gentle loops of foreplay that was never really consummated.

"I have got to use the bathroom," said Stacy finally, giving Alison a soft push that sent her floating.

"Oh, don't," said Alison automatically. "I can't bear it if you leave." In reality Stacy *always* had to go to the bathroom in the eye of a sexual storm and Alison usually enjoyed the few minutes alone, but if there was one thing she had learned from other relationships it was that it was never a good idea to become complacent. Stacy liked to hear that she would be missed, it took less than ten words, and the payback was terrific.

Stacy didn't actually preen, but there was just enough air of self pleasure about her to make her all the more lovely.

"I must," she said. "And don't hold your breath—I've been looking forward to using a flush toilet all day long."

Stacy climbed the ladder and stepped out of the tub into the moonlight. It was enough to take Alison's breath away, and it did. She threw a long, white terry cloth robe about her—was there nothing that was not in that bag?—and tossed her curls back.

"Come and give me a kiss," she said, holding her face close to the ladder. Obediently, Alison swam close to the side, and as she kissed Stacy her question about the bag was answered, if not wholly. Perhaps there was something that was not it the bag, but that something was not handcuffs. Alison was surprised to hear the little snick of metal as they closed around her right wrist, and then Stacy swung her through the water and swiftly pulled her left arm up behind her to secure it through the ladder. My, buoyancy was wonderful!

Stacy drifted though the glass doors and off down the hall before Alison could do much more than make a surprised noise. She contented herself with testing the play on the cuffs. Stacy had pulled both hands behind her head and cuffed them through the top rung of the ladder at about neck level. It was not a position which allowed for a tremendous amount of movement, but with a little experimentation Alison found that she was able to half float on her back, her head propped on her hands.

She stretched out her feet and closed her eyes. In a little while, she knew, she was going to have to deal with phoning—if the cellular phone would even work this far out. Then she would have to decide what steps she was willing to take to protect the integrity of the body. If, as she suspected, Sarah Embraces-All-Things had been overdosed with the antidepressants to make her light-headed in the sauna, then an autopsy would be crucial. But just for the moment she was content to float, feeling completely full of peace. She had a beautiful, sexy girlfriend who wanted to stick with her despite her shortcomings. She had a wonderful new house, a cat and friends she loved. In spite of her illness, she was a rich, rich woman.

A cloud passed in front of the moon. Alison heard the sliding door open.

"Stacy?" she asked lazily, hardly bothering to open her eyes. Stacy did not reply, but that didn't worry her. Stacy was a little deaf in her left ear, and she didn't always hear the first time. Alison twisted her head to the side and started to speak again.

She didn't get the chance. She felt a hand pass over her face from behind as if to caress her, and arched up to feel the touch. Then, without warning, someone standing above shoved her under water as hard as she could. Alison gave an involuntary gasp, and sucked in a mouthful of water. When she tried to break the surface, her head was forced down so hard that it slipped through her arms.

Now her elbows were in front of her face, and she stuck them up protectively as she tried to break the surface for the second time. The gesture was automatic, which was a good thing. She had sucked in a nose full and was far too busy choking and snorting to mount any kind of defense

I'm going to die! she thought wildly. What was it—six minutes that you could go without air before brain damage? Healing mineral water, she thought crazily.

She heard a splash and a scraping sound, and then suddenly everything went dark. I've died, she thought. So why haven't I quit choking? With her feet on the bottom of the tub, she pushed up as high as she could, shoving her head back through her arms. There was a loud thud and a shock of pain along her nose. From the taste of salt in her mouth she knew her nose was bleeding

It took her a moment to realize that what she had hit with her forehead on was the lid of the hot tub. While she had been struggling beneath the water her assailant had pulled the lid across the tub and, presumably, locked it down tight.

The instant she realized what had happened she ceased to choke. Her nose throbbed and bled and she was still handcuffed in a tub of hot water, but she was no longer possessed by the terrible panic.

Tentatively, trying to find a spot on her head which would not hurt if used as probe, she raised up again and pushed against the lid. It was difficult to find a spot neither bruised or bleeding—she had not just been shoved viciously in the face two times, but her head had hit off the ladder and sides of the tub as well—and was a vain effort anyway. The lid did not lift so much as an inch.

She floated silently for a moment, not sure what to do. Having space to breathe, she was no longer in immediate danger, but she was still supremely vulnerable. Had the woman or women—it occurred to her for the first time that this could have been the work of a team as easily as an individual—meant to kill her? Would a cry for help bring a rescue, or another attack? Her assailant could be even now standing a few feet away from her, listening from the outside for a sign of life. She had no doubt that it was the killer who had attacked her—but had the attack been a warning or a final solution? And what had Alison done to set the killer off? What threat had she posed, stranded out by the gate as they got ready to burn the only evidence?

Alison drew her foot across the bottom of the tub, trying to ease her position, and hit something that moved, something that had definitely not been there before the attack. She felt it with her toes— rectangular, a soft case over a hard body, something that her fingers definitely remembered feeling. Of course! It was Stacy's cellular phone! Someone had stumbled across it in the dark, someone to whom it spelled danger and exposure.

For the first time, Alison thought of Stacy. Where was she? She should have returned from the bathroom by now—had she been attacked as well? The panic began to well up in her again, and she had to call on her deepest and strictest cop mode to fight it down. She was *not* going to die here, not if she could avoid being attacked again. All she could do for Stacy was hope for the best. It was too late to call out and warn her—all that would do was alert her attacker to the fact that she was still alive. Attacking Stacy, who was alive and strong and not in bondage, would be much different than attacking Alison.

Alison had not consciously prayed in a number of years—if there was a God, she had a number of beefs with him, but she found herself moving her lips, begging, promising. If only Stacy would be all right, she would truly become involved in good works, would truly tutor illiterate adults, volunteer at the Community Center, donate blood to the Red Cross instead of just thinking about it. She would be good and kind and generous and love even the skin heads and gay bashers. She would, she would, she would! It did not occur to her to make any offers concerning her sexual orientation or proclivities—she had never believed that God cared what she did in bed. That would make him a voyeur, rather than an almighty.

Her nose dipped below the surface of the water, and she pulled her head up with a start, realizing that she had started to, as Stacy called it, grey out. For the first time it occurred to her that if Stacy did not come back (and, oh please, God, make that not be so) and neither did anyone return to the main house after the campfire, then she might be in danger of eventually passing out from the heat. It had worked once—why not a second time? And what about the air—how tight was the seal on the tub?

She had no idea how long she hovered in the tub, sometimes floating, sometimes crouching on her feet, trying not to make a sound nor lose consciousness. Her arms ached—Stacy had only meant for her to stay in this position for a few moments—and her nose continued to bleed. She had to breathe through her mouth. Stacy had not come to her, and that meant that Stacy was hurt or dead. Perhaps dying, perhaps not beyond help if she could just reach her in time.

She heard a noise, stiffened and then relaxed the tiniest bit. Although her sense of perception was distorted, it sounded as if it were coming not from beside her, but from inside the house. Which meant, she thought, that it was a fairly loud noise. Could that mean a crowd, people returning for a tub before bed? She had to chance it. She raised her leg and kicked against the lid of the tub, screaming as loudly as she could. She didn't know whether to cringe or cry for joy when the lid began to move.

"Alison?" Oh, god, she had never been so happy to see Michelle in her whole life, even though she did go into lecture mode immediately. "Oh, for fucks sake, Alison, what the hell are you letting that woman do to you?! You could have passed out and drowned…"

"I know that!" Alison snapped, pushing herself up to breathe the cool night air. Oh, God, it felt good! "Stacy didn't do this! Are you crazy! Do you think Stacy would give me a bloody nose?" Her anger turned to concern. "Stacy! Where is she? Michelle, she was in the bathroom, see if she's okay—she might have been attacked, too!"

"G-hey! and Lisa went to check," volunteered Claw. She was standing back too far to see—Alison recognized only her voice. "We heard her shouting when we came in."

Now that she had mentioned it, Alison could hear Stacy shouting for herself—what sounded like a string of curses that would do a longshoreman proud. She was flooded with relief. Close on the tail of that feeling came a great wave of embarrassment. She and Stacy had played at parties, but it was totally different to perform for an admiring audience than it was to suddenly realize that she was dangling naked in front of a horrified crowd who thought Stacy had hit her face to the point of drawing blood.

"Stacy didn't hurt me!" she said again, summoning back the

anger. "I was attacked when she went to the bathroom! Don't just stand there—get the key and unlock me!" Luckily Stacy, after a couple of those annoying I've-lost-the-key situations that tend to kill the scene, always kept her handcuff keys attached to a large keychain. Nobody moved. They all just stood watching her, as if she were some kind of strange animal in the zoo, the member of a lost tribe who no one recognized or remembered.

"Get the key!" she shouted.

Someone stirred. Coming from the darkness into the light of the nearly full moon, Alison was having trouble seeing who it was. Michelle must have gone to see about the Stacy situation, or she would have had the key out and in the lock already, lecturing the whole while.

There was a familiar little click behind her head. Gratefully Alison pulled her hands apart and lowered her arms. It felt so good. She still had no idea how long she had been locked in that position. She turned her head. Persimmon was standing behind her, looking with distaste at Stacy's key chain, which unfortunately was a squeak toy in the shape of a huge penis, veins and all, topped with whipped cream and a cherry. A gift from Lawrence.

"Stacy," Alison said. She put her hands on the two sides of the ladder, but before she could pull herself from the water there was a great whir of activity by the glass doors, and out rushed Stacy herself. Michelle and G-hey! followed close behind like handmaidens.

"Are you okay? Are you hurt? Oh, my God, your nose!" Alison found herself drawn from the tub, wrapped in a robe, held, offered water, questioned, whisked into the kitchen and packed in ice all in what seemed like under a minute. All this while Stacy managed to tell her own story, which was simply that the loose doorknob had been missing from the inside of the bathroom door. Stacy had left the door ajar, but someone had come by and given it a great push from the outside, trapping her. She had become frightened when Alison had not responded to her calls.

"Thank God you're all right!" she said. "Thank God, thank God!" She held Alison's head, ice pack and all, close to her chest. "I was so afraid! I thought she had gotten you!"

Except for those first few comments of Michelle's, no one had said much at all, although they had all followed her inside. Now, however, Alison could feel a confrontation brewing. She closed her eyes. Stacy would have to deal with this. She could not. She felt herself beginning to slip into the same dull stupor of exhaustion that had claimed her two nights before, and wondered if her medication was in her pocket or back at the camp.

"Tea?" she asked Stacy in a low voice.

"You bet." Stacy was patting her as if to make certain she really *was* okay, this wasn't some nightmarish dream with a trick ending. She moved back from the table towards the kitchen and Michelle, still holding a towel in one hand, moved immediately into the space that she had left to do the same thing. Even Persimmon's seductive glow could not overcome her protective allegiance to Alison.

"I am going to kill Seven Yellow Moons!" Hawk exploded. "I should never have let her talk me into letting you..." she struggled for the right word and burst out, "Perverts! Perverts on the land! I don't give a shit if you own a backhoe! None of this would have happened if you hadn't been here! There's a reason that we don't want leather women on the land. We don't want anything to do with that shit! You," she swung around and pointed an accusing finger at Stacy, "you almost killed her with your little fun and games! What kind of sick shit was that—where would that have put us if she'd drowned because you were acting out some twisted scene?"

Alison closed her eyes, and then opened them again just a slit. Tired as she was, she didn't want to miss the scene this was going to provoke.

She was not disappointed.

"Are you insane?" Stacy roared from across the kitchen. She stormed around the counter, her robe flapping around her as if she were a supreme court justice on a rampage. "Do you *really* think that I did that as part of a scene?" She was right up in Hawk's face now. Everybody stepped back to keep from being caught in her vortex. "Because if you really do, then you are a hell of a lot more twisted than I could ever be! You fucking idiots—what do you think s/m is all about? You think I like to be beaten, so why not just drop a rock on my foot? Hell, why don't I just wear shoes that are two sizes too small—that'd be just like masturbating!" She paused for breath and Michelle immediately jumped into the void.

"And I'm so tired of hearing all this crap about how you shouldn't have let us onto the land, because our motives weren't pure enough! I have lived in the lesbian community for twenty years and I have kept my motives plenty clear, and I have kept my political values when everybody else was moving on. I have walked the way I talked! And that's what it's about—living in the real world, not how you act at some big lesbian summer camp!" Michelle was so pissed that Stacy had even stepped back. "And I am not a leather woman!" Michelle added.

Stacy took a deep breath, but Hawk cut her off. "I don't give a shit if you're a leather woman! You hang around with them—that's good enough for me! They taint the whole goddamn community, and it's people like you—normal women who stay friends with them who allow them to continue! I don't believe for a minute that any woman as fucked up as this one," she pointed a finger at Stacy, "could even survive in the world if it wasn't for women like you taking care of her! You think it's wrong that we have to retreat? Well, let me tell you something—it's not men we're retreating from! It's lesbians like you! And you," she turned to Stacy, "if you didn't handcuff her, who did? Who else would even have handcuffs in this space? Because I don't know about you, but I don't have to handcuff my partner—she *wants* to have sex with me!"

"You are so ignorant!" Stacy wasn't quite spraying spit, but you could sure see her gearing up. Her robe had fallen open—all she needed was a broadsword to beat against her breasts. "You think the reason you're not in the leather scene is because of your politics, but that's not it at all! You're not in the leather scene because you're too damn *dumb* to be in the leather scene! You want to know who tried to drown Alison? Well, it wasn't me! It was the same person who killed that awful Sarah!" She took a quick look at Alison to see if they agreed on this. Alison nodded beneath veiled lids. "You've got a murderer right here, right here in your elite little group, and we didn't have a thing to do with it!"

There was a collective intake of breath, which could have related to any or all of Stacy's comments—she had pretty much managed to horrify or offend everyone there.

"You brought the energy in," said Hawk, spacing the words out like stones in a stream. "If it hadn't have been for you and the whole way that your energy is shaped, nothing would have happened, and no one would have been hurt."

"You must be crazy!" Michelle finally bullied her way to the top level of the shouting match. "That is the stupidest thing I've ever heard! You wanted to bring good energy in here? Then you couldn't have picked anybody better than Alison! You should have paid her money to come in here and spread her energy around! She's kind and she works hard and she's intelligent and she's productive and she's been putting that kind of energy into the lesbian community for years! That is such bullshit to judge her by what she does in bed!" Michelle snapped her mouth shut in surprise. Oh dear, she had just defended the leather scene. Well, she never did like anyone else to criticize Alison.

"If she's got such goddamn good energy, then how come she's

the one who's seeing murder all over the place, when all that the rest of us see is an accident? Why is she trying to enforce her will on the rest of us?"

"She sees murder because she's a cop!" Stacy burst in scornfully. "It's not any different than you seeing a scorpion in the adobe because you know where to look! And she's not trying to enforce her will on anybody—she's just trying to let everybody know what really happened so that they can make some kind of educated choice about what they should do. *You're* the one who's trying to enforce your will!" Stacy quickly slid her eyes sideways to Alison, whom she knew good and well *was* trying to enforce her will. Stacy was not above exaggerating in the name of being the winner.

"And talk about bad energy!" Michelle was still one or two blows behind—in a minute she was going to deny being in the scene again. "Talk about bad energy! What the hell were you doing letting that woman run the show the way she was? That is the most racist thing that I have seen up close in a long time!"

This one surprised everyone but Persimmon into silence. "What are you talking about?" she asked in a hurt, surprised voice which let anyone who hadn't yet clued in know that they were lovers. "How can you say that when we've gone out of our way to try and be inclusive to women of color and women with different abilities?"

Michelle looked pained. It was obvious she would have much rather flung a retort at Hawk. Still, she wasn't going to back down. She seemed to have momentarily flown off her cloak of confused alliance and become once again the Michelle of old. "Yeah, and then you were taken in by a woman who strung together a bunch of the worse stereotypes I have ever seen! And you believed her, because in some way you believed in the lies—that of course a woman who was Native American would be a spiritual bully! And you created your own little segregation plan. You didn't confront her, you didn't ask the same things from her that you asked from anyone else. Maybe you were letting her drink out of the same drinking fountain, but you sure as hell weren't treating her the same way that you treated the white girls. And if that's not racism, then I don't know what is!"

Nobody knew what to say. Perhaps there would have been an eventual response, but it was at this moment that Alison began to cry.

Stacy was immediately solicitous. "Oh, Honey, and I didn't even get your tea! And after all you've been through!" She glared around the circle. Everyone looked a bit sheepish, obviously thinking that Alison was weeping because of her brush with death. She was not. She was weeping with pure frustration. She needed to talk to people! She needed to question everyone! She needed to get her two cents worth in the conversation, and she could feel herself slipping away again, so exhausted that she couldn't even coach Stacy in a side bar.

"Well," said Hawk, looking somewhat abashed. Even in her state of upset, Alison couldn't help wondering why it was that anti-s/m dykes always seemed so damned surprised if any of the leather women responded with fear or hurt. "But I do—"

"Oh, *shut up*!" sobbed Alison. "Just fucking *shut up*. All of you! I was almost killed, and all anybody cares about is a chance to..." She wanted to say advance their political agenda, but that was far too complicated to put into words. She hated to cry. It offended the butch part of her. It made her feel as if she was enacting every single female stereotype which she had scorned since childhood—the woman who cried to get her way, or because she was helpless, or stupid or inarticulate.

"Well, I..." tried Persimmon.

"Just shut up!" If she was going to bawl like a baby in front of the whole world, then at least she was going to call an end to the bickering. Michelle and Stacy, who had both seen this before, had wisely withdrawn—the former to check on the tea situation, the latter to stick her head into the small fridge. Everyone else began to drift away. They were tired, they wanted to use the hot tub and they were just as embarrassed to watch Alison cry as she was to *be* crying. Hawk knew when she'd lost the crowd—she stalked away, leaving a trail of water across the kitchen floor. For the first time Alison noticed that the sleeves of her sweater were soaked to the elbow—even in her abhorrence she must have reached into the tub in concern when the lid was thrown back.

"You okay?" asked Michelle, watching Persimmon's back as she went through the door. Obviously her burst of bravado had been just that—an uncontrollable explosion during which the truth must be said. Just as obviously, it was now over and the only thing on her mind was saying whatever it took to spend the night in Persimmon's bed. Alison felt a brief flash of irritation at the abandonment, not even disguised, but what could she say? She shrugged.

Michelle, interpreting the shrug just exactly as it was intended—no, it's not okay, but I won't push it—made final amends by bringing Alison's clothes in from the patio. On the top of the stack was Stacy's phone. A little pocket of water had formed inside the imitation leather case—there was a flattened bubble across the dead display screen.

"Oh!" said Stacy, taking it into her hand. She pushed power. No one was surprised when the light did not come on.

"You know," said Michelle, who had already reached the kitchen door, "I think it would be good if you slept in the back of the truck tonight, don't you?"

"Why?" asked Alison absently, wondering more about how she was going to summon the energy to sleep anywhere beyond the kitchen table.

"Well, because you can lock it from the inside. I think that would be a good idea, don't you?"

CHAPTER TEN

When Alison went to the job site the next morning, everyone acted the same way that the cats at home, K.P. and Tammy Faye, did after a really undignified altercation—all sitting in opposite corners, washing their feet and pretending nothing had happened. No one mentioned Alison's swollen nose. Okay, she was willing to accept that. She felt as if she had been stripped of all motivation. Her sleep had once again been fitful and she had woken feeling resigned. Everybody was going to stand around and ignore a cover-up? Fine. Okay. She'd done what she could—now her only goal was to get home with all family members intact. She was willing to wait it out and not say a thing to anyone on the outside after the gate was opened.

Her feeling lasted until about midmorning. Her problem, she thought, as she spread a second layer of adobe on one of the inner rooms, was that she really did have control issues, just like Liz said. And the problem with that was that it was one of those things that changed from a problem to an asset according to the situation. Control issues—very bad if you were an enlisted woman, great if you were a general. She was not a general here, but still she could not help worrying over the problem of the body, even though she could see nothing to do about it. She must have been a cat in a previous life—she certainly had the tenacity.

They did not have a full crew on the site—the Chain Gang, Sandpaper Woman and Lavender Crystalpower were missing. Tempers were short. It was the hottest that it had been. Rusha, who was obviously somewhere off in the land of infatuation, started the stairs in the wrong place, which no one realized until after a whole lot of work. Hawk was cross about it, and Michelle dropped a tub of adobe on her foot, splashing everyone around her so thoroughly that several women knocked off right then in favor of a mid-day shower. Scaffolding had been produced, and Liz who was working up on top, reached over the roof and dropped the coffee can with the keys onto the ground. Everyone ignored it, but later Alison saw several women quietly pocket their keys.

Gaya, who was the only one of the land collective who did not seem ready to knock heads, suggested that everyone take the afternoon off.

"We're building the funeral pyre down by the sweat lodge," she told everyone. Indeed, in the distance they could hear hammering. "We can use help."

Not my kind, thought Alison wisely. She took herself down to the Fun Camp, where Stacy was watching Ricki Lake on her little battery-operated tv.

"Ah, the great outdoors," said Alison crossly.

"Fuck you," said Stacy. "And you should ice that nose." She was cross, too. "Liz said we could go naked and do drugs and dance around the campfire with women who loved women. So far I've been scolded for having my shirt off and nobody even likes me. I could have stayed home for that."

Liz, who had followed Alison to the Fun Camp, got a cold Diet Pepsi and a bagel without saying a word. She set them on the kitchen table and then, taking a lunch box from her tent, sat down herself. The box was old—it was made of metal and had a picture of The Monkees pressed into both sides. From the box she took a mortar and pestle, a ziplock bag full of gelatin capsules, and a second bag full of dried mushrooms.

"*Oh*," said Alison, "but I see that you're going to fit in doing drugs."

She had not meant to make it sound as nasty as it did, and rather thought that she deserved it when Stacy said, "Fuck you!" again.

Liz, working steadily, had the mushrooms ground down and in the capsules in no time at all.

"Here's to you, Babe," she said to Stacy, passing her a plateful of capsules. She offered them to Alison, who held up a hand to refuse.

They had no more than swallowed them—with a bit of a snack to ward off nausea, but not so much as to kill the high—when over the crest of the hill appeared Seven Yellow Moons and Zorra. Trailing her by about a hundred yards were, Michelle and Persimmon.

The Fun Camp girls looked at one another. Stacy and Liz immediately perked up at the thought of a little diversion, but Alison could tell that they were also hoping everyone got lost before they really started tripping. Michelle, particularly virtuous, infatuated Michelle, was bound to be a real drag while tripping.

"How come you didn't wait for Michelle and Persimmon?" Alison asked Seven Yellow Moons when she breezed into the camp.

"I wanted the chance to establish dominance," replied Seven, settling into the best seat. Zorra did a little hello dance and stole the end of Liz's bagel off the table.

"Hi!" said Michelle in the most artificially casual voice Alison had ever heard. Alison had no idea what her purpose was in bringing Persimmon to Stacy's fire. Or perhaps she did. In just the same way Michelle had insisted on bringing her girlfriends to her family reunions, back when she still interacted with her family. This is what I'm doing, and not only am I doing it in spite of what you think, I'm going to get right into your face and make you accept it. No hidden agenda with Michelle.

It was Seven Yellow Moons who saved the day.

"I haven't had time to talk to you since you moved out here," she said to Persimmon— just normal conversation, as if thoughts of Janka and the baby were not lying so very thick in the air as to be practically visible. Belatedly, Alison remembered that Seven knew Persimmon from before—not only knew, but had been a neighbor.

Persimmon either didn't feel the tension or was a damn good actress. "Electricity, hot water—!" she said, making an expansive gesture, and she and Seven laughed together, as if it were an inside joke.

"I know," Seven agreed, wiping her eyes. "I thought I would never be the kind of person who cared about that stuff. I really did! I thought I would be a nomad forever—that I could live in my van on the road until I was eighty years old."

"I know," Persimmon replied. "But, it gets so much harder as you get older, doesn't it? I love knowing I can take a hot shower whenever I want. I love buying food that I want—not having to worry if it needs to be refrigerated."

"Or that it will freeze when the fire goes out," Seven added. "I've slept with more bags of potatoes!" Another shared laugh.

"And having my shop here," Persimmon continued. "I can walk down the hill if I need to take a break, and then just walk right back up. I don't need to drive! I don't need to worry about having a working vehicle all the time—I don't need to worry about the pollution I was putting into the air every single day. Now, I go out for a show or supplies about once or twice a month."

"Living right in your shop, that's efficient," put in Liz, who would of course be the first to recover. Any upset in Michelle's life was going to reach her only as a slow trickle down. "How come you weren't sharing the other side of Sarah's casita?" No matter how she disguise it, Liz just couldn't stop with the lawyer thing.

"Oh, I'm used to living in small places. I like to live alone. I'm

145

spoiled." Persimmon spoke easily, but Alison was willing to bet that if you fed those three lines into the universal translator they would have come out, "I just couldn't stand the woman!"

"Me neither," put in Stacy, just as if Persimmon had said the words aloud. "Do you think you'll move in there now?" She had pulled out the Dos Equis, trying to disguise the bluntness of the question by playing hostess.

"I haven't even thought about it," Persimmon answered. "It's too awful—don't you think? It's going to take a lot of time to process. And I'm happy to stay in my shop—we're hoping to generate some new members out of the retreat. We might need Sarah's place." She took a swig of the beer without hesitation, and laughed ruefully when she caught Alison staring at her. "I'm not really as hard core as Hawk and Gaya. They have a real point—Gaya's had some drinking problems in the past, and Hawk's mother is an alcoholic. It *is* a patriarchal thing in a way—I mean, anything that women do to make themselves slaves to the system is patriarchal, and the patriarchy cashes in on whatever it can. I can't even read a mainstream magazine anymore—all those ads of thin women smoking cigarettes and drinking liquor!"

"Nobody fucks you up like your parents, huh?" asked Liz with fervor, fixing on the thing about Hawk's mother. Fucked up parents was something on which almost everyone could agree.

"Nobody," agreed Persimmon. "But I don't see the harm in an occasional beer or an occasional joint—I'm very focused, I work hard, it's not going to hurt me."

Since a joint had been mentioned, Stacy got out her cute little stash can. She was just the same way about her pot as she was about the fire—no one should mess with the queen. She did roll a nice joint, though.

"So is that going to be a problem?" asked Seven with a furrowed brow. "You drinking or getting high? I mean, it sounds like a major difference in philosophy."

"Oh, no," Persimmon shook her head. She really was quite lovely, and Alison could easily see Michelle's attraction. Michelle loved femmes, though she could never admit it. Women like Stacy scared her and turned her off, but she lusted for women like Persimmon and Janka—androgynous with just a little femme spin that she could deny or justify. "I don't think it's going to be a problem unless I get right up in their faces. I wouldn't do it on the land. I mean," and here for the first time a look of concern crossed her face, "it's really hard. Isn't it? To find women who have similar goals. And not just the goals, but the passion to make it happen. It's

146

hard to find women you can really live with and work with."

"I can't even find somebody to *date*," groused Liz, taking a long drag on the joint. "I usually lose them right on the first requirement."

"Which is?" asked Alison. It was easier to slide into the conversation not speaking directly to Persimmon.

"She has to have a library card," Liz said.

"And rule number two?" asked Stacy, who was either already really stoned or had a hidden agenda, because she surely had this list memorized. It was a best friend kind of conversation.

"She has to have a job. Or the equivalent," she added, before Michelle even got a chance for a toehold. Michelle liked to argue about fucking everything. "She can be going to school, or have her own business or be independently wealthy. I don't care. But she's got to have something time-consuming that she's interested in, and she's got to pay her own way. If I treat, I want to know it's a treat, not a necessity." Everyone thought of Carla, whose therapy Liz had guiltily paid for six months after the big break up and trashing scene, but no one said anything.

Persimmon spoke first—since she didn't know Liz she didn't have to go through the filtering process. "Well, see, those things have just never been important to me. They're not important now. I've lived on a lot of women's land, I've worked with a lot of women who weren't wage earners. As a matter of fact, I kind of admire that. You have to really have passion to survive in this country without working for wages. What's important to me is women who have dreams about changing the system and are willing to do more than just sit around to see them come true. They have to be hard workers. *I'm* a really hard worker, and I can't stand to be around anyone who just sits around." She did not look at Alison, or even change her voice to suggest that anyone was being implicated, but suddenly Alison was struck with a bolt of paranoia that made it seem obvious she was the one about whom Persimmon was talking. She glanced over at Michelle—surely she had stood up for her, hadn't she?—but Michelle was gazing at Persimmon with a soft and sappy look.

"It's hard to find other women you can live with," said Seven, blithely unaware that anyone was being paranoid. "Canyon Land has been good for me because, even though we try to make collective decisions about the land, we don't actually live together. I don't know if I could do that again."

"I don't know if I couldn't," said Persimmon simply. "Collective living adds so much of a dimension to my life. I feel half alive without it. I want to be around other lesbians every day. I do my best work when I'm around them. This thing about hiding out in a little box in the city, not having contact with any other dykes unless you're dating—I think that's unnatural. I think it's hugely limiting. Look at how much more we can do when we're living and working together! Look at what we've accomplished here in a couple of days!"

"Yeah," said Alison, who was not going to let Michelle be lured down the primrose path of collective living without a fight, "we managed to kill somebody."

"Why does that have to be part of this experience?" asked Persimmon. The little lines that appeared around her mouth told Alison she thought bringing this up in bad taste. Michelle scowled at her, just in case she missed the point. Michelle, Alison noticed, was boldly holding Persimmon's hand. Somebody was going to be pushed into saying something soon, and Alison would bet money it was going to be Liz. "Death always happens, no matter who you are or how you're living. It's part of life. It's going to happen to all of us."

"Well, I hope it doesn't happen to me for another forty years or so," snapped Alison. "And I hope no one pushes it!" Sitting here and pretending that she was happy for Michelle and her new girl-friend, on top of being prevented from going for the police, was making her really crabby.

"Then don't surround yourself with bad energy," Persimmon chided gently. "Don't you think that was what killed Sarah? It didn't matter that it was here—it was going to happen anyway. I believe that. She killed herself with her hunger for power."

Alison could not reply. She knew that if she did her ugly alter-ego was going to reach right up through her throat as if she were in a budget version of *Alien*. Blood would fly. She hadn't been in this big a twist in a good long while—she had forgotten how disconcerting it was.

"I'm surprised to hear you say that," said Stacy, relighting the joint. "About the bad energy. I guess I haven't really talked to Gaya or Hawk myself, but from what the other women say, I got the idea that they backed up Sarah I'm-Not-Really-An-Indian a hundred percent." She looked fairly pleased with herself. One more beer, and she'd be working foul play into the conversation.

Persimmon sighed. "Hawk and Gaya are good women," she said, slowly, as if unsure of what she was going to say. "Good women—sometimes they're easy to take advantage of?" She said it like a question, and they all nodded understanding. "When they believe something is right, it's not easy for them to adjust their beliefs to fit the circumstances."

"Get real!" exploded Liz, who must have been getting bored. She was as bad as Michelle. Somebody needed to hand her some knitting.

"Maybe," agreed Persimmon hesitantly, as if she was afraid this was getting way too close to talking bad about her family. "If you're really committed to admitting and fighting your own racism, there's not a lot of room to confront a woman like Sarah."

It was interesting, Alison thought, that Persimmon was the first woman who did not mention the blackmail angle. "Do you think she had something on them?" she asked, just to test the water.

Persimmon either looked surprised or did a damn fine job of pretending to look surprised. Alison was not sure which—she always preferred to believe the worst of everyone.

"Like what?" she asked. "I mean, what could they have done that they cared that much about people knowing? You know, no one cares about an illegitimate baby all that much any more these days."

"You know, I can't agree with you about this living with other lesbians thing." Too late, Alison realized that what she had really wanted to ask about was the blackmail theory. Oh, well, she was committed. She could bring it up later. She had to stop getting high during interrogations. "It's not that clear cut. I mean, it's not just live-on-the-land-with-other-dykes or else hide-in-the-city. I don't think I hide in the city. Michelle and I have lived in the same building for years, and now we own a house with Janka." Oops, she hadn't really meant to out Michelle, but she wasn't going to lie to cover up, either. "We've all worked in the gay community, and we've all put a lot into developing an extended lesbian family. I think that's just as valid."

"Gay community. What does that mean?" asked Persimmon.

"What do *you* mean?" asked Stacy, who was as bad as Michelle about butting in if she thought Alison was going to be dissed.

"I mean, doesn't 'gay community' mean that you're actually working on a lot of men's issues, like AIDS?" Tension jumped up a notch all around. Everybody liked a philosophical discussion, especially when they were high.

"AIDS isn't a 'men's issue'," said Liz. "Anybody can get AIDS. Lesbians can get sexually transmitted AIDS—I know, because I know women who are HIV. We just like to pretend that we can't get it, and that way we don't have to worry about using dental dams."

"Yeah, anybody can get it," agreed Persimmon. "And if it had first manifested itself in the lesbian community, do you think that gay men would have rallied to support us the way that we've rallied to support them?"

There was a long silence. Nobody, even Stacy, who loved faggots, thought that gay men would have been running Meals on Wheels for dykes.

"That's just what I mean," said Persimmon, leaning back in her chair and taking Michelle's hand again. "I think that most of the time when women are working in the 'gay' community, what they're doing is putting their energy into a bunch of men's issues. I mean, listen to yourself—lesbian isn't even in the name! I don't want to do that. I only have so much energy—and it seems to be getting less and less as I get older, and I want it to go directly to other lesbians. No matter what I do here—if I cook a meal, if I build a house, if I plant a plant or clean a room, that energy goes directly into other lesbians. That's all I'm saying. I like that. I think more women should find ways to do that. If we did, if we focused our energy onto each other instead of filtering it through men and straight women, then there would be enough for us to accomplish incredible things. That's all."

"I work on the lesbian archives in Denver." Michelle didn't want to go down looking like a total sellout.

At the same moment, Liz said, "Do you know that Michelle has a male child?" Oh, well, thought Alison, we all saw that coming.

There was a long silence. Didn't take a Betazoid to know why that topic just happened to come up in conversation. Michelle cast daggers at Liz, who looked supremely pleased with herself.

"Not my..." began Michelle finally, and then stopped. Even stupefied by lust, she could not bring herself to disown Sammy. Maybe, thought Alison, there was some hope for her yet.

Persimmon squinted up at the sun.

"We have to go," she said. "We're going to take a sweat."

Liz jumped up. "Oh," she said, her voice full of innocence. "I'll come with you!"

Persimmon shook her head politely. "Not this time," she said. "We're going to do a ritual sweat. You know, a spiritual kind of thing. I think it's important to keep in spiritual contact with the women you're close to—it heads off a lot of problems." She stood while Michelle gave Liz a big bear hug—Alison could hear her hissing, "Die, bitch!" into her ear.

Off they walked up the hill, hand in hand, their heads together. That was going to be one hell of a sweat, thought Alison. She'd bet souls were going to be bared and motives confronted.

It was not until she turned back to the keg that she realized she had never gone back to the issue of blackmail.

Seven stood as well. "I'm going to go help work on the pyre."

"That must be a hell of a pyre," remarked Liz, who was starting to get that bright eyed look.

"It is," agreed Seven. "I think it's more of a monument by now. That's okay—it's like the AIDS quilt, it kind of gives them something to do with their grieving."

"What did you think about all that?" Alison was barely able to wait until Seven was out of sight. "Do you think that Persimmon knows who killed Sarah?"

"You really are too tenacious," said Stacy, taking a long pull on her beer. "Frankly, it's getting to be boring. I don't know if you belong in the Fun Camp anymore."

"Well, I think..." Alison prepared to whip herself up into another frenzy, evoking the law, sanctity of life and the difference between right and wrong.

"Oh, stop," said Stacy, holding up a hand. "I can't bear it. I really can't. If that woman was not dead already, I would kill her myself. I may kill you instead. Everyone would cover for me."

Liz nodded agreement.

Alison sulked. Liz and Stacy, who were both starting to get those tripping smiles, looked out across the desert. Alison thought about tying them both to an ant pile. This had to be the worst vacation she had ever taken, and it wasn't just the murder. If she was going to be honest, the murder didn't really even have anything to do with her, although she would never admit that aloud. But she could not bear being so controlled and thwarted. And that didn't even touch on Michelle—it was quite horrible watching her best friend and traveling companion embarking on a course of action that was bound to shake their world like a snow globe.

She looked out in the same direction in which Liz and Stacy were staring. They had the best clouds down here. They stretched away for miles and miles and changed slowly as the wind took them. They were really doing some interesting things, and she supposed they were even *more* interesting to Stacy and Liz. Stacy had certainly begun to do a lot of drugs lately. Of course, Alison had known from the beginning that Stacy was a party girl, as Stacy herself had pointed out the one night she had mentioned it. Alison supposed it was just a case of sour grapes setting her own mouth in such an ugly line.

As if reading her mind, Stacy turned away from the clouds with a sigh.

"All right," she said. "All right, all right, alright! Let's catch the murderer. Anything to make you happy! Where's my notebook?"

"Well," said Alison, feeling a bit guilty. Why did she always have to be the one who rained on Stacy's parade? It would take couples' therapy to figure that one out, she supposed. "I mean I…"

"Oh, don't worry about it," said Stacy, sweeping through the camp like a particularly festive whirlwind. "It doesn't matter. Anything is fun right now." Her face had gotten very pink, and her pupils were huge. The last time Alison had seen eyes like that was when KP returned from night hunting with a bat. "And besides," she added, the need for discretion and butch-stroking totally overridden by the mushrooms, "you have no idea how to organize your information."

"And you do?" asked Alison, stung. Maybe she should have taken that extra hit after all, because Liz seemed to think this was quite funny. They could not even continue the conversation until she had finished laughing, wiped her eyes and blown her nose twice.

"I know how Kinsey Milhone does it," said Stacy, who had finally located her heavy Goretex briefcase, which matched her coat. It probably cost fifty dollars or more. Alison wondered if she could find something comparable at the flea market. Technically, she was supposed to have her gun on her person at all times, even off duty. The shoulder holster didn't always cut it, and carrying a purse offended her butch persona. Of course, if she took as long to find her gun as Stacy did to find anything, it wasn't going to do her or anyone else much good.

"There!" Triumphantly, Stacy pulled a marking pen (fine point) and a huge cube of sticky notes from the briefcase. She looked at the stuff she had unloaded on the table—two notebooks, spiral and looseleaf, a psychology text with a drawing of Freud, Jung, Piaget, and Margaret Mead all together at the beach, her sunglasses, a red and gold scarf in case she had a hair crisis, a Patricia Cornwell novel with a dozen dog-eared pages marking awkward sentences to be shared later with Liz, Oil of Olay sunscreen because one never knew and an unopened pair of black hose for the same reason. Stacy was a bit paranoid about being an older student—she certainly was not going to be a frump as well. She put her sunglasses on and then made a *really obvious* decision not to deal with the rest of the stuff. Lawrence was coming—he could pick it up. What was the point of having money if you couldn't hire out your dirty work? Did anybody think that Patricia Cornwell still cleaned her own floors?

"Now," she said, "what Kinsey always does…"

Alison could not bear to hear a conversation about the personal habits of Kinsey Milhone, a being whom only she seemed to realize existed solely on paper. Anything was better than that. "Stacy, Kinsey is a made up character. I, on the other hand, am a real police officer of flesh and blood."

"Kinsey always gets the killer," said Stacy, pulling up the lid of one of the coolers to act as an easel. The beer was gone, it didn't matter. They were going to have to start hitting the keg, like the little people. "And she always gets laid, too. You can't go wrong with a formula like that."

"Well, I don't think—" Alison began. She didn't know why she was in such a resistant mood, but she was.

"Fine! Fine!" said Stacy. "Don't do what Kinsey does. Do what Kay Scarpetta does. Head right up to that house and perform an autopsy. Hurry, while everyone's still doing adobe. I think I have a stryker saw in my bag." This time, both Stacy and Liz laughed until they wept. There was nose blowing all around.

Stacy began to wipe off the inside of the cooler lid so the sticky notes would work better. After about three minutes, it became obvious that she had gotten into the Zen of it and was going to wipe all day if not stopped. Alison mentioned this, and there was a short, tart exchange during which Stacy assured one and all that she *had* used sticky notes before and was quite proficient—it didn't take college. Liz went off into another gale of laughter. Stacy picked up her note pad and spent a moment looking at the pretty neon colors. Alison sighed.

"Okay, what Kinsey does," Stacy began. She looked at Alison and thought for a minute. "I read an article in a book," she said. "And *it* said—"

"Stacy, I'm not fooled," Alison protested. "I wouldn't have been fooled even if you hadn't already attributed this to a fictional character. You don't read anything but mysteries."

"What's with Kinsey and her home being blown up?" asked Liz, transferring her attention from the clouds to the conversation with no transitional remarks at all. "I mean, hasn't her garage been destroyed three or four times? Didn't it burn down a while back?"

"Well," replied Stacy, "what I want to know, *is* …"

"Tell us what Kinsey does," she commanded hastily.

Stacy, of course, didn't have the generic yellow or pink sticky notes that Alison and Liz used at the office. She had a big cube comprised of neon pink (two shades) yellow, orange and green. She divided it, handing the yellow to Liz and the green to Alison.

"What Kinsey does," she said, clearly pleased with herself for bending Alison to her will, "is she puts everything on notecards. Of different colors. For different categories." Alison looked blank, so she simplified. "Like, pink might be everything we know about Sarah."

"Let's make green everything we know about Sarah," said Alison hastily. She was afraid that if Stacy wrote they were going to spend all afternoon looking at the pretty loops the pen made.

"Control me, Alison. Make me do it your way," teased Stacy in a husky, fuck-me voice that Alison had to ignore in order to proceed.

"We know that she was pretending to be Native American," she wrote quickly on the top note. "And we know…"

"No, no," insisted Stacy who must have had a Kinsey Milhone home detective book in her briefcase. "One fact to a page. That's how she spots the pattern."

"What is it with these straight-girl detectives and old men?" asked Liz, suddenly coming to life again. "Kinsey, and V.I. Warshawski…"

Alison rode right over the top of her. "And we know that she claimed to have MS, but suspect this was also untrue." She handed both notes to Stacy, who stuck them to the upraised lid of the cooler.

"I want to write," complained Liz. "I either need to participate, or I need chocolate. Maybe both."

"You can be in charge of things we know about Sarah's death," granted Stacy graciously. "And I'm going to channel Aaron Elkins—I'm going to be in charge of interconnected monkey business. Anything strange. And there's chocolate in the other cooler."

Everyone settled down quietly for a few moments, Liz with a Hershey's kiss nestled securely in her cheek. After a few minutes, Stacy stood up again.

"Okay," she said, "who's ready?"

Liz held up a handful of notes. "Incidentally," she said as she handed them over, "I found out what the Chain Gang is called when operating as separate entities."

"What?" asked Alison who was still writing.

"Jane, Anne, and Katherine."

Alison who had still been expecting Falcon, Eagle and Owl, was confused. "I could have sworn they went together."

Stacy began to laugh. "They do go together," she said. "They're three of the wives of Henry the Eighth. We talked about it last semester, when I was taking that history class." She turned to Liz's notes. "One," she read. "Sarah either died in the sauna or was moved to the sweat after she died." She stuck the note on the cooler. "Two, we suspect she died of heat stroke, but can't prove it because there hasn't been an autopsy. Three—Stacy says her medication could make her pass out and it appears to have been tampered with. Four—no one admits to seeing her after dinner." That was it. Liz organized well even when she was tripping, but she couldn't make facts appear.

Stacy nodded at Alison as if she were running a third grade class room. Alison read her own notes before handing them over.

"One—Sarah claimed to be Native American and used it to control people."

Stacy frowned. "What are these initials on the bottom?"

"SU," said Alison. "Suspected untruth." She read on. "Sarah claimed to have MS—SU. Three—Sarah was blackmailing at least one person here. Four—some people think she was blackmailing Gaya and Hawk as well, but nobody knows why."

"And Persimmon," said Liz unexpectedly.

"What?" asked Alison.

"And Persimmon," repeated Liz. "I mean, she was the fourth member of the collective, right? We kind of keep skipping her because she doesn't do the money and power thing. But couldn't Sarah have been putting pressure on her as well?"

Alison wrote, 'Or Persimmon' on a note and handed it to Stacy. She resumed reading. "Five—Sarah didn't always practice what she preached. She had her own soap in her bathroom."

"Ah!" cried Liz. "The motive! It was another soap-related death!"

"It's just meant to show what kind of person she was," said Alison. Liz doubled up in laughter over her own cleverness, and proceedings had to be halted for a few minutes. There was more nose blowing, and bit of conversation about Kinsey Milhone and several other fictional characters of whom Alison had not heard, but to whose sleuthing skills she apparently measured up poorly. Liz also found a pretty rock while taking a pee and there was a bit of speculation about how it was formed and the ice age in general. Finally Alison was able to turn the conversation back to the murder.

"We know that Sarah liked to humiliate other women in public." Alison read her final note.

"Now, I know quite a few women like that," put in Liz. "She didn't go under the name Mistress Mad Dog as well, did she?" More gales of laughter. Perhaps they would never track down the killer, but Liz was certainly having the time of her life.

Stacy prepared to read her notes, giving first a brief speech that included but did not limit itself to Aaron Elkins, his protagonist, her favorite book and what she thought about the made-for-tv-movie. There were also a few comments about how cool the clouds looked.

"Okay," she said finally. "One—the gate was closed and the keys were taken so that no one was able to get in and out."

"That was because of the retreat," protested Alison.

"I get to write down things that are strange, and I thought that was strange," said Stacy. "How do you know it was about the retreat? How do you know it wasn't about killing Sarah all along? Frankly, it looks to me like the perfect set-up—the only monkey wrench in the plan is you. If you hadn't been here she'd already be a pile of ashes."

"It's really hard to get a fire hot enough to burn bones," contributed Liz. "Crematoriums have crushers—you might think you're getting an urn full of ashes, but you're really getting an urn full of crushed bones."

"You're a ghoul," said Stacy. "Look at the pretty clouds while Kinsey and I solve the mystery. Two—Gaya and Hawk don't seem to have any ties to this community. I get to choose, " she added, forestalling a comment from Alison with an upraised hand. "I just think that it's strange. If I was going to start a little kingdom, I'd certainly want to do it where I knew a few people to begin with."

"I was just going to say that you could put that over by the note about Sarah blackmailing them. If they're new to the area, how did she get the dirt on them?"

"And where does Gaya get her dough?" asked Liz. Looking at the clouds was good, but not really enough to completely occupy her, even while tripping.

"We'd better have a questions category," Stacy decided. She handed the blue notes to Alison and picked up her own notes, then set them back down. "Actually," she said, "I think everything about this whole set up is weird."

"You don't have the cultural background," said Alison. She was going to add, because you haven't been out long enough, but warned by a small line that appeared between Stacy's eyes decided it was a bad move. She moved quickly into questions. "Where did Gaya get her money? Where are she and Hawk from, and why did they decide to settle here? Whose idea was the retreat, and how did they advertise it and pick applicants? Whose idea was sealing the gate? Why didn't anyone else go to the sweat lodge while Sarah was in it? Who was in it with her? How many people here was

Sarah blackmailing? Did she have anything on Gaya and Hawk, and what was it? Whose idea was burning the body? Who attacked me in the hot tub? And why? Actually," said Alison, handing her notes to Stacy "just about everything is a question. And I have a couple of strange things to put down."

Stacy traded her pad for Alison's notes. Alison scribbled and Stacy arranged pretty patterns. Liz wandered off a few feet and squatted down, looking at the rocks. She popped one in her mouth, just as Alison had seen G-hey! do earlier.

"What is that about?" asked Alison. "Is that some kind of new spiritual thing?"

Liz spit the rock out into her hand and looked at it again. "G-hey! told me. She's studying to be a geologist. Sometimes you can tell what they are by how they taste."

"And how does that one taste?"

"Like chocolate." More laughter. Liz plopped herself down on the ground, barely avoiding a cactus, and began picking up pebbles one by one and examining them. She hummed a little tune to herself.

Alison handed her list of strange things to Stacy, who must have been getting bored, for instead of reading them she sang them like an opera soprano. "Who were the people on horseback? Were they really just neighbors, or did they know Gaya or Hawk from before? Hawk speaks Spanish fluently"—at this point Liz abandoned the rocks and became the chorus—"Fluent Spanish, fluent Spanish" was repeated ten or twenty times all up and down the scale.

"I am going to go and get my gun," said Alison, after Stacy and Liz ended with a huge encore finale that included throwing out their arms and beating their breasts as if they were Valkyries. "And then I am going to kill you both."

"Well, *there's* an idea," said Liz, which for some reason started them both off into giggles again. "Incidentally," she added, "people on horseback came this morning, and Hawk told me—well, she told Lavender, but I was listening—that they're two of her artifact contacts. You know, the people they give the pottery and bones to when they turn up."

For some reason, this irritated the hell out of Alison. It just did not seem right that Liz had been able to infiltrate the system out of which she had been basically banished. Crossly, she gathered her things and stalked away. If it hadn't been for the fact that she was sure it would kill her, she would have walked all the way into town in a huff.

The best plan seemed to be taking a nap. She headed back down towards the casita in which Sarah Embraces-All-Things had lived. Liz had mentioned that the Chain Gang had been spending time at Sarah's old place, but Alison was willing to bet that they were busy with the pyre.

Sure enough, the building was empty—so empty in fact, that it was a little creepy. Generally, Alison did not worry about things like ghosts or deathbeds. It was not so much that she was a rabid disbeliever in any other world as that it seemed one of those things just best not to think of—if there were ghosts there wasn't anything you could do one way or the other. Yet even she could not deny the heavy air of sadness? disappointment? that seemed to swirl out of the room that had been Sarah's. Perhaps petulance was the word— it was as if the peevish air of complaint and control with which Sarah Embraces-All-Things had surrounded herself in life had lingered behind her, souring like cabbage in the compost.

Or, perhaps what Alison felt was the genuine grieving of the three young women who had considered Sarah Embraces-All-Things their mentor. She stood in the doorway of her room curiously, looking for their traces. Much of the decoration had been removed—she assumed that the God's Eyes and dream catchers were now adorning the pyre. Her blankets and clothes were untouched—she did not know if the Chain Gang was planning on imitating the old customs of the Native American tribes who sent their dead to the afterlife with a packed suitcase, or the ones who allowed friends and relatives to pick from belongings no longer necessary.

There was a huge, round ball of crystal glass hanging in one of the windows. The window was open just enough for a tiny breeze, and the crystal was moving, spinning a rainbow across the shadowed walls of the room. It flashed a patch of red across Alison's face. She watched the colors travel around the room, landing on the bed, the bookshelves, the desk.

The desk. Alison went rigid, as if she had heard a frightening sound. The desk! Why hadn't she thought of that before? Sarah, from all she had heard, had enjoyed tormenting her victims. Perhaps she had kept little souvenirs for private gloating. Or, better yet, perhaps she had kept a journal! How could she have been so stupid? Still chastising herself, Alison moved across the room in a flash. She sat in the straight-backed chair and began opening the drawers. There was no need to be careful—Sarah was not going to come home and complain about her room being tossed.

But a quick search revealed nothing, not even the everyday

paperwork that followed most people around. No bills. No letters from home. No address book or library card. No birth certificate or college transcript or insurance papers or any of the things that filled a whole file at Alison's house.

She sat back in the chair with an exasperated sigh. It was pretty obvious that someone else had gone through the desk before her. Who? The Chain Gang, looking to cover up anything that might cause people to remember Sarah as anything less than a saint? Or had one of Sarah's victims wanted to make sure than her connection—her secret—was never discovered?

Alison leaned back in her chair, stretching her legs out before her. She was getting pretty tired of this unsolved mystery gig. She might as well take a nap—at least she'd feel better.

She noticed, to the right of the desk, a small corkboard with a notepad and pencil attached hanging on the wall. Pinned to it were some photographs and a child's drawing. The photos all had one thing in common—Sarah Embraces-All-Things. Sarah looking mystically at the clouds, seductively over her naked shoulder, standing in front of the ranch house with Persimmon and Hawk. Alison reached out to take one of the photos into her hand. As she did so her arm jerked the way it had been doing lately. She hit the bottom of the board, knocking it down to the floor.

"Damnit!" Crossly, Alison knelt on the floor. She was tempted to leave everything where it was, but it seemed a disrespect of the dead that went beyond the casual irreverence with which Liz and Stacy spoke. Somehow there were a great many more photos on the floor than had covered the board. Oh, okay, she saw now. Another handful had been pushed behind the notepad. She looked at each one as she stacked it on the desk. More Sarah pictures. Obviously she had picked out the very most flattering to display, but who could blame her there? Alison did the same thing herself. A couple of photos of other women. One of a dog. Two or three of various stages of the casita. Again, Alison was amazed at the way in which they had made the desert bloom.

Near the bottom of the stack was a photograph that did not seem to fit in with the others. It was the only group shot, and also the only photograph in which there were children. Alison gave it a cursory look, and then held it closer to study it. She picked up the photo of Sarah, Hawk and Gaya. That was weird. It had to be a coincidence, but it looked almost as if both pictures had been taken in front of the ranch house. She looked more closely at the children posing on the steps. Now that she was paying attention, she could see that the girl sitting in the front row was Persimmon—perhaps fourteen or fifteen years old. Couldn't mistake that birth mark. Oh, and there was Gaya, too. Boy, her hair had sure gotten a lot lighter. That was kind of odd—usually it was the other way around. Surrounding them was a gaggle of boys who had to be brothers, one with his arms around Persimmon's shoulder. In the background, by the door, was an older man she assumed to be their father. None of the apples in this family had fallen far from the tree—not only did all the kids look just alike, they all looked like him—same nose and cheekbones, even the same lanky build. You could see where Gaya got her height.

She flipped the photo over. On the back was written, "I'll call you when I get back from the Caribbean!" So why had Sarah Embraces-All-Things had a photograph of Persimmon's family?

"Did you find everything you needed?" A cold voice cut into Alison's musing. She jumped. Damnit, generally she would have had a trusty sidekick to watch the door. Unfortunately, they were all either tripping or lost in the land where this-time-it-was-all-going-to-be-different-and-last-forever. For a moment, she tensed, wondering if she was going to get hit on the head.

But the woman standing in the door did not seem threatening. She was one of the Chain Gang, the one with the shortest hair and the nose ring. An aura of despair seemed to hang over her, and she made no move to enter the room.

"No," Alison answered honestly. "I wanted to see if she had any personal papers. Anything that showed who she was blackmailing." She spoke bluntly deliberately—perhaps she could provoke the young woman to say in anger what she might otherwise guard. Which one of them was she—Jane, Katherine or Anne? And where were the other two?

The ruse failed. The young woman shrugged, as if it wasn't important. "We burnt everything," she said matter-of-factly. "Did you think we wouldn't? We thought that you'd be down here sooner or later. We did it that same night."

Which, thought Alison, got her off the hook for not being on top of things.

"So," she said slowly, working it out in her head, "then you must have known what she was doing. And it didn't matter to you?"

The girl walked across the room, reaching out her hand to touch the sweater thrown on Sarah's bed, the mirror hanging on the wall.

"I don't know that she was doing anything," she said, turning to face Alison. "But I knew that you thought she was. She was a sacred woman! Don't you understand that? That was all that mattered. Nothing else from the life that she had before. Everyone has a life before, everyone has done things that they're ashamed of! Why dig that up?"

"Don't you want to see the person who killed her punished?" asked Alison, falling back on her old standby. More than any other emotion in the world, she had found that human beings had a great capacity for revenge.

Jane/Anne—Alison was pretty sure that Katherine was the one who had been doing all the freaking out—shook her head. " Of course I don't! Not if it means digging up some dirty little secret from her past! Would I want that?" She paused, obviously searching for words. "What if you got shot?" she asked.

"Then I'd want my father to find out who it was and send them straight to the electric chair," Alison replied promptly. It was no secret that her capacity for revenge was even larger than that of the average citizen.

"Yeah, and if it was because you had done something bad? Something ugly? Like…" she struggled again, screwing up her face with the effort. Alison suddenly became aware of just how thin the veneer of civilization hung upon her—she had been through too much in the last several days.

"It doesn't matter," Alison interjected. She had no desire to drive this woman over the wall with philosophical discussion. "I'm just…"

"No!" Jane/Anne insisted. "What if you had been shot because you were running drugs or taking bribes? Or maybe just something that he could never understand. Then would you want your father to know? Would it make him feel better if he punished the killer, or would it make him feel better to believe it was just in the line of duty?"

Alison had not thought of this before, and the answer was no. She didn't, for example, want her father to go through her apartment and find all her leather toys. He wouldn't understand, and it would upset him. In fact, she had a deal with Michelle that in case anything happened to her she would clear out the apartment even before going to the hospital.

The girl must have read her face. "No," she said. "You wouldn't. So why fuck with her memory? You know," she said, moving restlessly around the room, "I had a friend who was in the military. A captain. And she told me that whenever there was an accident, they would go through the enlisted man's things before sending them home. They didn't want his wife or family to find out from his private things that he had a girlfriend on the side, or anything like that. It's the only decent thing that I've ever heard of the military doing." She turned away from Alison, who swiftly thrust the photo into the waistband of her jeans.

"You're not doing this for her," said the girl, turning back to face Alison. "You're not doing this for her, or her memory, or for anybody here. Don't fool yourself. You're not fooling any of us." She stepped over to the window and set the crystal twirling again. "Did you know," she said, "that Gaya spent the last of her money on this retreat? If you fuck it up, you fuck everything up. They've got to bring in some more women—they can't keep doing all this work themselves. Especially with Gaya being sick."

"What do you mean, sick?" asked Alison.

The girl gave her a pitying look, obviously wondering just how someone as stupid as she could manage to walk around alone.

"She has cancer," she said. "Haven't you noticed? She and Persimmon grew up in Los Alamos—don't you read at all? It's like a ghost town there now and hundreds of people, not just the men who worked on the bombs, but their wives and children, have cancer now. Why do you think she wears a bandanna all the time? She was doing chemotherapy before Sarah Embraces-All-Things started to work with her. You didn't think it was *her*, did you?" She threw back her head and laughed. "Sarah Embraces-All-Things was *healing* her—she's been in remission ever since she started her juicing and doing energy work! She's the last person in the world who'd want her dead!"

"Excuse me," said Alison, "I'm going to take a nap." There was no point in standing here and talking to this woman—they were on such separate sides of the fence that she might as well have been speaking in a different language.

But Jane/Anne was not quite finished. "She knew that she had done things that were wrong in the past," she said. "And she was making amends. She was totally dedicated to the idea of lesbian only land. She knew she might have to make some sacrifices, she might make some people mad, but she was determined to see that happen here." With this, she swung around, passing so close to Alison on her way out that they touched sleeves, and slammed the door shut behind her.

CHAPTER ELEVEN

It was late in the afternoon when Alison woke. She wished she had brought a can of Diet Pepsi down with her—she felt groggy and disoriented. Since she was trespassing anyway, she jumped into Sarah's shower, using both her nice soap and one of her big, fluffy towels to dry off.

She hesitated on the path outside. She really did not want to go up to the main house She had become a pariah there—the woman determined to besmirch the name of Sarah Embraces-All-Things who was, at least to part of the population, becoming an icon. She wasn't in the mood for Stacy and Liz being silly, either, but at least they had food, and they had probably come down by now.

Half way down the path to the main gate she saw Michelle coming up the road.

"I want to get out of here as soon as they burn that woman," Alison said to her bluntly, the moment they were within earshot. "I'll bet we can get all the help we need to move those rocks then. They'll be glad to have us out of here."

"Alison," Michelle said, and then stopped, as if whatever she was going to say was just too much to put into words. It was not a good sign. "Alison," she began again.

"Yeah, yeah," said Alison, hoping to jolt her out of her spiritual cloud by rudeness. "We've heard that part. Let's just get on with it. Now, are you coming or not?" Immediately, she wished that she had not put it that way, reminding Michelle that there was a choice, but it was too late to take the words back.

"Alison," Michelle said again. "Old friend."

Oh, my god, thought Alison, she's been brainwashed. Michelle had never called her 'old friend', particularly in that Hallmark tone, once in the twenty years they had known one another. She opened her mouth in an attempt to cut off whatever was coming, but Michelle was quicker on the draw.

"I've begun to believe that everything happens for a reason," she said. "Don't you?" This question must have been purely rhetorical, because she did not pause as much as a breath for an answer. "I realize that I've been fighting being here, when what I needed to do was accept that I'm here for a reason, and just let myself *be* here."

I haven't noticed you fighting being here," said Alison rudely. "What I've mainly noticed is you falling immediately into bed with a stranger."

Michelle smiled a placid little Mona Lisa smile, which scared Alison much more than a screaming rage would have. "I fought that at first," she said. "Then I realized maybe that was part of the lesson I was meant to learn while I was down here. And I was right—when I accepted the unconditional love that Persimmon had to give me, then a whole universe of options opened up in front of me."

"Are you telling me that the universe told you to cheat on your girlfriend?" asked Alison. She resisted an urge to just smack Michelle on the side of her head and then drag her back to Stacy's camp by her hair.

Michelle looked momentarily irritated, but she caught herself and resumed her earth mother placidity. "We don't know everything about the way the universe unfolds, Alison." There was a gentle chiding tone to her voice, as if she were speaking to a child who had been asked several times to pay attention. "All I know is that I found myself here—a place I'd never been before, with women I had never met before—at a time when I needed to make some major decisions in my life. At a point when my dreams were in danger of dying."

This was just too much. Alison took Michelle by the shoulders and stooped to look directly into her face.

"Michelle," she said slowly, not so much because she thought slow speech would stick better in Michelle's rapidly emptying mind, but in order to keep herself from screaming. "Sam has colic. That is all it is. Babies get colic. They grow out of it. You are all worked up on endorphins from fucking and getting a full night's sleep. It is making you behave like an idiot." She had meant to soften that last sentence, but there just wasn't really another way to put it. It didn't matter—nothing Alison was saying was penetrating Michelle's placidity. Persimmon must have tied her tail in an absolute knot, thought Alison with a sudden flash of anger. Fine, if she couldn't get through to Michelle, then she was going to make sure that Persimmon knew exactly what she was fucking with. She tried again. "You just bought a house. I cannot make the payment by myself. When we bought it we agreed that we'd both live in it for at least five years. You have a new baby, and he would not be welcomed here. Don't tell me that you're thinking of staying here. It's just the sex, Michelle, that's all it is. And don't try to tell me you're not doing it—I'll bet you've been lying the whole time."

Michelle shook her head with a gesture that reminded Alison of Hawk the night Sarah Embraces-All-Things had died. There were three decades of stubbornness behind it—she was as unchangeable as the road on which they had crossed the desert.

"You're just not opening yourself to this experience, Alison," she said, in a voice so washed of emotion that it sounded computer-generated. "I wasn't either, at first. But I've realized now how foolish that is. I'm on the edge of an experiment that could shake the lives of hundreds of people—what am I doing fighting against it instead of embracing it? We came in here with a destructive attitude—I've given that up."

"You are insane," said Alison. "You have been brainwashed. Remember when you were a Jesus Freak? You might as well go join EST or Lifestream. You're thinking with your cunt instead of your head. You're going to wake up from this and look and feel like a fool." She had pulled all the plugs—there was no holding back. She could not reach Michelle unless she fired both barrels, and even then it might be too late.

Michelle shook her head as if she were amused. "Persimmon said that you would probably be threatened," she said. "You don't need to be. We'll still be friends. I'll still love you, no matter where the universe takes me."

"The universe is going to take you right back to *your* house in *your* truck," said Alison. She did not add kicking and screaming if that's the way it has to be, but the thought was right in the front of her mind. All right, ultimately she could not stop Michelle from making some mighty bad choices, but she would be damned if she would carry the news back to Janka alone. Michelle was going to have to do her own dirty work, even if she had to stuff her into a sack and sit on her the whole way home.

"How in the world could you stay here, Michelle?" She tried a different tack. "Do you want to live forty miles from the nearest neighbors—probably a hundred miles from the nearest dykes and have every single thing in your life dictated to you by a set of rules you didn't help make? No coffee? No sugar? Sammy won't be allowed to visit." She was hoping if she hammered this home enough it would turn out to be a weak spot, "and you'll have to get rid of that dog." She pointed to Zorra, who obliged by looking particularly cute with a stick.

Again, a quick flash of discomfort passed over Michelle's face. Ah-ha, thought Alison, she's not really lost to us yet. She could still be reprogrammed. She opened her mouth to go in for the kill, but again Michelle beat her to the draw.

"Can't you just be happy for me?" she asked in a voice that was rapidly becoming much less Zen and much more Michelle.

"No! No, I can't, not if it looks like you're doing this just to run away from something! If you had researched this and thought about this and made some plans about what to do about your house"—she hated to keep harping on the house, but she was going to be screwed if Michelle abandoned the patriarchy—"and your wife and your son, then maybe I could be happy for you. I would miss you to death, but if it was an honorable decision, I would try to be happy for you. But this isn't honorable! This is you trying to run away, and wanting me to deal with Janka for you on top of it! 'Oh, hi Janka, yeah, we had a good time and incidentally somebody was killed and Michelle decided that she wanted to stay with the killers. She wants you to send her stuff, 'kay? Is there anything for dinner?' All you're doing is being a coward, Michelle! You think if you don't come back then Janka will get in a tizzy and go home to her mother and you just won't have to deal with her." This last had been a shot in the dark, but it was easy to tell from Michelle's face that she had scored a bull's-eye. "Oh, Michelle," she said, "that is so slimy. Three years with the woman and you want me to tell her that it's over and you're moving to the Wanderground."

"I'm not moving!" snapped Michelle, all serenity out the window. "All I want to do is stay for the retreat! What's wrong with that? What? What's wrong with me wanting to have a dream again?"

There wasn't, in fact, anything at all wrong with wanting to have a dream again, so Alison set her face and looked up the hill towards the big house. She wished she had a cigarette. Michelle set *her* face and began taking deep breaths to calm herself.

"Well," she said finally, in voice that was probably not nearly as placid as she imagined. "I didn't want to fight with you. I just wanted to tell you what I've decided." She managed to make it sound as if *she* was being reasonable and *Alison* was being, at the very least, a controlling asshole. "You don't have to do anything. What I decide to do has nothing at all to do with you. It's about me, not about you. All I'm asking you to do is to respect my decision— and be happy for me if you can."

Alison said nothing. Everything had been said.

"Come on Alison," Michelle coaxed, her voice slipping back into the mode of earth goddess. "Open yourself to this experience! Open yourself to just being here!"

"I believe our experience here has been a little bit different," said Alison stiffly. "I imagine that it's much nicer having a cosmic affair than it is having someone try to kill you."

Michelle gave a huge sigh. "This could be the experience of a lifetime. When I realized that, instead of fighting it, trying to open myself up to it…"

"Enough," Alison broke in rudely. "I cannot bear this any more. I just can't." She held her hand up in front of her face, her palm facing outward as if she were directing traffic. "Do whatever you want. I can't stop you."

"Oh, that's such a good start! I mean, for you to let go of controlling!" Michelle grasped Alison's other hand warmly. This must be coming from the same place from which 'Old friend' popped up. She was becoming one of them. Soon all that would be left was her husk—her caustic wit would have been drained out into the desert wind. "I do appreciate your honesty…"

Alison jerked her hand away, absolutely furious.

"…I want to be honest with you, too. I've really decided to open myself up to this—I can't get the full benefit if I'm fighting it. I want to embrace it, and that means letting go in the same way that everyone else has let go."

Perhaps if Alison had been actively listening rather than trying to shut the words out of her head, she would have known what was coming. Instead, she stood with her mouth open as she watched Michelle lob her keys up onto the roof of the unfinished casita.

"You just gave up your keys," she said, as if only by giving voice to what she had seen would it become reality. "You just threw your keys up on the fucking roof! How are we supposed to get out of this hell hole now?! How are we supposed to get this body into town?" It did not matter to her that Liz had already taken the other keys down, something which Michelle obviously did not know. It was the whole gesture of it—committing not only herself but Alison to this project.

"Let go of that," Michelle urged, as if she were calling sinners down to the rail. "Let go! You don't need to control it! The universe will take care of it! Just let it! That's why…."she hesitated a moment and then said it all in a rush, "I've unlocked the walk-in. The universe will take care of that…"

"Michelle," said Alison in a carefully controlled voice that belied the rage in her eyes, "I haven't hit you since we were twelve years old. But I am going to beat you to death and take your body home in a sack."

"Don't do this!" said Michelle. She was trying to maintain the untroubled voice and air, but that was difficult while backing up almost at a run. "You'll be sorry later! Open yourself up to the goddess!"

"I am going to open *your head* up to the goddess," said Alison between her teeth. "I am going to kill you and throw you right into the fire with Sarah Embraces-All-Things. And I am going to tell everyone that you were really a transsexual!" Alison knew Michelle's deepest prejudices and knew this of all threats was bound to offend the very most.

Sure enough, Michelle, got a horrified look in her eyes. "I'm too short to be a transsexual!" she squeaked. She glanced quickly over her shoulder, measuring the distance to the big house.

"Napoleon was short. Hitler was short. Danny DeVito is short. Believe me, I will convince everyone. I will go national. I will be on dyke tv! Even Janka will believe it! I'll start a support group for women who have been taken in by you! They won't even let your bones be buried here, and I'll give them to your mother! And don't think you can run—I will hunt you down like a mad dog!"

Michelle took this as a signal to sprint up the hill. Alison followed close behind. She was not usually a violent woman, and she didn't really want to kill Michelle. She did, however, want to sit on her and bang her head into the ground a couple of times, and she felt completely justified.

"Violence against women! Violence against women!" Michelle wailed at the top of her voice, hoping to flush out an ally. This was her downfall. The effort of taking two extra breaths slowed her enough so that Alison was able to catch her by the back of her shirt. She twisted her collar into a knot and held her at arm's length as if she were a wet cat.

"Alison! Stop it! What are you doing?"

Alison cut her eyes to the side for the barest second. She had not heard Stacy and Liz approaching, and they were bound to interfere.

"Get away from me," Alison said in a voice that even she didn't recognize. "This is none of your business, and it's going to be ugly."

Michelle took advantage of Alison's distraction by swinging back with one foot, landed a hard blow square in the middle of her right knee. They both went over. Alison hit the ground with a bone jarring blow that was going to hurt later, but it barely slowed her. She was too angry to feel pain. Michelle, still intent on escaping with her life, was up in a flash, but Alison reached up and caught the leg of her jeans. She tried using her superior size to pull her back down, but Michelle planted a hard kick right in Alison's rib cage. It knocked the wind out of her, but she hung on stubbornly even as she was gasping for air.

"Stop it! Stop it right now!" Far away, as if from another dimension, Alison was aware of Stacy's voice. With a huge effort Alison pulled herself up Michelle's leg and got a hand on the waistband of her jeans. She was going to take her back to Denver even if it had to be in a jar and no one but no one was going to stop her.

"Stop it now!" Stacy had a double handful of her hair and was pulling her head back as far as it would go, maybe farther than it was *meant* to go. "Get her out of here!" That was probably shouted at Liz although by then the whole camp could have been there, and Alison still wouldn't have known.

There was another good kick in the shoulder, then someone grabbed her thumb and pulled it back until she was forced to let go of Michelle's waistband. Stacy gave her a huge slam between her shoulder blades, and suddenly she was face down in the dirt.

"Stop it!" said Stacy again from where she was sitting on her back. Alison tried feebly to roll free, but Liz planted herself on her legs.

"I'm going to kill her!" Alison hissed, pulling in a mouthful of sand for all her passion.

"You're just being selfish," said Liz, a disembodied voice above her. "Everyone wants to kill Michelle Martin. The thought of killing her myself is one of the things that's kept me alive this weekend."

Alison heard the scratch of a lighter, and a moment later Stacy was leaning over her and blowing dope into her face.

"I'll be drug tested! I'll be kicked off the force!" Alison tried to turn her head, but Stacy was leaning on her shoulder now, and she couldn't move.

"I don't care! You are going to have a heart attack if you don't calm down! Now just breathe in!" She put her mouth right over Alison's nose and blew in a huge shot of smoke that sent her into a coughing frenzy. Now that Stacy mentioned it, she *could* feel her heart pounding like a hummingbird's, and her whole head felt as if it had swollen up to at least twice its normal size. Stacy hit her directly with another mouthful of smoke, and she gave up, breathing it in as if it were penance.

"I'm fine now," she said, in what she hoped was a repentant tone. "You can let me up—I'm over it." She glanced around her limited field of vision—maybe Michelle was still within reach.

Stacy was neither fooled nor amused. "You *are* fine," she answered. "You're fine just where you are. You're not getting up until we've smoked this joint—and I might make you have a cigarette on top of it."

Alison went limp in submission. Michelle had already made

her escape anyway. Sooner or later she'd catch her alone. Stacy, who read submission pretty darn well, held the joint up to her lips this time, and Alison took a deep hit. She thought that she might be starting to feel high already, but it was hard to tell with Stacy crushing all but the most vital air out of her lungs.

Finally, the joint was finished and all three of them got up. Stacy and Liz brushed off a little dust, but Alison was still too angry to care.

"You know what you've done?" asked Stacy, who was lighting two cigarettes at once. "You have just destroyed any credibility that you had with these women."

Alison took the offered cigarette and looked up at the main house, her mouth set in a pout. She didn't want to talk about it.

"What in the world did Michelle do to put your tail in that kind of twist?" asked Stacy. She picked up her towel and shook it out. Belatedly, Alison realized that she had been on her way to the showers. It was just a cruel joke of the universe that she had strolled by in time to save Michelle's life.

In a tightly controlled voice barely above a whisper—she still didn't trust herself to really let loose—Alison related the story of Michelle and the keys.

"Don't you find this rather odd behavior for Michelle?" asked Stacy as she flicked the ashes of her cigarette. They had both broken so many rules already that nobody was worried about getting busted. "I always thought she was on such an even keel. Do you think she might have a brain tumor?"

"Ha!" said Alison, short and bitter. She took such a heavy hit that she sent herself into a coughing spasm. "You just don't know her the way I know her. First she was a Jesus freak. Then she did Lifestream for a while. Then she was a lesbian separatist—she goes cult every single time it looks like there's going to be a major change in her life. If we leave here without her, Janka and the baby will never see her again."

"Oh, don't worry," Stacy comforted, following the cigarette with another joint. No pretense here—she was sedating Alison as if she planned to tag her and move her farther up into the mountains away from the garbage cans. "We'll make sure Michelle gets back home. We'll just throw a bag over her head and kidnap her if we have to. And if it will make you feel any better, we'll let you beat her to a pulp while we're at it. But not in front of everybody else."

Alison, who thought that it *would* make her feel better, nodded her head, somewhat mollified. Liz, lured back by the dope, edged back down the road, eyeing Alison warily. Alison thought about making a quick move towards her just to watch her jump.

"And do you know *what else* she did?" she asked. She had suddenly realized just how very badly she had acted and she wanted, if nothing else, to make sure that her side of the story was heavily circulated. "She *unlocked the body*!"

There was a long silence. Liz and Stacy did not, as Alison had hoped, immediately echo her indignation. Alison tried to work herself up into a good Nobody-understands-me-and-I-am-*right* mode, but being high made it hard.

Stacy spoke first. "I am going to tell you what is going to happen now," she said in a firm voice. "No," she held up her hand. "Don't even go there. I don't care about your morals and I don't care about your obligations and I don't care what you're going to do after you leave this place and I don't care if this murderer is ever caught. I don't care! You have been acting just like a runaway train—you've been plowing through everything in your path and acting like there is no possibility of derailment. And you are stopping right now— even if we have to take you back to camp and hog-tie you. You are not putting yourself in any more danger! You're acting like a crazy person! This investigation is over! It was an accident! I don't care if you believe it, and I don't care if anybody else believes it, but from now on you are going to pretend to believe it! Michelle unlocking that body was the best thing that could have happened! The body is going to be burnt to cinders by tonight—do you get that? You don't have any more proof, and maybe that, and sticking together is going to keep us from ending up with two bodies!"

Alison tried to speak, but again Stacy cut her off. "No! Don't go there! Don't go anywhere but back down to the Fun Camp! It is over! You are done! You are not Jane Lawless, and you are not Kinsey Milhone—as you have pointed out to me so many times you are a real woman who can really get hurt! Stop it! It's not going to happen!"

Alison tried to speak again, but Stacy was on a roll. "No!" she shouted. "Now, you can come down to the showers with me, or you can go back to our camp with Liz, but you are not going anywhere else! And you're not going to tell anyone else Sarah was murdered and that you're going to haul the cops out here once you get back to town! If anybody asks you're going to tell them that you got hit on the head and don't remember the last seventy-two hours! I mean it! And you are not going near Michelle unless you want to apologize or I need you to hold the bag!" Stacy stood with one hand on her hip, shaking her back brush at Alison with the other. Stacy did have the tendency to go off on a tear now and then, particularly before her period, but this was really a good one. Watching it was kind of like watching Martina on a fine day. What form! What skill! Alison decided to ignore the fact that she was being scolded and just watch Stacy's eyes flash with their dark fire. It made it easier for everyone.

Stacy was not fooled. "Now, I mean this," she said. She had exactly the same tone in her voice that Alison's mother used to get when they really *had* pushed her to the limit.

"Do I have to bark like a dog now to show I understand?" Alison asked in a sullen voice, just to show Stacy that her spirit had not been completely broken. In reality, what she felt was huge relief. She had done everything that she could have done. She had fought the good fight, and it was out of her hands now. She wasn't going to admit to this, of course. Somehow, she felt her honor would be sullied if she did not at least give the impression that she had been thwarted against her will.

"You save that," snapped Stacy, again shaking the brush. "Right now I am just as mad at you as you are at Michelle. This has not been any fun for the rest of us either, you know, and worrying about what stupid thing you're going to do next has been just about the last straw."

Alison was sorry that she had tuned in for this last bit. Oh, well, she would swallow it. Stacy was right. If she let the murder go they should be able to ride out the rest of the storm in comparative peace. Lawrence should be coming soon. There was no sense spoiling it with a quarrel.

Alison tried very hard to look humble. "I want to come with you to the showers," she said, trying to suck up a little.

Stacy wasn't buying it. "*Everyone* wants to come with me to the showers. There are women standing in line to come with me to the showers. So you had just better watch your step and count your blessings and maybe I'll let you hold my towel!" Mistress Anastasia tended to surface when Stacy was on a tear.

Mistress Anastasia was good, although Alison had a tendency to go right into submissive, fuck-me gear whenever she heard her voice. If she had been a sheep dog she could have won the nationals—she trained easily. She crossed her arms and looked out over the desert. The clouds looked different than they had before. Was it possible a storm was brewing?

"Oops!" said Stacy behind her. She was looking back towards the house. "Quick, let's make tracks!" She grabbed Alison's elbow.

"Too late," said Liz in a resigned voice.

"Well, at least guard my back," said Stacy. "Don't let them attack me from behind."

CHAPTER TWELVE

Alison looked up the hill and bit back a groan. Down the hill were marching Hawk, Gaya, Persimmon and Sandpaper. Hadn't she been punished enough? She felt as if she had spent the weekend in various rings of hell—every time she had started to get used to the ambiance a new twist had been added. It was bad enough that she had acted so badly with Michelle, but now she was going to be confronted over it. As if she needed to be told!

"You have to leave," said Hawk bluntly from twelve feet away. "You have to leave *right now*!" She repeated herself as she got closer, as if what was said at ten feet might be understood better at two. "We *will not have* any violence against women on *our land*! We won't have it! You have to leave *right now*!"

Stacy lit another cigarette—what was the harm in it now?—and Liz picked at the dirt beneath her thumb nail. Neither said a word. This was so unlike them that, in a vague and crabby way, Alison realized they were embarrassed about what she had done, and at a loss for words to defend it. It made her feel persecuted and angry. Perhaps she was not entirely justified in attempting to beat Michelle up, but who were these women to judge her? They had known Michelle for a few days—she had known her for twenty years—and she was only going to rough her up a little.

"Fine," she answered, just as angry as if she had been the one wronged. She felt as if she had been. "We *want* to leave right now. You go down there and clear those rocks away from that gate. And then see if you can figure out how to get those fucking keys off the fucking roof where that fucking Michelle threw them." It was a situation that called for a lot of profanity. Up the hill, on the porch, she could see Michelle, anxious and upset from her body language, peering down at them. Alison felt a sudden flash of remorse. Making up with Michelle one on one would not have been a problem. There would have been a little sulking and pouting on both sides; a few apologies and perhaps an acknowledgment of temporary insanity and then it would have been over. It wasn't as if it was the first time she had tried to kill Michelle, and the tables had been turned a number of times as well. Michelle in berserker mode was frightening—she seemed to shoot up about two feet and gain fifty pounds, all of it pure anger. The balance had been kept pretty even over the years.

But Alison did not know if they would ever be able to make up in this atmosphere. Already they had pulled half a dozen women into the quarrel—Michelle had never *tattled* on her before, at least not after she had gotten old enough to stop running to Alison's dad. Was this to be the final and inner ring of hell—Michelle would stay here and they would never see or speak to one another again, except in cold letters fired through their lawyers about the house?

Persimmon interrupted her thoughts. "Alison," she said, her voice more concerned than angry, "are you even aware what's happened? For you to be using violence against your best friend…"

"Open the gate and get the keys and we'll get out of here," interrupted Alison. She was not about to be scolded by anyone. Maybe Stacy, if there was a promise of sex later. But not any of these self-righteous bitches who had stood in her way and then condemned her for being male-identified. "And she has a wife and a kid at home," she could not resist adding. "If she stays here, you're breaking up a good relationship and taking her away from her baby. Don't you judge me when you're doing that with your eyes wide open."

There was a little murmur among the ranks.

"Michelle is a grown woman," said Persimmon, trying to sound complacent, but succeeding only in sounding defensive. "She makes her own choices, and they have nothing to do with…"

Hawk cut it. "We're not talking about that," she snapped. "We're talking about you leaving. You, and your girlfriend and her…" she looked at Liz, apparently at a loss to think of a description that fully expressed her loathing.

"Love slave," suggested Liz who couldn't bear to be out of the thick of things for long.

"All of you, out!" Hawk was actually trembling with emotion, and suddenly Alison felt sorry for her. She had planned a nice little retreat, and what had happened? Somebody had been killed and riff-raff had infiltrated the camp as well. Alison had thrown a couple of bad parties herself—she could sympathize.

But there was really no way that she could say anything but what she did say. "Move the rocks and get the keys off the roof. We want to leave."

Gaya broke in, almost wailing. "I wanted so much to get away from male energy," she moaned. "It's like a curse! It just follows me!" She seemed about to burst into tears. Alison didn't want to see that. She hated to see anyone as big as Gaya cry. She knew this was a dreadful prejudice, but she couldn't seem to get over it. She just couldn't imagine comforting anyone that size and what was the point of tears if no comfort could be given?

"Move the rocks and get the keys," she repeated, since Stacy and Liz obviously weren't going to be any help on this one. She could not apologize to Gaya for the disruption of her dreams anymore than she had been able to empathize with Hawk. All she could do was try to get out of everyone's face as soon as possible.

"You must have a spare set of keys," snapped Hawk. "You sure as hell didn't commit in any other way! Why would you give up your keys if you can't even give up caffeine!"

"Why would I torture myself like this if I had the keys?" asked Alison in a weary tone that was really only three steps below berserker, and only that because of the large amount of nicotine and pot she had consumed. She hoped they could get this over soon, because otherwise she was going to blow again, and the first tantrum had exhausted her. All she wanted to do was sleep, and if these dreadful women would just leave her alone she could.

"I'm going to write about this!" shrilled Sandpaper. What the hell was she doing here? Alison supposed they had just brought her along as a weapon—she seemed like the kind of woman whose constant anger made it possible to use her like a torpedo—just point her in the right direction and let her rip. Michelle could sometimes be used in that way as well, thought Alison with a little pang. Would she ever again get to watch Michelle send back food in a restaurant?

There was a clatter of stones and sand above them on the road. Everyone looked. Michelle, Seven Yellow Moons and Zorra were approaching. Michelle was looking small and passive. She had her arms crossed in front of her chest, her hands stuck in her arm pits and her head was ducked. She looked as if she was afraid of getting hit. Alison's blood immediately shot up to full boil. Goddamn her— that was an act and she knew it! What about the time that Michelle had lost her temper and nailed her with a pork chop thrown from twenty feet? What about the time Alison had gone home with Michelle's ex (yes, yes, she knew she had acted badly) and Michelle had stalked them and waited in the yard and drenched them both with the hose on their way to work at six in the freezing morning? She had lost a day's work and a good pair of leather shoes over that. What about all the nasty comments to Stacy? The point was, Michelle was not without blame. Alison had done a hell of a lot of good things for her over the years—everything from bailing her out of jail after the King Day riots to lending her money to lying to her mother about where she could be found. The attack was an isolated and completely provoked incident.

"Hey!" said Seven, holding her hands out in a manner not unlike the gestures the Pope had made when he had blessed the crowd. "We're doing this wrong. We're losing track of the whole idea."

Everyone looked blank. What *was* the whole idea?

"Women living together," said Seven. "Remember that? A whole new way of communicating? Creating a different type of society."

"I...they..." Hawk was still so angry that she couldn't even choke the words out.

"Well, yeah," said Seven. "But there's going to be people acting badly wherever you are." She looked past Stacy and Liz with a kind of muted zeal as if, really, they were but a fly in the ointment to whom she had hardly even been introduced. Alison suspected that Hawk and Gaya didn't know that she had been down to the Fun Girls' camp even once, let alone that she stayed at Alison's house several times a year. Seven was really quite a good actress.

"Really," Seven persisted. "The three of you," she pointed to Hawk, Gaya and Persimmon, "are not going to make this happen without experiencing conflict. It happens with everybody. It happens in every dream. It's not conflict that's bad, it's the way that you deal with it. If you throw them out like this, what's that going to be but doing the same thing men have been doing for years? Those with the power oppressing those without the power. Maybe you've got food, or money, or you're camped at the well or you're just plain bigger, and so you use that power because it's easy and working things out is hard."

There was an uncomfortable silence among the four women. With a flash of insight, Alison realized that it was possible for Seven to manipulate Hawk—and she was sure the point of this was manipulation—in a way that she herself could not be manipulated, because Hawk, for all her dreadful social skills, did have a dream, did have a commitment to change.

"I can't," said Gaya, her voice heavy with weariness. "I can't bear to have these women stay here. I'm not saying they're bad people—I'm not going to make judgments. But we are just not working towards the same goal. If I wanted to be a part of this kind of conflict and violence I wouldn't have put all my money into this." She made a sweeping motion with her arm that encompassed the main house, the casitas, the garden, the windmill, everything. It was the first time Alison had heard her mention money. She must not do it often, because everyone looked a bit surprised. Alison couldn't help thinking that Gaya was really much nicer about being the main financier than she herself could have been. If *she'd* been the one with the big bucks, everybody would have heard about it every time there was a disagreement. She wouldn't even get a joint checking account with a girlfriend.

"They don't have to stay," said Seven soothingly.

"We don't *want* to stay," put in Alison.

Seven ignored her. "They don't have to stay," she repeated. Stacy gave Alison a pinch as she opened her mouth to repeat herself. Alison shut her mouth with a pop. Now that she had been made aware of it, she suddenly realized that there was a different air surrounding Stacy and Liz, as if they were in on whatever Seven was trying to do. "But wouldn't it be better—for all of us!—if they left on better terms than this?"

Everyone looked at everyone else. It would, thought Alison, be nice if they could leave on somewhat civil terms. In spite of the horrible tone of the weekend, she respected these women for having a dream and working towards it. She could blow it off if they hated her, but she didn't really *want* that.

"I agree with Seven," said Stacy quickly. Her voice was demure, and only another quick pinch kept Alison from turning and staring. Stacy and Liz were always being thrown out of workshops and movies and sometimes even hotels for behaving badly. They referred to themselves sometimes as the Bad Influences, as if they were a rock group. Why would Stacy care about being thrown off women's land?

"Country dykes need city dykes," said Seven, as if she had been reading Alison's mind. "And city dykes need country dykes. We all need each other. Lesbians are like a huge, interdependent bio-system. The elephant really does need the fish." She did not look at Alison when she said this, which was just as well, because she puffed up with indignation like a blow fish. Damnit, that was her line and Seven knew it!

"I don't want to end it this way," said Michelle. It was her first input, and everyone turned to stare. She spoke quietly—not like Michelle at all—and her head was still bowed. This time, Alison realized, she was not putting on a facade to elicit sympathy. She really didn't want to look at Alison, but equally she did not want to look at Persimmon. "I want to stay here for the rest of the retreat, but I need to have some closure."

Another long pause, with everyone trying to make nonverbal

contact with their own allies. Michelle, obviously, was a catch for the Mariposa women. She was a hard, capable worker, and she shared a lot of their politics. More important, Alison thought, was that keeping her here at Mariposa would mean that she was not going home with Alison and the Bad Influences. Michelle was like the one lamb of the Lord, whom the shepherd went back to seek when the others were all safe in the fold, although the Mariposa women would hate the analogy. Michelle, too, was the wronged party here. She could ask for things the others could not.

"What kind of closure?" asked Gaya. Out of the four of them, she seemed the one who was truly feeling more distress than anger. It made sense that she would want to seek an amiable parting, rather than just a confrontation.

"Let's do a healing," said Seven. She sounded to Alison like a used car salesman who had gotten a heavy dose of religion—Jesus would smile if you bought this car!—but no one else seemed to notice this. "I've done this before, and everyone has always felt better afterwards. We'll have it down in the sweat lodge tonight, after it gets dark." She spoke as if it were already a done deal, but Alison could see that Hawk and Sandpaper, at least, were going to need a little more persuasion.

"I think that this is too important for apologies," said Hawk. That's okay, thought Alison, you're not going to get any. If she ever had anything to say to Michelle, it wasn't going to be any of Hawk's business. However, Stacy's pinches made her keep her mouth shut.

"Our goals have not been shown any respect at all," Hawk continued. "These women have made fun of them, and sabotaged them and then attacked another woman. I don't see how that can be healed." She looked over at Alison with a vengeful eye. Hawk, for one, obviously thought that the best solution would require some kind of torture.

"They don't have to stay," said Seven. She must have taken a negotiation class. "But wouldn't it be great if we could part with better energy between us?"

Again, everyone looked at everyone else. Better energy sounded good to everyone. It even sounded good to Alison who, to her supreme frustration, could not catch the eye of any of the women she assumed to be her allies. Stacy and Liz were either giving the Mariposa women sympathetic, really-sorry-it-turned-out-this-way looks or gazing across the desert as if seeing a vision. Michelle, of course, kept her head down.

"I don't see how *these women*,"—my, it sounded nasty when Sandpaper said it!—"are going to have any respect at a healing when they haven't had any respect at anything else." She glared at Alison and Stacy who respectively returned a bland look (Stacy was pinching again) and a doe-eyed, misunderstood glance.

"They don't have to stay," said Seven. "But wouldn't it be great if we could just take all this bad energy between us and send it off the land?"

By UPS, Alison thought, but did not say.

There was a bit more fencing, and Seven Yellow Moons repeated several more variations of her one line. Finally, between Gaya's anxiety, Michelle's request, Stacy and Liz's sudden placidity and Seven's gentle, relentless pressure, a healing ritual was agreed upon by all parties. They all, polled like a jury, agreed to meet at the sweat lodge an hour after the sun went down. Towels, and warm clothes for afterwards, were required.

CHAPTER THIRTEEN

The Denver gals spent the evening down at the Fun Camp, Stacy cooking some kind of marvelous rice and vegetable dish with a side of cornbread in the dutch oven.

"How come you'll cook over a campfire but you won't cook at home?" asked Alison idly as she sat, stuffed, beside the fire.

"Hmm?" Stacy was a little distracted—she seemed to have her mind on something else. Alison repeated the question.

"Oh." Stacy squatted back on her heels beside the dutch oven, considering this seriously. "The Girl Scouts," she said. "I mean, I could tell right away when I was a kid that this cooking thing was for the birds. My mom and grandma were at the stove night and day—they cooked and they cleaned up and my dad and my grand-dad and my brother ate and then went in to watch tv without saying thank you. Wasn't anything I was interested in."

"I stopped going to my grandmother's for Thanksgiving for the very same reason," put in Liz. "It was like I had these two options— clean the kitchen while my uncles and cousins sat around, or watch my seventy-year-old grandmother clean the kitchen by herself— and neither one of them was good."

"Yeah." Stacy nodded. She pulled a scrap of cornbread out of the dutch oven and ate it with her fingers. "I did it for my husband when I was married—it was expected—and after I left him it was one of the many things I vowed *never* to do again."

"What else?" asked Alison, looking at the sky. Again she wondered if it was going to rain.

"Well, never to let somebody fuck me when I didn't want to just because he thought it was his right. That was a big one. Never to cook when I didn't want to. Never to be afraid of dressing the way I felt like dressing because of someone else's reaction. Basically I vowed to be as selfish towards myself as most men are."

"So how come you'll cook over a campfire?" Alison repeated. She was not really concentrating on the answer—she was thinking about the healing ritual. She had not been able to shake her conviction that Seven Yellow Moons had cooked up something with Stacy and Liz while she was sleeping, but great innocence had been expressed when she suggested it.

"Girl Scout camp was a different world," said Stacy, still occupied with the corn bread. "Women ran it. That was the best part—no matter what happened, no matter how hard or what kind of crisis, women handled it. Nineteen year old girls, actually, when I look back. They seemed a lot older then. I felt totally empowered by everything I learned to do. Building a fire was empowering. Building a shelter was empowering. Carrying a backpack was empowering. Cooking over a fire was empowering. It was all about taking care of myself, not taking care of a man."

"We better go," said Alison, an eye still on the clouds. Actually, they probably had another good fifteen or twenty minutes, but she knew how Stacy was.

Sure enough, Stacy needed to change her pants and fix her hair and find her jacket. The result of all this fussing was a bland, generic look—no jewelry, hair in two braids—that made Alison wonder for a moment if she was getting ill. Then she realized that Stacy was simply dressing to fit in—showing her commitment to the healing ceremony.

As they walked together across the desert they could see other women coming from the main house and the tent village. They could see the funeral pyre, down on the edge of the arroyo that, farther up the hill, passed by the main house. It was like a stark skeleton against the sky and, as Alison had guessed, was festooned with the trappings of Sarah Embraces-All-Things' room. It was huge and elaborate—way bigger than it needed to be. Alison supposed that was the monument aspect—half a dozen women's grief had managed to raise something quite spectacular in less than forty-eight hours. The structure had two levels—one that was about twelve feet high, against which a heavy, lodgepole ladder was leaning, and a second perhaps five feet lower, on which was piled a huge mound of wood, obviously from the collapsed shed that Alison had noticed on the tour. Again, it seemed to Alison that there could have been easier ways to do it, but she supposed that the height satisfied a sense of ritual.

The entrance to the sweat lodge was lit up by two torches stuck into the sand on either side of the door. They were a little late—women were strung out all along the deck, undressing, putting their clothes in neat little piles, glasses and jewelry inside shoes.

Seven Yellow Moons was standing by the door. People were talking, but it was pretty low key. No one was looking forward to a good time, and few of the women nodded or even looked at Alison. Michelle was clear across the deck, her back turned, but

Persimmon—maybe in the name of reconciliation—made a point to come by and say hi.

"You've got a twig in your hair," she said to Alison, reaching up her hand to the side of her head before she moved away.

Stacy sent a long, hostile look after her. She considered grooming Alison her job and no one else's. She'd rather that Alison go around with a smudge on her face all day long than have another woman wipe it off.

As each woman approached the door, Seven sent her around the circular room to sit upon the benches that lined the perimeter. She alternated, sending a woman to the right and then to the left, so that Alison found herself sitting between Claw and Rusha, fairly close to the door, with Liz and Stacy across the room. She felt a little vulnerable, but that could have just been because she was naked. In the flickering candlelight, some of the women seemed completely comfortable and had fallen into poses of meditation, but others were fussing with their hair or trying to decide what to do with their hands. It didn't really matter how many times you'd taken off your shirt at a festival, there were always those first few minutes before you settled down, when you mentally compared your weight or breasts to everyone else. American culture is not as easy to shed as a sweatshirt.

Seven Yellow Moons, who entered the lodge after everyone else had found a place, sat on the floor cross legged. She had pulled the skin over the door behind her. Now the lodge was lit only by candles—four of them marking the four directions. Most of the women were in shadows, and by now there was little movement. Much as she hoped this would end in at least a neutral, if not friendly feeling between the Fun Camp and the land women, Alison hoped that Seven would hurry. Her back was beginning to hurt. She should have brought one of Stacy's lawn chairs.

Seven let them sweat for a few minutes in silence. Someone had cranked up the stove—it was really hot. Alison's breathing began to come fast and shallow. She was just wondering if perhaps this was really going to be a mass suicide—there's a sign of commitment!—when Seven reached outside the door and produced the wooden bucket. She stood.

"The highest motive of all," she said, "is to be like water. Water is essential to all living things. Nothing is weaker than water, yet for overcoming what is strong and hard, nothing surpasses it." She dipped the ladle into the water, lifted it above the rim of the bucket and then poured it back. Everyone followed the course of the water longingly with their eyes.

"We've had some negative things happen here," said Seven bluntly. "Things that have made us turn against one another, instead of remembering our common goals. Things that have made us forget why we came here. Tonight we are going to take all that negative energy and send it off the land, so that we can begin to see clearly again. But before we are able to do this, we have to let go of it." She again held up the bucket. "Water is a gift to us from the earth. It is only right for us to be willing to give a gift back. The greatest gift we can give this land at this moment is to let go of any hateful or harmful feeling that we might be harboring at this moment." She dipped the wooden ladle again. This time she brought it up to her mouth. "I felt angry with Sarah Embraces-All-Things because of the way she tried to control things. I give that anger up to the wind—I will not speak of it again." She drank. She drank with her whole body—the other women, envious, could practically see it flowing down to the tips of her fingers and toes. Seven Yellow Moons was in her forties, an age when American women are told to regret the changes in their bodies, to feel self-conscious because they are no longer young and firm. But her attitude as she stood before them in the candlelight was not self conscious, but comfortable and even regal. For a moment Alison rejoiced in just that one thing—that Calvin Klein and Oil of Olay and the Bodyworks had not managed to make Seven Yellow Moons feel badly about her body.

Now that she had drunk, Seven offered the dipper to G-hey!, who was the woman on her right.

"I've been impatient with everyone taking so much time to decide everything," said G-hey! promptly, as if she had rehearsed. Which, Alison realized, she probably had. Obviously any kind of ritual would go more smoothly if you had a couple of plants in the audience. So far Seven was receiving a very high rating for showmanship—she had made them wait and want, and had also voiced everything in the terms of 'we', so that no one felt attacked or blamed. A big ten for choreography.

"I'm going to let go of that," G-hey! continued. "I'm not going to bitch about it anymore—if I can't deal with it I can just leave." A tiny wrinkle between Seven's eyes told Alison that this last part had probably not been in the original plan, but what could Seven expect? They were dykes—they couldn't help editorializing.

A big long drink—Alison could practically hear the women around her hastily getting their confessions in order. Everybody wanted a drink. Again Alison commended Seven—no one was going to resist in this setting.

Somehow Alison had missed the affirmation of the next woman—she was already drinking. G-hey!, adding to the theory that she had been planted to speak first, was now acting as kind of an acolyte to Seven, following behind her with a second wooden bucket. She submerged a huge sea sponge, and then squeezed it over the head of the woman after she drank. The woman turned her face up to the water. There was a small but collective sigh of envy.

"I've been really angry at Alison," announced Salad, in front of whom Seven was now standing. "Because she kept saying that someone killed Sarah Embraces-All-Things, and I didn't want to believe that. But then I realized that even if she was right, I didn't have to let that affect me. So I'm going to let go of my anger towards her and not speak about it again."

There was a little stir in the sweat, kind of like the little ripple you get in a tightly controlled courtroom when something totally unexpected has been announced on the stand. No one actually spoke aloud, but the gasps and rustling were enough to make Seven turn a full circle, quieting each woman with a stern look.

The heat camouflaged Alison's flush. Every one was already red. God, it was hot! As Seven moved on, G-hey! took her bucket over to the rock pit and sprinkled water on them. A huge blast of steam filled the sweat lodge. Alison had to duck her head almost to her knees for a moment before the heat dissipated. On the other side of the room, someone was coughing. Someone who smoked in real life, from the sound of it. One of the candles had gone out, so Alison could not tell who it was. What the hell was Seven thinking? It was going to take a good twenty minutes to go around the circle—they would be lucky if no one fainted. Alison supposed it was all part of the confession ploy. And what was it that Salad had said about knowing she was right about the death of Sarah Embraces-All-Things? Had that come as much of a surprise to everyone, as it had to her?

As if reading her mind about the heat, Seven motioned to G-hey!, who put down the bucket and crossed the room to the door. She lifted the flap and held it wide. For just a moment a gust of cool air rushed inside, reaching its fingers clear across to the women opposite. Again there was that little courtroom stir, but Seven did not silence this one. Instead, she put down the bucket and reached out her arms as if she were gathering the heavy, hot air that lay above their heads into a sack. Gathered, she made a casting motion, throwing it in the direction of the door.

"We've let go of negative feelings, and we won't speak of them any more," she intoned. "Let the wind carry them far away, and cast them where no one will be harmed."

G-hey! dropped the flap, and crossed back to the pit, where she raised another cloud of steam. The cold air, which had seemed so refreshing, instantly became nothing but a memory. Or maybe not quite. Just from that one caress Alison felt herself more alert. For the first time, it occurred to her that *she* was going to have to say something when her turn came. She could not pass over her turn without looking as if she were the only woman there who was not willing to try for reconciliation, and besides, she suspected that by the time it came to her turn she'd be willing to do almost anything for a drink of water. She had a whole bundle of negative feelings, but which one was she truly willing to give up, to not talk about again? She supposed that all the Land Women were hoping that she would say she was willing to drop the issue of murder. Could she really do that? Then again, wasn't that what this was all about, really? Starting over? Everyone?

She looked across the circle, and for the first time noticed Michelle, sitting between Gaya and Sandpaper. She ducked her head to hide a smile—no doubt Sandpaper was making Michelle pay the price of defecting by constant political lecturing. Alison wondered if she were sorry now about the choice that she had made, and she also wondered what the reaction of the Mariposa women would be if Michelle were to change her mind again. Would she be allowed to leave freely, or would they attempt to change her mind with promises of Utopia or by painting Alison with the taint of evil? Michelle looked tired and worn. That, thought Alison, was something that she could agree to give up freely and honestly—her anger towards Michelle. Comforted by this decision, Alison settled back on the bench, trying to ease the ache of her hips and back without creating a commotion.

A second candle had gone out, and G-hey! had raised another cloud of steam with the water whisk. Alison had no idea that Seven Yellow Moons was standing in front of Stacy until she heard her voice. She had expected Stacy to say something about the animosity between the Mariposa women and the leather dykes, and in fact had planned on commending her for any attempt to bridge that gap. So Stacy's comment came as a total shock to her, floating disembodied out of the cloud of steam.

"I know who killed Sarah Embraces-All-Things," she said, her voice high and reedy from the heat. "And I felt angry at that person because of the position that she put us all in. I felt as if I needed to judge whether she had done right or wrong, and that I needed to act on that knowledge in some way. But I realize now that judgment isn't up to me. All I have to do is live my life the best way that I know how. So I am letting go of that anger and that knowledge and I will not speak of it again."

Again there was a ripple, though the increased heat made everyone react more slowly. The whole thing, in fact, was beginning to feel almost like a dream. Several of the women, Alison could see by the light of the two remaining candles, had slipped down to sit on the floor. She didn't know how Seven and G-hey! were able to take the heat standing and moving. Salad was on her feet also, handing around a bucket containing bundles of fresh sage. Alison took a bundle and, imitating Lisa, rubbed it over her face. It helped some. What was Stacy talking about? She knew who had killed Sarah Embraces-All-Things? Alison was confused, and the heat was making it almost impossible to concentrate. She knew that she could go outside if it became unbearable, but she also knew that it was considered bad manners for anyone to return to the sweat once she had left, and she didn't want to miss anything. If only she weren't so near the end! Claw passed the water bucket to her, and gratefully she squeezed the sponge over her head. She wanted to do it again, but Rusha was waiting with her mouth open and her tongue out. Alison passed her the bucket and then slid down to the floor. It was cooler down there, though not by much.

She had missed what Liz had said. Now Persimmon was talking. "I've been angry that so many women have chosen to put their energy into worrying about the death of Sarah Embraces-All-Things instead of turning it towards something useful. That whole house could have been done if we had tended to it the way we tended to gossip and speculation!" The statements of letting go were getting more and more editorial, Alison noticed. She was surprised that Seven didn't say anything. "I'm happy that so many women have chosen to put this behind them. I choose to put it behind me as well. I will not speak of it again."

Nice for the killer, whoever she is, thought Alison.

Now, as Persimmon drank long and gratefully, Michelle was speaking. "I know who the killer is, too," she said.

Another chorus of gasps, and from somewhere in the back, beyond the reach of the one remaining candle, someone called, "Who? Who killed her?"

Seven frowned. Alison couldn't really see her face. This time there was more than a ripple—this time Alison could hear actual words being said aloud, questions asked.

"But that's not the anger I choose to let go of," came Michelle's voice out of the semi-darkness again, rolling over the chatter. She did what Seven had not been able to do—silenced them all. No one wanted to miss anything. "I came here angry. I was angry at my life, angry because of the dreams I had let slip out of my fingers. I was angry at my friend because she didn't understand. I choose to let go of that anger, and not to speak of it again."

Even in the darkness and discomfort, Alison's heart was warmed. Of course she knew that, no matter what the promise made here, Michelle would not really let go of her attack. She would make her pay for that for six months. But still, it was good to know that Michelle was as concerned about their friendship as she was.

Quickly, calculating from Michelle's place in the circle, she tried to estimate how long it would take Seven to reach her. She thought that yet a third bucket was now passing from hand to hand, following the sage, and that all the women who had already spoken were drinking from it. But those whom Seven had not yet reached were still dry, dry as a bone, dry as the bones of Sarah Embraces-All-Things would be once the pyre was lit. Alison started. Where had that particularly nasty image come from? Now that it was in her head she could not rid herself of it. The dryness in her throat seemed to her to be caused by the very same flames that would obliterate Sarah Embraces-All-Things. No wonder, thought Alison, on the verge of delirium, she had been unable to keep Sarah from burning, when she was the one carrying the fire inside her.

She let her head loll forward for a moment. As if in a vision she remembered the moment when Sarah had spewed fire into the night. Beneath it, like a painting showing pentimento, Alison saw the photograph of Persimmon and Gaya with their brothers on the steps of the ranch house.

She snapped her head back up. Again she had missed a confession, and she didn't want to miss one. Not a word. They were too telling. The heat was breaking down barriers that she had not been able to break down any other way. She herself could tell that, unless Seven approached her within the next several minutes, she would sing like a canary, telling Seven every detail she wanted to know, plus a handful that she did not.

She remembered, as a child, hiking with a pebble in her mouth, and surreptitiously slipped her ring off her finger. Her mouth was so dry that even sucking did not moisten it much, but it was better than nothing, and it gave her a focus. She had to concentrate now— if she forgot what she was doing she would swallow the ring and probably die. She had no desire to be tossed up beside Sarah Embraces-All-Things like an afterthought.

"I tried to…" began a voice not far to Alison's right. She could not see who was speaking in the dim light, nor could she recognize the woman from the sound of her voice. It was merely a hoarse croak, the way that Alison imagined her own voice might have sounded a moment before. The woman speaking did not know about putting a pebble in her mouth. "I tried to…I almost…I only wanted to frighten her! I just wanted her to stop asking questions! But everyone came so fast and I was scared and the door wouldn't open—I would have let her up in a minute—I only wanted to frighten her!"

It was a measure of her heat and thirst that Alison almost permitted this garbled confession to pass right over her head. But there was something about the despair in the voice of the woman that wrenched her back to focus. What was she…oh, my god, she was talking about the scene in the hot tub! Someone had just confessed, and she had no idea who it had been! She had lost count of the women between herself and Michelle, and the light of the one remaining candle was far across the room. She could barely see the women next to her.

She felt the barest whisper of a cool breeze, and realized that someone had slipped out the door. Maybe the woman who had just spoken. Maybe someone else. She had no idea. She had no landmarks. She tried to pull herself back to the moment, tried to figure, by elimination, who the speaker had been. It had not been Persimmon, or Salad or G-hey! or Rusha or Claw. It had not, of course, been Stacy or Michelle….that was as far as she could follow the thread. It was only a repeat of what had been happening all weekend—she knew who had not, but she never knew who *had*.

There were still a number of women left to speak, but once again Seven halted.

"I can feel all that bad stuff leaving," she said, in a voice that was just a little too perky for Alison. It made her feel as if she were at a New Age Amway convention.

Seven Yellow Moons must have caught the inflection herself, for her next words were measured and slow. "I can feel it," she said again. It was much too dark to see her face, but all trace of the cheerleader gone. "We can do anything when we work together. We can make this land blossom. We can create a lesbian nation!"

Personally, Alison had doubts about making the desert bloom. They were going to be lucky if they ever got anything besides a small garden to grow in this climate. Outside, as if to give lie to her doubts, there was a sudden roll of thunder.

"We can make our dreams become reality," said Seven Yellow

Moons. "We need to focus our energy if we want to achieve harmony. The energy of women is the energy that moves the world. Armies made of lovers cannot fail."

But, thought Alison, armies made of ex-lovers can't even get out the front door. Not for the first time, she wished that lesbians had, as elephants were rumored, a secret bone yard, where ex-lovers would just wander off to die when it was over. Then she was ashamed of her cynicism. Not for one moment had she tried to accept the healing for what it actually could be—a chance to make up with Michelle at the very least, a chance to become a peripheral part of a whole new community at best. Instead she had blocked Seven's good intentions with dry wit, and had been totally unable to, as others had vowed, give up the idea of exposing the murderer. She didn't want to let go—something told her that the answers she sought were all but ready to tumble into place. But wouldn't that make her sacrifice more fine? Wouldn't it mean much more for her to give up the murderer to the mill of the Goddess when she was within reach than it would have meant for her to have abandoned the quest when it had seemed hopeless? And wouldn't it be better as well to commit herself totally to that abandonment now, when it still seemed like a choice that could be lauded, than after the funeral pyre was lit, when nothing could make it seem like anything but a hostile takeover?

"How can we work together when we know that one of us is a murderer?"

Were all of her good intentions destined to be shot down before they were even voiced? thought Alison. Like a well-trained retriever, she could not keep herself from coming to full point at the sound of the question. The speaker was lost in the darkness, and the voice was a harsh whisper, as if meant to disguise, but Alison could not shake the feeling that the words were said by either Stacy or Liz. She could neither hazard a guess at their reason for speaking or her reason for suspecting. But there was a heightened air in the room that could not be attributed totally to the heat, once again almost immediately unbearable.

Seven spun to face the direction of the whisper. Suddenly before she could say even one calming word, the candle went out.

The darkness of the sweat lodge was different from the darkness outside. There were no flashes of moon or stars through the clouds, no far off lights from the main house. It was like being underground. The darkness made the heat seem suddenly unbearable, pulling on Alison like a sodden blanket of wool. She wanted to rise to her feet, bolt to the door. To hell with Seven—nothing she could say or do in this room was going to span the rift between the two groups of women. Lesbians, thought Alison in sudden panic, were simply evil. They could never produce or create or join together—the only thing they had in common was their basic evil and their ability to hurt one another. This probably wasn't an effort to heal at all—it was probably some kind of weird Jim Jones thing. The Kool-aid would be next. They were all going to die in just the same manner that Sarah Embraces-All-Things had died as if even from beyond the grave she was manipulating.

She was on her feet now, almost ready to give way totally to panic, ready to start the rush that she could feel from the women around her—a stampede. They were all too near the edge, both physically and emotionally, to react well to surprise. No matter how vehemently Hawk denied what had happened, no matter how many had promised to let the identity of the killer blow away with the wind, Alison knew that she was not the only one wondering if perhaps the woman who had killed Sarah Embraces-All-Things was even now sitting beside her in the dark.

There was the very faintest flash, not of light, but of lesser darkness, over by the door of the sweat lodge, as if someone had lifted the flap just enough to crawl through. Leaving the ship, thought Alison. All about her she could hear voices raised in question, speaking not to Seven or the goddess, but one another.

She stood. Around her she could sense rising and shuffling. Suddenly, from out of the darkness, the voice of one woman rose in song. Alison had sung with that voice many times on the road, but she had never before heard it sound so clear and calming.

"'Oh, it could have been me'," sang Michelle, going back instinctively to Holly Near, on whom so many of the older women had been weaned. There was an instant change in the room. Around her, Alison could feel women settling back onto the benches. One by one, they raised their own voices to join Michelle.

Alison began to sing with the others, but she did not sit down. Without warning, she felt a sudden hand on her shoulder. She could not say later what it was that had told her this was not Stacy or Liz, not a touch that was friendly or even accidental. Only a hand on the shoulder, but she knew immediately it was the hand of the killer.

She jerked herself forward and flung one hand up, trying to turn and grasp the arm of the woman who had touched her in the dark.

Two seconds too late. Maybe if she had tried to concentrate only on getting away. But groping for the other woman had left her wide open, unprotected. A wet towel came down over her head like a hood. She tried to push it off her face, but it was held tight at the bottom by hands encircling her neck, choking her. She didn't even have time to gasp, let alone cry out before her mouth and nose were clogged with a hot layer of wet terry cloth.

Without a sound Alison was down on her knees. The wood was smooth beneath them. Even through the towel and the singing, she could hear Seven Yellow Moon's voice again somewhere towards the back of the sweat lodge Obviously she had no idea that not more than ten feet away from her Alison was struggling for her life. From the sound, all of the women had settled themselves again on the benches that lined the room. That left the middle open—she was going to be killed, thought Alison wildly, within arm's reach of half a dozen women.

Her assailant forced her forward almost flat on the floor while she stood over her—if you are standing you have more power. Then, with her left hand, Alison felt a wad of cloth on the floor. Her mind, operating only in little spurts like a faulty bulb, identified it. There had been a couple of bulky towels near the stove—probably in case the stove or the rocks needed to be handled. Alison grasped it in her hand. Doing anything was better than nothing, and nothing was the only other choice. Her throat was being crushed. Again there was the sound of water striking the hot stones, not too far from her.

Water striking the stones. Water striking the stones, and there was a big cloud of steam so close to Alison's face that it burned the inside of her nostrils. An idea burst into her head with explosive brevity. She did not think about it. She could not. She was beyond thought. She was acting only on instinct now. With a huge effort, she pulled the bulky towel around her torso, and hurled herself forward, half dragging, half rolling, into the stove and the pile of hot rocks.

She could feel the heat immediately. The towel could not mask that and, given a moment, would be burnt through it as if it were plastic.

But she didn't stay there a moment. There was a piercing scream close to her ear, and suddenly the horrible pressure that had been closing off her windpipe was gone. She did not stay to become part of the bedlam that erupted around her—the women's voices breaking off in mid-song to become cries, the sudden movement that meant that everyone was on their feet again, the terrible smell of burning flesh. She scuttled crab-like towards the place where she thought the door of the sweat opened. She was kicked and stepped on, but compared to the pain in her throat, it was nothing. She hit one of the benches that rimmed the walls, and began working her way around the perimeter of the lodge. She would have hit the door within another few seconds, but suddenly the flap flew up, marking the space more by the cool air that rushed inside than any difference in light and dark. Still crawling, Alison made her way for the opening.

"What was that, what the hell…" Behind her, the other women were pouring out into the cool night air. There was a roll of thunder, and then suddenly the night was split with a half a dozen bolts of lightning. They struck far out by the butte, but the storm was moving closer. Alison could feel it in the air.

She needed to see the faces of the women as they came out of the sweat. Surely the woman who had attacked her—for the second time, she supposed—would not be able to compose herself completely. If she could just meet the eyes of every woman as she ducked beneath the flap…

She could not. Darkness and lightning are not something that can be controlled by sheer will—if they were, the face of the killer would have lit up like a pin ball machine. Instead, all Alison caught were flashes of faces both confused and confusing. The lightning, striking every ten seconds or so, gave only a disjointed picture. Flash—there was Stacy, flushed and concerned, Liz looking over her shoulder, her face drawn up in a mask of irritation. "Well, you don't have to push," Alison heard her say. "You're not the only one who's been in hell." Flash—there was Hawk, looking furious, her head turning from side to side, just trying to figure out who had done what to misbehave so that she could top the scene; Seven Yellow Moons looking absolutely stricken—"Was someone hurt? What happened? Is everyone okay?" Flash—there was G-hey! looking more excited than anything else, as if caught in the thrill of adventure, and behind her Michelle, pushing away from Lavender—"Alison! Are you okay? Alison!" Even in a state close to shock Alison's heart warmed for a moment at Michelle's concern. Perhaps she had been acting silly with lust, but for all her denial Michelle was no fool—automatically she had questioned Alison's safety at the hint of foul play.

Alison slumped down on a bench, her hand in her lap. If only she could see! If wanting made sunlight, then she'd march right up to the woman who had attacked her and who'd give herself away somehow—her heartbeat, her eyes, something she just couldn't control. She was burnt somewhere—the smell and the scream had told Alison that. Alison herself had been burnt on the back of the hand—it throbbed. But here in the darkness, the assailant was just another grey cat. *Un gato gris*, thought Alison, and in her pain and despair it seemed just as important as anything else.

About half of the women were going for their clothes, trying to ward off the chilly wind that was sweeping in across the desert in front of the approaching storm. So that was not a clue. Who could tell which one was covering up the mark of the stove? Alison cradled her right hand in her left. She knew that this was a moment which needed to be seized. She needed to speak up and answer the questions that were still flying around her head. "Someone tried to kill me!" But she could not bring herself to move so much as a finger. That flash of adrenaline that had carried her forward into the rock pit had burned through her and left nothing but a bitter taste in her mouth and a strong urge to cry.

"Are you okay? What happened?" Stacy on one side, Michelle, all-is-forgiven, on the other. One holding a water bottle, the other Alison's brown and green flannel shirt (tolerated by Stacy only for camping). A flash of lightning lit them up as if they were a *New Yorker* cartoon—meant to be funny, but a bit too close to the bone to laugh.

Two long draws on Stacy's water bottle and Alison's head began to clear. The pain in her hand did not diminish, but it could be handled, be pushed back to join that long list of things, (intimacy issues, Marta Goicochea, her student loans) that could be dealt with later. None of the water got into her stomach, but was sucked up immediately by her tongue and throat. Perhaps now she could speak. She opened her mouth.

"Jesus Curr-rist!" Michelle threw the curse out into the wind as they were suddenly hit by a fine wall of water. They should have realized the rain was going to sweep ahead of the lightning and pretty darn soon, too. They all had counted one-thousand-one, one-thousand-two, after the thunder when they were kids.

There were a few short moments of milling and cursing. Right at this moment nobody gave a tinker's damn about *what* the hell had happened in the sweat lodge—it was all about not getting cold and muddy when you knew there was no hot water. Michelle, clutching Alison tightly by the arm, led a retreat across the fifty yards to the unfinished casita. The stones bit into Alison's bare feet, but it was only a short dash, and then they were sheltered, free to watch the magnificent storm through the holes that had been left for windows and doors.

"Put on some clothes," Stacy fussed, pulling her own turtleneck over her head. "You're going to get sick." Her tone told Alison that she suspected nothing of what had happened in the sweat lodge—*she* was concerned only about colds and sore throats on the drive home. Liz had brought Michelle and Alison's clothes with her—a perfect example of an emergency truce.

Alison obeyed. The moment during which she could have spoken easily and naturally had been lost in the rain. The most she could manage was fumbling with her clothes

"What's this?" asked Stacy, brushing Alison's damp leg and bringing up a palm covered with sand and what looked like a bead. No, it was a flat red pill, identical to those found in the pocket of Sarah Embraces-All-Things' jacket. "Just what were you doing in the fire pit?" Then, with no pause for an answer, "And what do you have in your hair? What did you back into?" She brushed at Alison's head, bringing back two fingers that sparkled.

Alison pulled away impatiently. This was not the time to worry about her hair. She was freezing cold. She pulled on her sweatshirt, wincing as she forced her hand through the sleeve.

About half of the women were dressing. Some—the younger, hardier ones—were standing by the windows naked, watching the storm. As long as their clothes were dry for later, they weren't worried. Steam was rising off their bodies, giving the room an otherworldly kind of look whenever the lightning flashed. Everyone was doing one of these two things, and on top of them most of the women were also drinking water and asking questions about the scream in the sweat lodge. The talk died down to a trickle. It was not, thought Alison, that anyone had stopped caring or being curious. It was the pure magnitude of the storm—faced by something so wild and glorious it was impossible to remain focused on anything else.

Even if she had known who the killer was, thought Alison, and could prove it, she would not have shouted out her name at this moment. It would have been like trying to persuade onlookers to apprehend a pickpocket during an earthquake—foolish and futile.

There was a particularly deafening roll of thunder, followed by a display of lightning that couldn't have rated less than a ten. At least, if it came bigger, Alison didn't want to see it.

"Look at that!" someone cried. At first Alison, shrugging her jacket over her shoulders while still battling the voices within, did not bother to turn her head. She'd seen lightning, and it was going to happen again.

"Oh, my God!" cried another, barely distinguishable above the babble that risen from both windows. This time Alison lifted her head. Had the lightning struck nearby? She stood on her tiptoes to see above the six or seven women straining and pointing in the nearest window.

It was fire, all right, but not from the lightning touching down. Someone had set fire to the pyre where Sarah Embraces-All-Things had been laid. Alison craned her neck to see how it had been done in the down-pour. Oh, of course, the second platform—the upper tier had kept the wood dry. That was clever, but it meant that it was going to take a little time for the upper platform to catch fire, particularly in the rain. It might not go at all. No sooner had this thought crossed her mind, than there was another cry. The first had carried a hint of entertainment about it—they were stuck out here in the rain, there was no tv, and it was kind of cool to watch a body go up in flames, particularly in such a dramatic way and when in effect, it resolved a really ugly conflict. There wasn't going to be any arguing over going to town once the corpse was gone.

But the second cry held a strong tone of terror—so strong that Alison pushed her way up to the window. She drew back in amazement, and then passed her hand over her eyes, as if to assure herself this was not a hallucination brought on by a combination of heat and adrenaline. She glanced at the women on either side of her—no, their open mouths told her that they were seeing it, too—and then back to the fire had flamed up to light the entire pyre, and on the top level the body of Sarah Embraces-All-Things had *risen to its feet*.

CHAPTER FOURTEEN

Alison stood silently. On the pyre, Sarah Embraces-All-Things pushed back the tattered quilt that had been wrapped around her and still clung to her shoulders. Her long hair blew wildly out behind her in the wind which also pulled at her long skirt and shawl. Decided not to do the sky clad thing after all, thought Alison stupidly, and then shook her head. What was she thinking? She of all people knew that Sarah Embraces-All-Things was not alive—she was the one who had given CPR until the body had begun to grow cold. Yet she could neither shut her mouth or tear her gaze from the woman standing on top of the pyre, lighted by the flames that leapt beneath her.

Get hold of yourself! her internal cop voice said sternly, This is just a scam! It can't be anything else!

With a tremendous effort, she tore herself away from the window and turned towards the inner room. She was not the only one to have come up with the scam theory—fully half the women there were doing a quick count. Find out who wasn't there, and you'd find out who thought it was funny to dress up like Sarah Embraces-All-Things and dance on her grave.

Except that everyone was there—even Zorra. Alison could see it passing across all the faces at almost the same moment—fifteen, sixteen, seventeen, and then there's me and that means that…

There was another cry from the window. Alison turned in time to see the ghostly figure raise her arms to the sky as if to implore. Not ghostly, really, because she looked pretty damn solid, but what else would you call a woman who had raised herself after three days of death?

"She can't rest!" said a voice at the back of the room, a shrill falsetto that disguised the speaker. "She can't rest until her killer is found!"

"That is such bullshit!" Hawk who had pushed up so that she was standing almost directly behind Alison, was quite literally foaming at the mouth with rage. A drop of spittle hit Alison in the chin. She wiped at it with the cuff of her shirt. "I don't know what's going on, but I bet I know who's behind it!" Hawk stepped uncomfortably close, especially considering the spit thing. "This is your bullshit, isn't it?" she snarled, putting out such a spray in her anger that Alison was forced to turn her head. "Isn't it!?" She jabbed her finger into Alison's chest.

"Oh, that works, doesn't it?" Stacy to the rescue, once more decked out in her generic dyke camping clothes. She hadn't been able to force the braids again—her hair was pulled back into one of those poodle skirt ponytails. "Alison can raise people from the dead now? And from a distance! Boy, even Jesus had to be right there to lay on the hands!"

"She didn't raise anybody from the dead!" hissed Hawk through clenched teeth. It sounded unpleasant, but cut down on the spitting.

"Well, she sure as hell was dead!" Stacy shrilled back. "I found her, I know! That wasn't any live body that you put in that refrigerator!" Stacy, who was actually pretty darn good in an emergency, sounded uncharacteristically hysterical. Alison, pushing out from between Hawk and the wall with her good hand, stole a quick look at her face. She had been around Mistress Anastasia enough to know when it was real and when it was acting. Definitely *acting*. She remembered her earlier conviction that the Fun Camp girls and Seven Yellow Moons were in cahoots and the sweat was a set up. Were they somehow behind the specter on the pyre?

"It's not her at all!" hissed Hawk. She had pushed her head forward and was bobbing it up and down in front of Alison, as if she were a cobra, just waiting for the right opening. "It's a scam!" There was more, but it was lost in the general commotion.

"...don't care how hard it's raining, I'm going to spend the night in my car..."

"...what's wrong with that dog, is she sick?..."

"I'll show you!" Hawk hissed into Alison's ear, taking hold of her head with two hands to a make sure this message did not go astray. "I'm going to go and find out who that is!" She broke away about three seconds before the internal limit at which Alison had decided to bite her arm in self defense, and dashed out into the pouring rain. Hardly anyone noticed. They were all still crowded around the door and windows, watching the figure who stood atop the burning tower. Again, she was beseeching the sky. The wind tore the quilt away, and they watched it fly out into the night and disappear. The Sarah specter bent double as if in pain. There was something a little funny about the way that she moved, thought Alison, but she did not stop to analyze it. She was already on her way to the door. She had wished for a miracle that would show her the face of her killer. And wasn't this the answer? Who was the most likely to be upset over the reincarnation of Sarah Embraces-All-Things? Wouldn't it be the killer? Hawk had been hostile to any suggestion of foul play from the very beginning—she also had a lot to lose to anyone playing the blackmail game. She obviously relished her role in the Mariposa community, but she did not control the purse strings. If Sarah Embraces-All-Things' secrets were ugly enough, if either Persimmon or Gaya could be turned against her, Hawk could easily find herself back in the land of wage workers. Her head bowed down in preparation against the wind, Alison made for the door.

She was not the only one, however, with this idea. There was a great deal of scrambling and shuffling. Alison was not too shy to push, but before even that worked a firm voice spoke above them all.

"Stop it! Calm down!" Persimmon, standing in the unfinished door way as if she were a sentinel. "Just everybody calm down!" Alison, prepared to push past her in a big, ugly scene if necessary, was surprised by her next words. "Alison, you come with me. This is obviously some kind of stupid joke, but Hawk's freaking out. The rest of you," she pointed back towards the wall on which they had been working the day before, "that whole wall's going to come down if it gets any wetter. Gaya, Michelle—there're tarps in the tool shed—get everybody on it."

Gaya seemed about to say something, but Persimmon rode right over her.

"Do it now," she snapped. "If that wall comes down, the whole building is going to come down!" She turned and ran into the rain, Alison close on her heels.

She was instantly drenched to the skin. Her jeans and sweat shirt offered so little protection against the furiously falling rain that they might as well have been made of paper. Paper, in fact, would have been an improvement, for paper could be torn off once it was soaked, unlike Alison's clothes, which suddenly felt as heavy as armor. In spite of this, she struggled forward against the rain, trying to catch up with Hawk. They were going to have this out once and for all—if she had to, she would rip Hawk's clothes right off her body to expose the burns she must have suffered when she hit the stove. Involuntarily Alison's hands flew up to her throat, touching the circle of swollen skin. Hawk had unusually big and strong hands for a woman. For a moment, Alison was sorry that in her haste she had not called for backup. Then she shook the fear away. This was not going to be a towel over her head in the dark—

this time Hawk was going to be the one surprised. And Persimmon was there to help—at least *she* seemed to realize that Hawk had gone off the deep end.

The rain had immediately saturated the clay and sand soil. The excess water was raging down the hill, funneling into the arroyos. Alison found it difficult to keep her feet. Twice, she fell and was aware that Persimmon had done the same. But she was driven by obsession, pulling her forward, chilled to the bone, against the driving rain. It was no longer just a matter of right or wrong—it had become personal now. Hawk, she was sure had tried to kill her, and she would be damned if she was just going to look the other way, soothed with fine speeches about choice and the patriarchy.

Hawk was almost at the base of the pyre now. Behind her, Alison was vaguely aware that Persimmon had gone down a third time. Alison shielded her eyes with her hand and looked up. The beseeching figure of Sarah Embraces-All-Things had disappeared. As Hawk climbed up the ladder that leaned against the side of the pyre, her silhouette was outlined in flame from the still burning fire. Alison caught the ladder beneath her. For a moment she thought of just tipping her backwards—the harm that Hawk might suffer in the fall seemed like nothing but a justifiable payback for the pain and terror that Alison was sure she had suffered at Hawk's hands. But the ladder, made from two of the lodgepoles that the Chain Gang had appropriated, was big and heavy, nothing at all like the aluminum one that Michelle kept in the garage, lovingly groomed. There wasn't time to get around to the other side and push, and anything else, if it moved the ladder at all, would land it, Hawk and all, right on top of her. Alison mounted the first step just as Hawk slithered over the side of the top platform.

The fire, she saw as she climbed the ladder, was still burning strongly, but only the wood that had been shielded from the storm. It did not look as if any part of the top platform had caught. Maybe the back corner had flamed up for a moment, but it looked as if the rain had doused it almost immediately. It should be safe, Alison thought, trying to think of it as an affirmation, and not a prayer. Still, she gingerly tested the side of the platform, shaking it with both hands, before hoisting herself over the side. She wasn't stupid—she looked for Hawk as well. She didn't want to be slammed in the head or pushed over the side. But Hawk was clear over on the other side of the platform, and the sounds that she was making seemed more shocked than threatening.

There was no one on the platform with the two of them. No woman, no apparition. No body, either. What there was, was a skeleton, and it didn't take more than one evening of prime time tv to know that it was human. The skull lay exposed, looking up at them almost as if it had been waiting, and might nod acquaintance at any moment. There was a long shock of black hair attached, and in it was tied one of the leather bands that Sarah Embraces-All-Things had affected. The arms of the skeleton were arranged on the chest so that the hands appeared to be clasped. The strangest, and possible most frightening part of the scene was that the skeleton appeared to be dressed in the same clothes and jewelry in which Sarah Embraces-All-Things had been laid out. The silver pin that looked like a lizard twinkled in the light from the dying fire below.

Hawk regained herself sooner than Alison. Alison, to be frank, was ready to back right down the ladder and out of these women's lives at this point. This was too fucking weird for her. If they wanted to lie down and sleep with a murderer, more power to them. All she wanted to do was get the gate open, and at the moment she was so wired with fear and excitement that she probably could have moved the rocks by herself.

"This is just…" Hawk was obviously trying to recapture the tirade that she had started in the casita, but the effort was frankly in vain. As inexhaustible as she had seemed to Alison earlier, the rain, the shock, was wearing her down—she stood staring at the skeleton. Alison knew exactly what she was thinking, because the same thoughts were going through her own mind. This had to be a hoax, because it couldn't be true, because it went against all conviction of logic, and if you didn't have logic, what did you have? A world of chaos that might at any moment erupt with zombies or werewolves or all the other things that your parents had told you firmly were not under your bed because they weren't *real* and if Michelle didn't stop telling you those stories she wasn't going to be allowed to spend the night anymore!

But, logic or no logic, rules or no rules, there was the skeleton lying right there at their feet, close enough to kick if either of them took a small step from the edge, and even if somebody was a really twisted kind of joker, where the hell were they going to get a skeleton? It wasn't as if they were sold alongside joy buzzers and rubber dog vomit. Even a professional practical jokester didn't travel with a skeleton in her suitcase, just in case. And what had happened to the figure that they had seen raising its arms to the heavens?

There was a thin cry, barely loud enough to pierce the sound of the rain, from beneath them. Alison, taking the very barest of steps backwards, looked over the edge of the platform. Oh, bad move.

The ground seemed to rush up to meet her, becoming one with the wall of water that engulfed everything as far as the eye could see. For a moment, Alison felt distinctly lightheaded. Not now! she told herself sternly, going into cop mode again—if you couldn't keep yourself from getting sick every time you pulled somebody out of a car wreck, then you might as well ask for a desk job.

She closed her eyes for the briefest of moments, and then looked once again over the side of the platform. This time, it was a cop's look, a look that calculated the top platform was high enough to hurt if you fell, but wouldn't kill you. Below them, her face barely distinguishable in the rain, stood Persimmon. She was smart not to come up—Alison did not know if the platform would hold all three of them.

Persimmon cupped her hands around her mouth and called again—a question, perhaps, that the wind caught and translated into a wordless wail. Alison looked away and back, first at the skeleton dressed in the clothes of Sarah Embraces-All-Things, and then at the face of the live woman standing across from her.

A third call. Hawk made a motion as if to step around Alison, but she held her ground. It was a very small space, high in the air, and it had not been designed for two people and the remains of another. For either of them to move at all around the small space framing the skeleton required the cooperation of both—neither of them wanted to tread on either Sarah's clothes or the bones within them.

Alison was not cooperating. Hawk, she was determined, was not going to leave the platform until they had settled the thing between them.

Hawk made another move for the ladder.

"Get out of the way, you..." her voice trailed off—she was apparently unable to think of a word bad enough to describe Alison that did not buy into patriarchal insults. Alison was impressed, but not impressed enough to move.

"Why did you do it?" she asked. Hawk's movements had brought her closer, but she still had to shout into the rain. "Why did you kill her? And where did you put the body?"

Alison had not thought Hawk, whose range of emotions seemed to all center around anger and domination, capable of showing such surprise on her face. There was a flash of lightning, and for a moment her face looked as clearly exaggerated and defined as that of a mime who has just encountered an imaginary elephant. Then they were plunged again into darkness, leaving Alison with the picture of Hawk's startled look burned upon her retina.

"What are you talking about?" Hawk cried, adding with almost childlike glee, "You asshole!" Hooray! she had thought of a name generic enough that sexism could be avoided.

"Stop it!" shouted Alison. "Stop it! Just stop lying! You've lied to everybody about everything—now just stop! It's not like I can do anything about it, anyway!" With a quick, hard gesture she indicated the bones. Perhaps she was foolish to play her hand so bluntly, but of course it was obvious to Hawk that without the body she had nothing but her suspicions and a story that grew wilder by the moment.

"You asshole!" screamed Hawk again. "You're not pinning this on me!" She made another move towards the ladder. Alison could see that a tussle was not far away. Would Hawk try to throw her over the edge? Probably—she had tried for her life twice already. Did Persimmon and Gaya, wondered Alison, know what exactly Hawk had done? She hoped not—she could live so much easier with the idea of isolated evil than the thought of conspiracy. But she could not count on it, could not count on the other woman helping her if she were attacked a third time.

Yet, even though the disappearance of the body meant the disappearance of her case, she *could not* let this woman go until she had forced a confession from her. It was as if she were driven by a kind of madness that did not allow retreat. She turned, and with both hands threw the ladder away from the platform.

She could not hear the crash that the ladder made in the mud below, and the water that it threw in all directions was lost in the rain. She had to be satisfied with the look of horror on Hawk's face and, frankly, it was pretty satisfying.

"You fucking *bitch*!" she shrieked, finally jolted right back into her evil, pre-enlightenment ways.

"Tell me why you killed her!" Alison screamed in reply.

"I'm going to kill *you*!" Hawk screamed back. She came at Alison with a suddenness that surprised her—she had counted on slow, careful movements on the little platform. Hawk's fury, however, seemed to have overtaken her self-preservation. Her lunge almost took them both over the side. Alison scrambled aside just in time. A bit belatedly, she wondered if the surprise she had seen on Hawk's face at the accusation of Sarah's murder had been genuine, and not just, as she had assumed with fierce scorn, another attempt at deception and denial.

It was neither the time nor place to ponder. Hawk lunged again, and as Alison scrambled backwards her foot slipped beneath her on the sodden branches of which the floor of the platform was made. She came down with a crash that made the platform creak and shudder alarmingly. Even more horrible—a broken leg could be fixed, but graveyard horrors lived forever within the mind—she had landed directly upon the skeleton! She could feel the bones of the rib cage snapping beneath her weight and for a moment the need to save herself from human attack was far outweighed by the need to crawl from the cold embrace of the dead.

She flailed wildly for a moment, trying to find a purchase without putting her hands down into the bones. Her sensible cop mode had fled completely—now she was entirely within that realm of the brain that has been fed since childhood on horror movies, *Tales From the Crypt* comics and campfire stories. Like a slow boil finally coming to a head, Alison felt her whole mind engulfed in a riot of gore and terror, through which she could barely hear that little voice still trying to tell her to get it all together, she was a cop after all and the *X-Files* was just on tv.

Luckily, Hawk seemed almost as taken aback by her dive into the skeleton as Alison herself. For a moment she hesitated, hanging above her like a great moth pasted to the sky, too wet to fly. Below them they could again hear the tiny, reed-like cries of Persimmon.

Alison again struggled to rise. But the platform had not been constructed for wrestling, and this was the last straw. With a huge and startling snap, her right leg plunged through the sticks.

The sound of the breaking branches seemed to waken Hawk from her momentary lapse—once more murder flared in her eyes. Perhaps she thought the tower was going, and wanted to make sure that she got in a few licks while she still could. With a jerk she lunged forward.

Alison, unable to rise, flailed frantically in an attempt to defend herself. Her right hand landed on something hard—she clutched it and swung upwards in a frantic arch.

There was a solid smack that sent a jolt of pain through Alison's arm. Hawk hovered above her for a moment, an astounded look on her face. Then, suddenly, she crashed forward, unconscious, on top of Alison.

Alison looked at her hand. With what had she hit her? To her revulsion, she saw that she had picked up the skull, and was in fact still holding it as if it were a bowling ball, a finger in each eye socket. She dropped it as if it were on fire. She tried to heave upwards, to roll Hawk off her. She did not want to be stuck in this position of vulnerability when the other woman regained consciousness.

Hawk, however, was a big woman, and Alison was flat on her back on a flimsy platform made of branches, with one leg dangling in mid air. She struggled until she was sweating and gasping in the rain, but she still could not move her. Even more dismaying than the thought of Hawk coming to and beating the shit out of her was the cracking and moaning of the platform during her struggles. Whatever else happened, it was obvious that, unless she could find a way off that platform much sooner than later they were both going to plunge into the fire that burned below them.

Alison wanted to cry. Like the phantom of Sarah Embraces-All-Things, she wanted to raise her arms to the heaven and cry, "Enough! Haven't I endured enough?"

The cries below them had resumed with new and frantic energy, and though she could not hear the words, Alison tried to draw some comfort from them. "Put the ladder back up, you fool!" she screamed back, knowing that her voice, like Persimmon's, was lost in the wind, but unable to lie there without making any kind of effort at all.

As if in response there was a smack against the top of the platform and the two top braces of the lodgepole ladder appeared. It should have been comforting, but the manner in which the added weight made the platform sway made Alison sick with apprehension. Keep calm, she chided herself. Lie still and in just a few minutes…

There was a terrific jerk. The platform had finally been pushed to the limit—it was going over. The whole structure was falling slowly to one side. Probably not enough of a drop to kill anyone, repeated the cop voice in Alison's head, but it was little comfort amid the creaking and crashing that was engulfing her as she lay helpless. One of the supporting beams—the one that had been licked by the fire—cracked suddenly in two, and that corner of the platform plunged drastically. They seemed to fall through the bed of fire, though before Alison's fears of being burnt alive could blossom, they had plunged beyond the flames. The whole thing seemed to take such a long time. It was as if some celestial director had decided that this scene would have a much bigger impact in slo-mo. First the downpour of rain, now falling right in Alison's face. She had to turn her head to keep the water from running up her nose. That would have been an irony—if she had survived two attacks only to be drowned by rainwater.

Now bits of flame were falling around them. They were going to be killed, thought Alison, there was no doubt about it. It was a freeing thought. No need to spend any more energy fussing or resisting—just become one with it. Her dad would be sad, but Michelle and Janka would take care of him. Stacy would get a new girlfriend, and Alison had life insurance to take care of the house payments. Those loose ends wrapped up in less than a second, the specter of Sarah Embraces-All-Things flashed once again into her mind. There had been something strange about that silhouette—and furthermore, it was something that she had seen before rather recently, something she had seen while at Mariposa. Why couldn't she remember it?

Finally the twisted director had had enough. This was going to be her Emmy scene. With a sudden jerk that shot them back into real time—two seconds were again two seconds, rather than an eternity—Alison hit the ground with a bone-jarring thud that knocked the wind out of her completely. This was rather a mercy, actually, because her foot twisted up beneath her with a jolt of pain so intense that it could be borne only by concentrating with all her might on something else—breathing, for example. She gasped for breath, trying not to think of the pain that had shot clear up to her hip.

They—Hawk was still draped across her which didn't help the breathing or the foot problem at all—had landed on the hill that sloped down to the arroyo. The ground was covered with several inches of water, all rushing down hill. Alison struggled first to breathe, and then to move. Another sharp jolt of pain through her leg convinced her that the latter was a bad idea. Better just to wait for help. She could not help but think of the road to town, and what a dreadful, bone-jolting trip that was going to be.

Then, suddenly to her dismay, she realized that the water was starting to sweep them downhill. Dismay is not really the right word at all—she was much more upset than that, but frankly everything had started to get a kind of cold mist over it.

Still, for all her becoming one with hell, she attempted to put out her hands to try and break the skid. The wet clay offered less handhold than a snow bank—it didn't crumple or pack, but slipped beneath her hand with only the slightest contact. They were, in effect, hydroplaning.

"Come on!" she thought, but did not scream, because it was too much of an effort, and besides, she had given up resisting. She could hear voices behind her and wondered distantly if Persimmon had been on the ladder when the pyre had fallen. That would have been certain to slow her.

Maybe Alison had been too busy thinking of other things, or maybe she was just plain dumb, but until she hit the bank it had not occurred to her that the arroyo which they had walked down during the tour was now going to be filled with water. In Denver a river was a river—it wasn't a dry bed one moment and a raging torrent the next. Because that's what the arroyo was now—a torrent. Before Alison had fully realized what had happened, her head was underwater and she was slammed against the rock wall on the opposite side of the wash. She jerked her head above the water and scrabbled for a hold on the rock, clinging for dear life.

Held facing the rock by the pressure of the water, she realized that the fingers of her free hand were wrapped tightly in Hawk's hair. Alison was more or less backed into an eddy. There were a number of dangers in this kind of rampage of water—you could be crushed beneath the boulders that the water was so blithely tossing about, you could die from hypothermia or you could be pulled under the water and die a death that was as much suffocation as drowning. For the moment, Alison herself was safe from the last, pressed against a stone out of the main torrent.

Hawk, however, was bobbing like a tuna on an unmanned line. Already, Alison's arm was fully extended, and the water wanted more. Alison was not sure if she could reel her back without losing her own tenuous footing—she was not even sure that Hawk was still alive. She could certainly not tell if she was floating face up, although she did her best to raise the head just in case luck was with them. It hadn't been so far, but that was the thing about luck, wasn't it? It was random. It was like a roulette wheel. Being struck by lightning one moment didn't effect the odds of anything that happened the moment after.

Alison had taken lifesaving a time or two back when she thought she still looked hot in a bikini, and she knew there was little she could do from the position she was in. Even in optimum conditions a water rescue was dangerous—an attempt in this water would be suicide. It was really only a matter of moments before she had to make a choice—Hawk's life for hers, or her life for Hawk's.

CHAPTER FIFTEEN

Thwak! There was a tremendous thud onto the rocks above Alison's head. She almost did not look up—things had been falling about her so fast and furiously over the previous five minutes that she had gotten a little jaded—but the shouts from the opposite bank made her lift her head. She had to push away from the rock that she was hugging with her free hand in order to see what was happening above her, which made the pressure on the arm with which she clung to Hawk's hair almost unbearable. She was only able to hold the position for a moment or two, but it was enough. Less than ten feet down stream, in a cut where the water had risen over the level of the banks, Persimmon had dropped the lodgepole ladder across the arroyo. On its side, one of the long poles of the ladder was beneath the water, the second just above the surface. Immediately, Alison saw the desperate plan. It was obvious that she could not continue holding Hawk above water. Perhaps, if she was forced to let go of her, her body would catch on the ladder long enough to be retrieved.

Or perhaps not. Perhaps she would slip between the rungs or even beneath the lower side. Perhaps it was too shallow for Hawk to pass beneath the ladder and she would be pinned to the bottom and be drowned, if she were not already dead, by the good intentions of her lover's sister. If Persimmon could get into the water as a catcher, Hawk's chances would be as good as winning a lottery, but Alison knew that she could not wait long. Already she could feel her fragile grip slipping.

Hawk's only real chance was if Alison went downstream with her.

She was facing downstream with her right hand in Hawk's hair. The hold was tentative, but it was the best that she could do. It was now or never. Alison pushed away from the rock and threw herself into the stream.

It seemed as if there was virtually no time between the moment of release and the moment they were thrown against the ladder, but there must have been, because Alison's nose and mouth were once again filled with sandy water. She spat it out in angry mouthfuls, trying at the same time to see what had happened, and which part of Hawk's body had caught above the water. That she was caught was unquestionable—Alison could feel her hand still tangled in Hawk's hair, but the horrible, unrelenting pressure on her arm had ceased, leaving just a dull ache to compete with the fresh pain that the short trip downstream had shot through her leg. They were both plastered now against the ladder, just as Alison had been plastered against the rock. Alison pulled her right leg over the bottom upright and straddled a rung before she tried to move Hawk. Luckily, both Hawk's right arm and chin had caught across the top upright. She would not have lasted in that position long by herself, but it had kept her head above water. She was, in fact, beginning to stir. Alison murmured a little prayer of thanks, and reached down to grasp her by the belt. One of Hawk's legs, like Alison's, had wrapped around one of the rungs, which was probably the only reason that Alison was able to reel her into a semi-upright position, holding her against the ladder with her own body. The movement sapped the very last of her strength. All she could do now was hope that rescue came before she lost her hold.

It was almost immediate. Persimmon, her arms over the top upright of the ladder and her feet upon the bottom, begin working her way out to them. She had taken off her jacket and she was coming quite quickly, considering the circumstances, and she was talking the whole way, long before she was close enough for them to hear.

"Hang on," she was saying. "Hang on, hang on, hang on, just a couple more minutes, we're almost there, hang on, hang on, hang on." Alison fixed upon the words as if they were a mantra. Something in her mind had been strained by the trauma—she was no longer thinking in the orderly cop fashion that she preferred. It was as if all of her concentration had converged on one goal—holding Hawk and herself above water—which left everything else free to swirl in the background. She heard her mother's voice, chuffing, 'I think I can, I think I can…' reading a bedtime story from a children's book, and smelled lilacs and bundt cake on the same breeze, a mixture she hadn't smelled for ten years, since her grandmother had died. 'Baby's crying,' said Janka in her head, and Alison heard Sammy weak and far away. 'Baby's crying.' She saw again the fire leap up on the funeral pyre, and the figure raise its arms on the platform. The figure turned its face towards her, and through the darkness and rain and across the field Alison saw that the face was Gaya's.

There was a new and different kind of movement, and Alison

was jolted out of her hallucination. Persimmon was pulling at her hands, which were holding the ladder tight as death beneath Hawk's arms.

"Let go, Alison," Persimmon said. "You can't hold her much longer. Let go, and let me take her. I'll come back for you."

For a moment Persimmon's face was close and clear. Then, swirling around her like the water that threatened to engulf them, Alison was again lost in a crazy salad of voices and images from inside her head.

'Don't let go of the baby,' said Lawrence, standing in the middle of her grandmother's kitchen, dressed in one of her house dresses. With a fabric pen someone had written, 'See you in the Caribbean!' on the shoulder of the dress.

'The boy just can't accessorize anything,' said Stacy, standing with her hands on her hips. She handed Lawrence a large straw purse with flowers on it. They were both dressed in flowered shirts and shorts, sunglasses and sandals. Gaya walked in through the kitchen door, wearing her old khaki shorts and red pumps. Arm in arm she stood with Lawrence, comparing handbags. 'See you when we get back from Trinidad, mon,' Lawrence said to Alison in a heavy, fake Caribbean accent. 'You won't know me!'

"Alison! Alison! Are you okay?"

Dazed, she looked up into the face of her father. After a moment, it melted into Gaya's face. Gaya had lost her bandanna in the storm. That was what had made Alison think of her father— Gaya's hair was thinning, and her hairline receding. Without the bandanna she looked much less like Persimmon. "Are you okay?" she asked from the bank where she was holding the ladder secure as Persimmon leaned towards Alison.

"Let me take her," Persimmon said again. Her hands were pulling at Alison's, trying to move her to the side so that she could get at Hawk.

The rain, which had been pounding down upon them relentlessly, suddenly stopped. One minute there was a wall of water, the next minute there was nothing. The clouds moved away from the moon. Persimmon reached for Hawk, bringing her arm up beneath Alison's in an effort to break her hold.

For a moment Alison prepared to let go, to move to the side so that Persimmon could haul Hawk back to the shore. She could hold on by herself. She was sure she could. She could hold on for just a few more minutes, and then there would be someone to help her, to pull her out of the water and carry her to the house and roll her in warm blankets and take her to the doctor, who would give her something for the pain, something for the hallucinations. Surely by now the Fun Camp girls realized there was something wrong.

'Don't let go,' said Lawrence inside her head. He was still dressed for the tropics, but in full drag this time, a long flowing sun-dress and wig à la Diana Ross. 'Last chance.'

"Let go," said Persimmon right in her ear. "Let go!" She pulled on Alison's hand, and as she lifted her own arm above the water, Alison saw in the moonlight that the whole back of her forearm, up to the elbow, was discolored.

"Burn," she said aloud, so softly that not even she could hear it over the torrent of rushing water. Was it starting to slow now that the rain had stopped? Then, louder, "Get away from me!" She snaked out an elbow quick and unexpected, catching Persimmon beneath the jaw. Her head snapped back so hard Alison heard her teeth click together, a hard sound that gave her an instant headache in sympathy. For a moment, it seemed as if she was going to lose her grip upon the ladder and be swept against its rungs as help-lessly as Hawk—then she regained herself.

"Get away from me!" said Alison again. She sidestepped a few inches, hauling Hawk with her. Carrying Hawk, she could not real-ly move away from Persimmon. If she let her go, Alison thought desperately perhaps Persimmon would be fully occupied with sav-ing her sister's lover, and she could escape along the ladder to the other bank. Or perhaps Persimmon, who was not injured and had been in the freezing water for only a few moments, would gather Hawk into her arms and then reach out with one long leg to flip Alison into the river. In her weakened state, one good kick was all it would take.

"Get back!" she warned again. She let go of the top rail with her left hand, guarding Hawk's body with the right. She had been right—the flow of the water was abating just a bit. She took a hand-ful of Hawk's dark hair and pulled her head back beneath the water.

"Get away from me," she said to Persimmon in a voice so cold and hard that neither Stacy nor her father would have recognized it. "I mean it! Get away from me, or I'll take her with me!" She felt a small pang as she said this—if Persimmon was the one who had attacked her, then perhaps Hawk was not the killer, either. But Hawk's life was the only card she had left to play, and she was not yet ready to fold.

"Jesus Christ, Alison!" Persimmon cried, clearly appalled. "Jesus Christ! Are you crazy? I'm not going to hurt you! You just saved Hawk's life!" She made a grab for Hawk's head, but Alison jerked away, catching her in the chest with her elbow.

"I'll let go!" she warned. "Get back! I'm the only thing keeping her here!" She did not know from where she was summoning the energy to do anything at all but weep, but the cop in Alison had been counting coolly—she judged that Hawk had been under for about thirty seconds.

"Okay! Okay! Let her up!" Persimmon hastily moved a few feet towards the bank. Alison pulled Hawk's head above water. She began hacking and choking, which was a relief in more ways than one. First, it meant that Alison had not killed her. Second, it meant that Persimmon knew that Alison still *could* kill her if she had to.

"Let me take her," Persimmon pleaded. "She's going to die if we don't get her out of here soon!"

"Don't come near me!" Alison shouted back.

"I'm not going to hurt you! Just let me take her, and I'll come back and get you! You saved her life! Why would I want to hurt you?"

"You tried to choke me in the sweat lodge! I know it was you! If you don't want to hurt me, then why did you try to kill me?"

The expression on Persimmon's face changed completely. She looked—well, more repentant than anything else. She looked like a little kid who had done something she knew was bad, something she knew she could not explain to any of the almighty adults in her life, yet which had seemed like the only option at the time she had done it.

"I'm not going to hurt you," she said again. "I couldn't—not after this." She gestured towards Hawk, who was still coughing up water. "Just let me take her. I swear to God that I won't try to touch you. I'll send someone else back for you."

Alison believed her. What other choice did she have? Was she really willing to hold Hawk's head under water until she died just to keep Persimmon away from her? Emotionally, perhaps. The desire to survive is strong. Physically, there was no way. She knew that if she did not let go of Hawk soon, she was going to lose her own grip and be swept downstream. This way, at least, she had a chance.

Cautiously she loosened her hold and, swiftly Persimmon darted in and caught Hawk beneath the arms. They were much nearer the far bank than the bank on which they had started, and she crawled right over the top of Alison before she took Hawk from her and headed to shore.

Alison crept along behind. Fearful as she was of Persimmon lashing out at her, she was more afraid of clinging to the ladder in the water until it was too late. Already her fingers and feet would barely obey her commands. Just a few more feet, she told herself, first enticingly, and then sternly. Just a few more feet.

She felt herself swirled away from the ladder and thought with resignation, "Well, this is it, then." Now she would find out first hand all the answers about God and an afterlife and whether there was really a white light at the end of the tunnel.

But it was not the raging waters that had torn her loose. It was Persimmon's two hands clenched in the back of her shirt. Persimmon, still standing knee deep in water, had reached the place where the water had overflowed the bank, and was hauling Alison in like a big fish. Alison, before laying her head back and thinking nothing, thought of the way that she used to help her father with the net when he reeled them in. Persimmon could have used a helper—she hauled Alison awkwardly, scraping her back on the stones that had been uncovered in the bank, and dropping her abruptly in the shallow water with a splash that covered her head before going back to Hawk.

There was nothing that Alison would have liked better than to lie back in the mud and give herself over to the care of others. But she did not know yet if she was safe, and it would have been worse than irony if she had survived the fight, the pyre, the flash flood only to have her head held beneath ten inches of water. Fighting, she knew, was not possible, but perhaps she was still able to retreat. She tried to scramble to her feet, but her body would not respond. Enough was enough, and after all she had put it through she was lucky to be half sitting in freezing cold water. Real lucky.

Hawk, with Persimmon's help, was sitting. She rubbed her eyes and shook her head. She was filthy. Alison looked down. So was she—the water had deposited a layer of sand and mud thick enough for fossils.

"I don't want you on this land ever again," said Hawk in a weak voice, focusing on Alison. "I don't care what it takes, and I don't care if it's the last thing that I do on this earth—"

"Stop it!" reproached Persimmon in a stern and forceful voice that Alison had not heard before. "She saved your life! You'd be dead if it wasn't for her!" Hawk snapped her mouth shut in surprise as Persimmon turned back to Alison. "I'm so sorry. I am so sorry. I can't explain it. I just lost it. The heat and everybody talking about Sarah Embraces-All-Things—I just freaked out. I thought we were going to lose everything that we've built here, and it just freaked me out."

Alison put her hand up to touch her bruised throat—sorry

didn't really seem like nearly enough, but she had to admit that Persimmon did sound sincere.

There was a huge crash in the arroyo. They turned just in time to see the lodgepole ladder fold in the middle, obviously hit by one last boulder that had been dislodged by the flash flood. The water was receding fast—she guessed that they would be able walk across within ten or fifteen minutes, but until then she was stranded here with these two women, both of whom, to one degree or another, regarded her as their enemy.

Before Alison could reply, there were shouts from the opposite bank.

"Alison! What happened? Are you okay?" Stacy was all but shrieking, which bespoke her urgency, for she hated sounding shrill. It was so unbecoming. She must have stayed with the others, holding down the tarps, thought Alison, for she was fully clothed but soaking wet. Perhaps she had not even realized that Alison had slipped off after Hawk until the rain had stopped.

"Are you hurt?" bellowed Michelle in a roar that could have been heard clear up to the main house. Michelle produced adrenaline like sweat in an emergency—in a minute she'd be leaping across the arroyo in a single bound. Alison glanced over at the downed pyre—no wonder Michelle was worried.

"I'm okay," Alison called back. She tried to stand again, but could not. Maybe she hadn't gone to medical school, but she'd bet her next paycheck that she'd broken at least one bone in her foot. "I'm going to need to go to a hospital."

"We'll come across and get you!" Michelle seemed to think that any temporary superhuman powers she developed during a crisis spilled over onto whoever was standing close to her.

"No!" shouted Alison. "Go get the truck and bring it down here, okay?" Surely, surely the other women would help them clear the gate now.

Michelle opened her mouth, and then shut it. She was way too smart to bring up the key thing again. Stacy bent close, probably reminding her of the scaffolding. They both turned and started up the hill.

Persimmon had turned away from Alison and now had Hawk on her feet, moving slowly. She was, Alison realized, sending her upstream. She could probably cross on foot at the narrow neck, and then she would be able to go directly into the house.

She turned from them to look at the remains of the pyre, remembering the specter that had danced in the flames. There had been something—aside from spiritual speculation—about the ghost-like figure that still nagged at her. She could not put her finger on it, but she knew—if only by the hallucinations she had suffered in the water—that it was connected with Gaya.

She knew she should try to move out of the puddle in which she was sitting, but even that effort seemed far beyond her. Letting her head sink down towards her chest, she wondered if it was possible for her to fall asleep as cold as she was.She jerked her head up and looked again after Hawk. Persimmon had turned and come back to where she was sitting. Then she remembered Gaya with her bandanna off.

"That's it, isn't it?" she said to Persimmon, the light of illumination making her forget all caution. "That's what she was going to tell. Gaya's not your *sister* at all, is she?"

With a quick movement forward and then down on her knees, Persimmon clapped her hand over Alison's mouth.

"Shut up!" she whispered fiercely through clenched teeth. The wind had blown the clouds completely away from the moon. The face that Persimmon pushed up to Alison's own was ugly and frightening. "Just shut up! You have no right to come in here and try to destroy everything that we've worked so hard for!"

Alison sat still without struggling. Eventually the woman was going to have to take her hand away. They couldn't sit like that forever. Eventually, if nothing else, Stacy would come back and rip Persimmon to shreds for touching her darling. Alison wished, though, that Stacy had not followed after Michelle. She hoped Persimmon did not realize how exhausted she was, and that it had not occurred to her, as it had to Alison, how easy it would be to hold her face down in the puddle.

Persimmon looked over her shoulder at Hawk and then back at Alison. Something had changed in her. Where moments before she had seemed angry enough to attack Alison, she was suddenly resigned, ready to negotiate. Maybe she realized that, no matter what she did to silence Alison, Stacy and Michelle would know that she had come out of the water alive. Maybe she was just tired. Either way, she dropped her hand and sat back on her heels.

"Please," she said. "Please. Hawk doesn't know."

"She's not your sister at all, is she?" Alison continued as if there had been no pause. "The other girl in the photo—*she* was your sister. But Gaya's your brother. She's a transsexual. That's what Sarah Embraces-All-Things was holding over your heads." It seemed so obvious now that Alison could not believe she had not noticed before. Except that she had noticed. Little things like Gaya always wearing a bandanna and turtle neck—she was covering male pattern baldness and an Adam's apple. 'See you when I get back from the Caribbean!' had been a joke—Gaya had not been going to the islands on vacation, but Trinidad, Colorado, for treatments. Just as suddenly as the illumination had hit her, Alison also knew who had played the specter of Sarah Embraces-All-Things. It had to be Lawrence—it was the *way* that he had moved that had started her thinking about Gaya. They both moved like men.

"We weren't just brother and sister," said Persimmon in a low voice that sounded almost like pleading. "We were twins. The doctors said we were fraternal, two eggs fertilized, one xx and one xy. But what do they know? I know. I know here," she thumped a place on her chest that was probably meant to be her heart but which Alison knew from Biology 101 was more likely to be the spleen, "I *know* that we came from one egg. Something went wrong, that's all. They call them birth defects. The only difference is that Gary was born a man on the outside, when he was a woman on the inside."

Alison said nothing. She had no idea what to say to this woman before her, so earnest, so protective, so aware that the foundation upon which she had built her house was on the verge of crumbling. How could she comfort her? There was only one thing that would save her world—if Alison promised the secret would not get out. But that would mean covering up a murder, and that was comfort Alison was not ready to give.

As if she had read her mind, Persimmon leaned forward until their foreheads were almost touching. "Oh, God," she whispered, as if they were surrounded by listeners. "You think she did it, don't you? You think that Gary killed that awful woman." She rocked back for a moment and laughed. It was not a happy sound, but more as if years of bitterness and shame were being expelled in short, hard bursts. "She didn't do that," she said. "That's not her style at all. Look around you," she said, making a sweeping gesture with her arm that encompassed the whole of Mariposa. "How many women do you know who would be willing to sink this kind of money into this kind of experiment? Nobody is paying here, nobody but Gary." It was disconcerting to Alison how Persimmon had fallen so easily back into the childhood name while still using the female pronoun, but she said nothing, nor did she move. She did not want anything to disrupt the flow of confession. "Doesn't that tell you something about who she is? If she was really a man, do you think this is what she'd do? All Gary has ever wanted to do is be around other women! What man do you know who is willing to put this much money into an experiment like this, and then give up all the power over it?"

215

It was a convincing argument. All of it. It might have persuaded Alison to hold up her hand in oath, except for one thing.

"And he killed a woman to keep it," she said. "Do you expect me to overlook that?" Persimmon let out a great whoosh of breath that blew out her lips like the neck of a balloon. Alison's mother had used that same gesture years ago, when she was exasperated beyond all reason.

"She wasn't even around," she said, a patient I-told-you-this-before voice. "You know that. She was with Hawk, playing cards all evening."

Alison looked away, up the hill. She could hear the sound of voices by the gate. Somehow Stacy had finally persuaded the other women to pitch in and move the rocks. Not too hard, probably, after the infighting and the specter of Sarah Embraces-All-Things dancing atop the fire. She'd be willing to bet that they would not be the only ones leaving. She wondered if Michelle would go or stay.

"Yeah, that's what Hawk says," Alison answered, not voicing the obvious—wouldn't most lovers cover for their girlfriends?

"You still don't get it, do you?" Persimmon looked up the hill.

Realizing that if anyone else showed, Persimmon was going to close up like an oyster, Alison urged her on, "Get what? You mean, do I think your brother killed another woman to keep his secret, and then attacked me in the hot tub? Yeah, I do."

"Listen to me," said Persimmon, leaning closer. Under other circumstances, Alison might have thought that they were going to kiss. Considering the way things were, she pulled back a little, afraid Persimmon might suddenly revert to anger and bite her nose off.

"Listen to me," said Persimmon again. "Because I'm only going to say it once, and I'm only going to say it to you. There's no way that Gary was with Sarah that night. No way. Do you want to know why?" She must have assumed acquiescence because she did not pause for a sign. "Because I was the person in the sweat lodge."

"Oh, Jesus," said Alison, suddenly tired of the whole game. "Stop it! Just stop! Doesn't this say something to you? You're doing the oldest thing in the book, you're doing what straight women have done for centuries! You're covering for a man!"

"She's not a man!" shot back Persimmon, hovering over her as if she had never heard of personal space. "And I'm not covering! I'm telling you the truth! It might not be the truth that you made up in your head, but it's the truth that really happened! Is that what you really want to hear? What really happened? Or are you just interested in something that fits your prejudices?"

Privately, Alison thought that these two might be one and the same, but she held her tongue. "Tell me," she said simply.

Persimmon, as if suddenly realizing that they were alone—for miles in some directions—sprang to her feet. Again she looked up the hill.

"She was a horrible woman," she said finally. "A horrible woman. But I guess I don't need to tell you that, do I?"

Alison nodded her head. This, at least, was one thing they could agree on without qualm. Sarah Embraces-All-Things—or whatever her real name had been—had been a horrible woman.

"Do you know what her real name was?" asked Persimmon, again reading her mind. "Tiffany. Tiffany McDonald. I saw it in one of her letters. I went through her things. Of course I did! We were trying so hard to attract other women—and then along came *Sarah*. It was blackmail, pure and simple. Gary and I had to let her to live on the land, become part of the collective, or she was going to tell Hawk. You can imagine how that would have gone over."

Alison could. Hawk, with her rigid separatist leanings, saw what she wanted to see in Gaya, and would have been furious to find out that she had been duped. For the first time, Alison felt empathy towards the woman. She wouldn't have liked being duped like that, either.

"We knew that having her here would drive away other women. But what could we do?"

"How did she find out?" Alison asked curiously.

Again the blowing out of the lips and a pause. "She speaks Spanish," Persimmon answered finally. "Gary and I grew up around here. We shouldn't have come back. But we both loved the area so much, that when my grandfather died and left her the land…we thought we'd be safe—the only people still around who might remember us from when we were kids were old, and they didn't speak much English. And Gary didn't ever leave the ranch much. When he did, he went to Santa Fe—no place around here."

Alli esta el gallo, thought Alison, remembering how she had looked up the road to try and see the chicken herself. But in Spanish, just like English, there were specific words for male and female chickens. 'There's the rooster,' he had said, nodding up the hill towards Gaya.

"So she moved in, and you couldn't figure out a way to get rid of her," said Alison, trying to get the ball rolling again.

"Yeah. She was awful. It would have been hard enough if she had been who or what she said she was. But to have to listen to her lecture and talk about what 'the mother' wanted when we knew

217

she was a fake—we could hardly stand it! Gary was better at it than I was. Isn't that funny? In some ways, they were almost friends. I guess he learned that, growing up the way he did. Always being the outsider. Always being the butt of the joke and the weird kid that everybody hated. He learned to take a little friendship whenever it was offered—little pockets that existed without connection to anything else that happened. The blackmail—that was in another room when he was playing cards with Sarah, or brushing her hair for her." Her pronouns had changed, Alison noticed, as Persimmon touched on her brother's past. The story was sad. Alison was almost moved to tears, though she suspected that at this point she could be moved to tears by almost any country song or an Olympic flame commercial.

"And then you had the retreat, and Gaya couldn't take any more of Sarah's shit?" Alison suggested.

"You're really stuck on that, you know? I mean, sorry if this doesn't fit your script, but, no that wasn't what happened. We decided to do the retreat in spite of Sarah. We'd been planning for months. We'd already interviewed women and ordered supplies. What would we have told Hawk? But you saw how awful Sarah was. It wasn't just that we were afraid that no one would want to join the collective—we were afraid that women would decide to leave early when we opened the gate for you and Michelle."

Alison thought again of Lisa and nodded.

"It was a relief, really, when your girlfriend showed up. Sarah hated her—it gave her something to focus on, instead of just trying to mind-fuck everybody in the retreat."

"But?" coached Alison. She didn't think it wise to mention Gaya again. Either Persimmon was going to tell her the truth or she was going to cover—either way it needed to be done before Stacy and Michelle made it back down the hill.

"But it wasn't enough for her." For the first time since she had begun speaking, anger tinged Persimmon's voice. Up until this point she had spoken of Sarah in a resigned manner—reporting terrible behavior, past and done, with no option for change. Now, however, a kind of hate snapped out of her dark eyes. "It wasn't enough. I asked her to take a sweat with me. I was trying—we both were. Trying to see if there wasn't some thread of decency deep inside the woman. Trying to see if there wasn't some way that we really could live together. Why not? We didn't expect this to be Utopia. Who in the world is harder to get along with than lesbians? Who gets their feelings hurt more? Who has more rules? Who's more rigid? We didn't expect it to be easy—we thought maybe in some kind of loving setting that Sarah'd learn a different way to be with women. Because she did want to be with women. That was her saving grace. She did want to be with women."

And how many evil women have we forgiven and embraced and taken back into the community for that one thing? thought Alison sadly. And how many good women have been destroyed because of them? But she did not say anything because, in spite of her cynicism, there was still a part of her that admired Persimmon for going into battle in a sweat lodge, armed only with her love for women, standing alone and firm in her beliefs like the students who had stood in Tiananmen Square.

Up on the hill lights from a vehicle were now showing. They seemed to go down a bit, and then back up. Michelle probably was afraid to take the truck down the hill—she was afraid she'd get stuck in the mud, or even slide into the arroyo. Alison bit back a groan and then chided herself. She did not have to be in charge here. She could give it up and let Stacy and Michelle figure out a way to get her up the hill. All she needed to think about was the story that Persimmon was telling.

"They can't get down the hill," Persimmon said, shading her eyes as if she were looking into the sun. "Maybe I should take you up to the house." She looked in the direction in which Hawk had disappeared.

"My foot is broken," said Alison shortly. Her foot was not what was important now. Her foot would still be broken in fifteen minute, in an hour, a week from today. There was no rush to reach the hospital—nowadays they waited for the swelling to go down before casting. But the window on Persimmon's story was ephemeral, and closing fast as they began to hear voices on the hill. "What happened when you met her?" She was surprised to hear herself ask the words as if she believed them. When had she let go of the firm belief that Persimmon was covering and began to wonder if maybe, just maybe she was telling the truth?

"She was drinking," said Persimmon, still looking up the hill at the head lights. "That was one of the things she liked to do, you know. Break any of our rules. Flaunt it. If anyone else had been drinking, Sarah would have *demanded* that they be thrown off the land. But she liked to drink and smoke around Gary and me. Show us that she was above the rules, that she could do anything that she wanted to do, that we had no control over her." There was another pause, but this one was shorter. Persimmon, too, knew that time was running out.

"And she had something to tell me," she said, swinging around to face Alison. "I thought that maybe there would be a point that *I* could talk to *her* about the way she was behaving—point out that the things she was doing couldn't be good for her spirit and were bound to come around against her." Again came a harsh bark of disillusioned laughter. "I really thought that. I must have been crazy!"

"She wasn't open to hearing any of that?" asked Alison cautiously.

"Are you crazy? I must have been! She didn't even give me a chance to say good evening, or comment about the weather. She had something to tell me, she said. Drinking tequila in front of me, asking me to hand over her glass or the salt. She'd finally realized that she couldn't live a lie any more. It wasn't good for her—it was making a weak spot in her soul. Like that woman had a soul! My God, people debate about whether animals have souls, but they just assume that all humans have them, like they were assigned at birth or something! I've known Siamese cats who had more of a soul than that woman! Our secret, a secret that hurt no one was making a black spot on her soul? That woman could have hired on as a drug runner, a mercenary and it wouldn't have damaged her soul any more than the things that she had already done!"

Persimmon stopped. She was panting as if she had just been in a hard race. Now it appeared that people were coming down the hill. Voices only—because of the moon no one needed a flashlight.

"What did you do?" asked Alison. God, she was cold! She was shaking so hard she was afraid that at any moment she would be thrown back into the hallucinogenic state that had hit her in the water. They needed to wrap this up.

"I just listened," said Persimmon quietly. Alison noticed that she, too, was shivering. "What else could I do? She didn't have any decency—she couldn't be reached by anything that would reach you and me. All she wanted to do was use us up and throw us away. She was tired of living out here in the sticks, I guess. She wanted to go back to town a hero—she wanted to be the one who exposed the transsexual! The one who'd let decent lesbians know that a man was running the lesbian retreat! She could have dined on that for a year."

"That was really cold," said Alison, because it was. She tried hard to focus her concentration.

"Yeah. It was. She didn't think like other people. She didn't think about how good we'd been to her—and we *had* been good to her, despite what she'd done to us. All she saw was the chance to make a big splash, a big scene. That's what she loved. So all I did was listen. I wasn't about to give her the satisfaction of throwing a tantrum. It wouldn't have done any good—it just would have encouraged her. All I did was listen. Listen, and watch her pour that tequila back."

The voices were close enough now to identify. Stacy for certain, still sounding a bit shrill in her concern. Michelle, of course. G-hey!, perhaps, and also Seven Yellow Moons. Liz, thought Alison, must be either breaking camp or supervising the work crew at the gate.

"And then what happened?" asked Alison hurriedly.

Persimmon squatted down beside her again. "You're waiting for me to say that I hit her on the head, aren't you?" she asked in a voice soft and sad. "Or drugged her, or I don't know what. And I didn't. You can believe that or not—it doesn't make any difference now. I can't prove anything. Her body must have been washed down stream—I suppose someone will find it. Maybe the coroner can tell you that I'm telling the truth." For the first time, it occurred to Alison that Persimmon did not know about the switch that had taken place on the top of the pyre. She opened her mouth, and then shut it. This was no time to confuse the issue.

"I only did one thing, Alison. The rest she did to herself. I'm not proud of what I did, but I'm not sorry, either. She was a monster. She was a hateful, hateful woman, and in the end she killed herself. I might have left the 'in-use' fetish on the door, but in the end she killed herself."

"We can't get the truck down the hill!" Stacy's voice floated across the arroyo. "We're going to carry you up!" More voices, arguments and suggestions about how to get across the arroyo. Part of the bank had been washed away on the other side.

"What did you do?" asked Alison, soft as a whisper. The women on the other bank were moving upstream, looking for a better place to cross. Her teeth were chattering—she could hardly get the words out.

"I walked away. That was all. She wasn't used to drinking tequila—she only drank it because she thought it made her more Hispanic, more Indio, more of whatever she was pretending to be at the time. She passed out, I collected the empty bottle and walked away."

"Baby!" Stacy swooped in like a mother eagle, practically knocking Persimmon onto her butt. No contest about whose side *she* was on. "Oh, Baby," she mourned, stroking her hand through Alison's hair and coming up with a handful of sand.

Michelle was more direct to the point. "Jesus, Alison, you look like hell. You look like a truck ran over you."

"I *feel* like a truck ran over me," Alison replied. She tried to muster a little dignity, but she noticed that everyone else had taken the time to change into dry clothes and couldn't help but feeling a little resentful. She tried to scold herself, but could not muster the energy. She got to be a baby when she was hurt.

"Okay, that goes there and that goes on top and we're going to need two more people…" Michelle was the general, and G-hey!, Salad and Rusha were her troops. Dutifully, amid tongue-clucking and small sounds of sympathy, they laid Michelle's blue tarp on the ground, and covered it with Alison's two extra blankets.

"My god, what happened, you could have been killed…" Stacy did not wait for any answers. Alison didn't care. The noise was only meant as a litany of concern, just as her father used to sit by her bed and sing to her when she was sick. Stacy first pulled Alison's sweat shirt and then her flannel shirt off over her head. It wasn't easy—they were heavy with rain and dirt and stuck to her skin. She wrapped one of her big fluffy towels around her shoulders, another around her head. Alison felt her core temperature rise immediately.

Seven Yellow Moons was the medic in Michelle's army. Alison could feel her touching her foot gently, though she tried to shut it out. Even a gentle touch was far too much—she was throbbing with pain under no touch at all. To distract herself, she thought of what Persimmon had just told her. I only did one thing, and that was to walk away.

She was being swaddled in towels and blankets. After the horror and cold of the river—now nothing but a trickle that didn't even have to be waded, but could be avoided by jumping from stone to stone—the feeling of warmth and comfort was almost like going into shock. Alison could feel herself slipping away again. There was no fighting it—all she could hope was that she would land in dreamless sleep, rather than that place in her mind populated by the living and the dead together.

Stacy was sitting her up, holding a thermos to her lips.

"Come on, Baby. You're so cold. Don't go into shock now, Alison." She seemed far away, but still Alison responded to the urgency in her voice and opened her mouth and swallowed. The coffee was heavily sugared, probably left from the mid-afternoon pot and no more than lukewarm from sitting in the coals. Still, it felt like a molten finger of lava reaching into the bedrock of Alison's gut, and for an instant her eyes flew open with the shock of it.

"Where's Lawrence?" she said right into Stacy's face. "When did he get here?"

Stacy, who had been masked with concern, smiled for the first time. "Well, aren't you clever?" she said, low so that only Alison could hear. "And we thought we'd fooled everyone. Don't worry—he's waiting with a nice, warm bed for you."

Alison was vaguely aware of being rolled and lifted, vaguely aware that somewhere up ahead Michelle had taken Persimmon by the hand, draped a blanket around her shoulders.

"What about her medication, then?" she said suddenly and aloud, turning her face to the place where Persimmon had been last. "If all you did was walk away, then what about all those pills?"

"Shh," answered Stacy, a hand that reached out of the darkness to touch her face. "Shh. Go to sleep."

CHAPTER SIXTEEN

They didn't get to the hospital that night, of course. That was Denver thinking again. Denver streets flooded—cars were submerged on I-25 and when the water went down you drove right on through, shaking your heads and saying to one another, "Imagine! And two hours ago it was high enough to cover a Volkswagen!"

So no one in their little caravan—Lawrence driving Liz's van with Alison and Stacy in the back, Michelle and Liz in Michelle's truck with Zorra in the back—had even stopped to think about the washes that opened across the road that led back to town. Probably none of them had even noticed them on the way in—just a dry arroyo with its mouth up to the dirt track. Nothing to notice when it was dry—a vomit of rocks and mud that took a shovel and two hours work to pass after a storm.

They cleared the first two using their hands and a folding camp shovel that Michelle—of course—had in the back of her truck. By then, it was two in the morning, and everyone was sick with fatigue and stress, snapping at one another and dropping rocks down in the same places. There was a suggestion that they return to Mariposa for more shovels, but no one wanted to follow it. Rolling out of the gate had felt too much like escaping from the maw of a big snake, careless for a moment. No one wanted to return to see if it had wakened.

So because, as Alison had pointed out in a brief moment of waking and lucidity, no one was going to do anything until the swelling went down, and five Advil was as good as anything you could get from a druggist, they had camped there in the road, beside the mouth of the third wash.

Now, in the bright sunlight of midmorning, Alison sat in a deck chair with her leg outstretched, her foot, her nose and her hand packed in the last of the ice from Lawrence's cooler. She had slept for a good ten hours without moving, and had woken stiff and sore from the beating she had taken—Hawk and the water—the night before. Though they had wiped her off the best they could before rolling her in the blankets she was still dirty and gritty—so nasty, in fact, that the thought of clothes had been horrible. Stacy had helped her into the chair, and then had covered her from with sun with one of Liz's sheets before going to help the others.

She looked down the road to where her friends were digging in the dirt. She had never thought that she would be jealous of that kind of manual labor, but she would have given five hundred dollars to be working there with them. A thousand if they had thrown in a hot shower. Stacy had left her a couple of muffins and the new *People* magazine, but nothing appealed, though she had managed to work her way through two cans of Diet Pepsi and a whole handful of Advil. She was going to have to pee soon, and if she kept it up, she'd probably have to get her stomach pumped once they finally reached the hospital. Which might as well be in Denver instead of a strange emergency room in New Mexico, because of her swollen foot. Stacy was the only holdout—she would have arranged an airlift if possible—but Alison thought they might win her over. Everybody was tired and dirty—no one would be unhappy to see the Land of Enchantment in the rear view mirror.

Alison squinted towards the road project, and pulled down the brim of Stacy's hat to shade her eyes. Someone was coming her way. Height made it Liz or Michelle. Blonde hair—it was Liz.

"How's it feel?" asked Liz, pointing towards the ankle. She was almost as filthy as Alison herself, with a broad band of mud across her forehead where she must have tried to push her short hair back. She wasn't wearing a shirt, which Alison figured must be her way of celebrating their escape—wasn't no one who was going to tell Liz Smith not to hang her tits out in the sun! The fabulous tits of Liz Smith, in fact, looked as if they were getting a little too much sun.

"It's okay," Alison replied, even though she really felt quite wretched. Whining wasn't going to do anything but stress everybody out. "You need to put on a shirt."

"My thought exactly. I'll bet you could get into Mensa, too." Liz climbed into the camper, leaving Alison wondering if her tone had been joking or snappish. Probably the first with a flavor of the second, she thought. Everyone was trying to be a good sport, but it had gotten to the point where trying really was the operative word.

Liz climbed back down the steps, holding a white, long sleeved man's shirt in one hand and a bottle of Lubriderm in the other. She dropped the shirt onto Alison's chair and the plastic bottle into the sand and then stood there beside her, trying to brush the grit off her arms and torso with her hands. Alison knew what that felt like— she had done it about five times already. It was rather like rubbing yourself with a really fine grade of sandpaper, and it left you with the feeling of starting a huge dig—you knew this was just the first of many layers, leading right back to the Mesozoic.

"So, how did you get Lawrence involved in that little show?" Alison asked. If Liz was crabby and didn't want to talk, then she'd just better get out of range. The night before had been such a nightmare of emergency and exhaustion that questions had just not been possible and Alison had quite a few she wanted answered.

"Oh, that was the easy part," replied Liz, somewhat preoccupied by a hair that had dared to grow in the skin surrounding her left nipple. Liz had made it very clear that she did not intend to age gracefully, and part of this war against time had manifested itself into a phobia about stray body hair. She went to the gay electrolysis place down on Broadway regularly and chatted up the queens while they all got rid of those annoying chin hairs once and for all. She tried—unsuccessfully—to pull the hair out with her fingers. "Nobody jumps at the chance to wear a dress like Lawrence."

"We had to do something to keep you from getting killed," put in Stacy, coming up behind her. She looked wiped—they all did—but she had still managed a perky note with her cute green cap and some bright fish earrings that she must have broken out just for the occasion. If she had known what the trip had in store, thought Alison, she would have brought something tasteful featuring little gold shovels. Stacy sometimes reminded Alison of an upscale version of the teacher who drove *The Magic Schoolbus*.

It was on the tip of Alison's tongue to blurt out, Well, that worked *real* well, but she clicked her front teeth together and held her peace. She was very aware of being the crew member who was not pulling her share—she didn't want to be a big, crabby baby on top of it. No doubt everyone would be nice and understanding, but it was like the crying thing—it didn't make her feel better, it just embarrassed her.

Stacy, luckily, was way too pleased with herself to notice Alison biting her tongue. "And guess whose idea it was!" she sang. She reached into the van and pulled out the battered copy of Shakespeare with which she had been struggling the whole trip. "Cause I was reading *Macbeth*!" She did a little congo line song and dance.

Alison's knowledge of Shakespeare was limited to a couple of bad movies and all the same lines and plot angles that every reading American has picked up by adulthood. She knew that Hamlet said, 'Alas poor Yorick' and that Lady Macbeth had a bloodstain problem and that there were three witches, whom Agatha Christy thought should be played as three normal Scotswomen looking sly. None of which was helping out here.

"Huh?" she said. Ordinarily she would have been filled with pleasure by the sight of Stacy doing the conga in her fish earrings, but at the moment she felt too awful.

"Probably the only useful thing for which Shakespeare has been used for what—five hundred? three hundred years? How long has he been dead, anyway?"

"Not long enough," said Liz, who was not only mad at the world but raising a welt on her breast as well.

"Stop it!" said Stacy, "You're making me sick!" She handed the book to Alison and popped into the van, returning a moment later with her Swiss Army knife, which had tweezers. She handed it to Liz.

Michelle called from the creek bed—just as grumpy as Liz— and Liz and Stacy went off to help move something big.

It was obvious Alison was going to have to bide her time. She hopped behind the truck and took care of the peeing problem so she could go back and arrange herself in her chair like a big spider hoping for something to fall into her web. She glanced over at the road crew and again felt a huge longing—they were talking and laughing and had probably shared all their secrets. Everybody knew what had happened but her!

To pass the time, she opened Stacy's book to the marked page. Doggedly, she read several pages of mostly incomprehensible verse until she finally caught the storyline to which Stacy had referred— Hamlet hiring the mummers to put on a play about murder in the hopes of flushing out his uncle, whom he suspected of killing his father.

Her spider sense told her that someone had wandered into her web and she looked up quickly. Lawrence was heading for the cooler sitting in the shade of the truck. Like Michelle, he looked *way over* this little adventure.

"Tell me what happened!" Alison whined. "Tell me, tell me tell me!" It was possible to whine a little to Lawrence, as she did not have to worry about maintaining her butch persona with him. It was kind of like talking baby talk to the cat—who cared if he thought you were an idiot?

"Well," said Lawrence, doing the limp-wristed thing, as if at any moment he was going to tell Alison that she looked absolutely fabulous. That was the good thing about Lawrence, he could always rise to an audience. "I was supposed to come and get you all this morning. You know? But you should have *seen* how badly that little weasel I went to visit acted. Steve?" He made it sound as if he himself were unsure of the name and needed a little confirmation. "Honey, I have never met anyone so rude and pretentious in my whole life. And put out? Let me tell you, on the Internet it was 'My big dick' this and 'My big dick' that, but when it got up close and personal it was 'I have a headache' and 'I'm too stressed out.'"

He paused, and Alison automatically said, "Hate him. He must die." Lawrence liked a little audience participation at key moments.

"Well," he continued, gratified, "I don't need to go to New Mexico to be forced to look at one more faggot's bad art work. Because that was all the action I was getting, and honey, I can do that in Denver. So he said, 'Let's go out for Chinese' and I said, 'Oh, why don't you pick it up. Order whatever you like—make it expensive and I'll pay you back when you get here. My treat.' But no sooner was his sorry little tail out of the driveway when…"

"But when you got here," Alison broke in, "what happened? What was the plan?" She knew interrupting was not the best way to handle Lawrence, who believed even a walk down the block to 7-11 should be turned into a story, but she also knew that in a minute somebody was going to holler and that was going to be the end of this segment.

Lawrence gave her a miffed look and, as punishment, went into the *Reader's Digest* version.

"Left early. Got here early. Stacy said, 'Gotta problem, go park the van down the road and come back here and play the dead bitch.' Did. End of story." He stalked off, carrying a can of Diet Pepsi. Stacy must have brought at least a case—either that or the blue cooler had a magic pitcher effect going on.

Next into the web was Michelle. This time Alison reached right out and grabbed her hand and pulled her down on the chair with her.

"What happened?!" she demanded. "Why didn't you guys come after me when I went after Hawk? I could have been killed! I almost was killed! Where were you?"

Michelle's face clouded over with remorse—more than anything in the world she valued being a good friend—loyal, protective and trustworthy.

"I know," she said. "I didn't want to butt in on Hawk's freak out, but I knew you'd been gone too long. I did start to follow you." Nothing need be said about the fight—it was Michelle's job to be there whenever Alison needed rescuing, and vice versa, regardless of any tiff.

"And then…" her face lit up suddenly. "Oh! You don't know, do you?" Without waiting for an answer, she jumped into the back of her truck and then came back out, carrying something carefully in her hands.

"Look!" she said. She opened her hands to show Alison a tiny, perfect black puppy with pudgy ears and closed eyes. "Zorra started having puppies last night just as you went after Hawk—seven that lived! Isn't she beautiful?"

Zorra herself came down out of the truck, followed by a chorus of tiny cries. She had a very expressive face for a dog—it was obvious that, while she appreciated and adored Michelle, she felt the puppy department should really be run by someone of the same species. Like herself, for example. Michelle returned the puppy reverently. Alison could see that if she and Janka weren't really firm, they were going to end up with eight dogs.

"It was a really difficult birth," continued Michelle, as she climbed back out of the truck. "Seven said that if we hadn't been there to help, Zorra and the puppies all probably would have died. We're supposed to take her to the vet's when we get home to make sure she's healing okay. Does our vet take dogs, or only cats?"

"Michelle!" said Alison impatiently. Fuck the dog, she wanted to hear the story.

"Oh, yeah—so I started down the hill, but right then the dog thing started happening. I couldn't leave. And I knew Persimmon was out there, too. I knew she wouldn't let anything happen to you."

With that she went off to help the others. Alison did not call her back. What was she going to tell Michelle about Persimmon? What was she going to tell any of them?

By the time that the next victim showed—not from the wash, but rather from the road that lead back to Mariposa, Alison did not recognize the car, nor did she recognize the driver. The driver, in fact, looked almost like a man. She shaded her eyes and stared frankly. She was bored, she was crabby and she felt bad. To hell with manners.

The car stopped some fifty yards away and after a short pause, Lisa jumped out of the passenger door. She walked cautiously towards Alison as if not sure of her reception and then stopped ten feet away.

"Hey," she said to Alison, her voice cautious.

"Hey," replied Alison, wondering what the tentative vibes were all about. She didn't think she had offended Lisa. Well, okay, she had offended everyone, but she didn't think that she had offended Lisa in particular.

"I heard you took a really bad fall," said Lisa.

They went through the whole thing about the road being

washed out and how it really didn't matter because no one would put a cast on her foot until the swelling went down, anyway, an explanation of which Alison was rapidly tiring. Maybe she should get a leaflet printed. Then Lisa stood there silently for a moment or two.

"What are you doing here?" Alison asked finally, when it looked like this might turn into an all day thing. She looked down the road at her own gang. They obviously knew the car had stopped, but nobody was coming over to swap howdys.

"Umm." Lisa stammered, started and stopped. "I need to tell you something," she blurted out all at once. "I need to apologize to you." Her voice was high and thin with stress, and the sound of it brought back to Alison something she had heard the previous night.

"That…that was you talking in the sweat lodge last night? That *was* you in the sweat lodge last night." First she asked, and then without waiting she confirmed it, remembering the voice which had wept out of the darkness.

"I didn't mean— I never planned—" Lisa wrung her hands together and then fell back a step or two in a manner totally at odds with Alison's invalid status. Since it was obvious she expected to be bullied, Alison felt that she at least ought to make the effort.

"You didn't mean to!" Alison cried. The attempt fell a bit flat— she just did not have the energy to work herself into full indignation. "You broke my nose!"

"I didn't," said Lisa. She was looking at Alison hopefully in that way cats will look at one another when one is getting old or ill and there is a possibility of a change in the pecking order. "And your nose isn't broken—the swelling's already gone down."

"Well, you could have," said Alison sulkily.

"Do you want to hear this or not?"

Alison nodded. It was too hard to push it.

"I was in the kitchen—I heard you. I just wanted to ask you— to beg you to let it go. To just let her secrets die with her! But when I came down the hall I tripped on the cellular phone. You were going to call the sheriff, weren't you?"

"Yeah," admitted Alison, wondering if she was in a dangerous position and where the hell this all fit in. Oh well, she guessed she was safe—unless Lisa pulled a gun out from beneath her shirt. Then they were all screwed.

"Yeah," said Lisa. "I freaked out." She looked hard at Alison. "You're really cold, you know it. I mean really cold hearted. I still don't see what gave you the right to hurt everyone there, just because you were living in some kind of old west fantasy. Just because you were being Little Joe Cartwright or the Rifleman—protecting the bad guys from the lynch mob so that a judge can hang them later after a fair trail."

"Fuck you," said Alison. She was tired of defending herself and trying to be diplomatic. She hoped Lisa *did* have a gun—she certainly felt bad enough to die. "Fuck you and fuck everybody who looks like you." Alison was an old George Carlin fan. "Just fuck you." My, she was more crabby than she had thought. It was nice that Lisa had wandered by—it gave her a chance to be ugly to someone with whom she was not going to have to spend eight hours in a car. She only wished she could get a little backspin on the fuck yous—she was so tired that she sounded like she was ordering a burger.

"Well," said Lisa, who was not visibly wounded. "I just wanted to say I was sorry. I didn't mean to put you in danger. I wasn't trying to kill you or anything. I mean, you were already cuffed and Stacy was in the bathroom…" She shrugged, as if punching someone in the nose and locking them in a hot tub was just a case of girlish hijinks—you know, like tipping over a privy. "When I realized what I'd done, I tried to get her. But the doorknob came off in my hand and I went for help." She paused again, looking at Alison expectantly as if waiting for forgiveness or confirmation.

"Well, that's a hell of a gracious apology," said Alison. "Forgive me if I'm not impressed." My, being a bitch felt really great. She ought to mine this for all it was worth. "So what was your little secret? Killed someone? Fucked a guy?" They were only ugly shots in the dark, but she could tell by the way Lisa stiffened that she had, totally by accident, hit home.

"You people," she said in a low, angry voice, after the pause had slipped far beyond comfort. "Who gave you the right to judge me? Tell me that!"

"I wasn't judging you, I was just being ugly to you! And you started it with that half-assed apology!" Alison knew it sounded first grade, but she had never been one to let a false accusation pass without protest. She was constantly in trouble for things that she really *had* done—she couldn't afford to be called on those she had not. "I was just guessing! What do I care who you sleep with?"

"Well, Sarah cared. A lot. And she thought that a lot of other people would care, too." Lisa's face was red—a blush that went down her neck and onto her chest. Alison grew florid when she became upset as well—she hated the look and feel of that kind of blush, and associated it with soon being out of control. If they didn't watch it there was going to be spit spraying.

"So that was what Sarah had on you?" she asked cautiously, ready to duck if she needed to. "You were sleeping with guys, and she was going to queer your chances for the retreat?"

"I wasn't sleeping with 'guys'," answered Lisa, stiff and hostile. "Boy, that's what kills me about dykes! They can be so promiscuous—they sleep with their friends, and their exes and any damn stranger they 'fall in love with' and when I sleep with one man, Charlie, one more time—someone I've known and loved and lived with for years!—then all of a sudden I'm the enemy! All of a sudden I'm not worthy of any lesbian money!" Alison had been right in predicting the spittle.

"Oh!" she said, the light bulb finally going on. "The grant! She threatened to take away your grant, didn't she?"

"Yeah," said Lisa, her voice flat with disgust. She looked back towards the car. "At least, she threatened to tell about it! What a fucking hypocrite! Her whole life was a lie, and she's going to bust me for one night with someone I felt sorry for! That's all it was about—I felt sorry for him! I felt sorry for him and he had never treated me badly. Not once in nine years of marriage—not even after I left him for a woman. But in your eyes, it would have been better if I had slept with someone like Sarah Embraces-All-Things, who was a liar and a cheat and liked to hurt people, just because she was a woman."

Alison held her tongue. What was she going to say on her own behalf? That she didn't care who her friends slept with? Because she did care—there was nothing that could get all of them going faster than a rumor of bisexuality. She'd had friends before who had gone back to men and she had drifted away from every one of them. For her, it had less to do with sleeping with the enemy than it had to do with watching them enter another culture. The strides that women had made in the work place and legal field did not seem to enter the sphere of male/female relationships—one by one she had watched these women slowly assume the full burden of housework, of children, of cooking—packing for him when he went away and writing to his parents at Christmas. It was that which she had not been able to watch—not the handholding. She had seen many lesbian relationships that were unbalanced, but the imbalance between men and women had seemed so...so sanctioned.

But she said nothing. That was a thesis, and Lisa was only going to be here for a few moments. Already Alison could feel her trying to retract the strands of her rage.

"But I am sorry," Lisa said, and for the first time Alison really believed it, because she could tell the by effort that it took her to say it. "That's why I left when Charlie showed up looking for me. What kind of thing was that to do—try to scare you like that? I didn't want to be in any situation where I would even think of acting that way. I could have killed you!"

"Yeah," Alison could not bring herself to extend forgiveness, but she softened her voice and her face. "Did they take back your grant?" she asked.

"I don't know," Lisa replied. "I just don't know. I don't think that Sarah told them about Charlie and me before she died. I don't know if Charlie showing up at the gate was going to fuck it up for me. But I couldn't stay any longer."

They both stood for a moment, looking up the road with their hands shading their eyes, Charlie waiting in the car. It looked to Alison as if the major part of the work was done, but all of her friends were still standing around, poking at boulders with their toes while they smoked cigarettes. Belatedly, Alison realized that they were being tactful. Alison supposed that, even from down the road, it had been obvious Lisa had something she wanted to get off her chest.

"Well," said Lisa. "I guess that's it." She looked back at Alison, and for the first time something akin to a smile crossed her lips. "Forgive me if I don't say 'See you around'."

"Forgive *me* if I say I never want to see you again," said Alison. It was not much of a peace, but at least they had not departed in screaming or threats. If they came across one another at a festival they would be able to exchange a quick and casual hi.

Lisa turned towards the car and then turned back. "Oh," she said. "I almost forgot. Persimmon asked me to give you this when I left. She didn't think you'd be able to make it out yet." She put her right hand into the pocket of her shorts, pulled out a prescription bottle and tossed it into Alison's sheet draped lap. She turned again. This time she walked four or five steps before she turned back.

"You know, don't you?" she said, rather than asked. "You know. Who was it? Who killed her?"

Alison had twisted the lid off the bottle and was looking inside. She lifted her head and looked Lisa square and honest in the face.

"No one," she said. "I was wrong. It was just an accident."

CHAPTER SEVENTEEN

No sooner had Lisa slammed the car door when the Fun Camp crew, plus Lawrence, descended upon Alison and swarmed about her like a flock of hungry reporters.

"What was *that* all about?" asked Liz, elbowing Michelle as if she was about to beat her to a front page story.

"Why didn't you come over?" asked Alison. She replaced the lid on the medicine bottle in a preoccupied manner, concealing the note that had been folded up inside it in the crease of her hand.

"I don't think so," said Stacy, who was still dragging on an American Spirit. "She might as well have had a neon sign over her head. I thought the cone of silence was going to descend at any moment. Come on, don't dick us around—did she do it?"

"Do what?" asked Alison. She was tired and in pain and figured a little payback was due for the way that they'd kept her in the dark all morning, feeding her little bits of information here and there as if it was some kind of cloak and dagger need-to-know only situation.

"I got five bucks riding on her being the one who tried to drown you, five bucks on her being the killer—which if she is, by the way, we'd better get hopping, 'cause they're getting ready to go—and ten bucks on both." Liz was standing too close and talking too loud and smelling bad on top of it. Alison wrinkled her nose delicately and tried to turn her head without being busted—she didn't suppose she smelled like a bouquet herself.

"I'll tell you what," she said. "All four of you just sit down and tell me what you did and you know and then when you're done I'll tell you what Lisa said."

"Oh, for Christ's sake," snapped Michelle, who was probably the one with whom Liz was betting. "Just tell…"

Alison put up her hand. "I am going to cry again if I don't get my way," she warned. "And then I am going to cause a big scene and insist on going to the hospital and make every one of you stay in the emergency room for five hours until they have time to see me. "

Well, nobody wanted to see any of *that*. There was a little grumbling, but everybody gave in more or less gracefully. After all, Alison *was* the one who was injured, and she *was* being a mostly good sport about it.

"How did you figure Lisa was involved with anything?" asked Alison, a little heady with her newfound power. Or maybe it was just the Pepsi and Advil combination.

"Well," said Stacy. She perched on the end of Alison's chair, and then figured from her grimace that this wasn't such a good idea. There was a small pause while the cute beach chairs were unloaded because, as Michelle said, I'm too damn old to be sitting on the ground.

"Well," said Stacy again. The very last of the Dos Equis had been broken out and she gestured with the bottle as if it had been a pointer. "You know how you never let me do cop stuff?"

"No," replied Alison, "but I do know how you never let go of anything." Being even borderline pleasant was getting more and more difficult. Maybe they *should* go to the hospital—even if they wouldn't cast her ankle they might give her painkillers.

"Well," said Stacy, ignoring her. "After you left, what we did was make up a chart for everybody." She flipped up the lid of the cooler that was sitting by the truck. On the inside of the lid was a whole Mardi Gras of the neon post-its.

"So what does it mean?" asked Alison after a long moment.

"It's an alibi index," explained Liz, who had been sucking her beer down like it was the last ten minutes of Happy Hour on campus. "What we did was reference everybody according to where they were when you were attacked and where they were when Sarah was killed."

Alison was silent and it was not a happy silence, either. Stacy and Liz were telling her that, tripping, they had come up with a better solution than hers by doing *paperwork*?

Stacy, who was quick to sniff out hurt butch feelings reassured her. "We were in a much better position to gather information than you were," she said. "Everybody came down to our place to relax and nobody thought we were up to anything but conversation when we were asking questions." Her face was gloating. "But we were!"

Liz pointed to the far right of the lid, which was dominated by green notes. "This was the group of women who had pretty solid alibis for both times. They were either covered by more than one person, or they had an alibi with someone who seemed to have no connection with them. Like, G-hey! had an alibi for Rusha, who as far as we know, she had never met before. The middle group"—the darker shade of pink—"had no confirmed alibis, but had no motive as far as we could see."

"Not counting just Sarah being a butthead," Stacy broke in. "We had to figure that out—otherwise everyone had a motive."

"This," Liz pointed to the notes on the far left, which were shocking orange, "was the group that we were interested in. They both had no acceptable alibi—for example, Hawk and Gaya covered for one another—plus had a motive."

"*I'm* on that list!" protested Michelle.

Stacy held up her hands. "Fair is fair," she said. "You were alone both times and you were right on the scene and soaking wet when Alison was attacked."

"And what was my motive supposed to be?" Michelle obviously couldn't decide whether to get all puffed up with indignation or just go with it. Being the murderer could be kinda cool.

"Sarah Blackmails-All-Women could have been threatening to call Janka about the Persimmon thing," answered Stacy. "Hell, we didn't know. We guessed on all the motives. They were all just based on gossip. I mean, it seemed obvious that she had something on the home girls—who'd put up with her otherwise? And she was yanking Lisa's chain right and left, according to Alison."

"Plus Charlie showed up yesterday," added Liz, rubbing her hands together with vindication. Lawrence had been putting together an hors d'oeuvres tray out of the rather pitiful remains of the supplies and she snagged a handful of pretzels. It was the wrong time of day to be eating chips and salsa, but everyone's clocks had been messed with, so it didn't matter.

"He *showed at the gate*?" Alison squealed like a straight girl. "And you *didn't tell me*?"

Stacy patted her gently on the shoulder, a touch used for invalids. "Alison," she said, just before stuffing a handful of Fritos into her mouth. She continued as soon as she had cleared the crumbs. "My darling. My sweetness. Light of my life. You were a madwoman. You were one step away from running through the streets foaming at the mouth and attacking everything that moved."

There was a long silence while Alison sulked and everyone else stuffed their faces, waiting for the sulk to age. Liz broke out a joint and passed it around and there were a few comments about how pretty the clouds were. Alison finally gave in when Liz and Lawrence started picking up pretty rocks—in a minute they were going to be putting them in their mouths.

"If her husband came by yesterday, why didn't any of the

Mariposa women see him until today?" she asked coldly, letting them all know that it would be a cold day in July before their subterfuge was completely forgiven. She felt just the way Nancy Drew would have felt had plump but pretty Bess leaped up and announced she had not only solved the mystery herself, but had in addition arranged counseling for Nancy's controlling personality disorder.

"He stayed in his car. Lisa was going to leave after the sweat, but the downpour and everything else changed all that. So anyway, we kinda knew who we were looking at," continued Stacy. As usual, a little downtime meant some self-maintenance. She, like everyone else, had been through a whole heck of a lot without washing, so she was going to need an hour or so just to get up to speed. She had decided to start slow, by pulling a wide-toothed comb through her hair. "And we kinda also knew who we weren't looking at. Like G-hey! and Salad, for example—we knew we could approach them for help and they almost certainly weren't mixed up in any skullduggery." Stacy looked please with herself for working skullduggery into the conversation. "They were clear because they were from Denver and hadn't met Sarah before they got here."

"And who could blackmail *them*?" asked Michelle, who was doing a version of the combing thing with her fingers. "I mean, they were practically doing a public orgy—I have a feeling there wasn't a whole lot that could have embarrassed them." She sounded a little scornful, as if nice girls really should be blackmailable.

"Yeah, they're pretty upfront," commented Liz, as if Michelle had meant it as a compliment. Michelle gave her an annoyed look and tried to move upwind.

"So, since we had kind of an idea about whose tails to twist, we had kind of an idea about how to twist them." Stacy was settling the whole hair problem by braiding it up in one french braid pulled so tight that it was giving her features a whole new cast. Alison had to remember that the next time she needed to send her in undercover. "It had to be something around Sarah and something around this place. Those were the two things everybody had in common."

"You figured this all out while you were *tripping*?" Alison could not help asking in a petulant tone.

"Yeah," answered Liz. "We also figured out a plan for world peace and how to put fruit trees in my back yard without taking out the fence."

"So Lawrence showed up a day early and—ta-da!—a star was born. Now tell us what Lisa said and then let's roll. Even if they *won't* put a cast on that ankle, let's at least stop and rent a motel room and shower and wipe off the car seats." Stacy's one flaw as a camper was that she really couldn't bear to be without hot water for more than a couple of days. She and Alison had gone to Michigan the year before last and mid-week she had left Alison working on the community quilt, jumped in her car, driven seventy-five miles and rented a room so that she could *really* wash her hair. While she was at it she had spent the night and then had a manicure with French nails before returning to wow the leather girls.

But there were just some pieces of the puzzle that were still not fitting together and without them Alison did not know how to respond to the note Persimmon had sent her in the pill bottle.

"I still don't get it," she said. "How did Charlie find..."

"Oh, he came and parked down the road with me and we played cards all afternoon. He's a faggot. He might not know it yet, but oh, honey." Lawrence flapped his hand in the universal queen symbol. "He followed me in, actually. We had both stopped at that little store in town, but he didn't know where to go from there. And of course, I had a map."

Michelle fixed an accusatory eye on Alison, who looked the other way. Okay, okay, her loose handling of the map had resulted in it falling into the hands of straight men. (Or maybe not, if Lawrence was picking up the right signals. Then again, Lawrence thought everyone was gay. It frequently figured into the adventures that were always leaving him stranded in uncomfortable if not actually dangerous places.)

"So what was with this guy?" she asked. "Was he like stalking Lisa or what?"

"Oh, I don't think so. Not at all." Stacy had produced a huge box of wet wipes, the kind that you carry in a diaper bag and was using them one after another to clean her skin in two inch patches. "He was a nice guy. It was more of a rescue than anything. I guess that after Lisa left for the retreat he went over to her apartment to do the cat thing..."

"Actually, it was the plant thing..." inserted Liz, moving in on the wet wipes.She held out her hand too and Stacy passed her a stack. It did feel good to get some of the grit off her face, although she had the feeling that she was probably just moving most of it from one spot to another.

"The plant thing, the cat thing, whatever. So then...actually," she said, looking at Liz, who had unbuttoned her shirt and was wiping down her tits with the same big old strokes that you might use to wax your car, "I don't really remember what the rest of his story was. Lawrence and I were brainstorming at that point."

"Don't kid yourself," said Liz. "You and Lawrence were sucking rocks and becoming one with the goddess like the rest of us. I only remember because I took notes."

"Why were you taking notes?" asked Alison.

Liz shrugged. "It seemed like a good idea. I believe there was about half an hour there when I thought I was Marge Piercy."

"This followed a short period of believing she could sing like Nancy Griffith," said Stacy. "All in all it was a pretty interesting afternoon."

"So I see," said Alison. "So, again, why did the hubby not break down the doors and come gunning up the road for Lisa?"

"Well, he didn't want to intrude," said Liz, "but he was concerned. When he went to do the plants…"

"How in hell did she think she was going to keep him a secret if she had him house-sitting?" asked Michelle. "Isn't that a little obvious?"

"I don't believe the fact that she *had* an ex- husband was a secret," said Stacy. "I don't even think the fact that he had a key was secret. I think she was living in a condo they had owned together?" She looked at Liz for conformation.

"Or something," agreed Liz. "*Anyway*, when he went over there for whatever fucking reason he went over there he ran into the neighbor…"

"Wait-wait-wait-wait-wait-wait-wait—!" protested Alison. "What do you mean, you don't think that was the secret? What are you talking about?"

Stacy gave Alison a look that, had it not contained so much fondness, would have been pitying. Actually, even with the fondness it was pitying. It was like the look a mother would give a favorite but slow child.

"Well, there had to be some secret, didn't there? I mean, that's what blackmail is all about, isn't it? There has to be a secret. I can't blackmail Liz about being into kink because the whole goddamn world *knows* she's into kink. The fucking *DA* knows she's into kink!"

"And wants to have a three-way," said Liz, in a tone that gave no clue as to whether this was the truth or just another bit of wittiness.

Stacy ignored her. "And, like we talked about, what secrets are bad enough for blackmail? To dykes? Especially separatist dykes? Especially separatist dykes who are handing out grant money to poorer dykes?"

"She was fucking him," agreed Lawrence, who was visibly

239

tired of either just this conversation or all conversations which did not include him. "He didn't say it, but I could tell by the way he acted."

"I thought you said he was gay," objected Alison.

"So what has that got to do with it?" asked Lawrence, raising an eyebrow. "I mean, I've fucked women myself."

The thought of this was so very mind-blowing that for a moment there was total silence as everyone tried to imagine, or tried not to imagine, Lawrence in bed with a woman.

"*Anyway*," said Liz finally, with a little shake of her head as if to displace *that* image, "when he went over to the house…"

"But I thought…" began Michelle.

"No-no-no-no-no-no!" Liz shook her head rapidly, her eyes closed. "I can't do this any more! My files are going to crash in just about half a minute if you don't let me finish!"

"Finish," said Alison. Stacy was still contemplating Lawrence with a woman and Lawrence himself had gone into the van for more beer.

"He went to her house. He met her neighbor. She was a dyke. She told him that a friend had told *her* that Sarah Embraces-All-Things had gone to the same retreat. She didn't think Lisa knew Sarah was going to be there. He knew there was bad blood between the two of them. He got to worrying that Lisa would be trapped. He came out here. That's all!" Liz wiped her brow as if she'd run a marathon.

"And after we told him that Lisa was okay, that we'd seen her, he agreed to wait until after the sweat," added Stacy. "We told him it would just be easier and cause less commotion and might get him in and out without getting castrated. We didn't tell him that he'd made Lisa a prime suspect. You know," she added thoughtfully, "maybe Lawrence is right. Maybe he is queer. He certainly didn't seem very impressed with my tits."

"You conducted this interview with you shirt off?" asked Alison. She was not even able to work up any indignation.

"Well, there we were," said Stacy defensively. "I mean, this whole vacation was supposed to be about mind-altering substances and frolicking naked in the desert, wasn't it? I wouldn't have signed up if I'd known it was going to be about dead bodies and how bad leather dykes are. I'd have asked my mother if I could go to Y camp instead."

Alison sat still, saying nothing. Thinking. Okay, so the Fun Camp girls had set up the whole performance. "I take it Seven Yellow Moons was in on this?" she asked rather curtly.

"Oh, yeah," assured Liz, who was peeling down and doing an improv sponge bath right there. "God, I stink. I hope you have something that fits me," she said to Lawrence, "'cause I'm not putting those back on. I may burn them."

"A service to everyone," murmured Michelle, but it didn't have a whole lot of sting. It was hard to zing someone who had really already beaten you to the punch. Besides, Michelle didn't smell that great herself.

Alison, whose energy had been totally sapped by wiping down the bottom half of her face, sank back into her sheet and tried to think. "So Seven set things up…" she said aloud, organizing in her mind. "With Salad and G-hey! as plants."

"Because we would have been too obvious," said Stacy. "We were pretty clever, weren't we?" She looked very pleased with herself. In a moment she was going to try to use skullduggery again.

"So there was going to be this whole confessional overtone to the sweat. Is that it? And then what—everybody was going to see Sarah rise up from the grave and the murderer was going to flip?"

"Except that Salad got a twist in her tail and screamed too soon." It was hard to get good help in the skullduggery business. Stacy looked as if she'd like to give Salad a good slap.

"That wasn't Salad who screamed," said Alison absent-mindedly.

"Well, then who was it?" asked Michelle.

Alison barely heard her question as she asked, "And when did you take the body off the pyre? And what did you do with it? And where did the skeleton come from?"

Much louder Stacy asked, "What do you mean, take the body? What are you talking about?"

Liz was more to the point. "What the fuck?" she asked.

"Well," started Alison and then broke off, confused. "I just assumed you would know." Quickly, or at least as quickly as allowed, she told the story from the point of her exit in the rain to where Stacy and Michelle had appeared on the bank of the arroyo. "I just assumed you moved the body," she concluded. "I guess I thought Lawrence did it while we were in the sweat."

Lawrence shuddered delicately. "You assumed *wrong*, girlfriend," he said. "What kind of ghoul do you think I am?"

"Well, who in the world…" started Stacy. She had gotten out the Oil of Olay again.

"*Why* in the world?" asked Liz. "And who's the murderer? I thought you found that out last night, but you didn't, did you?"

Alison was secretly pleased that she had not broadcast her conversation with Persimmon on her face in the same way that she usually broadcast her cards at poker. She shook her head, trying to look regretful. She had chosen to play her cards close to her chest because, frankly, she had no idea what she was going to do once they reached a telephone. Did she report a crime for which there was no evidence and in doing so expose a motive that would destroy a community? What was the point in that? If Persimmon was to be believed, it wasn't even a crime. She closed her hand around the bottle in her pocket and leaned her head back against her chair, wishing that sleep would overtake her then and there; that she would awake home in her own bed, clean, her ankle cast and the smell of coffee and muffins wafting up from Janka's kitchen.

Stacy, reading the look, was suddenly remorseful. "What are we doing sitting around here drinking beer? You should see a doctor! I think you're still suffering from shock." She stood up and went into whirlwind mode—everything in her path was suddenly closed and folded and packed. "Let's get this show on the road! You," she said to Alison, "need to lie down. And I don't give a shit about them waiting for the swelling to go down—you're seeing a doctor unless you look a whole hell of a lot better by the time we get into town."

Stacy as the Tasmanian Devil was a force with which to be reckoned—glances were exchanged and everyone agreed, without a word, to give in gracefully. They were under way within three minutes and it only took that long because Liz had to pee.

Alison, carefully tucked into long back seat of the van, was surprised when Michelle sat down beside her. She had been vaguely aware of a bit on reorganizing and negotiation, but had not realized that Michelle had been part of it. If Michelle was here, that meant someone else was driving her truck and, as they all knew, her truck was a high control area. Such a high control area, in fact, that Alison's first words were, "What is it?" If Stacy, or even worse Liz, was driving Michelle's truck, then something was up.

Michelle heaved a great sigh. Oh, dear, thought Alison. She hoped it wasn't about Persimmon and Janka and doing the right thing opposed to living one's dreams. She was just not strong enough to play the voice of Michelle's conscience any longer. She willed Lawrence to step on the gas, to get them out of the area *right now*. But of course the road was even worse now than it had been going in, and all he could do was lumber along in first gear.

"Suppose," said Michelle, leaning her elbows onto her knees and then her chin into her hands, "you knew someone who might have lost her mind."

'Suppose you knew' was a little game that Michelle and Alison had played for nigh on twenty years. There were a lot of dykes who would have disapproved of it, but it suited them just fine. It was like the high court language that Alison had read about in the novels of James Clavel—it allowed information to be passed and even apologies to be made with no loss of face.

"Temporarily or for good?" asked Alison, cutting right to the chase. If she'd thought she could sleep, she would have told Michelle to go away. But, jerking over the rocky road, there was no possibility of that, so she was a welcome diversion.

"Temporarily, probably," replied Michelle, sighing again. "But suppose it made her act kind of like an idiot?"

Alison mulled this one for a minute. Where did Michelle want to go?

"Well," Alison said finally, "everybody acts like an idiot now and then. *I* certainly do." She paused another moment. "Does this woman need to make any restitution?" she asked. Playing 'Suppose' was kind of like playing 'Hot or cold'.

"She kind of already did," said Michelle. "I mean, suppose that she acted like such an idiot that she kept someone else from doing what was right?"

Mmm, thought Alison, that had to be the keys on the roof.

"She already made the restitution?" she asked.

"Yeah," agreed Michelle. "She had the opportunity and kind of a moment of clarity."

What the fuck was she talking about? wondered Alison. What had she done to make up for standing in Alison's way about the body?

Then it hit her. "Oh!" she said, so surprised that she forgot they were even playing. "You were the one who snatched the body!"

Michelle looked out the window. Alison could not tell if she was just thinking, or if she was miffed because Alison had popped out of role.

"Yeah," she said finally, it was that awful Sandpaper! Going on and on about the matriarchy and lesbian space and what a bad person you were! How you shouldn't even be allowed to *be* a dyke and she didn't really believe in laws, but there should be a *law* that kept people like you from *calling* themselves dykes because it was an embarrassment to the rest of us…"

Oh, thought Alison, definitely the wrong track to take with Michelle. She didn't like to hear anyone talking bad about her friends, not even if all they were saying was things she'd said herself.

243

"And then she started talking about male children and Lydia had to butt in there about how I had one, and she just looked at me like...I don't know what! Like I was some kind of monster!"

"Like you were just as bad as me," said Alison quietly.

"Yeah," Michelle agreed, not seeing the pain in her eyes. "Like I was just as bad as you! Because of Sammy! And they just all assumed that I was going to give him up, because that was what was going to be good for their community! She was so damned patronizing—'Well, every man is an exception to someone, City Pony. Every rapist is some woman's son.' And I thought, 'This woman is crazy!' And that made me wonder if you weren't right—if somebody hadn't killed Sarah, and if the evidence wasn't going to go up in smoke."

Alison turned her head, unable to watch Michelle's face.

"So what did you do?" she asked quietly, wincing as Lawrence hit a particularly big pothole.

"Well, I hadn't read Hamlet. I wasn't really trying to freak anybody out. But they had two bundles ready to go—wrapped in quilts. Sarah's body, and the bones that were supposed to go back to the Navajos. Nobody wanted to handle either one. So I took charge when no one was around. Nobody even wanted to hear about it—nobody even asked how I got Sarah's body down the hill and up on the pyre. Even though I had a story ready."

Alison nodded. Of course Michelle would have a story ready. "What were you going to say?"

"That Liz helped me, and we used the wheelbarrow—which I did. And I tied the quilt at the corners and hoisted the bones up like that while everyone was having dinner and getting ready for the sweat. I knew Liz was an outsider—nobody would ask her about it. Nobody wanted to talk about it anyway. They were glad that it was done."

"The clothes?"

Michelle shrugged. "They were sitting there beside the body. You know, they wanted her to go sky clad. I guess I just figured that if anybody did climb up one last time, maybe that would confuse them. Maybe it could be passed off as magic instead of a switch. They were ready to believe in magic."

"And the body?"

Michelle looked uncomfortable. "Well," she said. "I didn't know what to do with it. I couldn't really move it far by myself. So I just dragged it back into the walk-in before the kitchen crew came in. Shoved it under the back shelf with a bunch of boxes in front of it. And pretended I was coming out with vegetables for dinner.

They won't get to it for a week at least." She turned away from the window. "So anyway," she said "there it is, if you want to send the cops in."

Alison said nothing. She held the note from Persimmon in her hand and thought of the words: 'It was an accident. All I did was walk away. There weren't any pills involved—the only medication I ever saw Sarah with were these. She emptied two bottles into the fire that night—she was 'healing' Katherine from her depression. She dropped this bottle and did something with the other one when she went outside to cool off.' Alison felt the melted lip of the plastic bottle, and thought of the little red disk that had clung to her skin after her dive into the sand pit. She also thought of Persimmon reaching up to take a twig out of her hair, and Stacy saying, 'What is this stuff? It's glowing.' The name on the bottle was Katie, and Katie was just one of the many nicknames for Katherine. And probably Persimmon was telling the truth about that, and everything else as well. Except one thing. Which was that with a bit of phosphorus paint on her fingers she marked Alison so that she would be able to pick her out in the sweat lodge.

She thought about that, and about all the things that everyone had said to her. About who would be punished, and an experiment as important as anything from the seventies. She thought about Seven Yellow Moons and G-hey! and Rusha, good women who would be hurt by the arrival of the sheriff, and Gaya, who would be hurt worst of all. Gaya, about whom Persimmon had said, 'What if she had a false leg? What if she was born without arms—would everyone condemn her for getting a prosthesis, for changing the way that God had sent her into the world?'

"So," said Michelle after a pause so long that they were now on a paved road, "What do you think I should do? Do we need to stop and use the phone?"

"I don't think so," said Alison. "But I do think you should send them a little postcard. Because it would be a shock to find that body again."

Michelle took her hand, the one that was not swollen, and they rode like that all the way to town.

---

1 *Tell Me What You Like* - New Victoria Publishers 1993

2. *I Knew You Would Call* - New Victoria Publishers, 1995

3 *Give My Secrets Back* - New Victoria Publishers 1995

IF YOU LIKED *IT TAKES ONE TO KNOW ONE*, YOU'LL LIKE THESE OTHER EXCITING MYSTERIES BY KATE ALLEN

TELL ME WHAT YOU LIKE An Alison Kaine Mystery
Meet Alison Kaine, Denver's most exciting lesbian cop! The story starts with a botched vacation and ends with the murders of two local lesbians. Trying to track the killer, Alison finds herself the next target. Is Stacy, the lovely leather dominatrix with whom she is sharing her kinkiest fantasies, at risk or a suspect? In this fast-paced, slyly humorous novel, Allen confronts the sensitive issues of S/M, queer-bashers and women-identified sex workers within a multifaced lesbian community. $9.95

GIVE MY SECRETS BACK An Alison Kaine Mystery
A dead writer, a missing sister, a leather contest and a host of ghosts from the '70s combine to create this riveting mystery, which stayed on Lambda Book Review's best seller list for a year. Denver cop Alison Kaine and her friends are as complicated as ever – numerous reviewers have complimented Allen's ability to write so insightfully about the lesbian community. $10.95

I KNEW YOU WOULD CALL A Marta Goicochea Mystery
Author Kate Allen, well-known for her Alison Kaine mysteries, sets this new mystery series in the lesbian ghetto where the characters live 'close to the bone.' When Marta is drawn into a caller's life she finds herself in the middle of a murder. "I cannot say enough about this excellent book," says Patricia Roth Schwartz in *Sojourner*. $10.95

SIX MYSTERIES BY SARAH DREHER

STONER McTAVISH   The first Stoner mystery introduces us to travel agent Stoner McTavish. On a trip to the Tetons, Stoner meets and falls in love with her dream lover, Gwen, whom she must rescue from danger and almost certain death. $9.95

SOMETHING SHADY   Investigating the mysterious disappearance at a suspicious rest home on the coast of Maine, Stoner finds herself a prisoner / inmate. Can Gwen and Aunt Hermione rescue her before it's too late? $8.95

GRAY MAGIC   A peaceful vacation turns frightening when Stoner finds herself an unwitting combatant in a struggle between the Hopi spirits of Good and Evil. $9.95

A CAPTIVE IN TIME   Stoner finds herself inexplicably transported to a town in Colorado Territory, year 1871. There she encounters Dot, the saloon keeper, Blue Mary, a local witch/healer, and an enigmatic teenage runaway named Billy. $9.95

OTHERWORLD   All your favorite characters—business partner Marylou, eccentric Aunt Hermione, psychiatrist, Edith Kesselbaum, and of course, devoted lover Gwen, on vacation at Disney World. In a case of mistaken identity, Marylou is kidnapped and held hostage in an underground tunnel. $10.95

BAD COMPANY   Stoner and Gwen investigate mysterious accidents, sabotage and menacing notes that threaten members of a feminist theater company. "Sarah Dreher's endearing creation, Stoner McTavish, is on every list of beloved lesbian detectives." $19.95 hardcover $10.95 paper

MORE MYSTERIES FROM NEW VICTORIA

DEATHS OF JOCASTA by J.M. Redmann
What was the body of a woman doing in the basement of the Cort Clinic? Could Dr. Cordelia James have performed the incompetent abortion that killed her? Micky Knight has to answer these questions before the police and the news media find their own solution. "Knight is witty, irreverent and very sexy." $10.95

DEATH BY THE RIVERSIDE by J.M. Redmann
Detective Micky Knight, finds herself slugging through thugs and slogging through swamps in an attempt to expose a dangerous drug ring. The investigation turns personal when her own well–hidden past is exposed. Featuring fabulously sexual, all too fiercely independent lady dick. $9.95

MURDER IS MATERIAL A mystery by Karen Saum
This third is the Brigid Donovan series (*Murder is Relative* and *Murder is Germane*) finds Brigid investigating the fiery death of a self-styled Buddhist guru and the kidnapping of a young woman. $9.95

FIGHTING FOR AIR A Cal Meredith Mystery by Marsha Mildon
Jay's class of scuba students goes out for their first open water dive. All goes well until a young Ethiopian loses consciousness and drowns before the dive instructor can get him to the surface. $10.95

NUN IN THE CLOSET A Mystery by Joanna Michaels
Anne Hollis, the owner of a women's bar is charged with manslaughter in the death of a nun. Insisting she's innocent, Anne appeals to probation officer Callie Sinclair for help. The case grows more complex and puzzling when another nun is murdered, and Callie discovers that sex and money are involved. $9.95

IF LOOKS COULD KILL A Mystery by Frances Lucas
Diana Mendoza, a Latina lesbian lawyer, is a scriptwriter for a hot new TV show featuring a woman detective. While on location in L.A., she meets blonde actress Lauren Lytch. When Lauren is accused of murdering her husband, Diana rushes to her defense. $9.95